How Like an Angel

SWEETWATER FICTION: ORIGINALS

TITLES IN THE SERIES:

Greetings from Cutler County: A Novella & Stories
by Travis Mulhauser

How Like an Angel: A Novel
by Jack Driscoll

One Mile Past Dangerous Curve: A Novel
by Darrell Spencer

How Like an Angel

A NOVEL

Jack Driscoll

THE UNIVERSITY OF MICHIGAN PRESS
ANN ARBOR

2008   2007   2006   2005   4   3   2   1

A CIP catalog record for this book is available from the British Library.

Library of Congress Cataloging-in-Publication Data

Driscoll, Jack, 1946–
     How like an angel : a novel / Jack Driscoll.
          p. cm. — (Sweetwater fiction. Originals)
     ISBN 0-472-11471-9 (acid-free paper)
     I. Title. II. Series.

PS3554.R496H69 2005
813'.54—dc22   2004017260

For Lois—without whom, nothing.

Acknowledgments

A number of these chapters, often in earlier versions, appeared in the following journals: *Blue Mesa Review*, *Mid-American Review*, *Portland Magazine*, and *West Branch*. Two chapters were nationally syndicated in newspapers as part of the PEN Syndicated Fiction Project, and two sections were aired on NPR's *The Sound of Writing*.

My heartfelt thanks to Pete Fromm, who read an early, almost unrecognizable version of what this novel eventually became, and offered both hope and valuable advice at a crucial time. To Amy Cherry, whose optimism and encouragement buoyed my spirits and helped me regain both my faith and my footing. To Sue and Paul Newlin, who asked all the right questions. And to my great and longtime friend Nick Bozanic, whose insights and compassionate final edit led me closer to the book I wanted to write.

Look. It's empty out there, & cold.
Cold enough to reconcile
Even a father, even a son.
                    —*Larry Levis*

ONE

Squalls

"We're just plain bad for each other, Archie," Z says, cutting, characteristically, straight to the point. Still, she *has* consented to this drive—"One hour," she says. "Tops." After all, what's left to say that can possibly take any longer than that? Probably nothing. Nonetheless the Caddy is full of petrol, the hour already fleeting and, by her own reluctant admission, she concedes again to that unmistakable, deep-seated something we just can't resist about each other.

I've owned this land yacht, a ruby red 1975 convertible, for longer than I've known Z. Power seats and electric eye on the dashboard and a trunk you could share with a small rhinoceros. A take-charge Coupe DeVille that I lucked into with a ridiculously lowball estate sale bid.

We're here on good tread—the snow slashing so hard into the headlights that we're momentarily blinded and staring dizzy-eyed into the tunnel between these fields of last year's standing corn. But this is not a storm we're cruising through—these are Michigan lake-effect squalls that slow us, sometimes to a crawl. But once they open up, the road is slick-black and entirely inviting, my arm around Z like old times, the world wildly alive again, and the radio loud.

"Archie," she says, turning the volume down a few decibels.

"We've been down this road how many times before? And to what end?" When I don't respond she says, "You do realize, don't you, how hopeless this is? How completely insane?"

I can tell she's softening, making this the most delicate moment of the drive so far—one wrong utterance and it's over, and this time no doubt for good. Nonetheless, I launch into this speech about real caring and trust over the long haul. I argue that on a sliding scale maybe we've slid as far as we're going to into that marital dead zone all couples fear, and from now on the momentum's thrust is up, up and away. It's the kind of testimonial you can only ever deliver straight-faced to someone you honest to God love, and actually mean it. Impassioned assertions that do not, however, as I've discovered firsthand, stand up well against the lessons of either logic or experience.

Z's an artist, a master glassblower with a degree from RISD, and I remind her how often she's argued her theory that anything can be transformed by art and love. Absolutely anything.

"This marriage?" I ask, flicking the wipers off again as we finally exit another squall. But this one's different, dissolving so slowly at the thin, opalescent blue rim of first light that it feels mystic. And I get serious chills when a swan emerges from that same dense snow behind us, with its wings outspread not three feet above the wet and shiny hood. It's that close, and Z whispers, "Archie," and I hit the brakes hard. On black ice as it turns out, and we're spinning now into a series of 360s, the top-heavy front end of the Caddy hesitating just long enough at the apex of each wide swoop for us to glimpse the torture of that enormous white bird's interminable somersaulting on the pavement.

We come to a stop in an empty field, the engine stalled. Z is holding my hand, squeezing it, and the radio is suddenly all static, like the snow, and Z is humming some made-up song. Just staring out the tinted windshield and humming, like she's been stunned. I can tell already that one of the swan's wings is broken, and one eye is completely shut, and the wind keeps lifting its neck feathers.

I don't want to move a muscle, but the gasoline fumes are strong and I'm afraid that the car might blow, so I switch the ignition off. And maybe it's the tinkling of the keys on the key ring—I'm not sure—but Z lets go of my hand and leans forward and takes off her navy peacoat and says, "Here." She says, "Please, Archie. You've got to go help it. You've got to."

What's most humane in this situation would be to put the swan out of its misery as quickly as possible, and by whatever available means. But try explaining that to the woman you've loved and are losing and so desperately want back in your life.

"Look, there's an inch of ice on its wings," I say, though I'm not sure how that matters exactly, except perhaps to solve the mystery of this terrible accident we've just witnessed.

"Go get it, Archie," she pleads, and she starts to cry because the swan is staring back at us with its one good eye, from me to Z, back and forth like that.

"You don't just walk up on wounded things," I say with absolute certainty. "Not on wild things, Z. Listen, I don't even have any gloves with me," which sounds like the chintziest and most insensitive and cowardly excuse in all God's creation. "Listen to me," I say, but she doesn't. Instead she lowers her face deeper into her hands and I notice, really for the first time, when I touch her hair, the first hints of gray, and how, unlike me, she's not wearing her wedding band. Which frightens me so much that I get out of the car and breathe deeply into the cold air to try and clear my aching head.

And it begins to snow again. Enormous feathery flakes floating down slow motion and so thick that when I wrap Z's wool coat around the swan and pick it up against my chest, I know she can only imagine in what direction I've gone, where it is I've bolted to under pressure this time. The only reason I don't call out to her, like someone lost and panicked, is that this bird has actually leaned its face against mine, and seems to be asleep.

Even more so when I lay the swan in the back seat, collar up, those black anchor buttons fastened like a line of poker chips down the center of its breast. It would be comical if it were not so damn sad.

She says, "Archie, look," and I do, this time in the rearview mirror, and what I see is that orange bill opening and closing as though it were trying to speak. Because I can't get the car started there is nothing we can do. The plumes of pink sulfur from the emergency flare I've already lit are visible on the road's shoulder. But nobody is driving this far outside of town on a Sunday morning. I imagine parishioners attending early Mass, and lighting candles at the feet of St. Francis, birds perched on his fingers in the Church of the Sacred Heart where Z and I were married in a tiny private ceremony.

Z, now huddled under the Hudson Bay blanket I stash in case of winter breakdowns, asks, "Is it really true that swans mate for life?" I nod, close my eyes, and wonder if the other is up there circling and circling, and then I crack the window and listen for that unmistakable slow whistle of its wings. I hear nothing, and I realize that it's not in me right now to confront the loss that sound would mean.

Z says she needs to say a couple of things, which she worries might sound foolish, but I tell her no, that nothing could with such a beautiful creature dying so close to us. She has no idea how soothing the music of her voice is. No earthly idea.

"We go way back, don't we, Archie?" she says, and I nod yes, her head on my shoulder, her right arm draped over the seat back where I know her fingers are fluttering slow, final dances for the swan. Then Z asks me if I remember *Swan Lake*, which of course I do—the only ballet I ever attended.

"Yes," I say, "every last detail"—the tight black strapless satin dress she wore and the way the camera shutter seemed to stop in mid-click, and that handful of white rose petals she threw toward me, laughing on those mammoth granite stairs outside the theater. And how she flapped her arms as though *she* might rise and fly, a raven, I thought back then, or a crow, or yes, a rare and elegant black swan.

"Archie," she says again, "don't you wish sometimes that we could retrieve the best parts of our past—just those—and hold onto them forever?" I swear to her that we can, which I know is a lie. "No," she says. "It's over. This time it has to end. This time for good."

"I know that," I tell her, and although true or not true, I want to believe that nothing ever really dies. But Z is already reaching for the swan, and crying again, as there must always be a first to cry out among the great flocks that take off by the thousands to migrate home. And then pair off, and because the world is sometimes like this, one must go on alone.

T W O

The Pig

In the end I did not contest the divorce. There were no grounds really. Just too many minuses in the marriage, as Z said. Too many wrong messages played out over time.

What's done is done, I conceded finally. And, with the DeVille recently pronounced dead with a seized engine, I considered myself fortunate to end up free and clear with this quiet and reliable, though high-mileage, ebony hearse my father left me in his will. Along with his well-oiled 1908 Holland & Holland double-barrel 16 gauge, and the deed to his getaway cabin with its eighty-five secluded lowland acres on a slow stretch of the Platte River where old lunker brown trout tuck in under the cool dark shade of undercut banks covered every summer in thick wild iris, rose hips, and spirea. Ruby-throated hummingbirds aflutter all day by the dozens on nearly invisible viridescent wings. If I concentrate, I can hear the holy water riffle far downstream. All of it clearly posted, plus a warning sign at the end of the rutted two-track drive that says LOCATE ANOTHER ROUTE TO PARADISE. And, as the fair-minded, no-nonsense judge made perfectly clear at the settlement hearing, two short weekends each month, and a portion of every summer, to spend with Rodney.

He's sound asleep beside me, the radio still tuned to WTCM. I crank it up so I can better hear Willie through the thick, insistent summer static: "Mamas don't let your babies grow up to be cowboys." It's one of only two or three classic country western tunes Rodney halfway likes, and it's time for him to wake up anyway. He's wearing my faded red-fringed childhood chaps, and cowboy boots with plastic silver spurs, and a fancy double holster packing two like-new six-shooters loaded with fat rolls of caps. Around his neck a tightly braided multicolor lariat tie. The entire outfit rescued from that mothballed attic war trunk above the funeral home the evening after my dad signed the agreement-to-sell papers. A real find, I thought back then, and now packaged and gift-wrapped and finally passed along to Rodney—all late birthday presents he opened last night on the screened-in porch, but without much enthusiasm. I could hardly get him to even try them on. And he ate only a sliver of the chocolate cake I'd baked, decorated with ten thin white candles arranged to form the letter *R*. Outside a full moon glowed, and the bright, corpulent white asses of thousands and thousands of fireflies throbbed above the water.

Which is why I was staring out there when he sneaked up and hugged me from behind and whispered in quick, panicky breaths, "Dad, I wish we could stay together forever. Like it used to be, I mean. Before you and Mom stopped having any fun." I nodded slowly and lowered my head, and I said back to him, "I know, and I want that too, more than anything in this world."

But here we are, just a few cruel minutes from the drop-off, Z's term for the Pig, an out-of-the-way pork-rib BBQ diner located exactly midway between Honor and New Buffalo, on old Route 31. As good or bad a rendezvous point for an in-state kid exchange as any, I suppose.

Rodney yawns, and even before opening his eyes, he sings, "Let 'em be doctors and lawyers and such." Then he unfastens his seat belt, and abruptly turns and draws, both barrels ablaze as he opens fire into the dark rectangular cavern of the hearse. "You're dead," Rodney says, as if the ghost of his grandfather were suddenly metamorphosing into flesh and bone and blood right before his eyes.

Rodney's named after his grandfather who is, in fact, back

there, not at rest in a top-of-the-line In God's Care casket, but rather packed tightly inside a box of White Rhino shotgun shells reloaded with his ashes.

On his deathbed almost a year ago, the two of us alone in the private, fourth-floor hospital room at dusk, he unexpectedly stirred and opened his eyes, flat gray, and I just stood there with this terrible, deep thrumming in my heart. Then, as he cleared his throat, I bent closer to him than I'd been in years, and he whispered in my ear, "Persona non grata, Arch. That's what the whole schmeer boils down to—a nobody's nobody unless you can forgive me. You suppose you can do that before I cut and run? Can you do that for your old man?" he said, the clear surgical breathing tube pinched inside his nostrils.

When I didn't speak, he bit his lip and grimaced, and, after another interminable couple of seconds, he said, laboring for breath, "For me?" Followed by this pained, open-handed gesture as if he half expected me to drive a twelve-penny spike right through his palm—nail him good one final time. I said nothing again—only stared and stared until his fingers balled slowly back into a fist, the knuckles glaring bone white on the starched sheet cuff, the thumbnail nearly purple. In that dead silence the bleep of the morphine pump sounded as loud as rifle fire.

Although I knew he was much too sick and weak, shrunken, what was left of his lungs continuously filling with fluids, I wanted him to cast off those covers, lower the iron bars, and emerge from the partially cranked-up dying bed and hit me. Dared him, really, my chin jutting out like some punk street tough. I'm not even sure why anymore, except that I'd both loved and hated him a million times over by then and I guess I just wanted him to acknowledge that and fight back one last time.

The room smelled like ether, my voice a high-pitched wheeze when I finally nodded and swallowed, my throat dry and scratchy, and I said, "Yes." I said, "Absolutely," which also meant, "So there. So what?" as if to confirm that life's paltry and perplexing incongruities could never, even here at the bittersweet end, be so easily undone.

He nodded, and the rain quit in the sudden calm that overcame us, and, without pity or recrimination for once, I said, "Look at that," as a last brief burst of golden sunlight poured through the corner window. His bottom lip quivered, and he sighted down the skinny length of his needle-bruised arms, and squeezed the imaginary trigger just once, the recoil pinning his shoulder blades even deeper into the two narrow indentations of the pillow.

"Promise me," he said. "If not for you, for your mother then," and he grimaced until I agreed to wade out chest-deep into the river, and there, one late-October night under the resplendence of the northern lights, scatter his ashes skyward. "Our final secret, Arch," he said in a thick watery voice.

I stood perfectly still, watching the slow rise and fall of his ribs under his thin cotton gown. A few additional words formed on his lips but were not spoken, and again I said, "Okay. You got it," and he smiled weakly as I drew the blinds to let him drift a little further away, his index finger pointing up, a gesture exactly like I use around my son whenever I hear blues or snow geese passing on their long migrations home.

The hardscrabble parking lot is empty, and I pull in right under the smirking pink neon Petunia Pig sign blinking on and off above the overhang, painted white to resemble an out-of-proportion ankle-high picket fence. Rodney says he likes the way the pig's outline shimmers and blurs across the shiny black hood of the air-conditioned hearse. What he hates about the hearse is the fake, lingering perfume smell of the hothouse flowers. Hates it, hates it, hates it, he says, and I immediately conjure up image after aromatic image of feathery black orchids in ornate water bowls and cachepots and smoked glass vases. Followed by intricately tiered arrangements of unspotted-pink Mona Lisa lilies, the most fragrant oriental hybrid in the hemisphere. And, wafting up again out of the distant past, my dad's perennial, unconditional first-choice condolence pick—"Oh, God knows, nothing beats the moist, intoxicating scent of alabaster gardenia straps," he'd say to anyone who asked. "No question about it. All others—well, let's just dub them lesser flowers. Substitutes." I never said so, but I much preferred the spicy redolence of paperwhites, which I'd sometimes carry from the hearse to the burial plots. I once secretly plucked a bunch from a casket spray and made a tiny bouquet of them for my mom. "Cruel," she said. "So young and already so cruel," when I told her how those older kids—those morbid-minded smart-offs I both feared and despised—had already started calling me Pansy or Flower-Boy. Or said, "Morning, Glory," and tried to trip me as I made my way to the far back of the school bus.

Rodney insists the collective, undiluted stench will stay buried alive for all time inside the velvet drapes and pleated upholstery. It reeks from way down deep in the pores, he says, and it makes his eyes water and itch. Overkill, he calls it—a new favorite word of his—and I don't doubt he's right. But to be perfectly honest, I've grown immune over the years to even the most pungent floral smells. Except, of course, in sweet memory everlasting.

"Dad," he says when I ease the hearse into park and switch off the ignition. "How come you and Mom can't, you know, not fight so much?" To which there is no new way to respond anymore, except to shrug and turn away, and swing open the heavy hearse door, and step face-first into the windless, almost unbearable heat of the day.

Inside, the waitress sits sidesaddle on the Formica counter edge, arms folded, her long dangling tanned legs crossed at the ankles, left one over right. High arches, silver toe rings on her middle toes. It's the first time I've seen her wearing those clear plastic flip-flops, toenails polished crimson, and the white double-hem of her starched uniform a steam-ironed sheen across her thighs. Over the past seven months I've known her as Kea and Corynn and Star and Scallop and Trinity-Lee. Today the plastic nametag above her breast pocket says "Ray."

If it was late and I was flying solo, I'd no doubt abandon my best behavior and give into the temptation to sit on that thinly padded chrome swivel stool directly in front of her, slouch forward, and order up the homemade sausage tops and slaw. A couple quick hits of Tabasco to pique the taste buds, and maybe splurge with an Old Milwaukee longneck instead of my usual cup of steaming black coffee. Or, as I sometimes do in this ungodly swelter, a glass of ice-cold sun tea with extra lemon. She's got sleepy lips, and hooded quicksilver eyes—light-shining wolf eyes—which appear to stare right through me as I pass. Hair as thick and black as Elvis, and styled not all that differently. I like her and I like how she sometimes smells like fabric softener when she breezes past. Still, I can't imagine her take-home's worth the hours or the heat, the interminable waiting around for slumming, road-weary customers like yours truly to sweep her off her feet. But I'm glad she's here. Lately, whenever she speaks my stomach walls contract a little more than I'm used to. Maybe one of these days, after Rodney's on his way back home with his mom, I'll stick around. Maybe.

Rodney leads us to the rear booth by the window where we always sit, waiting for his mother who, as the oddsmakers would say, is a lock to arrive at least a half hour late. It's a bet I'd surely take, though I've long since steered clear of the bookies and the numbers, and those dark smoky pool halls where I once believed I could run the table deep into the twenty-first century.

"Right on time as always," Ray says. "Score one more for the undertaker," and she licks and makes a check mark in the air with her index finger.

"I told you before already," Rodney says, "he's *not* an under-taker."

"Oops," she says, "I forgot."

"He's a river guide," Rodney says, a half truth, half lie, since I've refused lately to hustle and schmooze those long-winded, over-Velcroed multimillionaires who pay me top dollar plus tips to lead them—always in gentlemanly weather—to the spawning beds of the steelhead or salmon.

"Yeah, for sure—on the River Styx," Ray jokes, and Rodney says back, "No, on the River Platte," and I smile up at her and listen for a minute while Jerry Springer discusses life choices with a pair of anorectic cousins in love. Little matching Irish stiffs—sixteen-year-olds with skinny braids, and nose freckles, and identical high foreheads. Silver tongue studs they simultaneously flash for the camera upon request, and I can see now from a reverse-angle close-up how desperately they squeeze the life out of each other's pallid, almost translucent hands.

Ray smoothes her apron, and says, "I got news for those two kids—up there in lights is the last place they want to be."

The TV is anchored and tilted slightly forward on a swivel bracket above the grill. It's that kind of joint—a stand-up oscillating fan with tattered, multicolored 4-H ribbons streaming out. A framed dollar bill on the wall, and pitted ice cube crescents you can scoop from your water glass and press to your pulsing temples or throat, or rub back and forth across your exhausted eyelids. Whatever it takes to compose yourself in this no-man's-land, this purgatorial middle distance where, once again, you're condemned to give up your one and only son.

"A slice of watermelon," Rodney says, because he can see it glistening inside the glass cooler. And because it's the kind of food his mother has raised him to prefer. A devout chopped-raisins-and-nuts-mix convert all the way, which is fine by me, and I wish I had the willpower to follow his lead. In his current kid vocabulary are tabbouleh, radicchio, ginseng, sorbet, Dean & Deluca. He's more spoiled than I'd like, and smart and already well-versed in the language significant privilege provides. Sometimes in good humor I'll razz him by intentionally mispronouncing certain words, altering a context: "No, Dad, not para*sol*," he recently explained to me. "Para*sail*." A to-do beach vacation concept I find downright alien, though come mid-February he and his mom fly off again for a week in the Caribbean.

Z's a hardcore health and fitness disciple, a vegan of late, a devotee of purest-state edibles, plus a gallon of bottled H_2O per day, minimum. Whenever she wears anything low-cut or V-necked her protruding collarbone still drives me pretty feral. She's living proof that it all works: from the micro-nutrient supplements to the high, ankle-weighted leg kicks—three sets of fifty reps—and painful stomach crunches.

"Just water for now, thanks," I say, and I have half a mind to retrieve my dad's minor-key requiem cassette from the hearse so

Ray could play Ravel's "Pavane for a Dead Princess" while Rodney eats in silence. After all, the frail, pale-skinned anorectics have already broken into magnificent, fitful tears in front of the surprise guest psychiatrist who warns that their affair will be short-lived at seventy-one pounds apiece, and wilting.

"Vermin sleaze," Ray says. "Entirely rodent. What a complete and total turnoff. Look at them, supposedly educated adults so dead to the world. It makes *me* want to gag. Those poor kids—they don't stand a snowball's chance." Still, the audience applauds their mothers' shrill and practical and simple advice: The food's getting cold, so snap out of it girls, and pick up your mortal forks, and dig in. Otherwise, bye-bye. It's your funerals.

Set before them is a five-star meal. There's a single oversized plate of oysters Rockefeller, a dozen at least—appetizers for feasting on before the main course of beef Wellington, followed by crème brûlée for dessert. But the two cousins turn toward each other in unison instead and passionately kiss. And the applause turns to groans and sighs, and Rodney spoons out the dark shiny seeds and lifts the watermelon to his mouth, the sweet pink juice dripping across the light greenish rind to his wrists. He glances out the window again, and, at least in late-afternoon silhouette, he appears to be a handsome, happy enough, well-adjusted little kid.

"How sad," Ray says after the commercial break, elbows out, hands on her hips. "Like those freaks are in danger of saving *any-body's* life. Look at them. They won't let their daughters get a word in edgewise."

Ray shakes her head and shrugs again and slides me the check as the phone rings, and right then Z's white ragtop Beemer pulls up alongside the hearse, the fiery sun reflecting bright blue from the dark-tinted windshield. The silver-framed vanity plate says ZELDA.

"Mom's here," Rodney says, as he always does, wiping his sticky hands and face on the napkin. But it's not Z who steps out after a long minute during which nobody utters a single sound. It's some open-shirted hairy guy wearing ultra-black ball-hugger Spandex biking shorts, and wraparound sunglasses hanging from a lanyard around his neck. I've never laid eyes on him before, but as he slams the car door and stands there buttoning his boxy aloha shirt, Rodney says, "Nope, it's Omar."

"It's who?" I ask.

"Omar," he says again. "Mom's friend. He owns the new health food store and restaurant in town. You wouldn't like it."

"Oh?"

"Uh-uh. You'd maybe like Omar though. He used to play World Cup soccer. Mom says he was a big star in Brazil. Like a national hero."

"And now?" I ask.

"Now? Oh, he's just kinda our backyard goalie. Sometimes me and Timmy Reminschnider line up penalty kicks after dinner. Both of us at the same time from not very far out on the grass—'cept we hardly ever score. If we want, he'll even wear a blindfold to give us a chance. He blocks our shots just by the vibrations. That's what he says. Really, he's pretty neat. Plus I like his accent, and how when I ask him he walks up the back stairs—the whole entire way from back on the grass—on his hands."

I still can't tell if Z's riding shotgun or not. But I'd bet no by the way big star Omar of the Corumba Titmice pantomimes a clownish, serpentine dribble right up under our window, his arms horizontal as if he's gliding toward us slow motion, the tight muscles in serious bulge mode above both knees. I'm sure, by the way he stands with his feet spread apart, legs bent, that he intends to cap off his grand entrance by performing a standing back flip in his Birkenstocks.

Although I say nothing I'm seething under my breath, my poker-faced Omar stare-down conveying absolutely zip. Rodney presses his forehead against the thick, wavy pane, and that's exactly where Omar knocks. A quick rap-rap with the back of his knuckles, followed by an emphatic double thumbs-up fisting of the heavy air. Rodney waves through a fit of giggles and that alone constitutes a more upbeat conversation than my son and I have had all day.

Omar points at Z's car, points like he's a one-man rescue party, and it's time now to boogie back home, pal, just you and me.

Think again, I say to myself—think long and hard—because there's no way in hell he's driving away alone with my kid, and I don't care how many kiddy penalty shots he's blocked at dusk in Z's backyard. In loco parentis my ass.

"So he's there at the house a lot," I say to Rodney—a thinly veiled combination statement/question—and when he doesn't respond, I ask, "Why didn't you mention him before? I mean, how does this square with anything? How's this happen?"

He sighs in a gesture strictly St. James, strictly maternal. He says, "Rule one," meaning that it has already been agreed to by all parties concerned that he doesn't rat out either parent on private, personal matters. No matter what, no blown secrets, no taking sides—it's outside his jurisdiction, remember? But already I feel outnumbered, ganged up on.

"Dad," Rodney says, "you don't need to worry—he drives me places all the time. In his car a lot, but in Mom's car too."

"Drives you where?"

"Oh, like to Mohawk Planet to play miniature golf, or to ride the adult waterslide with me. Or to Double-Double's for super scoops of Superman ice cream. Homemade. Mom says from the cows standing right behind the fence. Guernseys. You can pet 'em afterwards if you want. Their tongues feel like wet sandpaper. They're really hot."

"Is that right?" I say, my heart wild in its ribcage of pins, and doubling in size, as if to swallow me from the inside out any second now.

Rodney nods, a single demonstrative nod, and then he adds, "Plus he bought me a long-haired hamster, too."

"A hamster."

"Mm-hmm—Gilroy. A rare, winter white Russian hamster. A dwarf. This little," he says, and cups both small palms in front of his chest. "For my birthday. He said, 'Runt'—that's what he calls me to be funny—'every growing Montessori dragon in North America needs a pet.'" I force a brief, not entirely understanding fatherly smile, and Rodney says, "The cage wheel's red and white. It looks like one of those old speeded-up barber's poles when Gilroy gets running faster and faster. His hair's so long you can't even see his legs go. Just his tiny pink feet if you get down low and close enough."

"If there's anyone here," Ray shouts, "last name Angel, he's wanted on the line. Urgent like." She's looking directly out at me from the kitchen, from above those Dutch doors that form the two separate halves of a sow's enormous pink rump. Then she covers the mouthpiece, and slow-rolls her eyes and says, "Yow." And by the time I press the clammy receiver to my ear, Omar has already stolen my seat, and a healthy gulp of my untouched ice water, and he's slapped down a ten-spot to cover the late-afternoon health snack, slapped it down like a cheap bribe.

"Who this time to the boneyard?" I ask, repeating what I'd heard my dad say to me some nights when he was exhausted and dozing off in front of the TV and the black rotary-dial business phone awakened him upstairs.

"Everybody's safe and accounted for," Z says, though my heavy breathing makes clear that it's not exactly all quiet on the mid-Michigan front. So let's forego the bear-with-me-I-can-explain-this-unexpected-call because "You can't," I say. "A deal's a deal, and this one happens to be legal. In triplicate. As far as I'm concerned, that's it, to the strictest letter of the law, just like you wanted. Remember, you're the one who served the papers, Z. So don't come on to me now with any after-hour amendments. And no more surprise attacks. No way."

"A surprise attack of conjunctivitis," she says.

"Try some Visine and a pair of Polaroids," I say. "Works miracles."

"Excuse me?"

"Visine," I say again. "Polaroids."

"And what exactly is that supposed to imply?"

"Don't know, except that we're here—me and Rodney—like we're supposed to be, right on the button, and you're still down there, right? So why don't you tell me."

"Ah, business as usual. Fine, go ahead . . . point and shoot, Archie. Let me have it—both barrels. Fire away, which I'm sure you will."

"Any wonder why?" I say. "I mean . . . come on, we're talking about Rodney here. What'd you expect?"

"Can't you be reasonable? I'm three hours away, and highly contagious. And anyway, Omar's already there, isn't he?"

"Couldn't tell you," I say. "What's this . . . what'd you call him—Gomer? What's he look like?"

"*O*mar," she says. "As in Sharif. As in shockingly dark and tall—great deltoids, hair like Antonio Banderas. As in one half of the adorable fornicating couple. Carnal tunnel syndrome. There: isn't that what you want to hear so you can spontaneously combust again and ruin everybody's day? Do you really believe I'd send someone I couldn't trust—in *my* car to pick up *my* kid?"

"*Our* kid," I say. "Ours. It's your car, but he's our kid."

"Hallelujah, what a dad! But just for the record, you're the one I worry about on the highway. You're the accident waiting to happen, not Omar. He's a better driver by far than I am."

"Terrific, but if he's headed this way . . ."

"Oh good—just what we need, another ridiculous hothead score to settle. Well, you're nothing if not predictable, Archie, I'll give you that. Always lobbing one hand grenade after another. Bombs away. Can't you concede something, anything, so I know it's at least still possible? Say . . . say it's hot out today. Say the sky's pale blue."

"It's hot out today," I say without hesitation. "The sky's pale blue."

"What a comfort. Now, can we just back up and clean-slate this conversation and begin it over again? Like two reasonably intelligent adults? Like parents? It shouldn't be all that difficult to improve on this start, should it?"

Uh-huh. Right, I think, and I pause for an approximate ten-count, as if to slow-scan the Pig, and then I say, "Okay." I say, "Let's see . . . I guess not—sorry. Except for me, nobody else in here quite fits the Omar profile."

"Mustache?" she says? "Brazilian? About your height—a little thinner?"

"Not a sign," I lie, but he's impossible to miss when I look out at him, posing and sizing me up, giving me the sneaky once-over out of the nervous corner of his left eye. I'm trying hard not to lose my grip so early in this reconfigured conversation, but I do with the stakes so high. I say, "Not unless you mean Don Ho huddled up in the back booth with our son. That him, Z? That who we're talking about here?"

"There's no need to malign him. He's only trying to help out, to do me a favor. So, if it's all right with you . . ."

"It's not. And correct me if I'm in error, but I don't remember discussing any middleman errand boy. Do you?" I say, hissing into the phone like a pissed-off snapping turtle. Then I answer for her, my face muscles tightening, my back teeth beginning to ache: "No—not by a long stretch. So on that front, meeting adjourned. There, how's that—calm and reasonable enough?"

"What if it were an attractive middle*woman*? Any concessions then?"

"Get off it," I say, momentarily glancing over at Ray. She's staring right at me, baleful-like, sad-eyed, as if it's perfectly clear in the midst of this public melee that I'm all alone fighting the good fight in a losing cause.

"That's not an answer," Z says. "That's your typical deflection response whenever you don't want to talk."

"No difference," I say. "None. A guy, a woman, that's hardly the point," my face a grotesque oblong cabbage-red reflection in the toaster's glare as I turn away into the kitchen.

"Talk about hypocritical," she says. "Go ahead and deny it all you want, but your real gripe is that you're jealous, Archie, aren't you? Fine, but why is it you *still* need to suck up everybody's oxygen?"

It's true, I'm nearly hyperventilating here in hell's kitchen where there's no circulating air at all, and where, because I'm too slow on the comeback, Z says, "Selfishness, that's why." She says, "That and arrogance and self-pity all rolled into one. My father's right, how could I have loved a man so damn obstinate?"

"Principled, you mean."

"No, downright obstinate—and so out of touch. How does that even happen—from an antique four-poster canopy to a feather mattress on the floor? You've pared it right down like you always insisted you wanted. Your books and your fly-rods . . ."

"Less to rescue from the fire," I say, and she says back, "Oh, right—'Simplify, simplify, simplify!' Rodney says you've gone and surrounded the property with bat houses."

"Natural insect control," I say. "Over twelve hundred mosquitoes per brown bat per hour. Works wonders."

"So does a bug zapper," she says.

I let it go and we both listen in silence for a moment as the current crackles in the line, the voltage surging through every curly-tailed, buzzing pink neon porker tube in the diner.

"What's for dinner?" I ask, part bad joke, part desperate hope, and she says back, her tone turning suddenly quiet and sober, "Don't flatter yourself. Dinner does not include you, Archie. There's nothing here for you anymore."

"Rodney's there," I say, barely above a whisper. And in the giant silence that follows I can hear somebody playing "Danny Boy" on an electric keyboard, all the lovely Irish sadness vanishing just like that. An exit march for the famished, perishing anorectics. In the booth, Omar is being held at gunpoint, both fluttering hands raised operatically high above his swirl of shiny dark curls, and the heat from the rotisserie of sizzling pork ribs at my back is making me sweat murderously, runnels of it down my ribs and spine and underarms.

"Archie," she says, "please don't." She says, "If you pull up front or into the driveway, the new neighbors next door are going to think somebody's died . . ."

As she talks I watch Omar goofing and tousling Rodney's hair right in front of me, and it's awfully abrupt but I say, "Sit tight, I'm on my way." For good measure I half slam the receiver down, and open the oinker's ass-crack wide to the walls with a high-drama ka-bang, and I just stand there, sweating bullets and breathing fire, and staring out at the startled odd-lot symmetry of Rodney and Omar.

Directly above me, Jerry Springer offers a pleading shrug to the beleaguered young couple, followed by final condolences to their parents, to *all* the disfavored normal mothers and fathers out there whose crazed, new-millennium crackpot kids keep starving themselves to death for God knows what.

"For love, and just possibly for a little understanding?" Ray says, her eyes narrowed on the TV screen. "Some tenderness, people? Sweet Mary mother of God, they're only kids. Is that so difficult to grasp?"

Nobody answers, and for a split second I'm certain she's going to puncture her palm by pressing, full weight, on the shiny steel receipt spindle by the cash register. But she doesn't. She freezes me again with the deep poured-silver gaze of her eyes, and slides the check all the way down, slowly and carefully.

And Jesus Christ I can't remember ever feeling so uncertain about what to say or shout or pray for under my breath. So I simply point at Rodney and gesture for him to follow me outside. He does, without argument or hesitation, holstering his sidearms and scarcely lifting his feet as he clicks his worn boot heels behind me across the faded, scuffed-up linoleum floor.

I slide behind the steering wheel, and turn the key in the ignition, and hit the power locks, and wait for Rodney to buckle up. Once he does I ask, "Which way?" half hoping he'll point us back toward the territories, where I'd sure like to make another desperation run into the heart of bear and badger and wildcat country, deeper in than we've ever been. Pitch a tent. Build a campfire and roast some hot dogs and marshmallows. Talk with my son.

"You know how to get there," Rodney says in a hushed, subdued voice, his fingertips brushing back and forth along the black vinyl altar of the dashboard. Right below the greenish, opaque plastic St. Christopher my dad refused to remove despite the church's insistence that it posed a potential safety hazard. "And don't start any trouble at Mom's this time, promise?"

"Why would I do that?"

"Because Mom says you're just like Buster when he used to chase and snap at his tail. She says you never learn, you just spin around in the same nutty circle getting nowhere and making everybody around you dizzy whenever you don't get your way."

"Get my way? When's the last time *that* happened?"

"I don't know. I just wish you and Mom wouldn't yell, that's all. I hate it."

"Hey, give your old man a little credit," I say, but he won't. No look or smile, so I offer a contrite, lopsided nod, and straighten up in the seat, and shift into reverse without another word. I haven't smoked a single cigarette all day—at least not in front of Rodney—but I reach now for the pack of Lucky Strikes in my T-shirt pocket. The T-shirt reads: HE WHO DIES WITH THE MOST TOYS, STILL DIES. I don't have a proper change of clothes with me. Only my dad's dry-cleaned black three-piece funeral suit still hanging in back like a ghost behind the clear plastic wrap. And his stiff black shoes and pocket Bible: "To every *thing* there is a season," and it's already getting on toward late July, in the year of our Lord, 2000.

I hit the blinker and turn out of the parking lot into the sporadic, southbound Sunday traffic. And I think, So this is what Z and I have been reduced to, a few strained minutes in a neutral, public place like the Pig, which never worked to sort out a single thing of any consequence. And the telephone's an inevitable disaster whenever we've got pressing issues to address. Omar, for starters, although I tell myself he's just a distraction who will outlive his old-world charm and be history in another six weeks—out by the autumnal equinox. Which is none too soon, though it's possible I suppose that Rodney could do worse than have a stepfather who blindfolds himself to give the neighborhood kids a chance at becoming the next great Pelé.

Still, the whole thing ticks me off big-time. I don't mean to, but when I punch the cigarette lighter a little too hard with the heel of my palm, Rodney winces and inches away even closer to the door, where he sits on his hands, and stiffens and turns away. I can see his blurred, blank face in the passenger's-side mirror, his eyes closed as if, for the remainder of the drive home, he's going to take up residence inside his head. He's going to blot me out entirely, the same way I used to do in the car with my dad.

"Sometimes it sticks," I say. "Sometimes . . ." but it's a weak-minded appeal, and when the lighter pops a few seconds later I pretend not to notice. "Listen, I'm sorry, buckaroo," I say. "Really, I am. It's just that—you know—that charade back there. Talk about being sandbagged. Just between you and me, it was a bit more than I bargained for, y'know?"

He's only half listening at best, and it's clear I'm in trouble when I can't even get him to join me on the chorus as Johnny Cash belts out, "And I fell into a burning ring of fire."

The man in black, I think, and I slide the cigarette behind my ear, and concentrate on the road, remembering how I used to pilfer my dad's Pall Malls, one each night, and how I'd drag deeply on that unlit unfiltered cigarette, pretending I was instantly grown up, and long gone from there. Then I'd exhale, and every good thing I imagined—every single impossible one—seemed so real in such a vague and unreal way, and so absolutely gettable.

THREE

Civil Twilight

We're traveling at funeral speed past the west lawns of the big houses, headlights on, the neighborhood shadowed by elms I thought certain should have died out down here by now, the branches loud with blackbirds.

In this slowly fading crepuscular light the ginger-colored hair of the two Reminschnider children playing croquet appears to be metallic as they look up, the mounded, mulched circle of seasonal flowers much too top-heavy and red, oversized heads drooping at the base of the aluminum flagpole. Rodney waves, but his impassive-eyed friends do not wave back, the lacquered mallets resting on their shoulders like ax handles or baseball bats, the multicolored wooden balls dead still on this lawn of a hundred leaning wickets.

Out of nervousness Rodney begins clucking his tongue, just as I used to on those interminable, seemingly aimless evening excursions with my dad who'd spent all afternoon in the basement among the deceased, making them presentable, he always said. Or even beautiful, though I never understood back then what beauty had in common with the grave, or the crematorium. I remember the incessant moans of mourners gathered in the separate coffer-ceilinged viewing parlors downstairs. And I remember, right after Rodney was born, how I swore to myself every single night before finally falling asleep, that any kid of mine would know me better by the joyous, living/breathing sounds of the out-of-doors: loons, marsh frogs, whistler swans.

Fact: The ratio of plastic pink lawn flamingos to the real living thing in this country is seven hundred to one. A statistic my ex-father-in-law mentioned to me one time, the two of us streamer fishing for kings on the gravel beds of the Little Manistee. He owned major stock in the company that mass-produced these substitute, endangered exotic birds, and referred to himself as a true-blue, late-century pioneer. Self-made, he said, an entrepreneur in the sweet, sweet science of amassing lots of American currency. Invest aggressively, he preached without a hint of irony, and pray they *all* die out—every last damn breathing shitbird on earth. It'll send the stock right through the ozone, and add years of hourly comfort to your life. To Z's life, he amended. Hell, the future's there for the taking, for those in the know, so take, take, take, and by whatever means necessary. That's the key, so chuck the principled nice-guy routine and get with the goddamn program. Look, the world is what it is. I didn't cook up the rules. I'm just here to help you understand them. It's a simple matter of getting you re-centered, realigned. That's all. Just remember that instinct is no more than force of habit, and what I'd like to understand—what's bugging me is: Where in fuck's name are your survival skills? Where in the goddamn hell is your staying power?

No way was it meant as a joke or an exaggeration. I wanted to tell him how much I appreciated his impassioned mission statement, but that I was not some journeyman fortune hunter beset by nightmares of living too low off the proverbial hog, and that some things you just couldn't—no matter what—put a price on. Instead I said, "C'mon, Brock, you don't believe all that—you can't possibly," the Golden Witch glinting as I twitched it a few times under the clear skin of the tailwater while I reeled in. I'd already limited out, having tailed and released all five silvery-sided salmon in the knee-deep back eddy, while he had landed none. And cursed them all, and ignored every not-so-subtle angling tip I floated his way—unwanted advice from his out-lander river-bum son-in-law. A pair of late-leaving cedar waxwings danced and kissed in the air currents above us, and I pointed up and shrugged and said, "Who really needs money that badly?"

It must have been the tone I used, given how his jaw locked tighter and tighter as he stared straight ahead from the thorny underbrush of his eyebrows, his neck knotting up and turning scarlet, his pulse about to rupture. A wave of new fish nosed into the trough in front of us, a whole parade of them, but he only nodded once in acknowledgment before backing slowly out of the riverbed and onto the bank, where he announced, "I do. I need the money. For another fucking worthless goddamn fishing pole." Then he carefully broke down his brand-new custom three-piece Sage nine-weight, saluted me from under his long-billed cap, and proceeded to snap each deep purple graphite section over his knee. It sounded like pistol fire in the cold morning, the first light snow of the season beginning to fall.

He's the one who convinced Z to think first and foremost of marriage not as a sacrament but as a potential blood sport, a liability—especially ours, a shotgun job, as he called it, a hostile takeover—and to protect her killer trust portfolio with armor-clad prenups, meaning as little common property as necessary. Separate last names, so forget that touchy-feely hyphen crap—St. James–Angel or Angel–St. James. What's this world coming to, for Christ's sake? And separate checking accounts, separate long-term security investments. No hard feelings—but consider the rules of evidence, the discrepancy here between bride and groom both in earning potential and in current net worth. Do the math. You'd have to be born ass first from the Great Mother not to see the gross inequity in that, he said. "Numbers don't lie, Captain Ahab, so let's screw all that river-worship crap and get a few things straight right up front." Noble advice, I guess, against any sudden, drunken urge of mine to cash out prematurely.

Z does not use the word "rebel," with or without a cause, or "passion" to describe that holier-than-thou behavior of mine, which she considers futile, if not downright mortifying. "For crying out loud," she'd say. "Rodney's embarrassed half to death by these watchdog displays. And about what? The Federal Reserve renaming its currency after fish and waterfowl? It's not going to happen, Archie, and I don't care if you were only joking. See this fistful of unpaid bills? Would you rather I wrote them out, or would you like to do it?" Point taken, and with it my silent admonishments these days to save the birds, to save us all. Because that's what it's about, restraint and forgiveness, as my dad reminded me on his deathbed, and, like magic, the palpitations subside.

"I'm hot," Rodney says, and I press the electric window buttons and turn the air conditioner back on high for the final hundred yards or so. Out of nowhere, a rollerblading replica of a younger Suzanne Somers steps up over the high granite curb to the sidewalk and brakes and genuflects all at once. She's fully plugged in and makes a wide canary yellow sign of the cross with her handheld Walkman as we glide by, her dangling gold crucifix appearing to wink between her mushed-up, silicone-enhanced, high-end breasts. I learned long ago—and I learned it the hard way—that there are no sure things in this life, but if I had to put my money on what she's listening to, I'd go with AC/DC's trademark "Highway to Hell." Z insists I ought to keep abreast of what's current in the culture instead of always theorizing and carping—my God—about how this generation's music will be their cross to bear.

All I know for sure is that the gray-faced, overweight black lab on the rollerblader's expansion leash is panting badly, so I pray silently that they're headed for the lake. She's wearing tight shiny white shorts and one of those designer sports bras and a white helmet with matching knee and elbow pads, fancy new fingerless gloves, a water bottle attached like a .38 to her waist. Perfect glossy mag–ad bleached-white teeth, and a single war-painted white zinc oxide stripe down her nose, and enough matte black pencil around her eyes to excite Rocky Raccoon. A Roller Slam queen, perhaps, on a different street, in another town. Here, under the invisible daystars, she looks only rich and foolish and beach-singed the color of darkened caramel. Unlike me, she looks for all the civilized world like this is exactly where she belongs, among these wealthy Lake Michigan waterfront estates.

"The Vansipes," Rodney blurts out. "The Sparrows . . . the Kastenbaums . . . the Cavells . . . the Bauchs." It's as if he's counting down, in reverse alphabetical order, all the way to *A*, to Angel, although it's Z's maiden name embossed in sparkling silver on the mailbox. "St. James," he says, as we approach the house, all four thousand plus square feet of it, replete with frosty central air, fold-up treadmill, and stationary bike permanently positioned in front of the monster, high-resolution flat-screen surround-sound satellite-feed TV. A call-for-action entertainment center where, when Oprah walks on stage, she looms as large as the Vatican.

In the master bedroom there's a two-person Jacuzzi with different-colored underwater lights, and jets powerful enough to realign a damaged spine. Seaweed loofahs hanging from every gold-plated, swan-shaped shower neck, and all the shower curtains 100 percent hemp.

The Jenn-Aire state-of-the-art kitchen includes electric gourmet gizmos that peel and de-seed and microslice everything from maraschino cherries to bloodroot to roasted garlic to—sure, why not—Brazilian dates.

We're talking a suburban domicile with tamper-proof windows and locks. And a security system to deter intruders like yours truly just in case I decide to sneak up some night under the cover of darkness to get a glimpse of Z one more time in her glassblowing studio behind the house, the gas furnace ablaze.

Whenever I dream about her, I'm right there sponging her bare neck and shoulders and back with ice water to cool her down. Her hair's pulled back into a ponytail, and she's wearing goggles. Glass wind chimes and gazing balls hang everywhere, with an unimaginable spectrum of colors, and it's the blue fire's natural updraft and not any breeze through the window screens that makes them pulse and shimmer incandescent in the dying light.

"*Zelda* St. James," I say, because Rodney and I are speaking in code now, attempting to lay the groundwork for whatever might or might not go wrong next.

There's no BMW in sight. No Z and no blindfolded interloper diving toward the dying, overinflated vibrations of simultaneously kicked soccer balls. The place seems deserted, the morning newspaper still rolled up in its plastic orange wrapper on the stoop, the blinds lowered tightly to the eggshell semigloss sills. Z is undaunted by the upkeep costs: housekeeper three days a week, and all yard maintenance—summer and winter—contracted out. Twenty-first-century splendor comes at considerable cost, but that's the price, Z says, of living a life a cut above.

"All set?" I say, and I cock one thumb, and then the other, imitating Butch Cassidy and Sundance before their final, fatal charge, though I'm sure Rodney could care less about either of those desperadoes. In fact, he's already unstrapped his six-guns and left them on the seat beside the spurs and chaps and lariat tie, the cowboy boots kicked off into the foot-well.

In the side-view mirror the rollerblader is no more than a blur or a ghost, vanishing into the distance. There's no human movement anywhere. Except, of course, for Rodney who is right this instant thrusting both hands into the deep cargo pockets of his baggy, down-past-his-knees Patagonia shorts, as if he intends to pull them inside out like a final disclosure on the nothing this weekend has turned out to be. Instead he simply shambles away, chin on chest and not a single wave or over-the-shoulder backglance at me, as if I'm no longer present, or never was. His unlaced Nikes' heels light up red each time they touch the ground. I rest my head on the backs of my hands, and grip the steering wheel hard as I follow him all the way with my eyes until he opens the front door, and disappears inside.

~~~~~

FOUR

How Like an Angel
Came I Down

"Life goes on," my dad used to say returning from one of our evening drives, "but rarely long enough to get it right."

The year was 1969, and Lonnie McQuinlin had not been honored with a hero's burial, or with a flag-draped casket or a military salute. Unless you consider the occasional, distant small-arms fire from somebody shooting rats that drizzly March morning at the Hazelton county dump.

He was certainly not the first to have arrived stateside in a black plastic body bag. But he was the first to have arrived, gutted by shrapnel, at our back door. My mom said I wasn't supposed to gawk, not then, not ever. But it was Saturday morning, and she was out grocery shopping at the Grand Union—double-coupon day—and my dad was just about ready to head down to work, making what he called a decent enough living at this ancient art. His red tie was clipped to his short-sleeved white shirt, and he repeated what he'd told me at least a hundred times: that life is a dangerous and bumpy ride—each minute of each brief disappearing day—and that everybody eventually meets his maker, young and old alike. But it's nothing to fear or dwell on, certainly nothing to lose any sleep over. There's a tiny dark speck of death waiting in that very first breath we take, he said, that first consecrated stir—the original beginning of the inevitable end. And if the deceased happened to depart from this particular mid-Michigan municipality, then more than likely they'd stop first at Angel & Sons Funeral Home, before the eternal traveling on. He never once referred to himself as God's assistant, but for years that's how I thought of him. I thought, maybe that's how we got our Angel surname.

Fact: The world's population has recently exceeded six billion. War, therefore, is only one of many practical, necessary evils. Because of this, Lonnie would never turn nineteen, his history already unremarkably complete, and so brief: son of Paul and Bridget E. McQuinlin, decent, noncombative blue-collar folks who purchased an affordable, low-end, electroplated, single-hinged E-25 particle-board casket. I'm not 100 percent positive, but it only makes sense that they'd pause and press their throbbing fingertips to the two-point brushed-gold finish and slate blue rails of the more expensive, guaranteed-to-last-forever models with the raw, pearly blue silk pillows and flowing velvet or satin insides.

What I do know is that Lonnie played class-D high school football, and referred inaccurately to himself as "The Torturer." Nose tackle. And in his senior year, following the final losing game of another losing season, he hot-wired a car, a new shiny maroon Buick Electra with beige leather upholstery, and drove it without a valid license or disguise all around the downtown on the busiest shopping night of the week. Stopped at stoplights, used his turn signals. Honked and saluted a group of bare-legged cheerleaders standing forlornly outside Papa G's in their letter sweaters and bobby sox, and shouted "Go Badgers" out the open passenger's-side window without exciting a single smile or word of response. Several hours later he abandoned the car at the limestone quarry, an empty Seagrams nip on the seat, and the front bumper not three feet from the eroding bluff edge. But not before he removed the AM/FM tuner and the Buick's fancy hood ornament, for a keepsake, he told the judge. As a first offender, he opted for the armed services instead of jail. He had pale red hair, an unctuous, nasal voice, and a sullen-faced, autistic younger sister named Michelle who pointed and pointed at the two cobalt agates someone—possibly her—had placed during the viewing on Lonnie's permanently sealed lids. He looked like some grotesque jungle reptile staring up at the high, hammered-tin ceiling, all pop-eyed and almost alive, housed in an army uniform, his cardboard chest conspicuously absent of medals. No collar stars. No Silver Star or Purple Heart. I thought maybe someone would at least play "Taps," but nobody did.

When my dad finished ad-libbing and embellishing the obituary out loud over dinner, my mom got up from the table, and turned off all the burners on the stove, and did not come back to join us. From where I sat, picking carrots out of the steaming casserole she'd worked on all afternoon, I could see her lying on the couch, the hand shielding her eyes still wearing her oversized oven mitt.

"Appears your mother's not feeling well," my father said, but he did not go to her. Instead he excused himself as always, and a few minutes later I heard the industrial Hoover start up, and the muffled roar of vacuuming from downstairs. I hated his chronic inattention to my mom at such crucial moments, hated how he'd push his chair back so slowly and quietly, and get up without another word, and simply toss his balled-up napkin onto his plate and walk away from us like that.

"Mom," I said, "are you okay?"

At first she didn't answer, but when I stepped closer she sniffled and said, "Yes, sweetheart, I'm fine, I'm okay," but I could tell she wasn't.

After that night she got worse and worse as each week passed and the war dragged interminably on. I remember how one time she stormed into the living room, and turned the TV volume all the way down, and stood right smack in front of my dad, her back to a silent and baggy-eyed and war-torn Walter Cronkite. She stood mute for maybe a full minute like she'd all of a sudden forgotten what *she* wanted to report, and just needed to collect her thoughts. When she did speak, her voice breaking, she asked my dad to renounce, once and forever, all faith in such a savage

Christian God, and in a bloodthirsty political regime that sacrificed its own children to a foreign conflict we did not deserve to win. Couldn't win, never ever could that possibly occur.

Before he could even respond she accused him of complicity—another word I didn't know back then—and of turning on the evening news each night solely to listen to the body count. She called it a sick, morbid fascination with the dead, and then she held up and shook his thick, black obituary scrapbook in one hand and his Rolodex of the deceased in her other. "Give them here," my dad said, leaning forward and squaring his shoulders, and shooting her a look I'd never seen from him before, frosty-eyed like a sniper. "Now."

She wouldn't, and for a split second I believed he might pick up the heavy, cut-glass ashtray from the floor, and heave it across the living room, stale mangled cigarette butts and all. Not at her, but rather to combat in no uncertain terms her growing hostility on the home front, and to make clear to me the absolute absurdity of such an accusation, and maybe settle this current border dispute for good. To my surprise, he said and did nothing until my mom retreated back into the remoteness of the spare bedroom at the head of the stairs, back into her silent martyrdom, closing and locking the door behind her. That's when he turned toward me and said simply, "Not so." He said, "That's the depression in your mother talking. It's a dark and angry scourge she's fighting, and I just want to set the record straight so you'll know what's what around here. Mark my words—when she gets hysterical like this, when she has these . . . episodes, delivers these . . . whatever they are . . . high-falutin pontifications, she's not mentally competent like you and me. She exists in a different world and says things she doesn't mean—hurtful, ridiculous things that she ought better keep to herself." For good measure he repeated what he'd said, but much more caustically: "They're not true, Arch. Believe me, son, they're just not so."

"I know," I said, but I noticed that it was only during the live TV death segment that he'd lower the newspaper to his lap, fold his hands, and watch helicopter after noisy helicopter lift off with all those young American corpses.

As my mom had often pointed out in her more forgiving moods, he was not a naturally warm and spontaneous man, his affections and sympathies practiced and reserved for those grieving souls who stopped briefly by on wake nights to pay their last respects. "Godspeed," he'd say, patting their backs or shoulders or squeezing their hands. "God bless." As soon as the last of the latecomers left, he'd loosen his tie, and quickly close up shop, and hustle upstairs to catch the last inning or two of the Tigers on the new seventeen-inch color Sylvania console.

I'd be waiting vigilantly for him, and he'd say, "How we doing?" and I'd give him the score, same as he always did, by referring to Detroit as the good guys: "Good guys five, bad guys zero."

If the Tigers were behind he'd say, "Okay, 'bout time for a rally." Then he'd grab a cold beer from the fridge, and untie and kick off his stiff black wing-tips, which always smelled like shoe polish. And wedge a couple of throw pillows behind his head, and start in with the serious chatter, as if the two of us were together at the ballpark, instead of sinking side by side into that overstuffed, sod-colored barge of a couch. "Look alive," he'd say, "look sharp," and sure enough, there'd be Wert at third, spitting into the perfect pocket of his glove. And Tresh at shortstop signaling two outs, and Stormin' Norm Cash at first, holding the base runner close. Sometimes I'd close my eyes, and pretend we were cheering from the box seats right behind home plate, the volume turned down so low I'd have to sit forward and strain and strain to hear Denny McLain's tailing fastball pop in the catcher's mitt.

But I guess my mom could hear it clearly enough, given how she'd get out of bed, and kind of float into the living room in her most enduring resentment. And stop directly in front of the tube, a bluish, electric aura surrounding her loose thin nightgown so that she resembled a spirit or a ghost. She'd say to my dad, hair loose on her shoulders, "Ah, back from the ghat?" Always an edge to it so I could tell right off it wasn't meant as a joke. But he would half smile anyway, like she'd delivered another pretty witty one-liner.

Then she'd leave for the bathroom, staying in there for a long time, running the water, turning it off. Swallowing more pills, I concluded, since there were more and more of them all the time, the opaque orange containers lined up neatly like 12-gauge shotgun shells on the medicine shelf. Painkillers, antidepressants, sleeping pills, the labels typed neatly with long strange names I couldn't possibly pronounce.

They never seemed to help much though. At least not to rid her of that deeply pained and dispirited expression I'd noticed getting worse and worse all the time. My dad referred to her affliction as a chemical abnormality. Abnormal was right, given how she suddenly butchered her hair one day, hacking away so that it was short and real jagged in the back, which made her look much older and strange and even a little scary, a real mess. In the right light her whole face would turn ashen and contort, furrowed lines appearing where she'd never really had any before. And her neck skin thin and brittle as parchment, like she was about to shed it for something new, something softer that someone might actually desire to caress or kiss or even just look at close-up. Worst of all were her eyes, the way they glazed over and seemed to recede farther and farther, as if into the damp, dark entrance of train tunnels. She left such an immediate and odd impression that I stopped inviting any of my friends over anymore, without apology or explanation, and they quit inviting me to their houses too. I even overheard Georgie Glaspey, a backstabbing kid I mistakenly liked for awhile, say one time at school that she looked as if she slept each night in a morgue drawer, a walking stiff.

One afternoon, right out of the blue, she put on her sewing glasses, and picked up her small wooden hoop and began embroidering Bible phrases onto the white linen Sunday tablecloth, right above where our three place settings would be. One said, *Sorrowful even onto death.* Another: *Where there is no vision the people perish.* All in crooked, cursive red letters and dangling threads. My dad was never much for us saying grace, but he bowed his head and read aloud, *Man is born unto trouble, as the sparks fly upward.* I wasn't sure if I should say "Amen" or not, but when I finally did, my mom, blank-faced and unblinking, lifted her fork and knife although no food had yet been passed. Then she started in with this slow, metronomic rocking back and forth, shoulders bony and hunched, those two elongated candle flames collapsing and bending upright again and again, imitating the exact movement of her body.

I noticed that her cheeks were waxy and tearstained, and, without another word from anyone, I got up and gently lifted away the yellow measuring tape draped around her neck. "I'll put it over here out of the way," I said, and then I served her a decent portion of mashed potatoes and meat loaf slathered in gravy. But she ate almost nothing—a few tentative bites. Later that afternoon my dad took me aside and said, "Follow me, son," and for the first time ever, while my mom napped fitfully upstairs, he led me tiptoeing down into the embalming room. It didn't smell like death or disinfectant nearly as much as it did the Wildroot and talc and Lava soap he used to spruce himself up every single morning before heading down to work. "Well?" he said, kind of clicking his teeth. And there among the chrome scalpels and vein tubes and mouth formers, he assured me that—God willing—my mom would come to her senses soon enough and resume her rightful place in the creation.

"Unlike her," he said, pointing at the woman lying loosely covered on the cold stainless steel table, the massage cream as white and shiny as Noxzema on her face, so I couldn't really tell how old or young she was, or how pretty. Only that she was more frightening than anything I had ever seen. "It's okay, she won't bite," he said, and winked, and rocked back on his heels in a way I didn't much like. But I stepped closer anyway, without hesitation, focusing on her eyelashes so thick and black and perfectly curled. I don't know why, but I imagined how carefully my dad would lift her into a stiff sitting position after awhile, then reach behind her with both his hands and clasp the padded silk underwire bra to get her dressed and ready for proper viewing. The white enamel coffin in its wheeled frame waited off to the side, the silk-lined lid propped open, soft and billowy like a summer cloud. Would he eventually carry her to it in his arms? I wondered. Or simply wheel it over right next to the table and slide her in, fingernails trimmed and polished, burial jewelry already on.

As if I'd asked him a question, he nodded and said, "Sure, why not?" He said, "You're never on the road, and it's calming work, Arch. Quiet, respectable, solitary. A lot like you."

I didn't care for that connection at all, but I stayed silent as he continued: "No wrongful deaths on the job," he said. "Or even any injuries. Nobody losing fingers or toes like down at the foundry, and nobody serving you walking papers during slow times. But that's not why you do it. No, not even close. You do it out of devotion and necessity. You do it to dignify both the living and the dead," and as he talked he raised the woman's head, raised it real gently, and spritzed sweet-scented water from a bottle, beginning right at her widow's peak. Rosewater, I think, or camphor. Then he began stroking and combing her wet hair straight back, long and shiny-black, and, after a minute, damp-drying it with a clean blue bath towel. Except for her slightly lopsided lip-line, she seemed so at ease with him, like maybe this was a vacation spa or something. It was right then that I heard the water swirling through the pipes from the shower drain upstairs. Which meant my mom was already awake. "Living proof," my dad said with an edge, "that even middle-aged manic-depressive women function pretty damn well when they decide to get off their high horse and rejoin the world." That cold, scoffing tone I'd hear in his voice from time to time was always directed at the living, always, and it never ceased to give me the chillbumps.

"Maybe you'll want to take over the business someday," he said. "Grandfather to father to son. I can teach you when you're ready—a practical play-by-play hands-on education. Just remember, son, two things: First, there's no turning back the clock as we live out our days. And secondly, the future belongs to no man. Although we never know exactly where or when, Mr. Death has already scheduled a visit. It's inked there somewhere on his master calendar. But don't think of this as working *for* him, and never, ever think of it as a job of woe. No. Think only how what matters, when a loved one stares into the casket, is appearance. How good the dead look—how peaceful at last, their bodies made beautiful again by the expert laying on of Angel hands. If the mourners do not avert their eyes, if they smile or cry or especially if they're overcome enough to touch or kiss, then you've more than provided a service. You've earned your money honorably. You're an artist, a *re*-creator. This is not cosmetology, Arch. This isn't something you learn in a beauty college, or at a wax museum. This is an ancient and serious calling, a mission of human closure, and something for you to think about as the future man of the household. We'll be partners—the day you start: no climbing the ladder, no bucking for promotions. Fifty-fifty right from the get-go."

"Mom told me I could be anything I want, anything at all," I said. "An astronaut even, or a herpetologist, or even a second Magellan."

"Well, sure, she's right about that. You sure can—within reason. It's your call. But I hope you'll choose this, if it's meant to be. Just the two of us, and in due time you'll inherit the whole shebang—house, funeral parlor, the hearses. Every part of it. We've got a long-standing, first-rate reputation around here. Did you know we're listed in the national registry of funeral homes? That's a fact—quality assessed. Top 10 percent."

Then he nodded, as if he'd sealed the deal. I did not plead my case any further, but in that instant under the blinding bright nakedness of the hanging fluorescent lights, I knew that I did not want to turn into him, or even into any recognizable version of him. Nor into my mom who sometimes scared me just as much with the crazy things she said and did, the two of them assigning more and more blame to each other's life choices all the time. To each other's private desires and failures.

Fact: The hands of the dead are always cupped and positioned with the left one over the right. Exactly the way my mom always cupped her cards. Even while playing Russian solitaire for hours at the kitchen table, housebound and killing the days, and checking them off with a fat *X* on the Angel & Sons Funeral Home calendar, a different color ink for each unmemorable, slowly dissipating month. Once, when I got home from school, I dropped my books by the door, and sat down across from her and started dealing a hand of Crazy Eights, simply to change the mood around if I could. But she never even lifted her cards. Instead, she reached over and touched my face in that soft, comforting way my dad never did—her palm cool on my cheeks and forehead, like maybe I was running a fever. "I'm not sick, Mom," I said, and she said back, "I know you're not, sweetheart—I know that." And, in that same extended breath, she bit into one of her knuckles and began this mournful, low-moaning, deathlike lament: "Ooooh, ooh, dear God," she said. "No, oh please—no, no, no," the whole time shaking her head back and forth, shaking it like maybe our time together was about to be cut short. In the late-afternoon glow, the lipstick on the empty scotch glass was as red as fresh blood.

A week later my mom ran off to northern Wisconsin to live with her younger sister, my aunt, Esther Westfall, and her new husband, Hubble. A goddamn scheming snake in the grass, my dad later called him. A layabout waster and a loser, a man enchanted by the quick buck, by excess in all things other than an honest day's work. I was only ten then, but my mom did not fight, in the ways a kid might hope for and even anticipate, for out-of-state custody. For love.

Nor did she return home after the private landfill business Hubble started went belly-up, and he and my aunt Esther left Armstrong Creek in a hurry for parts unknown.

It was wrong, and I knew it even then. But one night I silently picked up and listened in on the telephone extension as my mom said, "No," and then a second time as my dad pleaded with her to come back and be with us, promising to get her better medical treatment, a whole new battery of tests, new doctors with new ideas, and to try harder to work things out between them. He never mentioned the word "love"—not a single time—but he suggested couples counseling might be a place to start. She said, "Not now, Rod. It's simply out of the question. Cooped up like that day after neglectful day? To what conceivable purpose? No, I'll be away for awhile by myself, I believe. Possibly a long while. Hire a housekeeper," she said, because she was all done wasting away above the red-velvet wallpapered parlors of the dearly departed. "It's depressing. Every morning I wake it's the same sad bleak morning. The cruel coordinates never change. You're content, and I don't begrudge you that. I envy it—your personal organizers, your habitual routines. You leave nothing to chance, do you? But for me this is simply no place to find redemption, much less get well."

As an afterthought she said, "And I hate that you've already prepaid for our caskets and tombstones, as if we're as good as buried. Yes, I suppose it *is* prudent with a shortage of space, but it's so . . . so funerary and such a wrong-minded metaphor for the future. Can't you see that? Can't you see that I need to find my life before it expires entirely? And believe you me, Rod, when I take my final leave I implore you not to eulogize me in any way other than by a single poem. And do not consign my body for all eternity in that barren ground. Leave my side forever and ever undisturbed. I, for one, choose the almighty pyre."

I figured what I'd heard was at best a rough translation of how she felt. And that a lot more needed to be said in a language I could better understand, and that all the spoken and unspoken words back and forth between them added up finally to little more than another dead-end conversation, one more futile attempt to communicate. We'd been studying what our teacher Mrs. Trundy called cause and effect. I reasoned that's what this was: A leads to B leads to C and so forth, though I sure didn't use it as an example when called upon the very next day in front of the entire class.

We didn't hire a housekeeper. We stocked up instead on frozen TV dinners, and family-size cans of pork and beans and Dinty Moore beef stew. The cardinal rules in the house were to "make do," and "fend for ourselves," and that's what we attempted after our lives took such a gigantic turn for the worse. I helped out as best I could with the laundry and the dishes, rinsing and draping the dishrag over the side of the drainboard, just like my mom used to do after wiping down the table and the countertops and the stove hood. I even lined up peaches and mangoes to ripen on the windowsill above the kitchen sink, and I always slid the toaster cover back on straight. Pasted in the S&H Green Stamps every Sunday morning at the kitchen table, sitting right where she sat, my back to the dark and depleted pantry. I folded the bedsheets and tablecloth fresh from the dryer, and scrubbed out the black sludgy gunk from the oven corners and on the window glass. I imagined her hands whenever I'd pull on those rubber yellow gloves—I could almost feel her touch in the fingers. Still, nothing ever seemed the same again, and I hated how I had to beg and beg my dad with my eyes to please stop talking about her. Whatever he might say, good or bad or indifferent, had long ceased to matter. I wanted to hear it from her, no matter how skewed or scary that version of reality seemed.

It took maybe a month before she wrote to me for the first time—a long and melancholy handwritten letter, the words dark and sharply slanted on the scented, marbled midnight blue stationery. She talked mostly about the two young black bears—twins—that somebody, some wretched evildoer, shot dead at dusk (on All Saints' Day no less) in the field behind her rented, aluminum-sided double-wide. For the eyeteeth and claws, and left the steamy hulking carcasses right there to decompose. "Contemptible" was the word she used, and, when I looked it up in the dictionary, I thought it pretty much applied to what she'd done, too. Before I was born, she'd taught English literature for a few years at the community college in the next county over, but she'd been let go mid-year on an emergency medical leave, which never really ended, my dad said, and in all likelihood never would entirely. What she had wasn't like German measles or the flu. It produced an altogether different kind of fever, and no amount of bed rest and juice and antibiotics alone could cure it. "It's more like . . . polio," he said, "but up here," and he lightly tapped my forehead. "A *mental* paralysis." Although I didn't ask, I wondered if that same disease could infect me—it felt more and more like it already had. Like mother, like son—maybe I, too, had been born under what my dad called her unlucky star.

He explained their separation as a no-severance package—she was owed nothing, but I noticed he continued to send her a check each month. Sometimes I'd watch him write it out, always on the last day of the month, and I theorized that maybe there had been some judgment against him from the parish or from city hall, and that he didn't figure to face the consequences of even a single delinquent payment. Other times I'd see him forge her signature—Millicent Angel—on things, though I'm not sure what they were. Prudential Life Insurance forms, I think. A large, satiny sympathy card once to help ease old Mrs. Ironsides down the block into the sadness of her newfound widowhood, which I signed, too.

My mom said the silver tips of the bear fur shimmered in the moonlight, and that the constellation Ursa Major that night glowed almost violet and brighter than she'd ever seen. She ended by saying no single sadness was insurmountable, but that each one that befell us weakened both the spirit and the will to go on. I read and re-read that one sentence, and then ran downstairs and read it aloud to my dad, thinking it sounded a lot like suicide, like a desperate cry for help. "We'll inscribe it on her headstone," he said, but he was already slack-mouthed and quiver-lipped, and fighting back tears when he took off his glasses and turned suddenly and left to go sit outside on the long, cushionless wooden mourner's bench on the front porch.

I wrote her back that very night, the first of maybe a hundred or more seething, vengeful replies that I never mailed, crumbling each one up and throwing it away instead. "Come home" is what I should have said. Just those two words. The same ones I whispered over and over like a prayer while lying spread-eagle on my bed real late most nights, just staring up for hours at the acoustical ceiling tiles, and thinking this must be what it felt like to be floating alone and forever lost.

She didn't divorce my dad, nor he her, although I worried and worried that some crazy common law would kick in eventually to terminate that legal title of man and wife. *Statue* of limitations, I thought back then, as if the wear and tear of time on a life could ever be accurately sculpted.

FIVE

The Map

"Gone but not forgotten," the DJ says from his radio pulpit, meaning Hank Williams, "all-conference, all-world, all-being and beyond us now"—and he continues the country classics segment with "I'll Never Get Out of This World Alive." Nor will I if I don't pull over soon. I've already swerved once from the soft shoulder back onto the road, my eyelids heavy as whetstones. In my twenties I might have done enough speed to transport me partway to the afterlife and back. Tonight, the more difficult destination is to get just a little farther north, a few more necessary miles this side of yet another heartbreaking memory imprint.

To my right, just beyond the windbreak of leaning sycamores, the harvest moon adorns the turned-over sugar beet fields, the striations of light incandescent enough to induce animal spirits to stir and rise beyond those zoned-commercial billboards. I wish Rodney were here so he could ask, "Which animals, Dad?" and wide-eyed and all excited we'd begin the naming of those already extinct, and then those endangered, scarce, rare, never before imagined. A game I wish I'd learned from my dad to pass along to my son—the child inside the child inside the child—and on and on like that across the eons.

The gas gauge is bumping E, and the BP station I hoped might still be open is deserted and dark, except for the green and yellow sign high up in the sky. In the farther distance, the red lights of a transmission tower, and the DJ is now taking requests in honor of all the lonely wounded night riders in flight out there. This one goes out, loud and crystal clear, to Natasha from Grand Rapids who feels redeemed now that Patsy Cline's serenading us with "Walking after Midnight." Well after, as it turns out, and the hearse gets no better than twelve miles per gallon. What's worse, the filmy orange warning light has just blinked on, and I've long stopped beating those beautiful sad tunes into the steering wheel.

As I mentally re-map, I'm reminded that there's nothing else on this stretch of road except for a couple of white wooden road-side crosses, a dead flower wreath drooping from each. And somewhere along here is the Pig, though it seems a lifetime ago since I was last sitting there in the back booth with Rodney.

I hit the low beams and concentrate on how the left front tire inhales the burning, hypnotic yellow lines as if from the scaly back of some giant viper. The road begins to narrow and loop, the silver shroud of ground fog creeping up from all around those pregnant seedpod cattails lining the drainage ditch. The moon light's so luminous it makes me want to click off the headlights, and crush the accelerator, and really test the limits of this life.

No overheads in the parking lot and no security roof spots. Only the neon circle of the diner clock radiating like a halo from behind the counter, and casting a mossy glow into the window booths.

I'm sure it's only an optical illusion, or me hallucinating from lack of sleep and no food, but I swear someone's sitting in the far back. It's the same feeling I used to have about my mother, of her both being there and not at the same time. A kind of absent presence, if that makes even the slightest bit of sense. My dad insisted it didn't. He said a particular wash of light could play tricks like that on a person's mind, especially if they were addled or upset, but that the larger given world was *not* inhabited by ghouls or ghosts or hobgoblins. When all was said and done, it was still by and large a congenial, and recognizable, even sometimes know-able place.

It rarely seemed that way to me though, especially when he'd get irritated and turn abruptly away from me for asking certain kinds of screwy, irrational questions that I suppose to him must have bordered on the supernatural. "I have no use whatsoever for this sort of nonsense talk," he'd say. "I have a mortician's degree, and stacks of guidebooks for how to care for the deceased, and a copy of both the New and Old Testaments with highlighted pas-sages to summon in times of need. Yes, and an abiding belief in an afterlife, a better, less troublesome life than what has lately tran-spired around here. At least I hope and pray for that. But I know nothing about what you're asking. Trust me, come Judgment Day, Arch, all will be answered if that's what you're after, though no rational, clearly thinking person thinks like that. But from me, your dad? Unh-uh—nosiree. You'll get no such confirmation." As an afterthought he said, "And furthermore, ghosts trade places with the dead, not with the living. The dead happen to be some-thing I know more than a little about—and this, goddamit . . . this is not, nor will it ever come to be while I'm alive, a haunted house."

Eventually I outgrew those emanations—if that's what they were. But I've just finished peeing behind the hearse, and when I zip up and glance back at the Pig, I swear somebody's definitely there. Not that I can make out features or details—nothing any-way beyond that unmistakable, muted pink paleness of a face star-ing out at the exterior darkness.

I get back in the hearse and straighten a stubbed-out butt from the ashtray, and light up. And so does whoever is inside the diner, the glow-orange cherry of the cigarette brightening behind the wavy pane. It's definitely a woman's drag, long and pensive and lonesome and slow. Like a rescue signal every thirty seconds or so, a miniature late-night, safe-haven beacon, and all I have to do is step forward and be rescued.

Which is why I climb into the rear of the hearse for a Clark Kent costume change. And emerge seconds later through the rear door, a deeply depressed, beat-up wretch miraculously transformed under the glittering stars in my dad's custom-tailored burying suit jacket and shirt. It's weird how perfectly the coat fits through the shoulders, the length of the arms. But this is nobody's funeral, and I'm here only because whatever time touches, changes—places and people and circumstances. Sometimes for the better, and I'd gladly, in this fleeting moment, draw up a living will right on the spot, and leave every last good fantasy of love I own to the phantom booth woman whose Christian name I sincerely doubt is Ray.

But that's what I call her once I push open the screen door and step inside. "Hey, Ray," I say, "that you back there?" the whole floor seeming suddenly to shift and tilt, as if I'm stepping carefully toward her from the bow of a McKenzie drift boat, or from a dream. I even pause and listen for that reverberating, heavy-wooden-hull song in the current, those peaceful, somnolent water notes trailing each deep swirl of the oars. It's pure music to my ears, the pink-tinted moon of the clock reflecting like heavenly fire on the water.

When I reach out to steady myself, she takes my hand, and stands on the tiptoes of her thin-soled plastic flip-flops, and pulls me close to her by both lapels, and presses her cheek against mine. "Look at you," she says. "My goodness—so formal." Then, like magic, we're floating away, the oscillating fan, with its sudden gusts, splashing her damp hair forward against my face. What she whispers is no more than the slow, orchestrated burble of water over stones. I want to tell her that the trout will begin rising soon from those pools under the overhanging cedars. Listen: already you can hear the first tentative slurping pitch of their lips on the surface, the feed rings spreading outward. Or is it the soft wet kissing sounds Ray's making now on my neck?

It's a wild-hearted guess, but I open my lids half-mast and lean back on my heels and say, "So you've been waiting for me."

"For something, all my life."

"Archie," I say. "Archie Angel," and we shake hands.

"Your stomach's growling," Ray says, and, as she sits me down, I'm convinced the hard wooden booth is really a bow seat, the drag chain anchor slowing us almost to a stop. She says, "Don't move, I'll be right back," and I watch her until she bobs mid-river out of sight around that first sharp elbow bend into the kitchen. Outside, the moonlight keeps leaching away, and I can barely make out the hearse anymore, except for the hood's shiny black mirror of stars flashing like fingerlings toward some even deeper, spring-fed bottom pool below the ancient, ice-age boulders.

There's a luna moth stranded at the window, the dull, artificial light on my face his single passion for the night. Even when I drum softly on the glass with my fingertips, he stays, and Ray slides in beside me with two frosted mugs of beer, a clean ashtray and half a pack of Camel straights. So maybe we're not floating the river after all, but rather sitting above it on the stairs of a primitive back cabin porch, miles from the nearest road phone and nothing but a deep well and zinc bucket and a tin dipper to lift to our parched lips.

"Cheers," Ray says, and the clink of frosties only heightens the mood, and I swear the great puzzle of grief on earth is solved in the split second it takes me to drape my arm around her neck. Then it's bottoms up, at least for me. She's already cupping my left knee in the dark cove below the table, then slowly fingering up and down the stiff trouser crease along my left thigh. It's been awhile since I've broken out in serious shivers and goose bumps, every dying nerve-end coming back alive under her touch. So when she leaves me again it's certainly not for dead—it's for the food I need before I pass out cold, that single guzzled ice brew gone straight to my head like eighty-proof.

I close my eyes, and just like that the smell of ribs on the grill reminds me why I cook over a fire pit at home most clear nights. And from there I drift immediately into that recurring dream where I always stop roadside late in the evening to lift a dead albino buck (the only one I've ever seen) into the rear of the hearse. Then I start slow driving away, the radio off, and when I check in the rearview mirror, he rises light as a ghost to his front knees, his carnelian-rimmed eyes staring right at me from under a wide, pure white, long-tined ten-point rack.

I can hear him breathing back there in that hollow casket space, though he makes not the slightest movement, not so much as a single blink or muscle quiver as I pull off the road and into a field of scattered blue spruce in the exact middle of nowhere. And park, and turn off the ignition, and get quietly out. There's barely enough lingering light in the early-winter sky to watch him bound away, which is what I want to witness once I swing open the massive rear door and stand back.

Instead, as always, he simply vanishes into thin air, a wild North American spirit mammal that I lift again and again with all my strength, and drive right here to set free in the season's first snow.

"Have at it," Ray says, as she returns with a plateful of steaming short-ribs smothered in barbecue sauce, and awakening me from that snowy far field to this other real-world moment at the Pig. At least it appears real enough, the way she ties the bib around my neck, and sits back down on the bench directly across from me.

I dig right in—all fingers and salivating mouth glands, and she says in perfect non sequitur, "What improbable, godforsaken lives we lead."

I agree but offer instead my compliments to the chef. "It hurts they're so good," I say, and she watches without comment as I rip the meat from the flat greasy bones with my teeth, and then start in sucking the marrow like some delirious crooning alpha wolf.

"Here," she says when I finish eating, and tears open and passes me a folded, moisturized napkin, which I unfold to its full civilized size and wipe my hands and face. Then I reach for a cigarette from the pack she's just nudged toward me. But I don't light up. Instead I strike a match and hold it out and watch her silhouette waver and dance on the far side of the flame point. Just before it burns my thumb and index finger, I blow it out. And light another, and another, and, right before I strike the last blue-headed match in the book, I confess face to tired face that she's occupied a certain place in my mind of late.

"Is that a fact?" she says, followed by an exaggerated whistle. Then she half stands and makes a wide oval of her mouth and leans forward, closing her lips carefully around that final tiny fire. Her cheek skin turns pale orange and I like the way her tongue tip

47

slides up my thumb to the flame and flicks it out. And how she opens her mouth wide, and backs away, blowing a nearly invisible smoke ring above my head.

"Feel better?" she asks, and I nod, Oh yeah, that I do, declining on the homemade apple pie. I've got no room left for dessert. I'm full, I explain, but the hearse is just about out of gas, so even if I wanted to leave, which I most certainly do not, where would I go anyway at this desperate hour? And why, especially now that she's just reached wrist-deep into the darkness above the table to take my hand. To lead me, I imagine, toward a makeshift bed or couch somewhere close by, which I hope isn't asking too much. She explains that normally, no, not a problem. But it's not her house trailer to offer. It belongs to her sixty-five-year-old mom, a long-enduring widow and recent—though not-so-major as it turns out—heart attack survivor whose cardinal rule to the wise, meaning her only daughter, is: Trust no man you've ever loved. After all, look where her vows left her, all alone at the end of a flat, dead-end drive in a senior citizen mobile home park called Dream America.

If Z were here she'd concur: Every woman needs an exit plan. My mom sure had one, a piss-poor plan as it turned out. And Ray's ready to hit the road herself come payday, she claims, now that her mother's back on her feet and swinging that terrible Lhasa apso in circles again by its hind legs, homespun dog therapy to straighten its spine. "Take it from me," Ray says, "three's a crowd, especially in that loony-tunes encampment."

Out on the road a transport trailer slows through the sudden downshifting of gears and the deep wheezing air of its Jake brakes, as if the driver intends to pull his eighteen-wheeler around back for a late-night delivery of sleeping heartland hogs. But he doesn't. He sees the hearse in his high beams, and continues on through the mushrooming gray dust cloud. In his wake, the hog smells merge with the belching diesel exhaust, and I can hear the retreads whine on the pavement long after the disappearing running lights go black.

Ray says, "Catch this—the whole tribe actually got together last week at the Rec for an emergency session to discuss the dif-

ferent warranty options on new skirting for their house trailers—
aquamarine or peach or lilac. And to bitch about too much noise
during garbage pickup, and about some fellow named Mr. Gig
who's decided, without association approval, to raise honeybees
in his backyard. Talk about being deep into the snooze."

"Parents—they're a handful," I say, averting my eyes, and Ray,
without a second's pause, says, "The two most mysterious people
in the history of the world: our own mothers and fathers who
crave our approval right down to the bitter end, no matter what
they've done to us. Which in most cases is plenty. They don't
mean to—but that's what they do."

Her chest heaves in a way that makes clear she's fully stoked
and ready to ignite on this particular subject, so I don't push. I
say, "To be sure—the road to hell is paved with good intentions,"
which sounds both diffuse and entirely trivial, and she says, "And
blah blah blah. Still, whenever they call us, no matter when or
from how far away, there we are, all happy smiles but unable to
conceal what we're really thinking. For a little while, sure, but not
for long we can't, and all I can think about anymore is getting
gone from here."

"Check out my place, why don't you?" I say. "One sane day
with me on the river, and all your incurable aches and worries get
washed away. Guaranteed."

"So draw me a map," she says, and I do, in careful landmark
detail, on the back of a clean pink place mat. No phone yet, I
explain. No lines out that far, though of course I'm not unaware
of cellular technology.

"But there's one at Buck's Bait and Canoe Rentals," I tell her.
"A sort of courtesy phone where I check in twice each week for
messages." It's also where I buy my six-packs of Rolling Rock and
cigarettes and instant lottery tickets, and then gas up in preparation for these painful and perilous round-trip journeys to the Pig.

Speaking of which, but Ray assures me that when I awaken
after daylight she will have poured into the tank just enough mid-
grade to get me to the Mobile station maybe eight, nine miles
down the way.

"Look at that," I say, pointing above the parking lot, where a shooting star unspools its line of silver light, like a perfect last cast across the heavens. When I squint, I can vaguely make out the meandering Eridanus. I'll bet there are forks and eddies and native sky fish—old soaks—so huge even the river-guide gods can't possibly land them.

Like certain lake-run browns on the Platte that have straightened my hooks in the outflowing currents, or stripped my reels right through to the backing. I promise Ray a riverboat or float-tube trip, fresh trout on the grill. Nothing pellet-fed or farm-raised, which is all I can think to say as we wade out arm in arm in a kind of tidal dance across the hard-baked gravel of the parking lot.

We're both still staring heavenward into the immensity of that infinite space, and I know it's only make-believe—escapist, as Z would say, childish—but I feel suddenly like a kid, content for a change, and immune once again to the incessant spinning away of the days. It's like I'm standing in some strange magnetic field, the starlight swirling in counter-clockwise patterns across the surface of the universe. Perhaps it's even possible that no one has turned up missing or beset by grief or dying anywhere in this numinous, stop-time moment. It's a comforting thought, anyway.

The hearse door opens and closes, but not before Ray says, "Goodnight, Archie Angel. Sleep tight," and I lie back utterly exhausted on top of the sleeping bag, hands folded across my chest. As happens often in the instant before sleep, the backs of my eyelids are mirrors, and this is what I see: two clenched fists raised in front of the superimposed face of my dad, and me, and Rodney. The boxing gloves are heavy and big. What's strange is that there's never anyone there to take a swing at us, so I don't know why that fighter's crouched pose frightens me like it does, or why my entire body aches so much some mornings I can barely roll out of bed. I'm always unmarked, except for that new stubble gray on my chin, and the crow's feet that seem to deepen a little more each time I squint into the sharp glare of the river, scouting for the elusive, wavering bottom shadows of trout.

All I know for sure is that no camouflage could ever be more deceptively beautiful than a river-born brook trout, its feathery white fins and tail nearly invisible even in the clearest quiet-water pools and shallows. And those spots on their sides, the purest, most serene reds and blues I've ever seen. Like rosary beads, I used to believe, looped between the fingers of the dead.

SIX

―――

The Deadstream

The deal my dad struck with Oleida Sergeant was simple and quick: a fancy funeral in full for the deed to her husband Benny's hideaway Deadstream cabin, including the surrounding eighty-five wetland acres—no public easements to the river and contiguous on all sides to state land. Sight unseen, though she described it as wholly disagreeable. Verdant and fungal, she said, and teeming with tree frogs that clung each night to the window-panes like giant throat-croaking leeches, and lime green salamanders, and sinkholes where a God-fearing man out fishing or walking—especially someone with such a crippling war wound—could disappear without a trace. Imagine that. "Or it can happen like this, so unexpectedly," she'd said a couple weeks earlier, and pointed back at her discolored electric-blue Olds Eighty-Eight, idling roughly in our driveway, the chrome grill a sharp icy glitter that hurt my eyes. "Go on. Go see for yourself."

It was February, the short and desultory melancholy month, as my mom used to call it. So still and bone-chilling cold that particular subzero morning, and although I did not yet know his name, I could see Benny Sergeant slumped forward in the front seat, like maybe the car heater had just given up the ghost. The snow was deep but light as air, and I'd been shoveling a path to my dad's collection of misprinted headstones out back. He'd recently purchased another, to make an even dozen—this one from somewhere in upstate New York, Utica or Schenectady, if I remember right. It was copper-colored and shiny like a new penny and said "Sister M. Susanne Smith—1912–1968." An *s* instead of a *z* was my guess once I sounded it out. Underneath the date, a raised garlanded heart the size of a small kid's fist, and an inscription that read "Pilgrim of Earth," and nothing else.

He never explained to me why he bought the stones and stood them up in three straight neat rows behind the funeral home, as if all these nonexistent strangers were interred in our backyard. Same reason, I concluded, that other people dragged in old bathtubs and painted the insides sky blue and stood them on end as front- or backyard Virgin Mary shrines. Or gray concrete dogs that sat all day and all night on their statuary haunches, holding lava lanterns or flower baskets in their mouths. Lawn jockeys, half-buried antique wagon wheels, ossified hunks of mangled driftwood.

The oldest marker dated way back to 1834. It said "Chester Padly," as if introducing the title of the poem that followed:

> *Passing stranger, call this not*
> *A place of fear and gloom;*
> *We love to linger round this spot,*
> *It is our father's tomb.*

There was a tilted crucifix to one side, and a chiseled rope of laurel, and I wondered sometimes if his name was really Chester Badly or Chester Sadly or something regrettable like that.

The smallest and plainest of the headstones said simply, "Our Dear Baby Ottis—3 months, 3 days." No matter how many times I dropped down on one knee to study its mysterious imperfection, I couldn't find anything wrong. Just another cursory death sermon embedded in stone.

"Oh yes, he's taken his final leave," Oleida said, "no question about *that*. Sometimes death catches us completely off guard, doesn't it? Early or late—death shows us no mercy. But who'd of thought, on our way to early worship at Blessed Sacrament. You know the one. The round brick church off Dwight Street."

She seemed so proper and calm—not a single stutter or tear—as she retied her scarf, her breath rising in small bell-shaped plumes as she spoke, her earmuffs the color of cranberry juice. But my father did not stay to listen. Instead he took off running in his slippers and terry-cloth bathrobe knee-deep through the wind-sculpted snow, and opened the passenger's-side door, and placed his fingertips for a few seconds below Benny's left ear. Then he shouted out, "Son, help—come quick and help me."

By the time I got there, Benny was flat on his back, one foot dangling from the open car door, the other trouser leg empty and safety-pinned back to the knee. My dad lifted and threw the single crutch onto the back seat, and started pressing down hard on the old man's chest with both hands. Followed by frantic mouth-to-mouth resuscitation. He'd pinch Benny's nostrils closed, exhale hard into his lungs, and then he'd pull away and whisper, "Breathe, breathe," and he'd do it again and again, over and over like that, the back of his neck beet red from exertion. I thought, when he finally stopped and slowly propped him back up in the seat, that maybe he'd really resurrected this old-timer from the dead, a modern-day Lazarus. True, Benny was awfully blue in the face and lips, but his eyes were wide open and clear, and my dad said, "Archie, go . . . turn off . . . the key." He was hyperventilating, and I said, "Okay, I will," and I hustled around to the other side, where I slid in behind the wide white steering wheel, and reached over and killed the ignition.

I swear Benny's veiny hand pulsed and turned palm-up on the seat right then, his cracked thumbnail brushing my leg each time my dad hugged him and squeezed his slumped-over shoulders. I guess it was only rigor mortis setting in, because I could see now that Benny wasn't breathing, the powerful V-8 engine already ticking and cooling down. That's when my dad started to really shiver, and he said, his words interspersed with deep and audible breath pauses: "What on earth was she thinking . . . bringing him here like this? Why in God's name . . . didn't she . . . drive him to the hospital? To the emergency room. In the first place . . . I do not . . . *save* lives. I'm no . . . paramedic, and secondly, I can't keep him here without a . . . death . . . certificate. I'll be shut . . . right down. Why," he said again to drive home his point, "would she do such . . . an . . . ungenerous thing?"

I didn't say a word, turning away instead from his icy stare, as if only Oleida herself could answer such a demanding and personal and complex question as that.

She was looking right at us, her coat sleeve pressed up under her nose and her legs raw where they stayed exposed between her dress hem and her zipped-up fleece-lined boots. It must have appeared to her like the three of us were about to continue on to church without her. At least that's how I figured it, once she turned away like she did, brushing snow from every headstone with her bare hands, exposing the misspelled names of those missing dead.

"Sweet God Jesus," my dad said, and I silently mouthed the letters: J-E-S-U-S. It was as close as I could conceive of to a prayer on the spot, and I wanted it to be solemn and correct. Inside my mittens, I imitated the slow, downward double finger motion my dad made, as if it were me reaching over and shutting this thin, white-haired man's eyelids in front of the Lord.

"Of complications," my dad would explain a few days later when I asked, because that's what life eventually does—it complicates and kills, sometimes without warning. "So you and me, Arch—we'll keep it simple if we can. We'll keep things positive," which seemed to me anymore to border on the impossible, and maybe even on the absurd, given how those low-murmured notes of bereavement continued to float up, sometimes two or three nights in a single week, from downstairs. Although my mom once asked me to in her deepest lunacy, I never did add up the number of funeral processions—what she called the terrible processions of souls—which originated from right outside our front door. So many uncountable sorrows, she said. She referred to them as Exhibit A, as if in defense of her secret leaving later that same month. I was missing her something terrible, praying and praying that she was better now, maybe even content with her new life from time to time, but I was silently cursing her too. It's like she was the one who had died, and whose departure had cast such a permanent pall over all our lives.

What goes around comes around, my dad said, but whatever he meant by that sailed right over my head as we drove north that spring to open up and air out the cabin for the first time. Our maiden voyage, he called it. And he called me the first mate, like maybe part of the trip would be by hovercraft or ferryboat.

He'd hired some local, small-operation sawmill fellow named Its—which I thought was pretty funny, a thing instead of a person—to drive out and turn on the breaker switch and prime the well pump, so we wouldn't have to worry about all that. My dad wasn't real handy when it came to any kind of do-it-yourself home repair, so I was hoping the place would be in okay shape— no king termites or wood wasps or busted windowpanes or anything like that. Ruptured screens. Raccoons or red squirrels in residence in the walls or ceilings. Leaky pipes. Mold or mildew covering everything. Otherwise, poof—end of our odyssey, end of our safe-haven getaway dream. I knew without question that was all it would take—really, that was it—to reduce our world yet again to smithereens.

It was a few months since my mom had taken off in the green Rambler on her all-night flight to Wisconsin—no, had *stolen* the car, as my dad pointed out. Grand theft auto, a felony, a legal and not merely a private matter. But he did not press charges, nor cancel the car insurance, and I took that in my child's mind as a positive sign she might someday relent, and return home to finish getting well, and to give life here with the two of us another chance. After all, marriage was a consecration. Marriage was forever, wasn't it—a blessed union? Until death do us part?

Which is why I didn't really mind traveling north to Honor in the retired hearse. My dad had recently invested in a new one, and he made clear he wasn't about to incur the debt of another car too. It felt a little strange, but I tried to think of it as a sacrifice, a necessary penance for having driven my mom away like we did, though I hoped deep down that I wasn't really at fault. At least my dad insisted I wasn't. He said, "Your mother's illness is nobody's doing," and explained that the forces of nature conspired against people in horrible, unintelligible ways, but that the winds of time would eventually shift. They always did, he said, and often when you least expected it.

But for me it was more like winter had sprung eternal, the days frozen and flat gray and indistinct from one another, like we'd been entombed in an unending season of sorrow and guilt and forever-deepening regrets.

My dad hadn't forgotten to take off the white funeral flags from the fenders. Still, cars pulled over to let us pass, or switched on their headlights, or even exited the highway, as if the foreseeable future needed no shiny black grim-reaper mobile creeping up to remind them of what lies in wait somewhere not all that far down the proverbial pike.

Then it happened—a warm blow moving down from the Upper Peninsula, an unexpected thermal rotation, I'd later learn. An inverse climactic shift my dad could not name or explain, other than to point to where the sun was unearthing hazy sheets of hoarfrost from the fields, the top halves of aspen stands silhouetted against the sky.

He turned off the heater, and cracked the window a few inches, and breathed in deeply and said, "A change of scenery, Arch. Shoot—sometimes that's all it takes," and he gave me one of those patented nods that I hadn't seen from him in a long time. Followed by a couple of pawing, loose-fingered right jabs that grazed my shoulder and chin. When I smiled and nodded back, it was as if to confirm that all those months of dolor and doom had been suddenly eclipsed, and here we were, father and son, following our AAA Trip Tic toward better, happier times.

My dad drove one-handed, relaxed for a change, and I loved the way we kept crossing the river, and how those rushing, deep swirling water sounds echoed up from under each bridge and culvert as we passed over, and how the only restaurant in Honor was called Money's. A man in chest waders walked out laughing all by himself into the sunlight, his suspenders bright rainbow-colored, his billfold still in his hand.

It wasn't much of a town really—the kind, as my dad said, that would take all of about ten minutes to complete a full and total evacuation. A one-ring-circus town he called it, and then he said, "Whoops," and pressed his finger to his lips as if to remind himself that outsiders like us shouldn't prematurely form and voice such negative opinions.

For sure there wasn't much to it: a single no-name gas station with a bunch of wooden pallets stacked out front by the street and a manure spreader for sale that someone should've at least hosed off. The pickup parked at the pumps had its tailgate down, its hood open, and as soon as the driver let off revving the gas, the engine started coughing pretty bad, the exhaust clouds as thick and purple-blue as newly formed bruises. A sign in the station window advertised ice-cold beer and blood sausage.

Our two silver thermoses lay side by side between us on the seat, coffee and hot chocolate. Plus a couple of prepackaged cold-cut subs with extra American cheese, and half a dozen pretzel sticks from Pluver's market, and a handful of individually wrapped goldfoil milk chocolates for dessert, so we didn't stop anywhere, though I wanted to. "On the way back through," my dad said. "Tell you what—we'll make it a ritual, how's that? We'll designate this day, March 28th, as the New Day of Our Dawning."

Once again I wasn't exactly sure what that meant, other than he'd just conferred upon the two us some sort of blessing or promise, and that was good enough for me. It's what a father was supposed to do, and it had been a long time coming. Much too long, as far as I was concerned.

In his own way, my dad was trying hard, doing his best. He'd bought me a two-piece Shakespeare fiberglass rod, and a Pflueger closed-faced spinning reel, and a hard plastic tackle box with double fold-out trays containing a dozen or so lucky lures: raised-eye Jitterbugs, Clatter Tads, different-colored five-of-diamonds spoons, Erie Dearies. I'd been practicing my distance casts in the backyard after school, trying to hit the huge target rings I spray-painted bright red in the snow. I'd click open the bail, and spread my feet wide apart, and really wing that three-ounce pyramid sinker, the thin blue monofilament line whistling out under the immeasurable arc of the sky. Every time I got snagged up, I pretended I was fighting a muskie or a northern pike, the same monster size I'd seen bursting fiercely yellow-eyed from the glossy covers of *Fins and Feathers* and *Michigan Outdoors*.

Just outside Honor we hung a right past the county sand and gravel pit that rose steeply above the town with its tiny post office and corner IGA, and then past the Fox Den Bar and Grill.

"Road name?" my dad asked, but there wasn't one that I could see. Nor any more boarded-up shacks or abandoned trailers for maybe another mile, although the first one we came up on had crooked black numerals painted across the mailbox, plus a semi-circle of yellow and white pinwheel daisies at the base of the post. "Here, fold this," my dad said, and he handed me the map, like he knew the rest of the way by heart. I figured the sawmill guy must've provided a trail of unmistakable landmarks to follow.

"Bingo," my dad said. "Checkpoint One." Then he pointed at the dilapidated Quonset hut, the faded white crucifix rusting above the door and, on the roof, a limp and tattered windsock. A combination airport and mausoleum, I thought, reduced to a cemetery of junked cars, every single windshield perforated with bullet holes, the headlights shot out, trunks sprung open in the weeds like silent screaming metal tongues. Parts cars, he called them, organ donors.

Plus a heap of about a thousand blackened cans from a trash fire. My mom would have called it a shame and a sacrilege, a human blight, and I envisioned her lowering the visor, and wedging the map up under the thick red rubber band, and snapping it like an exclamation point on such a worthless excursion. She sometimes mentioned faraway places where she'd like to go, "jetting off" as she put it, but this sure wasn't one of them. No Olivier's *Hamlet* performed here, no string quartet playing Schubert's "Death and the Maiden." No John Keats's headstone from which to make a charcoal rubbing to excite her unteachable, nose-gazing, nonexistent students she still talked about every now and again, never once mentioning that petition they signed against her. At that moment I was secretly grateful she wasn't with us, my dad's sudden good mood transforming even this junked-up landscape into a homely kind of beauty.

"If it moves, shoot it," he joked, still all keyed up, but we hadn't yet purchased a gun, and nothing did move that I could see. Except for the turkey vultures overhead, their wide wings outstretched, but they were gliding downwind, seemingly mindless of the two of us, and already way out of range anyhow.

I don't think I dozed, or even averted my eyes from the roadside for more than a few seconds, but suddenly, and without warning, everything had changed. No more scrubby small fields or rolling high-ground hardwoods—just those gnarled, petrified arms of the standing dead cedar trees reaching toward us from an enormous swamp. I'd never seen such barrenness, never thought before of a road's vanishing point as the absolute end of the world, the disembodied dark V of the void.

"Leaping Jesus," my dad said, and I sat forward, looking for him, the Son of God, to come crashing out through the thorny tangle of underbrush, giant hell dogs snapping at his bloody heels. The hearse was barely moving when my dad turned on the emergency flashers, and I secretly pressed down the passenger's-side door lock with my elbow, and the single word that sprang immediately to mind was "doom."

"This can't be right," he said, more to himself than to me. "Can it?"

When I didn't answer, he stopped right there and put the hearse in neutral. Then he said, "Figures," but nothing did except that we were lost, and that he'd as much as called it quits on ever finding the cabin—I could already hear the predictable, scratchy resignation in his voice, and in a certain way that was okay with me. I had to use the bathroom, and Honor wasn't all that far back, and I thought sure we'd just turn around and stop at Money's, a *one*-time ritual, assuming such a concept existed. Probably didn't, which meant we'd order a simple late lunch, most likely burgers or grilled cheese and fries, and eat up without saying a whole lot to one another, and pretend after a few days back home that we'd never even left. I'd mention nothing at school to anyone—no exaggerated fish stories from the tundra—and my dad would return to his work with the deceased, and that would be that.

Just another missed Kodak moment, as my mom used to say quite often—the predictable culmination of nothing. She was right about the snapshot part, there being few family pictures and not a single one of those square, clear plastic photo cubes anywhere. Which in a lot of ways made our lives seem fake and unimportant, even nonexistent. But some nights my dad would relax in his recliner and slide color negatives from those glassine envelopes of his and hold them up to the lamplight, like he was considering just which ones to enlarge and frame behind glass for somebody's mantle shrine or bookcase or time capsule. You wouldn't think even the deepest grief of surviving a loved one could manifest itself in such bizarre behavior displays, but sometimes it did. And my dad made no bones about his dead charges—that's what he called them—being remarkably photogenic once he was done attending them. Even that heartlessly messy teenage shotgun suicide: Joey Montjoy. Or as some kids called him, Joey-Joy, the loner who never gave a straight answer to anyone about anything. "Thereabouts," he'd always say. Or, "Close enough," or "Around there." He who, to this day, remains the youngest contestant to ever win the tractor pull at the three-county fair. I remember how my dad rolled up his shirtsleeves at dinner and said, "Well, here's where we separate the boys from the men. A next to impossible reconstruction, but if that's what his folks want, then that's what they get."

Until this morning he had rarely taken his Pentax out of the mortuary—an occasional birthday, my first communion—but he'd made a point of packing it this time, along with the pillows and extra blankets and a couple boxes of Diamond kitchen matches. I knew if I lit one, and blew it out, and held the charred tip up to the windshield, it would be the same exact color as the swamp—dead gray, the thin vapor rising from the still water like smoke.

"Pour me some coffee, would you, Arch?" he said, and leaned forward over the steering wheel. I don't know if it was something he saw, or just intuited, but he said, "This *has* to be the Deadstream. Let's give it another few minutes—we don't find anything by then, well . . . son-of-a-bitch there's a man-made two-track back in here somewhere, and this road can't go on forever. If it does we're going to end up in goddamn Warsaw or Cuba or someplace we can't get back from."

Before I could even unscrew the thermos top, he shifted into drive and stepped on the gas full throttle, the hearse up and planing like a boat. I actually stared into the side-view mirror half expecting to see an undulating wake fanning out behind us. Maybe *this* was the river, and we were following it out to the Big Lake, where we'd rig up my line with a swivel and a red and white Daredevil and begin trolling the shoreline north toward the Straits and Superior, all the way by water into the Atlantic Ocean.

We never quite went airborne, but I hung on as we rode those road swells until my dad finally hit the brakes hard and we fishtailed to a stop. I'd never seen him drive with such reckless urgency before, not even on that night he rushed my mom to the hospital in her nightgown, her wrists and thighs a bloody mess.

"Fancy that," he said. "There it is." He seemed short of breath, and his face was flushed, and I said back, "Here's your coffee," and I poured him half a cup. When I looked back up, the wavering blue flame of his Zippo moved back and forth in front of his face, like he was trying to locate something in the dark, rather than light a cigarette, which he took from his dry lips and slid back into the pack. I thought about holding out my hand and asking, "How many fingers?" just to be sure nothing bad had just happened—a stroke or a minor heart attack.

There were silver pussy willows budding everywhere, and fresh tread marks in the spongy black mud, but no chain across the two-track. "So I guess we'll just take our chances," my dad said. "I guess we're okay." But I still wasn't so sure *he* was, sweating and clearing his throat a lot, and his hand shaking noticeably as he reached over for the coffee. "Let's go look-see exactly what we've got here," he said. "What say we go air out the ghost of one Benny Sergeant?"

The ruts weren't all that deep so we didn't run aground. The frame bumped a few times, and my dad said something about the oil pan, but he never spilled a single drop of coffee, and he did not seem disoriented anymore, nor the slightest bit disappointed when we pulled up to the cabin. "Mm-hmm," he said. And then again, rubbing his chin, as if in calculated approval of all that had so far gone so well.

It was tiny in comparison to our hulking, turreted, pre–Depression era Victorian mansion turned funeral home—the only house in which I had ever lived. A fortress, as my dad sometimes called it, but what we ever defended there remains a mystery to me.

I was glad there weren't all those heavy domed shade trees around, like the ones that darkened and cooled the street out front. Here the sun shone straight down, and there were pockets of crocuses already poking up around the cement foundation slab, a forsythia bush trying hard to bloom, the weeping willow tendril veils a lustrous greenish yellow.

The logs were freshly stained, and the whitewashed mortar between them in halfway decent shape. It reminded me of a fairy tale house, smoke billowing from the blue-black stove stack sticking up through the roof shingles, and no appreciable sag or warp in the low eaves or along the roofline, certainly not a structure any wolf could blow down. It was maybe a little out of plumb, but that only added to the charm, to my dad's higher than expected approval rating. An eight, he said, which really wasn't half bad. All in all, the place looked pretty safe and durable. As permanent, I thought, as we needed it to be. Nailed above the door, what looked like devil horns—curved, sun-bleached spike deer antlers—and a sign underneath that said THIS AND NOTHING MORE.

I'd never even seen an outhouse before, but that's where my dad pointed, referring to it as your basic non-flush, utilitarian country crapper. It didn't amount to much—two oval holes in a wide planed plank, a bag of quicklime, and a gutted, dog-eared copy of *Gulliver's Travels* positioned midway between the openings. The thermometer on the wall read thirty-seven balmy degrees. I unbuttoned and dropped my pants, and lowered my fanny onto the smooth cold wood, and listened to the insistent and ceaseless confabulation of what I would later learn were spring peepers, mating swamp frogs, and the steady background sound of water purling behind me—the Platte River. From somewhere a grouse drummed its wings, and sunlight through the walls and door cracks seemed to widen and contract, as if even this sagging wooden structure were alive and breathing. Above me in one corner the cobwebs were tinted gold.

My eyes adjusted quickly, and I leaned forward and traced the simple scrollwork of initials with my fingertips: B.S.—1957. I wondered if any *two* people ever sat here, bent over together with their jackknives open, splinters falling away from each deep letter and date. Already Benny Sergeant was dead, and my mom was most likely marking time in other ways, in another out-of-the-way northern place. I was counting the days until school ended so that the remaining members of the immediate Angel clan—meaning me and my dad—could spend more time up here in God's country, not having to answer to anyone or anything for a change. Where the days would pass unhurried in pleasurable solitude, and where we'd be so completely cut off that maybe nothing bad would be happening anywhere in the world.

I liked just sitting so alone and carefree in the wild middle of nowhere, thinking and listening to all those invisible sounds, though I admit I didn't feel all that great about indelicately ripping out any more pages from the emaciated book.

My mom was the real reader in the family, the only person who'd ever read aloud to me, which she often did at night, her weight on the bedside one of the few guaranteed comforts of my early growing up. "Draw from it," she'd whisper, "when there is little left to draw comfort from." She had a soft, sonorous voice, and I'd close my eyes and listen, not to Jack and the Beanstalk or *James and the Giant Peach* or Dr. Seuss—books *I'd* buy and read years later to Rodney—but rather selected scenes from the Brontë sisters and George Eliot. And sometimes, to practice her Middle English pronunciation, Chaucer's "Parliament of Fowls." "How I love these brief interludes of clarity," she used to say. It was the only time she seemed remotely happy, and I knew she would have hated me sacrificing any more of those first eight and a half chapters to my baser needs. I remember in particular my mom reading to me about the king of Brobdingnag, and how next to him Gulliver was only six inches tall, no bigger than my hand. That was my favorite part, and I sure didn't want to use it or any other page for that matter. Unfortunately, my dad hadn't thought to pack a single roll of toilet paper or a box of Kleenex, so I had no choice but to rip out another couple, which I didn't even attempt to read.

I finished and zipped up fast when I heard my dad's light-hearted whistle, so uncharacteristic I assumed it had to be somebody else, somebody more cheerful, maybe Its, the sawmill fellow, come back to make sure we'd gotten in all right. But it wasn't—it was my dad, bent over and inserting the key, then turning it easily in the lock. He wrenched the knob and kind of lifted at the same time, shouldering the door open, and then shielding his eyes against the interior darkness.

"What?" I said, but he just stood there speechless for maybe a full minute, an eternity as far as I was concerned. "Let me see," I said, and wedged myself by him into the open space of the living room, where I yanked each of the black bead chains on the bronze stand-up lamp. "Look," I said, pointing at the two side-by-side shades suddenly aglow with pinholes of forty-watt amber light, a wide-banded silhouette parade of bears and bison and moose and elk. I liked the faint, sweet wood-smoke smell and the exposed rafters with the bark still partially on, and the syrupy-colored knotty pine walls.

The kitchen was more like a galley—everything crammed in together, and almost no counter space—a couple of linoleum-covered boards with thin, dull aluminum edging. You could see where bottle caps had left their jagged bite marks. Mismatched metal mugs hung by hooks above the sink, the tap water as cold as fresh snowmelt. I took a long slow drink, and my dad did too after sitting down and swallowing a couple of extra-strength Tylenol, and rubbing his temples in circles, rubbing harder than I'd ever seen anybody do. Then he pressed with his palms as if to stop the pounding. It got so quiet I could hear, as if it were suddenly amplified tenfold, the refrigerator's erratic hum.

"Dad?" I asked, but he cut me off and said, "Scout it out, Arch, and let me know what you think. Let me know if it'll do." I figured he already knew, but I played along, opening drawers and cupboards and turning on an old Philco radio that kind of whistled a couple seconds' high frequency, and then gave up the ghost with a loud pop. I found some tin snips and a cribbage board minus the pegs, and a single pink plastic geranium I snipped and slid stem first through a buttonhole in my dad's new wool vest. "All I need now is someone to dance with," he said, which was meant as a joke, but it came out awfully sad. I wished then that I'd offered him the square carpenter's pencil or folding ruler instead, or the indecipherable letter that began "Dear Vox," and the ink-smudged date. I could make out the word "love" in there too, at the very bottom, but nothing else.

My best find was a stack of topo maps on top of the refrigerator—fat black X's marking what I imagined must be secret hunting or fishing spots. Or maybe a trailhead to an old Indian encampment where I could unearth stone arrowheads, though I didn't yet know north from south, east from west. Only that my bedroom was over *there*, a trundle bed covered with a tucked-in, nubby blue bedspread already turned down, but no sheet underneath. I'd never seen a bed made like that before. Nor a closet without a door. Just this drab red curtain with pitted silver slide rings, which I whipped open like a matador's cape. And there, propped against the back wall, a single cream-colored artificial human limb. Nothing else. I didn't scream, but it sure spooked me the way it rested so casually on its worn heel, like it had just been outside kicking up the leaves or the snow or the wind or something, the rest of Benny Sergeant already housed peacefully in the next world.

It seemed a bad omen on such a good day, so I didn't say anything about it to my dad. I simply waited until he walked outside to unpack the hearse, and I grabbed and squeezed the wrought iron tongs around that bulk, and lifted and carried it to the woodstove. I opened the door, and lowered the leg onto the coals, black shoe and sock and dangling straps and all.

The fire turned from orange to gold, and then pure platinum, the thin film of creosote vanishing instantly from the window. I knelt and watched the laces and tongue smoke and crack, and then the entire shoe dissolve in a matter of seconds into thin white ash. The flaming toes curled slowly under and popped, and my dad, dropping his suitcase behind me with a dull thud, said,

"Let's hump it, Buster Brown, there's plenty more to carry in, and it's turning nasty out there—temperature's falling mighty fast." I stared upside down at him, pausing to warm his hands, and I reached back and squeezed both his ankles, and felt with my fingers up over the fleshy contours of his calves. Both knees were still attached, his whole body looming over me in that bright white firelight like a mortal god.

That night in a dream I saw him crouched and poking at the dying coals, and fanning them furiously with a bellows. Nothing caught, and the snow outside had fallen for days, or was it weeks already? It must have been because we were down to burning a walking stick I'd found, and the four bowed legs of the davenport, and the half dozen wooden mousetraps we'd already set to stop the incessant scratching in the walls.

When I called out to him, it was Benny Sergeant who turned around, but whatever he said sounded like footsteps clomping up and down an endless flight of invisible stairs to nowhere. Had he simply walked off without his wooden leg? he wanted to know. How was that possible— just how tired or forgetful or resigned would that old geezer have to be? And where was it now? Had I seen it and made some mental note of its whereabouts? Had I perhaps, like a good and practical-minded boy, put it aside for him in case he hadn't decided to die after all? Only I knew the answer, the cold confusion of telling the truth, and I screamed, "Get out—nothing here is yours anymore," and I opened the cabin door, and stood back to let his smoky humanless shape pass by me into the night.

I listened then to the howling voice of the wind, and then to my dad who took my hand and whispered, "This way, Arch— quick, this way, son," as he led me back inside, and turned the lock, and said, "You've been sleepwalking again, but you're fine now. You're with me in our cabin and you're okay—we're both fine, everything's all right," and he sat me down on the hooked rug in front of the stove, where he stoked the fire with two split dry logs from the copper washtub. He rubbed and rubbed my bare feet until the stovepipe turned cherry-colored and glowed, and he asked finally, "How long were you standing out there?"

but of course I had no idea. "You're freezing," he said. "Look how your teeth are chattering. You could have gotten hypothermia or frostbite. My God, you could have walked off and gotten lost out there."

Out the window I watched the drifting blue snow clouds mirror the moonlight, and I nodded yes when my dad said, "Stay right here," and left to go get me a blanket and a pair of dry wool socks. I wasn't going anywhere. Even if I'd tried to stand, I don't believe I could have, my cramped toes burning badly in my squeezed hands, my whole body shaking uncontrollably. I slid across the floorboards a little closer to the stove, and listened to the soft padding sound of my dad doubling back from the bedroom to cover me, and to hold the blanket flaps closed at my throat.

I knew next trip there'd be a double chain lock screwed high up on the front door, and that he'd apologize at least a dozen times on the drive back home for not having thought ahead about such an obvious and simple safeguard. He said, "You're safe and that's all that counts but you sure did scare the bejesus out of me, Arch. It is my fault though, my fault entirely, and I'm truly sorry about it."

He didn't say another word. He simply bent down and rested his chin on my head, and hummed softly some sad lullaby I didn't recognize. He stayed hugging me like that for a long time, both our faces reflected golden in the fire glass. It was, and still is, the single clearest love image I own of my past with him, an absolute miracle of memory.

And what I wondered—then and now—was whether I was all alone in my thinking, or whether other sons would gladly freeze a thousand nights over to get that close to their dads.

SEVEN

Loon Lake

Here's a Scottish saying my dad took to quoting whenever we'd head north, like a long-awaited weekend send-off: *Angels,* he'd say, *can fly because they take themselves lightly.* But *he* rarely did, and like it or not, that's me all over. I brood and obsess and often indulge excessive late-night ruminations, visions of calamity and eternal grief, and unexpected betrayals. I suffer the same quotidian nightmares without letup, grinding my teeth some nights until they ache. I ponder "in vacant or in pensive mood," as Wordsworth maintains, and postulate my son's absence into absolute panic on demand. Other times, and without warning, I'll recall, let's say, a certain day thirty years in the past. Two Angels: me and *my* dad, and we're not flying—we're slow-drifting out into Loon Lake, out over the deep drop-off, the heavy wooden ribs of the rented rowboat settling into the water.

We've rented it from early summer right through Labor Day—for a song, as my dad said. One small victory for the new-comers, the early-risers. It's perfect because we leave the boat right here, unchained and unlocked in the tussocks and cattails, like this is our own remote and private lake. Pretty much it is, given that I've never seen another person about. Never once, no matter what time of day. I've seen the loons though—two differ-ent pairs—plus their young who have grown now, and already I

69

can mimic those lonely shrieking off-key cries they make when-ever we arrive. A stable and quiet craft, my dad calls it, as opposed to the noisy and less seaworthy aluminum kind that leaves no margin for human error. And, because he is not a good swimmer, this makes all the difference.

It's why he lets me stand, smack-dab in the boat's damp center, feet wide apart while I cast and cast my silver and blue Johnson spoons, retrieving them across the weed beds with a jerky wounded-minnow motion. And with each strike I set the hook hard, the rod whipping taut above my head. I'm a natural, he says, entirely self-taught, and how can anyone learn that much about catching fish in only a few short months? Then he reminds me again that I both walked and talked at eleven months. Always a step ahead of the curve, he says, always the adventurer. He does not possess that same magic feel or touch anywhere outside the mortuary, that all-important hand-eye coordination. Nor the need to exceed simply tagging along, as he puts it, with the mas-ter angler. That's plenty, he says. It's a gift just to be out here in God's country relaxing like this, and he concentrates instead on the antiphonal lapping of water against the hull. The fresh early-autumn air and the turning leaves, the sumac blood red along the shore where a single sugar maple on the up-slope explodes orange like a sun above the cattails. Unfortunately, he never lets on what he's really thinking.

Sometimes we'll fish Loon Lake twice a day, early morning and evening, when it's by far the best. I can't get enough, though I wish my dad hadn't stopped bringing his camera after the first few trips. I mean, in most respects it's all right, and granted he gets plenty excited for me whenever a good-size pike struggles to climb away from the water, to shake loose the thick treble knot-ted in its jaw. Still, it would be nice, after four straight months, to capture at least one of these father-son trips. A shot or two of me out here in the boat, smiling wide-eyed and holding up a keeper—both wrists straining—its silver sides shimmering against all those vibrant primary autumn colors slow-burning and reflecting in the background. I'd like to frame and send one to my mom for her birthday—it falls this year on the first Sunday in

Advent. "That's me after another growth spurt!" I'd say on the reverse side. "That's me as proud and happy as I've ever been," and date it, and maybe in that way entice her to visit. At least set the thought in motion, which I guess I haven't so far.

"Got one," I shout. "Fish on," and after maneuvering it close enough my dad reaches over the gunnel and loops that long-handled net over the fish's head—another average-size pike—and pulls it to the side of the boat, where he clubs it with a miniature Detroit Tigers baseball bat. Whomp-whomp—without ever even wincing. Always twice between those flat, cold-blooded yellow eyes, the pupils falling away, not into the forehead like a person fainting, but down into the cheeks, disappearing like small moons. But what he's best at by far, after we get home, is slitting their luminous white bellies clean with his surgical scalpel, a line so fine and precise it's nearly invisible until he spreads it apart with his thumbs. Sometimes he'll slide out a whole undigested smelt or crawfish, and those are the nights I dream of monster pike and tiger muskies that swallow young ducks, jerking them under by their webbed feet, shaking them violently until they drown.

Here's another saying—my mom quoting Milton: *Tears such as Angels weep, burst forth*. It's an evening excursion and we've forgotten the club and the metal stringer and who knows what else. My dad's been doing that more and more as the weeks and months tick by—forgetting things—and I get the distinct impression his mind is elsewhere, that he's here only out of loyalty and habit now, his attention flagging more and more, which tends to half ruin the trips. At least I wish he'd talk to me—or smile or wink or something other than light up another cigarette and turn away. I suppose silent company is better than no company at all, but it does send a mixed message, doesn't it?

I don't say that of course, or even dwell on it all that much if the action's good, and the fish that hits this time is enormous, powerful in a way I've never experienced before, except in my imagination. Even after fighting him for twenty minutes I can still feel the weight of his tail fanning all the way down in the rod butt, the line cutting wildly back and forth through the water. I don't want to lose him—not this one, not so late in the season. "Please," I whisper to myself, wishing I had re-knotted with heavier leader after landing that last fish. My arms ache each time he head-shakes and lunges deeper. "Please," I whisper again, and tighten the drag, the rod bent almost double. And this time I'm able to nose him slowly upward and toward the stern where my dad makes the perfect scoop, a pro when the chips are down, when I most need him to come through for me. At this moment I love and trust him almost enough to believe he's right when he says, "Don't worry—we'll make do. We'll manage just fine with what we've got." He says, "Holy Moses." He says, "Jiminy Christmas," as he kneels prayer-like and reaches slowly into the blue braided nylon, attempting to lift this summer's trophy catch out by its gill plate, the insides pink as a tongue. No kidding, this fish must weigh a good ten or twelve pounds—far and away the biggest I've ever seen—and I'm still speechless and shaking.

"Shees. Look . . . at . . . him," my dad says. "Now there's one for the record books. Jeez-o-Pete he's a dandy. Good for you, Arch. Good for you, son. You sure got the magic touch out here, don't you? Holy Moses," he says again. "Never in my youth. I don't know where you get it from, but you sure as heck know what you're doing on the water."

"Yeah, really works," I say, referring to the extra treble—the trailer—that I wired to the lure just like the guy at the bait and tackle shop showed me. He said, "Be careful though," which is exactly what my dad keeps mumbling to himself: "Be careful . . . be careful now." A weak-minded caution, I've learned, whenever a northern pike this size thrashes back to life, a wild and violent-writhing single muscle-girth of silver torpedo. And next thing I know—it happens that fast, in a single blink—one hook has buried itself beyond the barb deep into my dad's thumb, the second treble catching him in the palm of the other hand.

It's as if the moment has stopped, and I can see myself, much more frightened than disappointed, and so utterly helpless to even move, the fish finning down and away, the net doing its slow-motion oval dance to the clear bottom of the lake. My dad does not scream or swear or utter any single thing. Instead he sits carefully back on the green plastic seat cushion, and stares into his hands as if they were mirrors, as if pulling them close to his face he can see the rest of his life fading beyond his hairline.

"Dad?" I finally say, and when he gazes up at me he seems both old and very tired, as if he hasn't slept in days, as if maybe now, right here in the watery middle of nowhere, he's going to choke up, and then he's going to cry.

He does neither. He waits silently for maybe a full minute, as if deep in thought, and then he says, "Bite the leader, as close as you can to the lure." He's forgotten to put the pliers back in the tackle box, so I lower the rod and move toward his cupped hands, the backs of them held out to me like a man protecting his last match from the wind. It's blowing now from the south end of the lake, the boat rocking, so I grab hold of both his wrists to keep from falling overboard. And then, sitting on his knees facing him, I put the thin, almost invisible line between my teeth, and watch the silver-blue of the lure flash the last remaining light across my lips. "Okay, free," I say, and using only his elbows he nods and pushes me away and sits down on the floor planks, shifting awkwardly between the wooden ribs and into the safe axis of the boat's wet center.

"Arch—get us back," he says, but I cannot pull both oars through the choppy water together, no matter how hard I try, my lips pressed closed with the effort. Too much deadweight to maneuver, so I slide across the seat from one oar to the other, back and forth, trying to straighten the heavy nose. But it's no use, the rowboat arcing around in a full circle farther out into the lake. In the waning light, at the level of the trees, two golden eyes descend smoothly into the reeds downwind and out of sight along the darkening shoreline.

My dad, like a man in handcuffs, says, grimacing, "Move over, son." He's standing right behind me, blood down to his elbows like the blood that drips down the silver sides of stunned and dying fish. Before taking one oar, he lowers his hands a single time into the cold, spring-fed lake water and then twists his locked hands back and forth until the oar handle comes out gleaming red beyond his thumbs.

"Row, Arch," he says. "For the love of God, row," and he begins his count, the rhythm steady as a pulse. It's just a kid's fear, I guess, but the lake suddenly seems to double and then double again in size, and I do not care anymore if I ever fish again, here or anywhere else. I only want for my dad to be all right and to not hold whatever this night becomes against me. "One," he says, "again, Arch—one, one," and I know if I try to count along with him I'll burst into tears.

Who's Milton? What's *Paradise Lost*? What does he mean—the "palpable obscure"? I won't know for years, although I can hear so clearly my mom's lulling recitations as I pull for all my skinny aching arms are worth, the lake widening and widening behind us the closer we get to shore. We're in perfect sync, and together we're going fairly straight, though my dad's already breathing hard and coughing a lot, and at one point he says, "Rest." He says, pointing up with both wounded hands, "Look," because there's Cygnus, the Northern Cross, though neither of us is well enough versed in the language of the constellations to even attempt to name or describe their animal shapes. All we can say is that they're so incredibly bright in the ocean of the sky tonight, bright enough to navigate by if we were ancient mariners—father and son—experienced helmsmen traveling home alone from distant lands.

It doesn't really take us all that long, half an hour at most, and my dad says, "I'm sorry," because stepping ashore at season's end so empty-handed is entirely his fault, and he hopes he hasn't wrecked everything with his clumsiness. "Have I? Have I, Arch?"

"No, don't say that," I tell him, which, if not an outright and transparent distortion, is at least open to interpretation. Here's mine: At eleven years old I land a once-in-a-lifetime northern pike, but out of carelessness or oversight or chronic inattention to the essentials, we don't have a single glossy colored snapshot. Nor any exact weight or measurements, nothing tangible enough to prove that there are, indeed, certain days unequaled on this earth, days and nights created to celebrate forever who we are together, and why. This one's gone, vanquished. Even the bragging rights. And in the painful retelling, it's a story, not about the granddaddy pike that got away, but about how my dad snagged only himself, a sorry excuse for a memory, or rather a memory run amuck. And how we left the rod and tackle scattered in the bottom of the boat, and two-stepped it single file up the dark path to the hearse, the blurry star patterns riffling across the hood.

So, when he told me to, I reached without a word into his left front trouser pocket for the car keys, and opened both doors, and helped him slide behind the steering wheel. I reached across his body and turned on the headlights, then shifted for him into reverse, then into drive. What I remember most is how he steered with his forearms, his fingers interlaced as if he were praying his way up the old logging cut, the wave of the high beams slamming over every rut into the darkness of third-growth pines. The needles gleamed, the air thick and lush with the scent of them.

The scales on his hands appeared green in the dashboard lights. As he put it, a fish out of water. He said something about his dad and trade-offs and surviving disappointments, about there being other days—"You'll see," but they were hard to imagine with this one having gone so wrong and not nearly far enough behind us yet.

"Radio," he said, and I turned it on just in time for Perry Como to serenade us with "Catch a Falling Star," which I surmised even then was an ironic blessing from above. By that I mean we didn't have to say a single other awkward thing. Instead we sang along, or he did. I mostly hummed the melody, my head pressed against the seat back so I could maybe see the stars if they fell.

All the way to the Emergency Care in Frankfurt I couldn't get that single tune out of my head. Not even as I sat alone in the waiting room, where I closed my eyes after awhile, and imagined my dad, mouth open, and breathing quietly those exact same lyrics. Maybe that's why I still heard them playing, over and over—that bit about love and pocketing even one star. I know it sounds far-fetched, but when I squeezed hard I swear I felt the silver-blue starlight knotted like a ball in my palms.

"Arch," my dad said, lightly shaking my shoulder. "Wake up." He said, "Look," and flexed his fingers and bandaged thumb, and, because I hadn't yet drifted all the way back from sleep, his amateur sleight of hand wasn't half bad. He said, "Here it is," as he reached behind my ear for the lure, both big treble hooks gone, and when he dangled it by the barrel swivel under the bright white ceiling lights, it flashed and glittered. Still bleary-eyed I flicked out an imaginary cast, and started to reel, and on our slow ride home in the hearse, my dad conceded, "Yeah, it smarts a little all right, but that's fair, I guess. That's what I get for being sloppy. That's life." Then he described the worst part, the doctor's tug and pull, the tetanus shot, and I got kind of queasy and quiet all over again, but I didn't ask him to stop with the painful and grisly details.

He said there were frozen fishcakes at home we could thaw if I was still hungry. He said we'd sleep in tomorrow if that seemed all right. He said a lot of things until the oncoming headlights through the fogbank momentarily blinded him, and he turned his eyes away from the road just long enough for me to glimpse a face I'd never seen before. A scared, ghost-like face I'd remember clearly, but wouldn't recognize until many years later when my own son stared at me in a certain way, and like my dad just did, I'd ask Rodney, "What?"

In the affirmative, "Nothing," which is only what I said then, staring straight ahead at the illuminated, slightly moonward slant of the road. Followed by my dad's slow consenting nod, as if the true worth of our lives on earth could ever be acknowledged by such a simple and necessary lie. "Nothing," I said again to myself. "Really, nothing at all."

EIGHT

Buster, Copperfield, & Rhea

Fat chance this solitary river existence will ever again take a back seat to love, though I do admit to being more than a little charged about Ray's possible showing up. I can't at this point honestly say what I expect or don't, except that I've taken a liking to her. Still, I refuse to drive myself crazy trying to puzzle it all out ahead of time, the odds and the risks, the probable and improbable outcomes.

I'm stretched out with my cat Copperfield, the two of us reading about the worldwide decline in earthworm populations, when the Harley, engine killed, rolls down the gradual decline toward the river, following the contour of the footpath through the waist-high goldenrod and Queen Anne's lace. At first I don't recognize Ray in full road leather and black Darth Vader helmet shield. Neither does Copperfield, naturally, and he's already up and hauling ass away from the river and up and through the boxed strawberry and rhubarb beds, right past the old bleached-out wooden cross of a scarecrow. I follow his lead from the hammock toward the main garden, where there's sure no light saber leaning against the chicken-wire fence, but there is a primitive hoe and spade, for whatever protection they might afford. The goldfinches have scattered in a yellow cloud burst from the feeder, and Copperfield hasn't stopped or even slowed down. But I have, turning now to watch as Ray unzips her jacket and takes off her helmet and smooths back her hair with her fingers.

It's Friday, evening already coming on, and I'd all but written her off. Gun-shy, I figured, after the late-night costume ball at the Pig. Still, "offer stands" were my last spoken words to her, and so I'd been waiting around just in case, losing faith and gaining faith, caring and then not. Picked up and re-read *Bartleby*, and only afterward got duly depressed by examining too deeply the sedimentary layers of my life, how the years had already started to pile up and run together. All forty-one of them. Worse yet, I felt old, a condition born of apathy and emotional fatigue, and by each day's end, except when Rodney was around, I rarely even cared anymore. I'd stay up late and rise early and begin the new day with a nap, sometimes until noon when I'd brew that first full pot of coffee, and light a cigarette with each steaming cup I drank alone out on the porch. Maybe dress after awhile— weed barefoot between the rows of pendulous beefsteak tomatoes, and beets, and those fat leafy heads of romaine. Prize Deadstream vegetables grown from Heritage conservation seeds, and without any insecticides. I leave that good work to the ladybugs and the praying mantises, and the banked brush piles of blackberry canes placed around the perimeter. Companion planting. Onions and marigolds and horseradish root strategically scattered about, a confusion of smells to confuse the rabbits and skunks and deer. It all works—a healthy mixture of compost and leafmeal and humus and river water. And although I believe in interspecies communication, I do not make a fetish of talking to plants, or playing in excess any Mozart or Vivaldi or Chopin to help them clear their heads.

Sometimes, right before we leave for the Pig, Rodney will go alone into the garden, which he helped me put in this past spring, and fill a half-bushel basket to take home as a gift for Z. Or he and I will walk together across the soggy, thick moss carpet to the nearby bog, where we'll pick a couple quarts of swollen wild blueberries, their skins almost ready to burst. She always thanks him with a hug, always, but has never once since our divorce hugged me. Of all life's vagaries, I believe small hope of this sort dies last, if at all.

But my habit of late has been to spend a larger portion of each idle afternoon tying flies under the bright concentrated circle of a halogen light. I use only barbless Mustad hooks, a measure of sportsmanship not as extreme as one might suspect, and a must on all designated no-kill sections of certain blue-ribbon rivers and streams. A different array of flies for different days: dozens of bead-headed sculpins, and at least as many wooly buggers, and maybe a hundred or more gray and brown drakes just since this past Monday. Coffin flies, green weenie wets, crystal midge pupas. Plus a handful of original patterns: High-Vis Angel Gnats and Archie's Holy Hoppers, every fly shop in a seventy-five-mile radius always anxious to pay me handsomely in green for whatever volume I'm willing to sell, and in whatever season.

It was Z who talked me into marketing flies as art. Nothing museum quality, she said, but perfect for the living room and den walls of those outdoorsy types. A baker's half dozen nymph series, for example, recessed in shadow boxes, elaborate patterns, which, as she accurately predicted, never appeared beside her hand wares in the uptown big-city gallery catalogues. But they do bring in the easy dollars, especially around the holidays.

That's the deal: no deadlines or quotas to meet, so no supply shortfalls, nobody pulling rank and yelling his greedy fool head off at me to get with the program, to start busting my lazy chops for a change.

So quitting time's whenever I get the urge to knock off. We're talking approximately a buck fifty for simple five-minute patterns, give or take—double that for streamers or flatwings. It's a far cry from amassing a family fortune, but at least I'm not standing out on the Deadstream Road with finger-cymbals and a tin cup. The truth is, in addition to Rodney's support check, I contribute each and every week to a secret medium-yield (6.75 percent) Rodney fund. I've never once pilfered from it—not one dime. I submit freely that I've erred in other ways—substantial and regrettable—but this future provision for my son is sacrosanct. His St. James trust fund no doubt has him set for a sizable head start in this life, but what he'll inherit from me someday is a legacy born of love. So I save. Plus the value of this river property continues to escalate beyond my dad's wildest wild dreams of his legacy to me, not that I normally think of it in these terms, nor did he. Always way out of his element here, he nonetheless knew what this place meant to me, and passed it down free and clear on anybody's books, the taxes paid up years in advance.

Ray toes the kickstand down, turns sidesaddle, and sweet-talks me with a simple "Hello, Archie Angel. Surprise, surprise."

I grab two ice-cold beers from the cooler on the picnic table, and when I crack hers for her she says, "Merci." I like the way she French-trills the *r*, the wetness in the sound, and how her knees spread slowly and wide apart, her plant position decidedly pelvic, her leather hip-hugger pants soft and skintight.

"I agree, it's a bit off the beaten track," I say. "But looks like you found it all right. Welcome." Followed by a jabbering, overeager "How long did it take?" and "Nice bike," and "Wow, it's a scorcher—mid-eighties, the dog days of July. Oppressive as hell, but every day above ground's a good day on the river."

She smiles, toasts the moment, then presses the sweating can to her neck and forehead. And stares at the river then up toward the rumble of distant rolling thunder. The swing hangs straight down from the tree limb. "Go for it," I say, and by the time I'm back with a towel, she's already undressed to her tank top and panties and is soaring in great wide arcs, higher up by far than I've ever been, or care to be. A good fifteen feet at the apex, where her body seems to pause weightless for the longest second, head and shoulders tilted back, toes pointed into the broken cloud light. On the back-swing she yells, "Is it deep enough to shallow-dive?" and I duck out of the way and sound the all clear. "Deepest hole in the river," I say.

I'm sure she won't do it, but she pumps and thrusts full-force one final time, and sitting forward lets go of the ropes, and tumbles off headlong into the drink. It's a perfect entry, hardly a splash, and I can see her moving now like a ghost woman under the water, breaststroking slow motion along the sandy bottom, hair floating in and out. When she finally surfaces and stands on a sandbar maybe twenty-five yards upstream from me, the water barely reaches her hipbones.

"Come on in," she says, hands at rest on her hips, each rib visible, her sides heaving. "It's invigorating. It feels so incredibly good. What are you waiting for?"

I squeeze my eyes shut and when I open them and squint into the dying light she's still there, as gorgeous as a snowy egret. Whether I'm hallucinating or not, I savor the moment by watching her fall sideways; then she's up again, lunging backwards this time, just enough flutter kick to keep her swimming in place, her breasts round and buoyant. A tiny belly-button ring glints like a silver circle hook, a size-four Eagle Claw, the barb completely buried. If I had my lightweight Winston fly rod handy I'd tie a pink rose-hip petal to the 6X tippet instead—something soft and redolent—and see if I could drop it in that flat concave of her belly. Not an easy cast, but somebody put some money down and I guarantee I can cover this woman with flowers.

She slides under again, somersaults forward in a dead man's float, and comes bursting back alive, her humpbacked butterfly strokes like wild wingbeats on the water. The reeds and cattails along both banks ripple in the wake, and a school of minnows scatters up the burbling black feeder creek, the long-legged water striders striding full-tilt for the banks. Ray's all smiles and panting even harder by the time she hooks both elbows over the dock edge, as if it were a swim-up bar in Cancun or Monte Carlo. I dry her index and middle fingers when she spreads them into a V, and cross-legged I lean closer so she can take the lit cigarette from between my lips.

"One of life's great pleasures," she says. "A cigarette after a swim," and she inhales deeply, signals for the can of beer with her free hand. Sips it, closes her eyes. Moans a few minutes later as Copperfield rubs and rubs under her chin with his wide head, his post-fright purr motor louder than it's ever run for me.

He's a Manx—bobbed tail and pointy ears. But in size he rivals a Maine coon cat. His life on the Deadstream is, by and large, untroubled. Fat and spoiled, he hunts only out of need. Which pretty much means never, though there's no doubt that's how he stayed alive before showing up here half starved a year ago, immediately after Buster—a gentle, laid-back, pink-nosed husky and retriever mix rescued from the Humane Society—died of old age. In people years eighty-five, such as they are, but I'd only had him for six reasonably comfortable canine years, especially after we left Z's for good. Down there he was banned from all couches and chairs, Scotchguarded or not, and from begging table scraps at dinner or digging up and burying bones in the backyard. He hated leashes as much as I did the leash law. Both times I let him outside to run in the night it cost me a trip to Animal Control, and seventy-five bucks bail money to uncage him, double that the second time. He couldn't wait to get back north, where what was mine was his. Out of a mixture of sadness and inertia I'd decided to bag it on the companion front—just go it alone for a month or two and see how I felt about another dog then.

The first time I spotted Copperfield he was sitting on the dark newly turned earth of Buster's grave, and yowling into the wind like a dethroned king. I thought, bobcat, when he stared up at me with his wild yellow eyes and bounded suddenly back into the swamp. But next morning after a hard frost, I saw the tracks were much too small, and I put out a bowl of puppy chow, the only food Buster would eat toward the end. Copperfield kept a wary distance for weeks, even when I attempted to lure him in with a trail of woodcock or venison scraps that led directly to my hand. Or to coax him closer with a catnip mouse I'd stupidly bought for him at Farm and Fleet. I tied it to a length of monofilament and twitched it through the dying ferns, expecting he'd lick his chops and pounce on it with primordial vengeance. I thought sure, like me, he'd want to get buzzed for awhile after what he'd been through. Chancing nothing, he turned his back on it like a cruel joke.

Ray arrives and in half an hour he's euphoric, luxuriant. She says, "Good name: Copperfield. Not the illusionist—the original." She says Dickens rocks, and that she adores animals both domestic and wild. "Kingfisher," she says, identifying correctly the magnified double screech that echoes along the contours of the river, bend after bend and finally out of earshot beyond the steeply banked horseshoe where the bigger browns tend to nymph in the early mornings.

Her eyes stay closed, even as the daddy longlegs crosses her forearms, the grainy light falling lightly across her summer-bronze shoulders, the nape of her neck. Followed by long minutes in which nobody speaks, and I'm tempted to lead Ray blindfolded into the cabin, say, "Okay, open wide," and then watch to see if those quicksilver eyes feast in earnest on the floor-to-ceiling bookshelves—my mom's entire library. She never completed that doctoral degree she began at the University of Michigan in the early years of her marriage to my dad, but she did manage a master's between three nervous breakdowns, highest honors. She was a regular Encyclopedia Britannica of obscure literary facts and footnotes. It sounds obsessive, I know, but she could recite entire poems backwards—the first twenty-five Shakespeare sonnets and a ton of John Donne: "star, falling a catch and Go." "Just another asocial genius with a photographic memory," as my dad grew a bit too fond of saying. "A mind minus a mission," he'd say. "So take note, Arch. Take this as a warning." Occasionally, I still find pressed flowers turning to weightless, colorless dust between the pages.

I earned my degree at Kalamazoo College, a private and competitive in-state coeducational institution. Small and academically impressive but without the ivy walls or the archways or the vaulted library ceilings designed, I imagined, to make one feel tiny and humble among the stacks and study carrels found in those more celebrated East Coast colleges. An appealing campus overall but much too far away from any fishable river. I suppose I could have power-casted into the shallow sumps and mudflats nearby, blood baiting for carp or catfish or crappies if I'd wanted. I didn't.

To compensate I shot pool in the bars on the weekends, a respite from academic dabbling: religion, physics, Romance languages. Followed by a serious career choice ten years later when I fell so maniacally head over heels in love and married Z, and, for longer than I care to admit, sold six-figure above-market-value homes to an aggressive clientele eager to register with the town's

Newcomer Club. Then climb in earnest in their polished oxfords and blue-striped button-downs. Early thirtyish Harvey Wall-banger types. A client asked me one time—he was dead serious—if I thought it would appear sacrilegious for his beagle Tommy to sleep in a doghouse designed as a chapel. That night I tore up my appointment calendar and realtor's license/certificate in front of Z, the gas fire silently ablaze behind me in the fireplace. "What this world does not need more of," I said. Then I showed her a clipped-out newspaper article about a man sentenced to a year's probation for driving his lawnmower while intoxicated, but never outside the boundaries of his own yard. Ratted out by his neighbors to whom he had innocently offered a drink. I hoped I was making clear to Z how enfeebled my bowels felt, and how I couldn't stomach one more day of it, not without some extended downtime on the Platte. "So go," she said to my surprise, "but call in sick before you do." Instead I called in old. That's the message I left: "I'm old. I'm all fucking done."

I've never catalogued or inventoried how many collections of poetry my mom left me. I'll pull one out from time to time and turn the thumb-worn pages: "Beauty is truth, truth beauty—that is all / Ye know on earth, and all ye need to know." Exit this world on those simple terms and you've probably lived a decent enough life. My prized book is a rare, signed first colophon edition (1653) Izaak Walton—*The Compleat Angler*—a final gift from my mom. I have no idea where she got it, or how, but it's the principal reason I keep the contents of the cabin insured. It's the book spine I still brush most often with my fingertips, my eyes closed, as if I might re-read it blind, and in this way discover its powerful and fanatical river teachings all over again, just one more time. Exactly: Trust your feet in the dark waters, not your eyes.

My dad never asked if I wanted all the others. I simply drove down there and boxed and loaded each leather-bound set into the hearse—Zola, Turgenev, Kafka, Dostoevsky, whom I read sparingly these days, afraid of being lured too deep into the horrors. The compassionate Chekhov, Proust—the list goes on—while my dad marked with red numbered tags the remainder of the funeral home contents to be auctioned off. By that time he required around-the-clock oxygen, a portable backpack cylinder by day, a stand-up tank bedside at night. He could barely swallow without it, and he winced whenever he talked. So we said less and less, and, with each passing harsh winter month and one lung already partially removed and a second triple bypass and a still arrhythmic ticker, his willpower to resist assisted living weakened.

That spring I moved him and his few remaining worldly possessions into Enchanted Acres—the lesser of the two evils—which smelled like ammonia and milk and enemas, old and medical, a sort of briny human fermentation. And where the unapologetic last-stop gods of mercy quickly sucked up every last thin dime of his retirement savings. A churlish, waif of an RN named Jeanette led us—me pushing my dad's wheelchair—slowly through the drafty, undraperied corridors of pain to my dad's private boudoir, as she called it. Room 511—and I thought, Yes. I thought, *For it is written,* as we entered what I've since assessed to be the true epicenter of despondency and despair. A holding area for the near dead, the already written off.

Nurse Jeanette mentioned family hour in the lobby, a Steinway, a piano player, a sing-along every Saturday evening for those who still remembered the words and the music. Then she twisted open the blinds, and I locked the brake, and held fast as my dad got up and shuffled over and stood with his back to us, nodding at the panoramic view of the parking lot, all but obscured by the sudden snow. I could see the silent shame of surrender in his shoulder blades, the articulate hunch of his back. He looked to me at that moment both tiny and immense. The hearse, the third in a series of retired hearses he had made his transportation of choice, was still in his name, and would be legally until his death. "Continue to change the oil every three thousand," he said in his strictest, quietest brooding voice. "High-test only."

"Panther juice," I said, our standing joke, but all he said back was, "It's in your care now, Arch. In your . . . your trust."

I thanked him, and after a lengthy pause, and without turning around, so that I wouldn't see how cloudy-eyed and frightened he was, he said, "Bring my grandson, my namesake, to visit me

before I cross over. Better hop to it." The only time I did my dad
greeted us with a peremptory smile, his upper plate missing, and
his entire face caved in. He said the Salisbury steak they served
for dinner was decent enough, tasty but stringy, and no extra
bread to sop up the gravy. "Ought to be some bread," he said,
"and more salt. And someone to watch my back. I'm all alone
here, Arch." Then he futzed impatiently with the TV remote,
muttered through a consumptive wheeze of words some half-
formed indictment against ungrateful sons and grandsons that I
couldn't entirely decipher except by tone.

"What?" I asked in like-sounding response, but he'd already
nodded off in his faded plaid armchair, the semiliterate, over-
groomed QVC hawker marketing—exclusively here, and one
time only—bona fide stone fragments from the Berlin Wall. Sec-
ular relics, he called them. He said the phone lines were now
open. He said no Deutschmarks, please, and above the 1–800
number flashing on the screen, *he* flashed those of us still watching the most perfect replicate smile of a shark that I'd ever seen.
Within a week my dad would begin to cough up blood. And those
phones would continue to ring and ring. People ordering worldwide, shelling out the bucks they'd saved over a lifetime, the
interminable days and nights stitched together like one long and
silent scream.

It's possible Ray's fallen asleep, arms supporting her head on
the dock, the deep guttural thunder-growls creeping closer, and
Copperfield up and legging it double-time toward his oversized
cat door. He hates storms, and this one's about to break open
above us—I can smell it in the ionized air. "Hey, what say we head
inside before the rain?" I say. "The river's the wrong place for a
person to be if this turns electrical, and given the heat and humidity all day, I'm guessing it's going to get pretty dicey in a hurry." I
don't tell her that lightning cracks alive at approximately fifty
thousand degrees Fahrenheit, hotter than the sun's surface, and
that men are four times more likely to be struck than women, but
I'm sure as hell thinking it. And that even with a so-so survival
rate, the electrical charge is apt to char the neurons of the frontal
lobe and permanently alter personality. Mine's already been

altered enough. Furthermore, lightning is much attracted to cottonwood trees, which is what's hovering directly above us, mammoth and double-trunked and leaning almost to mid-current. "Hey, look up," I say. "Look how those clouds keep swirling and racing."

She doesn't. Instead she slowly ducks under one last time, then hoists herself with a sudden whoosh out of the water, and up the three-rung ladder. I'm holding the towel open for her, but she sprints whooping right by me and through the open gate into the garden, and by the time I get there she's biting into a giant ripe beefsteak tomato. She eats it like an apple, her wrists together as if in handcuffs, forearms covering her half-naked body. In this dying light Rodney's pumpkins are speckled blue, and the cover crop of sunflowers hovers above us like moons. The green pepper leaves have already begun to tremble, their silver undersides turning over the instant before the whole sky explodes in a single cloudburst. We're caught in the biblical downpour, the raindrops large and warm and plunking like hail on the river, everything suddenly earthy and musky-smelling.

Ray smiles and holds the dripping tomato out to me; holds it like an offering while I open wide and bite down, the seed cluster delicious and slippery on my tongue. We do this back and forth, back and forth until the tomato has disappeared, the garden drenched in thick rising mist and darkness. Neither she nor I picks another from the vine, or makes a single human sound. It's only in the immediate, first bright lightning flash that the two of us are fully illuminated, eyes focused on one another, and our arms gone suddenly slack and weak, our lips wet and glistening with desire.

The last of the beer's gone; the moon breaks through above the river in this season the Sioux call "moon of the red cherries," and I'm alone on the porch, Ray and Copperfield sound asleep on the feather mattress. Perhaps they are dreaming about birds. I've retrieved her sodden leather pants and jacket, the fat saddlebags from her bike, and spread them out across the green oilcloth on the table. She's the only woman I've slept with in this bedroom besides Z, and the first woman, period, in several months, if anybody's counting. And I am.

It's partly why I'm awake, sitting on the screened-in porch contemplating what this all means, or might mean if she decides to hang around. There's a breeze through the screens for a change, heavy with the scent of morning glories, and that's reason enough to be sitting up without a drink or a smoke, enjoying a peacefulness bigger than any I've known in years.

It's about time, given how I never lived on less than I did right before and after the divorce—a steady diet of alcohol and straight-up Kaopectate from the bottle and not much else. Dropped a quick twenty-five pounds and all but signed off for good. Had the white-coats come around back then, they would have seen LPs hanging like flat black Christmas balls from the snowy branches of trees on both sides of the river: Oliver, the Carpenters, Tony Orlando and Dawn. That dim vintage—the entire box purchased for a couple bucks at an Elberta garage sale.

They didn't shatter as I thought they would when I shot them with the .22. They spun in circles instead, the fish line invisible so they appeared to be floating. Sometimes when the wind came up at night, they sang in soft whistling voices so cold and beautiful I believed a church choir of ghosts had drifted through. "Oh Captain my Captain," I'd croon between choruses of dry heaves the next morning. "Oh Tennille my Tennille," and I'd fire the carbine one-handed from my waist, like the Rifleman gone suddenly berserk on blotter acid or an overdose of Dexedrine. Or I'd sit half trashed in the slight slur of the snow in the early A.M., recalling over and over how Z, in the end, had referred to her B.A. and her A.A.—life before Archie, and life after Archie. And almost everything in between as no life at all, a siege, and not a marriage. Such good early fun-lovers but in the final analysis such improbable and mismatched lifemates, so entirely mistranslated on each other's tongues.

I'd sing, "Cherish is a word," and take aim, and listen to the bullet ping through the vinyl and then whistle off into the dead silence of the winter estuary. "Tie a yellow ribbon 'round the old oak tree," and I'd slide shaking on the ass of my blue sweatpants a few feet closer to the shelf ice, and rack in another shell, and pretend I was mercy killing every shitty sentimental tune that ever came into existence. "My cherie amour," and "Silence is golden, golden," and once the ammo ran out I'd full roll and come up firing dry like some shell-shocked foot soldier belting out a medley of corny off-key love lyrics to his best girl back home. For her, whosoever she was, I stood ready and willing to defend her to the death. Sometimes I thought I had, waking flat on my back, and staring skyward, my arms outstretched like some drunken middle-aged snow angel.

There must have been fifty bullet-riddled records afloat in the perpetual slow-falling snow that hardly let up that entire month, the center labels different-colored reds and greens and purples. A kind of sporting clays for the weary spirit, I thought, and I'd chug-a-lug another beer and warble my falsetto invective against this cruel and maudlin world. Wa-wa-wa-wa-ta-da, nonsense dither that nobody I know ever needed to hear in the first place.

I've since taught Rodney to shoot, but never like that, though sometimes he'll hum to concentrate, something soft, something I don't recognize, his cheek pressed against the polished walnut stock. I'll say, "That's my boy," whenever he plunks a can, or mutilates the small black centers of the paper targets tacked up on the plywood sheet in front of the sand mound twenty-five yards away. He's good, doesn't flinch, keeps both eyes open as he feathers the trigger before he squeezes. Shows no anger toward anything or anyone, at least not when he's here with me. The safety's always on when he hands back the firearm, the engraved blue gunmetal barrel facing skyward. He makes clear that he never intends to hunt for real, except maybe with a camera. In truth, I gave it all up myself one October morning in a blind when a pair of returning wood ducks landed among the decoys and swam to within three feet of me. I held Buster, who always refused to retrieve but made for good hunting company, firmly by the scruff of the neck. I believed, by the way he watched, that he, too, felt blessed by those perfect white circles around the female's eyes.

Not a bad swap as it's turned out: the firearm for the camera lens.

This would be a great time-lapse shot: the hundreds of mayflies attached to the screens, and behind them, the bats spinning loose like shadows from the monochrome sky.

"Can't sleep?" Ray says. Turns out her name really is Ray, but spelled R-H-E-A, short for her mother's maiden name: Rheaume, French Canadian. For some reason it sounds like a trick question. She's standing right behind me, wrapped in a sheet. Then she comes around and plops down, straddling my lap, facing me, and brushes her index fingertip lightly against my chest, tracing a slow serpentine line from my sternum to my lower stomach and then back up. And kisses my eyelids shut before opening them again with the warm slippery tip of her tongue. "You all right?" she asks.

"Never better."

"That's good to hear, but what I can't help wondering is why a person wakes at two thirty A.M. to sit all alone in the half dark when there's company waiting in bed. Probably it's for a reason."

When I don't answer she leans slightly back away from me, a silver cat-like sliver of light reflected in both corneas. For an instant I believe she's going to croon and purr, a softer, soothing music, which I'd kind of like. But no. "The thing is," she starts in. "Well, first off, your body language is screaming loud and clear that you don't need this—which is so guy-like anyway, so full of . . . sorry, 'issues'—but just hear me out, all right?"

Something tells me I'm going to whether I like it or not, so I offer a flimsy reluctant nod, and she says, "It's like this: the clock strikes two and three and maybe the moon comes out, like tonight, or it doesn't—point is, who cares? Or there's a Russian or a Chinese spy satellite or something that grabs your attention. We're all paranoid in our own ways and there it is, and of course you're going to follow it. You're going to hold the moment."

"A spy satellite?"

"Whatever—doesn't have to be that either. Glowworms. Random images. Even abstract impressions. My point—what I'm attempting to get at—is that the mind's optical. It sees and then responds and that's how it makes connections, even if your eyes are closed." I open them on my own this time, and she says, "The human mind is massive and complex—even little minds, closed minds—and we don't control it, nobody does, with an on-off switch. The synapses spark nonstop your entire life. And within every single mind is a freethinking mind of its own. A sort of sound-alike, an echo's echo that talks to itself, to *you*. That's its function, to communicate, to figure things out. Especially if you're awake and sitting up alone—like this, out here—then something's going on up there. That much is undeniable."

"You're sure about that? Far as I knew I was up listening to the hours pass. It's what I do. Wake and drift out here and lean back in this very chair and by degrees I just fade away."

"All you're describing is a different *state* of mind," she says, "a different current of thought, and I think possibly a very dangerous one."

"Is that a fact?"

Rhea takes my hand, massages the palm with her thumb. "Fine, what's it to me? It's just . . ." but she doesn't finish. Instead she asks, "How about Copperfield then—you ever commiserate with him? Insomniacs do that sometimes. There's even a going national chain called Rent-A-Pet—dogs, cats, parrots, goldfish pairs if I remember right, with names like Wanda and Jaws and Moby Dick and Rambo and Satchel Paige—for this very purpose. I've seen the brochures. A kind of Lonely Planet Guide to improved mental health. Pet therapy. Works wonders from what I hear."

"Copperfield's heard it all," I say, "and then some," and I pause to let him back me: he's sawing catnap logs big-time in the bedroom. Other times he'll turn scrotal, and languorously lick his sizable private feline body parts. And glance over with an occasional, judicious mewling, "Shut the fuck up, Archie," and ball up at the foot of the mattress, head tilted back and to the side, both front paws curled like a miniature kangaroo. What's clear right now is that I'd rather do sets of late-night step aerobics than listen any further to Rhea's mental health theories. "So, if it's all the same," I say, "maybe we could put a lid on this particular line of conversation?" I don't have a clue where she intends to take it, but wherever that is, I'm headed hell-bent the other way.

"We'll begin with me then, since I don't have a cat," she says, "and I'm not verbally impaired at any hour, day or night. I find it helps to clear my head. Besides, now that we're awake and up anyway, what's to lose? And when's the last time a woman offered you her full and undivided attention?"

Or pinched my balls while doing it, I might add, though I don't. Instead I place my hands on her hips as if some great dance lift toward the bedroom is imminent, which it might be—"a double shot of my baby's love"—but the wordless stare she gives me says, "Don't." It says, "Isn't anything *else* about me of interest to you? The truth is you know next to nothing about me. And vice versa. Or is that the whole point of this?" Before I can even answer she says, "What are they? Raccoon? Fox?"

She's pointing at Rodney's collection of skulls lined up on the windowsill, where they sneer empty-eyed like miniature gargoyles, and slowly whiten over time in the late-afternoon sunlight. "Right so far," I say. "Opossum next, mink next to it. That smallest one's a hognose—a snake. Muskrat on the far end."

I reach up and smooth her hair back from her forehead, and say, "Are you thinking this is a good thing, stopping by, I mean?"

"Do you?" she says.

"I thought we agreed it was my night to pitch the questions."

"Oh, it is, but women prefer men who *ease* their way in." She laughs without embarrassment, and performs this seductive little butterfly jig with her eyelids. "Otherwise, you might scare me off, and you don't want me to dismount and take a hike so early in the trial period, I hope."

"No," I say, "I don't," though part of me thinks, Go on, slide into those leather road digs and press that electric starter and motor out of here before I ever even catch your last name, and save us both a lot of grief and explanation. Instead I ask, "What is it?" and she says, "Tomas," and I ask, "Spelled how?" and she says back, "T-O-M-A-S, just like it sounds this time." She says, "No *h*. Say it."

"Tomas."

"No, the whole thing."

"Rhea Tomas," I say.

"And that sounds okay so far?"

"Let the band play on," I say, and press my palms to the outsides of her thighs and shift our body weight slightly forward in the chair.

"Good, because I believe you have to love a particular name to ever really care for that person, maybe eventually even love that person. You have to say it and have it matter every, every time. If it doesn't, gig's up. Listen: Archie Angel," she says, a sort of bell-echo vibrato rising from deep down in her diaphragm. "Now *that's* got real resonance to it. Archie Angel, Archie Angel. Nice. Okay, next question?"

"Long-term storage? The place you return to after the ride-about? It's not your mom's, I think I'm safe with that. And fat chance your whole history's stuffed inside those two saddlebags."

"Sioux Falls, Chillicothe, Blue Jacket, Antelope, Wolfs Store to name a few. LA, which I can tell you is *not* a City of Angels. Hackensack, Baton Rouge. Just 'looking for love,'" she sings, "'in all the wrong places . . .' No northern latitudes after, say, late October, give or take. Winter's boring and cold, the roads always icebound or blown over, and I figure the 'Blessing of the Snow-mobiles' can go on perfectly well without me.

"Plus it doesn't hurt if there's a small-animal clinic nearby. I'm a veterinary technician by trade—MSU, 1990."

"No lie?"

"When I was a kid I volunteered at the animal shelter, week-days after school and all day Saturday. I wanted to adopt all the castaways, young and old, pretty and homely. Ever the rescuer. My mother was on me constantly to go into nursing, but sick people, that's not my cup of tea. Animals, now, they rarely complain. They know when you're trying to help them. And there's almost always work available—except during those stints when I play good-daughter nursemaid, and slave for scraps at the Pig. I've been at it this way for the last ten years now."

"How old are you?" I ask. "If you don't mind."

"Why would I?" she says. "Thirty-three as of May 12th. But maybe tonight we're both only eighteen—sad and horny and love-struck all at once."

I don't have the heart to tell her a guy can grow awfully old in a year or two out here alone. And that I've barely enough energy left to while away the days until I catch a second wind and head out yet again to rescue my kid at the Pig. Until he's what, fifteen, sixteen? Gets his driver's license—and guess what? His quirky, out-of-touch old man's not even around to underhand him a set of car keys. If he were, what could he possibly say anyway? "Sorry, no Ferrari in the immediate forecast, but take the hearse, son— it's a relic but it still runs like a charm, and believe me it's not all bad to make the girlfriend squirm a little on that first date. Keep it edgy, different. Be an individual. Show her a good time at the local burying ground, where your dad and his dad carried armfuls of hothouse flowers to the open graves. Point out the Angel family burial plot, still strangely semi-vacant. Or better yet, take a leisurely spin by the old funeral home. Show her the dogwood tree that never blooms under all that shade, the seedless bird-feeder that eventually fell in pieces to the ground. Show her where your roots lie. In Transylvania, as the school kids used to say and then howl like a chorus of drunken Boris Karloffs every time the school bus stopped out front to let your dad off. Try it, see what gives—you might be surprised."

Rhea lets go of the sheet and shakes both wrists above our heads like castanets, while outside the crickets suddenly begin to chitter, and the scythe of the moon cuts briefly through the clouds, hazy striations of light falling incandescent on her shoulders.

"Behind you," I say, but she's already pulling my head to her breast, her nipple slowly hardening in the fold of my tongue until she squirms and moans, her stomach muscles contracting. Then I deliver slow wet kisses all the way up to and into the swirl of her left ear. As I lower her carefully onto her back on the floor another sudden uproar of thunder erupts in the distance. And then again, way out above the Big Lake, beyond where the ore ships and oil tankers occasionally take refuge in the bay.

Some nights when I can't sleep I'll take a long walk alone, through the troughs and up the Lake Michigan dunes where I'll sit on the windblown crest, and stare for hours as the blue ship lights on the vessel stacks rise and fall and blur below the cloud line. Like water stars, I think, the surf booming flat on the shore. I always feel the shock waves, followed, after a momentary delay, by those cold underwater echoes that rise right through me and up into the sky.

Fact: A freighter's main anchor weighs over two thousand pounds. "Imagine that," I whisper to Rhea, and she grabs hold even tighter with her arms and legs, the swells already building from the wavy rhythms of our bodies, buoyant and drifting free in the moonlight.

NINE

The Return—1972

Parked right next to my dad's brand-new pewter-colored hearse, the Rambler looked dead. It stopped me in my tracks, the noxious blue cloud of school bus exhaust still hanging in the air, and that creepy, mackerel-eyed Bobby Wojnowski shouting his usual disappearing "Angel, Angel, Angel" out the open rear window, the yellow bus already barreling away down the deserted street.

Although I'd thought ahead to this day a million different times, I sure hadn't seen it coming. My mom had sent me a letter or postcard or newspaper clippings or something every month without a miss for the entire three years since she'd left. Famous quotes, rhyming poems I never really understood. Odes to Grecian urns and nightingales and one to the west wind, which I kind of liked. Sometimes they'd arrive postage due, and I'd have to leave Mr. Cutney, our mailman, eight cents in a sealed envelope. She never once mentioned a word about a family reunion. I even hinted at the possibility, but maybe not directly enough. I suppose I could have offered to take the Greyhound to visit her in Wisconsin. Which I'd thought a lot about, and by the time I was twelve and tall for my age, I'd even saved up a decent amount of money working for my dad as a fill-in pallbearer. Not that one is needed every other day, but it occurs more often than most people might imagine. But my mom would inevitably frighten me away with the crazy, unpredictable things she'd say over the telephone. Like she'd stopped writing to the president immediately after he stopped writing to her. "I'm onto him," she said. "I'm onto all those cagey, imbecilic, brain-washed Confucians." She said, "The scope of dispassion and political misunderstanding is immense," but she didn't offer an explanation as to what that meant, and I never interrupted to ask. I wasn't even sure she was speaking English. She mentioned Sodom and Gomorrah, and insisted that God and country had been supplanted by forces so evil that the world's death squads seemed naive in comparison. She listed, alphabetically, maybe fifty foreign countries I'd never heard of, all capitalist-inspired, greed-based imperial governments, she said, who cared nothing about their progeny, whatever that meant. She referred to us, the children, as sacrificial lambs, and predicted the greatest of the great and calculated human calamities was yet to occur on earth, the *eleventh* Biblical plague, and in all likelihood during my lifetime. "At first there was the word," she said, "and then, after God was replaced by a civil defense siren, there wasn't. Only thievery and noise and conspiracy." She said encoded in the world's masterpiece librettos were the final clues to the whereabouts of the missing four or five commandments, though no doubt they were uninterpretable in the present day anyhow. She said that Abraham was the greatest of mortal sinners. She hoped she was wrong, but conceded that human history—and some history it turned out to be—had left little doubt that all the agents of pathos had finally been bred out of the human cell. She said intransigence was now the leading killer worldwide, and that the world itself was a false and dangerous presupposition, a reflex against the final reckoning, which she called both Armageddon and the day of Kingdom Come. "World. Just a meaningless word," she said, "a dither, a pause, an intermittency. So drink plenty of milk, and honor the memory of your mother and father and your grandparents, and let us pity all earthly ululation." She said life expectancy in the year 2020 would be one hundred years if mankind survived at all, though such longevity-seeking added up—at least in her mind—to little more than a selfish and foolhardy crusade against mortality. And so forth and so on in our slow, persistent, hard-hearted, root-bound evolutionary decline. "Here's our future in a nutshell," she said, and all I could imagine were her hands held out to me, her doubled-together palms holding nothing but a few sun-bleached fossil stones.

Other times she spoke like a normal mom, and things would pretty much hang together—whole entire paragraphs. We'd talk about school, and I'd imagine her wearing eyeliner again, and blush, and maybe the right amount of Chanel, just like all the other mothers. She'd say, "Keep sending me those lovely report cards, Archie, I'm so proud of you." They weren't really all that lovely though—they were doctored-up Xerox phonies, but I figured our lives had become a giant lie by then, and I couldn't see much difference between a C and a B anyhow. I didn't hesitate to put a plus after every A. Really, you'd have thought I was headed straight for Princeton or Harvard.

Like I said, I hadn't seen my mom in over three years, and I did not want to see her now. Or I did, but I surmised bad things were about to happen, and that I'd have absolutely no way to turn them around. No matter how much I willed her not to be upstairs, I knew she would be, probably sitting alone at the kitchen table like she used to every day for months before she left, listening to her scratchy clavichord recordings. Ancient warped 78's that she'd so carefully take out of those thin paper sleeves, and play over and over on the stereo. Only once did I put one on, not thinking, I guess, that of course my dad would get up abruptly from his chair and turn it off, and confide to me in a foul mood that if the devil himself ever listened to music, that would be it. Not Little Richard, not the Beatles, not that oversexed phony-baloney Tina Turner whom he'd just seen that same week gyrate half dressed at best across the TV screen in spike heels right in front of a bug-eyed Johnny Carson. No, not *any* of those slop-bucket rock 'n' roll alchemists could compete with the goddamn clavichord. "Want real music, play big band," he said. "Play Dorsey or Duke Ellington or Benny Goodman." Then, as if interrupted by the long silence of his own awkward pause, he said, "Let me finish."

He said, "Please, your attention, everyone," though only I was there to watch him lift the needle arm and lower it gently onto track one of the great Count Basie and his band.

It sounds crazy, I know, but I believed if I stared long enough at the car and the hearse, back and forth real fast like that, they would eventually cancel each other out. There would be only an empty driveway, and a thirteen-year-old kid in a blue hooded drawstring sweatshirt and khakis who'd had another nothing run-together day, and was glad to be home alone for awhile, glad the weekend had finally arrived.

My chest felt hollow inside, my knees weak and rubbery when I tried to walk, but I didn't stop until I got to the car, flat-topped and boxy, designed, I thought, to assault the very physics of both beauty and speed. Its trunk was rust-pitted, chrome flaking like metal scabs from the rear bumper. My dad was a stickler about keeping all his vehicles vacuumed and Turtle-waxed, but there was no shine left on the Rambler. It had turned drab green over the years, like a government car, and even my reflection in the passenger's-side window seemed dull and pale, completely washed out.

Helpless, I thought, as I shielded my eyes and pressed my forehead to the cold glass. It sure wasn't much of a packing job or a fashion statement—more like somebody'd given up on choosing an outdated outfit after holding up a bunch of them in front of the full-length mirror. One by one, and then simply dumping the entire wardrobe in a giant panic of disappointment and despair. All these thin paisley-print skirts and button-up cardigan sweaters with Kleenex still balled and bunched in the pockets, and dresses wrinkled and folded in half on the back seat, the plastic pink hangers tipped and loose under the shoulder straps, the different-colored zippers partway open, the clasps unclasped. One dress still had the tiny white price tag safety-pinned to the sleeve. Matronly stuff you'd see prominently displayed in the picture windows of St. Vincent de Paul's or Father Fred's, or maybe at a church bazaar. Crazy dresses. Dresses with shoulder flaps that looked like folded wrinkled wings.

Up front, an open Rand McNally road atlas, and shoes in a

heap in the foot-well. Those same high heels with their aging upcurling toes she'd taken to wearing for awhile, and winter galoshes, a single, worn-out leather sandal, and what appeared to be a man's red house slipper.

The car door was unlocked, but I didn't open it. Instead I stood back and slowly turned around, concentrating on slowing my breathing, the blood's dull hammering alive in my ears. It was early May, and overcast, and fifty degrees at most. A few orchid and gardenia petals from last night's wake lay curling in the driveway. My dad had just purchased two new viewing-room kneelers, and the old golden-oak ones looked strange outside by the headstones, the last of the snow all but gone from under the scrawny hemlocks.

I wondered if my dad knew ahead of time that she was coming, and had decided to keep it a secret, a one-man welcoming committee. Or if my mom simply got into the Rambler early this morning in the chilly dark, and turned on the ignition and the heater, and somehow ended up here, climbing the back stairs like she always did, but this time hesitating, then softly knocking empty-handed on the door. I suppose it's possible that she walked around to the front and stood perfectly still under the awning's formal green darkness, where my dad's first glimpse of her would have been through that frosted oval of beveled glass. Some dim, half-recollected ghost-shadow from the past. What might they have said when they first saw each other, I wondered, and who was it spoke first across that threshold, and then closer together, eye to eye in the entryway? Or, true to form, did they defer yet again to that same unbearable dead silence I hated most in them? Those mute dinners, the silverware striking so loudly on the plates.

I couldn't fathom my parents kissing, or even extending a guarded touch, though I don't doubt my dad eventually stood back off the carpet runner to let her pass. And that my mom, eyes lowered, made her slow climb and shuffle up those rarely used front stairs and into the apartment, trailing her hand along the backs of chairs, across the credenza and the highboy, the worn spines of her abandoned records and books. Pulled a volume partway out—Shakespeare or Dryden or Milton maybe—then slid it carefully back with the thin heel of her hand. Thumbed the threadbare ribbing atop the brocaded couch pillows, and plumped them, and, perhaps, with the thermostat set at sixty-five, picked up and carried the coverlet into the kitchen, where she finally sat down at her accustomed place at the table, her back to the pantry. Pulled out her deck of playing cards from the drawer. Or browsed one of my dad's old Spiegel catalogues from which he never ordered a thing since that very first summer at the cabin when he purchased all that metal dinnerware, and a picnic basket and flannel sheets and pillowcases with a grizzly bear print for my bed. It's possible she poured a midday drink, complete with maraschino cherry, or didn't. Wore lipstick and perfume and surveyed the somewhat sparse yet beautiful furnishings she'd left behind, as if still laying claim or attachment to any of them, to any single visible thing.

Finally, there was nothing I could think to do but go inside and face whatever additional hurts and disappointments I knew were in store for me, for all of us. I swallowed hard, my throat tickly and dry as chalk, and I whispered my own first name just to make sure I could get a word out. Whatever eloquent, well-rehearsed killer tirades I'd perfected over the years vanished in a flash. I had no idea now what I'd say, none, and I wanted more than anything in the world for my mom not to address me with that one question: "Archie?" the way people who used to know you well almost always do. The simple truth was that we'd worked hard and long at becoming strangers and that even the purest pure heart in the universe could never ignore such a fact. No matter what amount of forgiveness might shower down around us, we'd be forever committed to the memory of our great cowardice to remain a family, and I didn't care how bad that family might have been. I simply did not care as I mounted the stairs, one at a time, the teakettle's whistle sounding a lot like an approaching train. It was my stop, and I felt sure, for the first time in my life, that when I opened that door and walked into the kitchen, someone I barely knew would be waiting.

Someone was. A woman whose face I might not have even recognized on the street, a face that did not appear happy or loved or reconciled in any way—wizened and bruised-looking and hardly meant for someone in her early forties. I'd never thought of my dad as an unusually handsome man, but next to her he would have resembled Joe DiMaggio or Tyrone Power, and she his frail and failing mother, her weight halved at least, bordering on skeletal. Of course, he wasn't there for the comparison.

I noticed the table was larger again, and I remembered how my dad and I had pulled it apart to remove the extension insert, as if the diminished size would help us forget who was missing.

Her hair had grown back, but the thin braid slung forward across her collarbone was going gray now, her hands tightly folded as though she'd been praying for a long time. No earrings or lipstick, and except for her foot lightly tapping the linoleum, she stayed still as a statue, her face sallow, transfixed, her eyes turned inward like she'd been permanently dazed or hypnotized. She was painful to study so intensely, which, because I couldn't help it, was exactly what I was doing.

Without meaning to, I expelled that long-held breath and said, my voice trembling, "Hi, Mom. It's me." For a couple seconds, nothing, like her mind had drifted way off somewhere else, way off in that private and forbidding other world she occupied all on her own. A deeper, I surmised, and much more intense world than my dad's or my own.

I said hi a second time, a little louder, and that's when she began looking me up and down, up and down until I filled her entire field of vision, and her eyes softened and slowly brightened way back in those inward-spiraling, deep dark sockets. Not smile-brightened, but more like she was startled awake by me actually standing there, not ten feet away. I took a few quick steps and turned off the stove and moved the screaming teakettle—what she always called a samovar—to the back burner. "We're all out of tea bags," I said. "And honey. No cashews or Ritz crackers either, I don't think."

Her lips hardly moved as she tried to talk through the tears. I was almost certain she'd suffered a stroke, or that it really was my grandma stepping back alive from that last black and white snapshot (circa 1959) ever taken of her in the high ladder-backed rocker she liked, and me that newborn bundle swaddled on her lap.

My dad's retractable silver ballpoint was right in front of her, but no paper, so I got out my wide-rule school notebook, and opened it to a blank page, and slid it across the table. Maybe she couldn't talk, but could still formulate and write down sentences. Which, after another interminable minute or so, is what she did. She picked up the pen and leaned her forehead into her left palm, and, in block print like a little kid, she strained to complete each giant letter. I counted them—seven, which took up just about the entire sideways sheet. She finished, and held it up to me, and silently mouthed the words: I'M SORRY! That's when she started to cry audibly, louder by far than any mourner's wail I'd ever heard floating up from the twin parlors downstairs.

"Oh," she said, "oh, oh," her purplish lips forming a perfect round circle of lament, a grief so deep I almost covered my ears. Although she did not say them, I heard in the sounds one long complex word that meant *holy*, and *lonely*, and, oh yes, *only*—that for sure—because only those fervent low moans could even begin to speak to what we'd say if we could. *No*, a thousand times over, and *don't go*, please, and *don't* ever love so poorly again that love has no chance to heal or grow, to attend to any loss or threat, any earthly estrangement or tragedy at all.

My whole body was shaking when I sat down, and reached out my hand, and hardly felt her patting it, as if everything from my fingertips back had suddenly fallen asleep. She was wearing her amethyst birthstone ring, but not her wedding band, her fingers so thin and crooked at the tips I thought sure they'd been broken, each one seeming to bend and flutter away from the others. I counted all ten, but they seemed like somebody else's.

"Listen," my dad said, clearing his throat. I hadn't heard him come in, but when I turned around his gaze was directed at me, his smile so brief and uncertain I wondered if it wasn't more a grimace. Or both, the clearest gesture of confusion I'd ever seen. His eyes shifted to my mom as she sat back, suddenly shy and remote again, the second hand on the wall clock seeming to falter each time it clicked. It was as if this moment defined her entire being, and the moment so full of longing and grief. "Listen," he said again, hands limp at his sides, "hadn't we better get the car unpacked? Your mother's moving back, Arch, back into her old room at the head of the stairs. She's not well, and we're going to take care of her as best we can, okay, son? All right?" He sounded like a doctor imposing restricted visits or something, and my mom too sick or tired to protest. "Any questions?"

He was talking to me, but staring her directly in the eyes, his face stern but still not entirely readable. I'd never been handed a written apology before, not from anybody for anything, not ever, but I took the sheet of paper and passed it to my dad, who folded it in half, and then in half again, and stuffed it unread into his back pocket. "We'll continue this later," he said, "after your mother's had a nap. We'll talk then, maybe order some take-out from the Peking Palace. She's had a long and nerve-wracking drive. We all have," he said as he straightened his watchband, and then waited another couple of tortuous seconds, just to be certain, I guess, that each of us recognized fully the terrible truth this indictment embodied. "We'll need to ease into things," he said. "We'll need for awhile yet for everyone in this household to go slow and careful." Then he nodded directly at me and his face twitched, and I nodded back like I understood.

In a conversation that lasted maybe fifteen minutes total, I'M SORRY was all my mom had managed to convey. Sorry, a word that I've since learned needs redefining on a regular basis. I could have said, "Me too," but I didn't. Nor did my dad. I figured we were apologized out—me to him, him to me, both of us to ourselves.

Before I closed the door behind me I said, "Mom, I'm glad you're back," an oversimplified and precarious approximation of the truth, but the truth notwithstanding. I almost added, "I like your shawl." But she did not look good in red and black, and I did not want to compliment her with such an outright lie.

Once outside, in the image my mind made of her so that I

wouldn't cry, she was beautiful and young, exquisite, really, and perfectly coherent in matters both big and small. She had not yet left or come back home, and showed no dependency whatsoever on prescription drugs or alcohol, no crazy war harangues to deliver, all visible scars gone from her wrists and legs. In other words, I'd created somebody else. Or maybe some*thing* else, not a person so much as a concept I grasped and held to all the way out to the car, where I began to pick up armloads of her clothes, even her underthings, slips and half-slips. I stopped for several seconds to try and smooth out the wrinkled front of a black satin dress with my flattened hand, the static lifting the fine blond hairs on my wrist. Then I buried my face in the fabric to see if I could recognize any scent at all, but I could not. So I turned around, and opened my eyes, and there she was staring down at me from the pantry window, her face illuminated, her bright red shawl still on. She rapped hard on the pane, as though attempting to thwart a neighborhood crime in progress. "It's me," I said again, but this time only in a whisper to myself. "It's me, Mom. It's Archie. We're okay now, you and me. Please, let us be okay, please, please, please."

Then she was gone, and my dad was there, waving down at me before he, too, stepped backwards out of the dying, late-afternoon light. My arms were much too full to raise my hand, though I'd wanted to, in a simple, unmistakable gesture of love.

I was thirteen years old, holding my mother's dresses and slips as high above the ground as I could. And as I started back to where the open storm door creaked on its hinges, I wondered if she'd gone out to dinner on a date, or danced cheek to cheek in any of these outdated outfits. I tried to imagine a succession of men over the three and a half years, their hands pressing the small of her back, her shoulder, her neck, and again I came up blank. Even though I tried and tried I couldn't imagine even one man. A grange hall and live music, an animated, middle-aged bandleader tapping his boot toe and singing into the stand-up mike—maybe two one-hour-long sets—and people laughing and drinking beer or cold cider and doing the Texas two-step, but my mom was not only partnerless, but nowhere in sight.

I felt like a stranger, bringing her clothes to her, and wondering whether it was ever possible to really know another person. Even one's own mother once she'd taken off, no matter for how long or short a time and for whatever impossibly complicated reasons. I figured, probably not. The vast and multiple configurations of our loss had multiplied into the singular shape of our loneliness. I had no answers except to hang and spread these clothes apart in my mom's closet so she'd wake from her nap and feel like she was back home in familiar surroundings. Mismatched shoes lined up, a new toothbrush in the holder.

I looked back up at the kitchen window. From this angle the clouds kept passing three-dimensionally right through the glass and into the house, the reflected treetops budding out in shiny green leaves. Like a dream or a painting or some kind of strange special-effects ultra-slow-motion film. Nothing you'd ever see in real life. Nothing, certainly, you'd expect anybody else to believe.

TEN

Infidels, Betrayers,
& Penitents

I t's a Sportster, not a hog, pure custom black except for the polished chrome pipes and headers, and plenty of throat as the
engine growls each time Rhea throttles down for the curves. I'm
on back without a helmet, which violates Michigan law, an
injunction, as she says, that should be reserved, and enforced, for
tinderbox American subcompacts, with or without airbags. But
either way she's unknown in these parts, and there's no back-
roads constable she can't outrun.

In the meantime I'm holding tight, my arms folded right
below her breasts. Her skimpy top is custom too, a jet black
match to the bike.

Rhea's got her leather bottoms on, but her jacket with its looping chains and slanted silver pocket zippers is back at the cabin,
absorbing about half a gallon of Neatsfoot oil. In the fish-eye
side-view mirror, my face takes on a striking resemblance to an
aging bottle-nose dolphin.

The Platte's still high and roiling from the last two nights of
flash storms, so the float trip's off for at least one more day, unless
that's what this is, the Harley in full glide through the curvy,
newly black-topped six-mile stretch of M-22. It's strangely lumi-

nescent, smooth and slippery as an eel, almost electric. Traffic's light, mostly because it's seven thirty A.M., and the pavement's already steaming itself dry in oblongs and circles as we pass through the slowly rising road vapor.

When she leans, I lean, a kind of dance with Rhea in the lead. We've got a thermos of black coffee and a couple of Bismarcks from the Benzonia E-Z Mart in the saddlebags. Continental breakfast, Rhea called it, a confection buzz for the early-ups. Last night as we ate goat cheese and crackers and drank vodka martinis, she had no difficulty whatsoever imagining the two of us on a train moving leisurely through the nineteenth-century Russian countryside. She said, "Let's do it. Let's get the day started first thing tomorrow by traveling somewhere exotic and old-time romantic. Like Dr. Zhivago minus the war." Sure, why not, I agreed, because on the whole it sounded to me after a couple drinks like an entirely workable plan.

Thus we're headed for the abandoned train trestle—an early, last-century logging route, where we can walk out on the ties, and stop dead center above the river. It's safe enough as long as you watch where you step and don't suffer from ataxia or acute vertigo. It's a prime place to bird-watch for great blue herons and kingfishers, if the watchers are quiet and patient, and restrained in their desire to cannonball their own slow-wavering reflections from the flat-top railing. I've done it a couple dozen times at least, setting a personal best just last weekend with a splash that measured a good fifteen feet up on the concrete abutment. No graffiti spray-painted anywhere. Just another new high-water mark that Rodney and I eyeballed together and then watched disappear. He gets a real kick out of it—his old man tucked up like a frozen turkey and yelling "Geronimo lives" before blasting ass first into the drink. Every single time I surface and look up, I see his apple-cheeked smile, every facial feature so fully distinct and alive. "Good one, Dad," he'll shout down. "Really, *really* good one," and when I wave back I can almost feel his hand close on mine. He hasn't taken the leap—I won't let him, not yet, no way—but he dares me to every time we come here to fish the deep gravel troughs behind the fossilized pilings and permanently stranded drift logs.

But more often than not lately, it's gotten so we don't even pack the rods and waders and landing net. Instead we'll take the Pentax, and our rubber-tipped walking sticks, two finely sanded and polished black walnut scepters, father-son caducei with perfect camber that I designed and carved earlier in the summer, and store in the hearse for this purpose alone. One adult, one kid-sized. We take the trip simply because it's a guarantee to make him laugh, this little king of a kid with his left-temple cowlick and crinkled-up dimple-innocent smile, his baggy shorts and T-shirts. He makes a wish each time. So do I—the same seemingly impossible one, as I flick the penny skyward from my thumbnail. Only once in my life have I seen one land so perfectly flat that the shinny copper circle floated and flashed for a full five or six seconds downstream before suddenly lipping under and out of sight in the tailspin.

It's impossible to come here anymore without thinking of Rodney. It's why I come so often, and most evenings, if I stare down long enough, I believe I can hear his laughter spreading out in invisible waves across the water, even when he's two weeks and four hours away in New Buffalo.

Because of the way the rivets are punched through the steel girders in a series of crosses, we refer to it as the Angel Church Trestle. Flowing underneath, the holy water, where all the diehard fisher-ghosts pass on their way back from heaven, once each year to fish the best stretch of hex hatch water in the state. Holy, I tell Rodney, precisely because no living fishermen but him and me appear to know anything about it. Always keep it our secret, I tell him. Or at least be very, very careful about who you lead here because a sacred place loses its sacred powers once its whereabouts have been given away to the wrong people.

Sometimes I'll sit alone for hours, my legs dangling as I listen to the browns and rainbows feed directly below me, their slurping water notes rising harp-like out of that deep, acetylene blue midnight light left by the moon.

I tap Rhea on her bare right shoulder, the signal for her to slow down, which she does, and I reach my right hand beyond her as we approach the overgrown two-track, and I point a single, emphatic, "There." No hesitation on her part—she brakes, downshifts through the gears into first, and stands up on the foot pegs like a jockey, and rides the bumps with abandon.

The two-track splits after another fifty yards, and she bears right like she's supposed to, the ground ferns soaking my knees. The timing's perfect, the submerged daylight just beginning to filter up through the lush green tangle of vines and leaves, fine spiderwebs of mist tingling my face and arms and neck. In the cold air pockets, the temperature drops a good twenty degrees, Rhea's entire body breaking into goose bumps. Her skin smells strangely like coconut and butter-fudge.

She never stops or slows down, not on her own, and not when I caution her that we're getting close. "Hey, Knievel," I say. "Back off. We're almost there."

For a second I believe she's going to drive right out onto the bridge, a highly improbable tightrope ride along one of the rails. Or worse—if she's been dazed or hypnotized (which she appears to be), she might veer completely off course any second as if to ascend upriver through the multiple and voluminous arches of light, full-spectrum rainbow colors.

I've witnessed this after-storm phenomenon only twice, and felt both times my spirit take flight, the whiteness so bright that I momentarily longed to disappear among those trillions of invisible yet glowing molecules of liquid sky. But never while approaching at this speed on a Harley, and I'm just about to chuck all faith in miracle crossings for a high-risk tuck-and-roll dismount into the earthly cinders. Before I do, I tap Rhea's shoulder one last time, and sure enough she sits and squeezes the hand brake hard and we slide smoothly to an angled stop.

"Jesus Christ," I say, and she takes off her helmet and points, her arm fully extended.

"Oh, my Lord," she says, because never in her entire life has she witnessed anything quite so lonely and lovely. "A natural shrine," she says. "A golden trail of golden spires."

I assure her we're not quite witnessing the birth of light or the Messiah's up-north surprise arrival, although the trestle, to be fair, does appear to be glowing, like some embossed biblical illustration of heaven's gate. "Still, let's not come completely undone just yet," I say.

She gives me a supplicating look, says nothing, and when I bend and pluck a sprig of wild mint, she genuflects, then opens her mouth, eyes rolling back in her head as if she's just lapsed into a seizure. I place the limp green leaf on her tongue, the fragrance strong in the air, like incense, as if altar boys have lined up and lit votive candles along the rusty, pockmarked railing, while those tiny, tornadic, after-storm whirlpools of silver continue to swirl downstream. I hear the quacking mallards just seconds before they alight, their two iridescent green heads rising from the cattails like ascending meteors.

"Trust me," I say, and I hand Rhea the thermos and Bismarcks before bending to lift her into my arms and kiss her as a yellow warbler calls "sweetie, sweetie, sweetie" in its shrill, single-word mimicry of love.

Rhea relaxes deadweight as I step from tie to tie, and she begins counting aloud the syncopated slapping footfalls. Thirty-five is exactly halfway, and I can walk it without ever once looking down, the spaces between just wide enough for a grown person to fall through.

Rhea is talking in tongues, eyes wide and elevated—vision this and hail that as if she's been seized by the taming power of God to recant all sin and shout his praise.

"I've never seen anything like this before, never in my life," she says. "Not even on peyote."

"A natural Platte River high," I say, and when I look over the railing the convex water mirror reflects a giant burning halo around the trestle: a resplendence of greens and reds and yellows. It's so bright I have to squint, the way I used to as a kid, staring and staring at the illuminated yellow sun slowly rising over the stained-glass shoulder of St. Francis, a single mourning dove perched on the crook of his index finger.

"How's this?" I say, stopping mid-trestle and hoisting Rhea's tight bottom onto the railing for an even better upriver view, her black combat boots dangling over the side. I'm hugging her from behind, medium pressure, and staring down. "Brown drakes," I say, and, when I point to them hatching below us, it's as if I've anointed the river from behind a gilded pulpit, the entire congregation of cedar waxwings emerging from both banks through these inexplicable, spiraling, cylindrical tunnel-whorls of colored light.

Thirty of them at least, and Rhea puts down the thermos and Bismarcks and spreads both arms as if *she* intends to lift off into this glorious moment, into the soundless flutter of yellow-tipped wings rising and diving. But she stays right there, her palms rotating upward, eyes turned heavenward. There's maybe three inches of iron ledge for her to hook her heels, but it's enough with me holding onto her hips as she leans, knees hyperextended and back arched, almost horizontally out above the water.

Maybe it's the angle, or the way the light is momentarily quenched by the sudden lone dark rain cloud—I'm not sure—but when she delivers a bewailing "No, don't go, don't go," those heavy *o*'s echo back from underneath the trestle as if resounding through a bullhorn. Nothing divine intervenes—the rainbows have already turned a softer glow and then pure white in the miracle of their disappearing, both color and form. Then it happens: the cloud passes, along with its spectral shadows, and the morning returns to a normal Friday morning in July: leaves and trees and seventy dark creosote ties spaced equidistant across an abandoned train trestle. Blue sky. Nothing otherworldly unless it's that muskrat's tail finning its tiny, flat-glare downstream wake, as if headed straight through the turbulent floodwaters only to dive suddenly into the river's deeper and secret sanctums.

"Looks like the service is over for today," I say, my arms straining now against the weight of her body, and I haul her back until she collapses again into a sitting position, head bowed, fingers laced tightly on her lap. I can tell before she even turns around that she's real close to crying.

"It's been . . . twenty years . . . since my last confession," she says. I press my finger gently to her lips to check those dark and forbidding thoughts. Believe me, I forgive all her crimes and sins and indiscretions entirely—past, present, and future, whatever they may be, mortal or not, and no additional penance necessary. Normal life will take care of that. But when I offer Rhea a steaming, aromatic first sip of coffee, she slowly shakes her head no.

"He didn't care about me," she intones, and eases herself down from the railing, and pushes my arm away when I reach out to her. Then she turns on her tiptoes, appearing to float light-footed like a high-wire walker in her heavy boots, not toward the Harley, but off in the opposite direction.

Whatever she means, this is a dangerous moment, and I try to distract her by saying, "Wait up, I neglected to mention that I want to show you something." Which, in fact, I do—an after-breakfast surprise, but to no avail. She doesn't answer or even slow down, the distance quickly lengthening between us. "You'll like them, I promise, really," but it's obvious that those bone pellets I discovered last week underneath the great horned owl's nest will atone for absolutely nothing. No, show her instead the powerful she-owl swooping down on the voles and mice, the sharp-curved orange beak and talons, and forget those half-digested bone fragments of the weak and innocent dead.

I don't immediately start after her, but I do shout loudly that there's an awful lot of thorny wilderness back there, and probably a tusked bush pig or a black bear sow with cubs. Which is no picnic should she unexpectedly run into them, and I'm just wondering if she's got a specific destination in mind, and a working compass to get her there by nightfall, and a six-volt searchlight since very little sun falls on this particular northern forest floor. And, not to be overlooked, a flap-hat and some mosquito netting, or at least a sufficient supply of Dr. Juice bug dope for those ill-bred, flesh-eating black flies that search and destroy in massive dark swarms this time of year. Hard to know for certain, but all-in-all it might just be the right moment for some reflection.

She stops at the end of the trestle, and turns to face me, mouth agape, and through the megaphone of her cupped hands, she says, the sounds tremulous and wavering, as if her tongue's been cut out, "A-n-y-w-h-e-r-e." Or is it "M-e-n-b-e-w-a-r-e"? I'm not sure—some sort of eerie death chant or warning. When I point to my ears and say, "What?" she crouches and begins to beat her arms against her leather thighs, and screech incoherently at the top of her lungs in some unintelligible, ear-piercing chimeric language. The glorious morning's beginning has taken a sharp, unexpected turn and I'm lost as to how to turn it back around.

She's on her knees, watching warily as I approach, and glancing from one side of the trestle to the other. "Please, tell me," I say, almost certain she's got in mind to leap one way or the other if I venture too close too fast. It's shallow down under her, and stump-ridden along this stretch of the river's hunched shoulder, and she's shouting, "Stay away from me, stay away," her open right hand batting aside every comforting, whispered word I attempt. Her body gestures are loud and clear: she is terrified and lost in some deep, inconsolable, completely remote bad place all her own. "Rhea," I say, "please let me help," and I stop three ties away, where I drop to my knees. We've already locked eyes, but only until she bows her head again. Then she says, in the slow cadence of confession, "Our father . . ." but it's not the Lord's prayer she recites. It's a story about Lake Penawawa, and a pickup truck with chained rear tires carving out a tight-turning-radius figure-eight on the glassy ice.

There's a girl, she says, standing just off-shore, a gorgeous old-growth white birch forest behind her. She's twelve years old, and freezing cold, her brother riding shotgun and waving to her each time the pickup muscles into its arc and S's back across, ice chips flying skyward in two bright silver-blue rooster tails. He's only nine, and easily bored, and still in love with his dad's chronic willingness to misbehave, to never entirely grow tired of kids' dumb and dangerous antics, their preposterous dares, their immortal, innocent-minded deceptions.

In a mother's absence, it's the daughter's obligation to worry, no matter how young she is, and no matter that nobody has ever voiced such a thing in her presence, but she knows. It's understood. She has skipped Mass to tag along on this day-long wilderness retreat, and she feels the weight of her presence deeply. She feels, in the clear comprehension of the unspoken mandate to intervene, enormous confusion and guilt and dread, as well as unspeakable contempt for them, for their tacit carelessness and conceit, their merriment.

Half a dozen tip-ups are set farther out, set since just before first light, but the pike have gone close-mouthed on this frigid February morning, and that's reason enough for something unpredictable and maybe even demonic to transpire. It's Sunday, of course, and the family should be sitting closely together in the center-aisle pew at Holy Cross, directly in front of the basilica's high altar, a faithful part of the faithful fold. *But my mother's there all by herself,* Rhea says, like some expectant widow praying with her rosary, and asking God's forgiveness. "Give us this day," she whispers, the organist pumping away and the choir singing "Rejoice, rejoice," but it's a harsh, cruel world out there, the looping figure-eight, with each pass, deepening under the tires, the chains glinting like skate blades. The girl, in fact, is wearing skates— they're new and bright white, the edges sharp, tiny silver bells attached midway up the laces. Which is the sole reason she's come along, to try them out. Certainly her mission's not to ice fish, and when her red mitten springs up like a flag, her father does not stop the truck, and open the door, and run to her the way he should if he were paying proper attention, if he weren't, once again, playing favorites. It's as if she's always borderline invisible.

"And lead us not," the mother continues, "into temptation," but the boy, whose name is Richie, keeps chanting, "Faster, faster," and his father accelerates even more. He's already let go of the steering wheel, which now turns on its own, following the smooth sculpted contours of the grooves. At certain angles, the girl can see clearly her brother's arms flailing like an exhausted swimmer behind the wavering, blue tint of the windshield. Behind the bars of the bright chrome grille, the engine whines and whines in its lowest gear.

There's nothing amusing about this, least of all the laughter splashing from the open windows, which itself appears all wrong in this ungodly climate, even sinister, something awful for the local news to report. So the girl bends at the waist and pushes off tentatively with her left toe, pushes again and again, and calls both their names as she glides toward them: *Dad*, she says. *Richie*, her breath rising in thin white puffs, her palms gone suddenly sweaty, almost numb.

It's maybe ten degrees—no windchill—and the tailgate's down, the minnow bucket and the gas-powered auger sliding from side to side across the black ribbed bed liner. She knows the ice is thick, a solid foot, clear as a cut-glass flower vase, but the truck's chassis is already so low she believes it's about to bottom out, and get stuck. *If it does*, Rhea says, somebody's going to have to cross all the way over to the south end of the lake where they started out only a few hours ago through the darkness. Where the smelt shanties—two dozen or more—are clustered along the drop-off, just out from the public boat landing. Ice Town—a generic name for these impermanent winter villages. She wishes she could still see the bluish plumes of smoke from their stoves, or smell the slow-burning ironwood, but she can't. They're completely cut off, and she's afraid—because only she is wearing skates—that it will be she, and she alone, who is designated to go seek help. It's a good half mile, and her legs are unsteady, and even though the sun's still out, dense snow begins to fall. Squalls. Naturally, there's no compass in the tackle box, no pink sulfur flares to ignite, and who'd see them anyway from inside those windowless huts? Somebody outside taking a pee? Somebody stretching?

Besides, she simply does not want to go knocking on strange doors bearing strange names like Walterhouse and Backalukas and Schmuckle and Yob, asking if anyone—any of the icemen staring down into their dark rectangular holes—has a wench or a tow rope. Perhaps a few minutes to spare because there's nobody else anywhere around to rescue her stranded family. No, she wants for none of this to transpire. She wants only to be kneeling in the safe refuge of Holy Cross in her Sunday best, right tight to her mother in prayer, perhaps secretly watching the lifeless dark eyes of the altar boys open and close, their hair combed, their parts straight and perfect. And the choristers so angelic in their lovely, complicated, mesmerizing Latin harmonies, their missals held out in front of them. On this day she wants to rise and walk up the aisle to the altar with its candles and open her mouth and receive the Eucharist. Or, if nothing else, to at least climb into the truck right this instant and drive straight back home for a breakfast of Canadian bacon and scrambled eggs and toast with jelly, another kind of blessing.

These are the reasons she shakes off both her mittens, her scarf and parka and hat. Pulls the thick knit lamb's-wool turtleneck over her head, unzips her snow pants from ankles to waist, and lets them drop away so that she's skating out only in her flowered long-johns, her pink pompoms and her silver bells, her fluffy white earmuffs. Maybe *this* will get their attention, get them to sit up and take notice for once. Although she will not likely expose anything more, she imagines herself suddenly older and naked before them, an act almost desperate enough to make her want to do it—really frighten them with an altogether different sort of daredevil, unforgettable midwinter thrill.

And it works—the pickup slows and stops, she says, and everything's going to be okay once again, though she's no doubt the defiler who has ruined their weekend fun, and look how badly she's shivering, hyperventilating now, both hands pressed into the hollows of her armpits. The headlights blink on and off like a warning, and she can see that her father is waving her away, all the while saying something she can't hear to her brother. She's within ten yards of them when the truck inches forward, then back, a kind of rocking to get them in motion again, and it's right then that the ice cracks. It's dull and brief, like distant rolling thunder, followed a couple of seconds later by this awful low-hemorrhaging roar right under her feet. At first she believes she's simply too cold and losing all coordination, but it's the nose-heavy front end of the pickup that tips suddenly forward and down. Not slowly like she's heard, but all at once, the windshield slapping hard against the icy black water.

Only the driver's-side door opens. But before anybody slides out, the entire bottom oval of the eight drops away into the lake, the water sloshing up in a single, perfectly clear high-ankle wave.

This time she does lose her balance and falls, and is swept backwards in a slow-motion 360, the snow and the sun and the sky swirling above her. When she looks back, the truck has vanished, all but the crimson emergency flashers, and then they're gone too, and there's her father, hanging onto the perfectly curved shelf ice by his elbows.

He calls her name a single time—"Rhea," amplified to a pitch she's never heard it spoken before—and without another word he pushes away and dives, and he's under for what seems a long, long time. "Come up," she whispers, "please, please come up," and presses her forehead hard to the ice, almost believing she can see her father and brother drifting by like ghosts, and that's when she begins to scream.

It's possible he hears her—he must. He surfaces, after all, his gloves and hat gone, but his glasses somehow still on, and she's right there, waiting on hands and knees for him, just inches out of reach. His unblinking eyes are wide open and, like hers, more silver than blue, bottomless, she thinks, as if to plumb the depths of the unimaginable loss and sorrow that's about to drown them all. It's his fault, nobody else's, his alone—and he knows it, and so does she, struck speechless now, both trembling hands covering her mouth.

". . . and deliver us . . ." the mother whispers, staring up at the magnificent hanging crucifix above the altar, the perfectly arched wooden feet crossed and bloody, and the girl's father, purple-lipped and gasping for breath, instructs his daughter calmly: "Don't . . . don't come any closer," as she begins to crawl toward him, her fingers splayed out on the slippery wet ice. "I'll only pull you in," he says, his teeth chattering wildly. Then he whispers, "Dear Jesus . . . where are your clothes, Rhea?" as if she, too, intends to dive for her missing brother. "Go, get help," he says. He says, "Save yourself if you love us," and he lets go without a sound—no good-byes, nothing—the open water closing silently above him.

That's what she remembers most clearly—those final words, and how his body disappeared without a human splash—and how it wasn't so much the cold, but rather a permanent deep ache that entered and numbed her entire being. How she got to the village she doesn't know, but two men in a shanty sat her down on an overturned bucket by the stove, and asked where exactly and how long ago, questions she could not answer. She told them she just followed the blind music of the bells across the lake, and pointed at her skates, and the men nodded as if they understood this whispered, universal language of shock and trauma.

In their absence a woman arrived, a large woman, skin and hair white as plaster. She smiled kindly and unfolded a dark woolen blanket, and wrapped the girl before pushing open the shanty door just enough so they could watch the silent fathers and sons fanning out across the ice, not more than ten feet apart in the strangely blue winter light. "A dragnet," she whispered, as she peeled and separated the sweet, glistening crescents of an orange, and fed them to the girl one at a time, this girl whose sleeves were still pulled over her clenched hands. The woman had line cuts in the creases of her fingers, and she preached like the Sister of Final Reckoning from some invisible text: "Remember," she said, "we do not die forever, just once in a lifetime before our eternal souls are risen. It's the living who must endure—who must forgive and go on."

"She called me 'a child of faith,'" Rhea says, "and I still hear that dream-voice of hers each time my father rises and rises from that black hole with his murdered son in his arms, the two of them hovering above me. 'Forgive, forgive,' but I don't, I can't, and I'm pointing and screaming up at them, sentencing them to be forever damned."

I just stare at Rhea until our eyes slowly disengage, and we simultaneously stare down in silence between the wooden ties. I can make out only the vaguest reflection of our contorted faces, and Rhea's hands steeple-like before they part, the same way my dad's used to while testing new kneelers for the viewing rooms. "Go ahead, try it out," he'd say to me after they were installed below the polished mahogany rails. "What do you think—they okay, Arch? Comfortable? Easy on the knees?" and I'd say, "Yes," though what did I really know or feel except that kneeling without a prayer always seemed such an empty gesture, perhaps even a sacrilege. That's exactly how I feel now, and in that moment I mourn all fatherly betrayals, my own included.

The birds have quieted, and Rhea, enshrouded now in shadow, says, "Listen," as if she hears the submerged flood-felled tree seconds before it thuds hard against the center piling, shifts its lumbering, waterlogged direction, and bobs up and down on its way out from under the trestle.

The water has not yet begun to recede, though the river's at ease as always with its sudden wild turbulence, the cuts deepening under the sandbars and blow-downs, the flooded tag alder trembling for miles and miles downstream, all the way to Lake Michigan. Sand and gravel shifting elsewhere and back all along the riverbed.

"We should leave," I say, and this time when I reach out to her Rhea squeezes and stands and does not let go of my hand. Says nothing, clutches it like a frightened little kid. And that's how I think of the two of us—just kids—someone's daughter and someone's son, all alone and much too young to be holding hands on an abandoned railroad bridge.

"I . . . I miss them terribly," Rhea says, quietly, almost idly, and I say, "Shhhh," once again pressing my finger to her lips, and staring right at her as if I understand. "Do you?" she says, and the nod I offer is slow and reassuring, like a father's nod. And yes—that too—like a surviving only son's.

ELEVEN

Zelda

It's 1990, the millennium's wrap-up decade, and I'm standing on a three-quarter-inch plywood casting platform, four separate different-diameter target rings anchored at various distances. The one farthest away—the anemic, curdled butter–colored one— is only twenty-five yards, but seldom does anyone other than me ever hit it. Especially not those eco-tourist tycoons who tomahawk the water surface with their high-dollar rod tips, and more and more that's been my clientele. No feel or finesse whatsoever, at least not until they reach for their wallets at the end of the day. So I'm actually relieved that Mr. Brock St. James has defaulted due to his backlog of pressing international business considerations. His daughter Zelda—she goes by Z—would like to come in his place, assuming he might prevail upon me in this sudden way to invite her aboard instead. As in what, I wondered? The starship *Enterprise*? But all I said was, "Sure, I suppose. Why not?"

She's twenty-two years old, and fresh out of a fancy East Coast art school. And she's here, hip cocked, because she's recently read *A River Runs through It.* Twice, and now *she's* hooked, she says, and smiles up at me like I'm some close blood relative of that particular Presbyterian fly-fishing trio, the wise angler-philosopher dad and his two sons. All this banter as we stand inside the resort right beside the stuffed fourteen-foot-tall Alaskan brown bear. As always, his enormous raised paw seems to ordain, in purest angry bear cynicism, my lighting out on yet another sorry excuse for a fly-fishing expedition. Out of the plush purple-carpeted lobby and into the great unspoiled northern Michigan outdoors, and this girl prattling on about what a fantastic film the novel would make.

Yes, I *have* read the book, loved it, too, I tell her. But I doubt a movie's in the offing. Much too literary. Entirely wrong kind of plotline. Unless, of course, Hollywood decides to transform it into a slasher-on-the-river flick, which wouldn't surprise me but would kind of alter its heart-song some, wouldn't it? "You'll see," she says. "Just wait and watch."

I shrug as she raises the striped red and white golf umbrella she's just opened to provide us some protection from the elements. It's a sweltering ninety-four degrees, the air syrupy, the single hottest day I've ever spent on this reputedly world-ranked golf course. Breezeless, a hundred plus humidity, the heat slackening not one bit all week. It feels a lot like Guadalajara must in mid-afternoon. It feels like siesta time where, under the generalissimo's sacred shade trees, the blue-ribbon wing-clipped fighting cocks sleep and dream of surviving yet another grim and bloody humdinger of a day.

I've got the fly shop's fancy camcorder with me, which I use so paying clients can later study their angling technique—back cast, roll cast, tower cast, etc.—or, in most cases lately, lack thereof. It's part of the sales package, but I'm tempted instead to stop the Imperial golf cart right here and shoot an impromptu close-up of Z on the famous thirteenth fairway, a 570-yard par-five dogleg. Something for me to review some sleepless night long after she sashays away on those perfect, poolside, chaise longue legs.

She's hatless and she's wearing tight-fitting khaki shorts. No shades, though I can't imagine why not on a day like this. And a white T-shirt with what I thought for sure was an image of Freud stenciled on front, his eyes bulging as if starstruck by Z's beauty and poise as we traverse the bumpy roughs. But no, "It's not the great mother-obsessed Sigmund," she says. "It's Degas," and I simply say, "Of course it is," as we glide down the recently shorn fairway grass in our humming electric cart, past the time-share condominiums, half a dozen expensive demo rods and reels piled in protective cases in the back. Equipment I endorse for the 10 percent kickback on everything I unload. It's quality gear. I own it myself, I say to any of the annoying cynics who ask.

The sad truth is, we couldn't be farther from those cold Montana and Wyoming trout rivers if we tried—Snake, Bitterroot, Musselshell, Flathead, Big Horn, all rivers I guided as I drifted through my twenties. By the time I'd turned twelve I'd already given up lakes in favor of fly-fishing the Deadstream stretch in front of the cabin, leaving my dad to watch safely from the porch. "Where there's water there's worry," he'd say, but the only serious danger I've experienced anywhere I've ever fished is right here at the resort.

Z and I are already headed for the largest of the manmade water hazards, where there must be a thousand globby corroding green golf balls clustered like a giant frog's egg in the algae. The effluvial ground clouds of nitrogen fertilizer and insecticide they spread in the dark predawn most days cross-pollinates—I'm dead certain of it—on the surface water, so who knows what's swimming around down there in the chemical seepage. Something you might luck into with a side of rancid beef and a grappling hook, something straight out of *Creature from the Black Lagoon*. There have been days, I swear, when the water began to burble and belch, a kind of glottal regurgitation that nobody but me appeared to notice.

I'm curious, but more than a bit reluctant, to test my theory about the water hazard being flammable, and it makes me plenty nervous when anyone lights up a cigar out here. "Between ten o'clock and two," I tell them. "Remember, the rod's an extension of your arm. Timing and rhythm, not strength, and always between ten and two," and I stand back and watch as clients flail their knotted Wonderlines into a breeze that smells sometimes like hydrogen sulfide, and other times like the armpits of burning tires.

For this they pay and thank me. And, more often than not, re-up for phase two, an actual guided trip on the Boardman or Platte—tubes, floatboats, knee-deep wading on the easily readable, flies-only, catch-and-release Pioneer stretch. It's rife with ten-inch stockers, pellet-fed rainbows you can't possibly overfish. They'll rise to almost anything at any time of day or night. I tend to speak sparingly on the river, hoping that when I do these beginning anglers will pay attention. Sometimes they'll spring for a Grand Marnier and a flaming dessert if I show sufficient interest in their ongoing, single-sided conversations about hog futures and the extravagant dollars dance they do on the ballroom trading floor. If at some point they inquire directly about *my* investment strategy, I tell them that there are schools of one-thousand-year-old fish frozen into the Antarctica ice, and that the invention of the fishhook occurred sometime around 8,000 B.C.

Directly ahead of us the aluminum sand-trap rake at the bunker edge keeps shooting fire bursts back at the sun. There's nobody else on the course so late in this sun-storm of an afternoon, the pointed red pin flags ablaze in the dense, undulant heat waves that shimmer, as Z says, like the molten, pre-liquid sinews of glass. She claims to have blown her share, having apprenticed over the last two years to the masters in the most famous glass classrooms of the world: Austria, London, Venice, Munich. She says the art of glassblowing is not unlike the art of having a baby, all breath and forceps and a lot of love and pain.

"What exactly pops out?" I ask.

"Depends," she says. "Optic pitchers, satin melon vases, oval bells and gazing globes. Thin, long-stemmed wine and champagne glasses—stemware's the potential best cash crop of glassblowers. French open heart-arch baskets. An assortment of art bottles," she says. Which makes what I lift from under the melting ice in the Coleman cooler seem fairly crude, even risky, but Z immediately closes the umbrella, twists off both caps, and we clink a toast to high- and lowbrow art alike. When we do, I notice no wedding ring or mega-carat engagement rock, but rather a raised burn scar on the back of her left hand. Occupational hazard perhaps? Could be she's telling the truth so far.

She's got major plans, she asserts, to open her own signature business worldwide—the Zelda St. James collection. Chicago-based. *Forbes*-endorsed, no doubt, once her powerful father calls in a favor. "Where else *but* the Windy City?" she says, and refers to it as the only Midwestern marketplace that does not suffer an identity crisis, does not strike Easterners as dowdy and desperate and entirely evangelical. Charlie Trotters, she says. The Art Institute of Chicago, the Navy Pier and the Sears Tower. Wrigley Field, of course, and gallery openings all the time and street vents and sidewalk life and traffic reports and just enough healthy urban chaos to keep folks young at heart and coming back. O'Hare, she says, for a quick getaway to anywhere. All city sights I've so far avoided like the plague. Which until this moment always improved my self-esteem, but for some reason leaves me feeling not unlike a muleskinner, and I almost reach up to bat away the swarm of invisible iridescent green flies. Above us the vapor trail of a silent jet divides the stratospheric blue like a feathery backbone.

"That's my future," she says, "something on the order of Waterford crystal or Fabergé eggs." Meaning high-ticket all the way, but that can wait because today is today, and she's feeling fishloric, she says, if that's the right word for wading the local rivers with our resident guide. And afterward a swim? After all, she's packed her bikini, she says. "It's balled up right here in my back pocket."

She doesn't exactly show it to me, but my imagination's mushroomed alive, the creative synapses sparking in overdrive, and I say, "Okay. No more farce-fishing. The Platte it is," and I bank the golf cart tight to the lip of the green, right back in the direction from which we just came. Probably another impulsive wrong turn, but who cares anymore? I've drawn four aces twice in one night already this fiscal year, which proves sudden good luck can sometimes conquer the odds, and I'm convinced—more so than ever—that the cautious discernments one tallies over time make eunuchs of us all.

So when Z puts her beer in the holder between us and leans forward I take careful notice. It's not a hyper-dramatic move she's just made, though in this heat any effort to stretch and shake hands with one's own lower extremities is worth at least a peek or two on this surreal, battery-powered retreat we're attempting across these contaminated, felt-green thermal fields.

Her fingers remain clenched around each thin ankle, her eyes closed now, head tilted back. She's smiling, that's all. She hasn't leaned left, hasn't fixed on me in any noticeable way. So maybe I'll just chalk it up to heatstroke when I decide to suddenly raise the stakes and escort her, not directly to the river, but rather to the cabin where she can change out of or into anything she desires. It's a hedge, I realize, but the truth is, no self-respecting brown or rainbow or brook trout is likely to rise from under the shade banks or root pools for quite awhile. Which means we need to kill some time, and I wouldn't mind a swim myself. Then maybe shoot some eight- or nine-ball in the air-conditioned back room of the Fox Den, the perfect place to hole up until the predicted cool front washes through. Midnight and a waning moon—that's really the time to go—and when I suggest that as a feasible plan Z promptly nods her approval. She says, "Sounds perfect. I'm up for some local color." Plus she's got nowhere else to be but with me, so why not just play it by ear until the more serious business of the river. "Let's do it," she says.

If it's there, I haven't picked up even a hint of irony, and I don't say another word. I like the shape her full lips make when she speaks, the slow animate mobility by which they form each slow seductive syllable. It's unrehearsed. It's much too natural not to be. She's not even sweating as far as I can see, though I'm wiping condensation nonstop from my eyelids, and my shirt's soaked completely through, runnels of it down my ribcage and spine. Could be she's heat-resistant from the long hours of sitting in front of blast furnaces, red-hot motes shooting out. All I know for certain is that there's something erotic about a gorgeous well-bred woman gone wild enough to blow intricate glass shapes from the fire.

I've flattened the accelerator, not setting any land speed records, but on this gradual decline there's almost enough speed for the breeze to tangle her hair, feathered out well past shoulder length with her head still tilted back like that, and her earlobe studded with three tiny carbon-colored crescent moons.

———

I own a Cadillac DeVille convertible with white reflector mud-guards, but no fuzzy mirror dice or high school graduation tassels, and no suicide knob either. I'm permanent small-town—there's no denying it, no Sunday *Times* delivered here on time, and yet there is a limit to the provincial.

Behind me a balled-up cigarette pack remains suspended inches above the rear seat, afloat like a lottery power ball, weightless in its vortex of quickly dying light. Whenever I brake, it drops. Whenever I hit sixty-five, as I've just done past the tiny hillside cemetery with its flat stone markers and flags and black wrought iron fence, it's up again, fluttering, the cellophane's high-pitched insectile whine like a vibrating needle in my middle ear.

Z, who's been watching it, reaches back now and backhands it to the floor. "Enough of that noise," she says, and when she turns around she's sitting closer to me, but only for as long as it takes her to give up on finding a decent radio station.

It's Friday night, and my pool cue is in the trunk among the fly-fishing gear. Which pretty much guarantees the beers will be free, although there is this guy named Its who used to open the cottage and make repairs when my dad first finagled it. No last name that anybody knows. Just Its, and he shoots a decent game even with those stubby, badly warped bar cues. He works for the pulp mill, but with recent federal cutting restrictions he's been demoted to part-time after almost twenty years, half his miserable existence, as he says. Nonetheless, as he's quick to point out, at least his sorry derriere hasn't been laid off or laid to rest. Not like some guys, and he's been able anyway to recoup a small portion of his losses with his chain-saw art. He takes his craft seriously, and it's clear he doesn't expect anyone to stroke his ego. But it's equally clear that you do *not* goof on him about being an artist, a craftsman. I doubt he'll abound any time soon in the glory of a genius lifetime artist grant, but he has, to his credit, racked up a few brief mentions in the *Honor Enterprise*, a local weekly. I'm quite fond of *The Female Pope*, though the piece I like best is his black bear riding backwards on a moose. It's called *These Moments They Are Not Rare*. The bear, cradling a flintlock rifle, is grinning, but the moose is not. Its says he's got something else in mind for me though: *Icarus in Waders*, a rod in one hand, a stringer of fat-bellied trout in the other, wings half melted on his back. He likes that myth, he says, and he's thinking he'll spray-paint the wings flat black like ash, and tip the feather ends with hammered tin. Pure oak, six feet in height, and let's consider as further incentive that he'll deliver it free of charge? A consignment piece I'm seriously considering, although we've yet to settle on a price.

He describes each new sculpture brainstorm to me while he muses and drinks—he "talks me through them," as he puts it, "clues me in" to the complex ways in which the creative mind operates—and I, his third eye, provide rapid-fire on-the-spot titles. I write down the ones he likes: *Ponce de Leon's Captive Spike-Haired Amazonian Bride. The Polygamist Dances Mambo Alone in the Gloaming. Woody Woodpecker on Steroids. Fugue of the Agnostic Crow. The Gargoyle Polka Crowd Pauses to Cry.*

Its has enormous arms and a barrel chest and, depending on his mood, a face that resembles either Oliver Hardy or Nikita Khrushchev. Mostly I like the guy, except when his eyes in a certain light take on that opaque color of a molting blue racer. He could, without a doubt, grab me by throat and crotch and clean jerk me above his head, hold for the count, and step forward, dropping me behind him to the floor. But then, as he says on a regular basis, there exits the last intelligent life form from this den of otherwise fallen angels.

His battered pickup is already in the parking lot, tailgate gone, the bed littered with empty beer cans and spent 12-gauge shotgun shells, the gun cradled, and no doubt loaded, in the rear-window rifle rack. A come-along and two chain saws, and a sleeping stone-deaf bloodhound named Him, a jug of water and a water bowl and a sizable bluish white femur. Bovine, I suspect, but who knows for sure. Unless you're upwind of Him, he doesn't have a clue you're around. I've learned never to scratch his dewlaps until he's awake and staring directly at me. Then he craves the attention. Moans and thuds his tail and slobbers all over the hand that loves him. Offers his fat paw each time I try to leave. Sometimes on my way out alone from the bar I'll slip him a stick of beef jerky or a pickled egg.

I can see through the window that Its is already at the bar, head down, his right index finger slow-tapping the edge of a shot glass of house bourbon. Before too long he'll be feeding coins to the Wurlitzer. It's loaded with vintage Marty Robbins, and Merle, and Tammy Wynette, a platinum compendium of good-love-gone-bad tunes. Plus the Sons of the Pioneers, and my favorite, "Wichita Lineman." But Its plays one record and only one, over and over, commencing approximately one half hour before closing. His anthem. F-10: Kenny Rogers's "Lucille," a catchy but somewhat sappy lament about kids and crops in the field and an untimely wifely defection.

"A goddamn accurate ball-buster of a ballad," proclaims Junior J. Fox—the ruddy-faced toothy wink-and-nod owner and bartender—almost as many times as Its has played the song. Hits pretty fucking close to home, Junior always says, and whenever he does a chorus of howls erupts from the parched throats of those six or seven regulars still hounded by the endless betrayals of female love. The deeper into their cups, the harder their angry, collective broken hearts wail.

"It's usually worth a few laughs," I say. "Really, they're harmless. Past-their-prime roustabouts just trying their best to get by."

"We've got honky-tonk cowboys in Providence," Z says. "Plenty. Gaggles of."

And just like that she's out of the car, laughing and dancing her way up the stairs. "Whoa, hold on," I say, "wait up," but she doesn't. She fingers her hair back off her forehead, opens the door, and steps inside like she's late for a group portrait. I can't quite picture her among them without me, but what I've learned already is that she's not the least bit reserved or shy. Or wasn't just an hour ago, sitting in her radioactive lime green bikini on the river swing and sipping a glass of white Bordeaux, her contribution to the dinner. I thought of Dryden's "All human things are subject to decay," a line my mom quoted from time to time in her final slow dying. But one whose truth paled badly in comparison to what I saw and felt as Z pushed away from the dock, and leaned back above the water, head down and lolling from side to side, legs straight out. As if to say in her silence, Screw the pessimist poets—they don't know shit from Shinola if they can't compose any better than that.

Far be it from me to disagree. I was tongue-tied, but with my brain still locked in overdrive. I thought, Why not capture instead in verse eternal that moment when an addled thirty-two-year-old recluse riparian lowers a lifetime of defenses and falls deeply in love for the first time? Add that to the canon of human reckoning. Keep it simple and upbeat and close to home.

Meaning no Kenny Rogers before midnight, but already he's pining away on Z's quarter by the time I enter, and Its in mid-spin on his squeaky bar stool is toasting this strange and beautiful and unaccompanied woman whose body language is equal to her exquisite musical taste. Either that or she's telepathic. Junior Fox, one hand suddenly risen from the elbow-deep steaming sudsy water where he's purifying beer mugs, appears to bless her, his index finger pointed heavenward toward the helix of silver and gold lights, where that team of high-stepping Budweiser Clydesdales circles in on gigantic silent hairy-white clodhopper feet for a closer look.

And rail-thin Cliff the Skinny, on his way back from the men's room and still wrestling with the stubborn zipper of his fly, stops, zips easily now, a sobering miracle of coordination entirely unknown to him after a sixth or seventh pee. He smooths his thin goatee one time with each hand before he folds them, and for a second I believe he's going to fall to his knees. Maybe he does but I can't be sure after every light in the place pulses and dims. Followed by total blackout, as if this sudden electrical overload is the result of Z simply being here in her tight shorts and T-shirt and slip-on sandals.

"Fucking-A." It's Cliff the Skinny, who's pretty much gotten by in this life by repeating only those two words, and perpetually readjusting his Texas belt buckle like a shield for what must be his undersized pud and testicles. At least that's the ongoing joke. Junior Fox, his vocabulary extensive by comparison, says, "Watch that goddamn mouth of yours—there's women in here." He pronounces "mouth" without the *h*, the *t* in "there" as if it were a *d*.

"Listen to your own self for Christ's sake," Erv Early says. "It ain't the mouth, it's them words come pissin' out that matters."

"Sure as shit you can say that again," Its chimes in, and Cliff the Skinny does. He says, "Fucking-A," louder this time, as if preaching from a dais, and the "amens" that follow make the first lit candle seem a churchly act. It's passed slowly from hand to callused hand to Z, and I can see now—just barely in the slow unblinding of the den—that Junior has lifted and placed a wicker creel onto the bar, and inside a whole stash of candles. Everyone reaches in for one but me. I'm still over by the door, frozen out of the conversation. And momentarily stunned by the exaggerated features of Z's illuminated profile, her ease, her making sense of this place, the occasional grunts, the deep whistled breaths that carom from wall to wall in this semidarkness.

Her skin glows, an image I already know will last and last in my memory. But it's a little eerie too, especially when Its leans toward her to light a cigarette from the flame. I can see in his left eye a look I've never seen from him before, something as clear and innocent and as far removed from here as infanthood. Z doesn't appear at all uncomfortable or alarmed. She simply stands there smiling at these lonely hard-drinking men she's never laid eyes on before.

I'm not sure they've even noticed me yet, so I screw my pool cue together and start tap-tapping the unchalked tip in front of me like a cane until I arrive at her side. I can barely make out the row of spellbound faces—cut-outs, I think—a north-woods cardboard tribunal staring back at us from above the bar stools like part of a stage set. Not one of these men is hatless, bills tugged low on their brows. Then someone—the recently furloughed Billy Vandyken, I think—says, "That the Angel? That you, man?" and when I nod it's as if I've given permission for them to reach toward this goddess of heavenly fire, all of them at once, their candles sputtering alive as Z touches flame to wicks, one after the other.

Coming slowly into focus behind them in the bar mirror, the ratty mule deer's protruding black glass eyes, his faded red Shriner's hat, last year's Christmas lights and bubblers entwined and corkscrewing up and around each brow tine like plastic green electric vines. Not a fox, but a mule deer. And there's my face right below him, as if I've hauled the enormous severed head of this ridiculously adorned Western creature all the way home to Honor on my back.

Z catches my eye in the mirror, in the smoky nebula of glass. She's straining now, as if seeing me for the first time, her T-shirt as white as snow. She has not latched onto me with her free hand, and I cannot tell for sure if she's waving at me, or waving me off. The whiskey bottles waver like buoys and these men with their lighted candles staring out at the two of us as if from a choir stall.

Outside in the truck bed, Him begins, in the four major keys of regret, a wail so lonesome that our human voices —should we ever speak again—will likely be forever deepened, forever changed.

I don't know why I feel like this, or why the sound of the pool balls is anything more than that—a clipped kiss-kiss of sound. Maybe it's the wavering body shadows cast across the green felt, or the way Z calls "cross side," calls without doubt or deliberation those almost impossible combinations and bank shots, and makes them all seem routine. We're playing teams, partners, and she and I hold the table against every challenge. Together, we're unbeatable. Junior Fox keeps bringing the beers and the candles. Everything's on the house, he says, until whenever the power comes back on.

I re-chalk my cue and break for maybe the tenth consecutive time and almost run the table, the circle of white surrounding the black numeral eight staring back at me like the unblinking eye of some strange nocturnal animal. It's a gimme otherwise, straight into the corner pocket where Z is standing, sipping a Red Dog. I can see the foam on her upper lip as she bends down and then licks it off. There's just enough light to see her nod and wink, and the hard English I execute keeps the cue ball spinning backwards in place for a second or two after the shot is made.

It's right then that Kenny Rogers in mid-song is back to finally wind down this crazy night with his classic country whine, the fluorescent overheads pulsing their blinding light back into those ceiling tubes. It's well past midnight, perfect timing, Its says. And now he's singing along on his way out to re-join his retired tracking hound who always gets to ride home in the front seat, stately, alert, ears cocked, I guess, in the service of what he used to hear in the criminal darkness. That's the ritual, same as always, the two of them following the same scent trail home. Only difference? The pickup's muffler hits an octave or two louder than it did last week.

"Fucking-A," Cliff the Skinny says, perfectly lucid and upright at this late hour for a change, his face all nose, all hawk beak. He's still holding his candle in one hand, and fiddling with his wad of chain-dangling custodial keys. He hasn't taken his eyes off Z all night and they get even larger as she licks her index finger and thumb and snuffs out that final flame. "Fucking-A," he says again, and Z agrees by rising on her tiptoes and kissing him on the cheek, and rendering him altogether speechless.

"Any time," Junior says, "we're always here for you." Which must make her one of us, one of this motley crew, and Z curtsies in courtly farewell.

We step outside to the white moon and the stars and the red Fox Den sign laboring back to life in the cooler air. And just like that the fishing trip ceases to be, at least for tonight, because ten minutes down the road I can't even wake Z to point out the shower of the northern lights. She's asleep right up next to me, her head on my shoulder, her hair fanned out across my cheek.

Driving her back to the resort by way of the back roads, I'm wide awake. So much so that the adrenaline's pumping, the rearview mirror adjusted so I can see the silver spangles reflecting on her face, the stars so bright in their explosions of light that I swear they are flying out right at us from the undersides of the shiny summer leaves. It's all around us, and for once I have no bone to pick with anyone or anything, no complaints with the world as it is.

Hart Crane: "I learned to catch the trout's moon whisper; I / Drifted how many hours I never knew." For all eternity wouldn't be long enough, and I'll promise even that if she'll only say or do anything to show that these final twenty-five minutes together will not be our last.

Maybe she senses this—after all, she's just pressed up even tighter against me. It's always cooler through the dips of these lush meadows, the air misty, which maybe explains why she's suddenly squeezing our held hands between her thighs.

I have never before heard or felt such a drum of hooves in my chest, the hammering blood-thunder rush of them kicking up sparks I'm certain will fly right out of my mouth should I even attempt to speak. So I say nothing, deferring to the night its trillion different circular collisions—a universe of flint and fire. Look how everything glitters and dissolves, those plunging, heavenly bodied meteors, blue-tailed in their inevitable burning forever out of sight. In their wake, so many dead planets, but on this night the river bequeaths its river cantillations, and the moon listens as we pass slowly over the wooden-planked bridge that creaks but holds yet another time.

It's here, slowing down, that I turn and kiss Z's forehead, and she, eyes still closed, reaches over left-footed and eases down on the brake.

We come to a full stop in the dead center of the dirt road, but she does not shift into park, does not reach to turn off the headlights or the ignition, or say any single thing. She kisses me back when I press my lips to hers, moist and drowsy. And the hoot owls hoot and the coyotes in turn withhold not a note of their mournful laments.

"They're never out of practice," I say. "Every night they're at it—such lovely sad songs. Listen."

She doesn't. She bolts fully awake, retracts her foot from the brake and says, "Let's go before they get any closer."

"They won't," I say. "They're afraid of us, and for good reasons," and she says back, "Just the same," and she suddenly slides away from me and locks the door.

I've never even attempted to put the Caddy's top up with the car in motion but at her request it works, the caught air in the canvas sounding momentarily like the whistle of a swan's wings. And once I do hit the gas Z's back beside me, calmer, and intent, as she says, on getting together again soon. It's been a crazy-fun night, and thanks, and next time up maybe we'll get some fishing in, too.

Though I'd intended to, I do not point at the Dog Star silently weeping above us, cousin to those coyotes who continue to sing skyward through whirlpools of glittering light.

"Most definitely," Z says, and she takes my head in both her hands and kisses me every few minutes until we hit the blacktop. Then she's off on a theory about how only occasionally do two entirely different natures intersect. The dance of all dances, she says. It's what she's always searching for in her art.

Above us the whirling, nacreous, blurred shapes of the wild star beasts begin once again to vanish. Night's slow emergence into day, and Z's holding up and wiggling two fingers directly in front of my face. Two weeks. That's when she'd like to drive back up if I'm not already booked solid. Or if there's a cancellation per-haps I could slot her in early? *Her* schedule's flexible—any excuse to get away, to return here.

I've never been blessed with the best orienting skills, and I feel nervous and lost in the over-willed, unlikely prospect of what might be, of what I want to be. Which is for her to not leave, especially so soon.

"Two weeks," I say, and Z, pointing up at the interstellar stri-ations of light, says, "Count on it." And because I want so badly to believe her, and because I can't really think what else to add, I simply nod. And then hit the high beams, the light flooding out-ward and up over each slight rise and crest.

TWELVE

Derald & Criseide

Objects that come to rest tend to stay at rest. That's what Mr. Hulgrottom taught us. But Derald Pozar, a kid who'd already stayed back twice and hated school and stupid teacherly dictums, disproved everything we'd learned that entire week by demonstrating an entirely other kind of physics. Derald Pozar, at fifteen years old, did a terrible, terrible thing.

I know. I watched all rubber-kneed from an empty, second-story classroom window as Sheriff Scamehorn led him away in handcuffs, my forehead pressed against the pane. I stared and stared and for the instant it took for the cruiser's rear door to close, I could see Derald looking up at me, the cold metal rope cleats dinging against the aluminum flagpole.

I don't remember if I waved or not. Probably I didn't, and it's certainly possible that he couldn't have seen me from that distance anyway, the glass maybe reflecting the late-October sky clouds as it sometimes does that time of day. Also, why would I be in there, in the newly soundproofed music room, when no class was even going on? And what crazy impulse would make me acknowledge him or anyone under such disturbing circumstances?

Questions I can't answer for sure, not without a bunch of hesitations and second thoughts. But I can say without pause, and

136

without misconstruing a single second of those secret few moments away from homeroom, that the porcupine was huge. I'd estimate a good forty or fifty pounds—and it seemed even bigger after one of the deputies outlined it with bright, highlighter-yellow chalk on the black pavement. The American flag was still there too, folded on the ground like it shouldn't have been. And our first-year principal, Dr. Laday, a soft-touch disciplinarian as my dad one time called him, a left-wing liberal educator, had about a million quills lodged deep in his neck and shoulders, and even slanting down his spinal cord. I was glad when I couldn't hear the slowly disappearing screams of the ambulance sirens anymore, knowing he was that much closer to the emergency room, and to those trauma-trained doctors I prayed could save him, and somehow save us all

At lunch someone said, "Paralyzed," someone else said, "No, dead." But the rumors were quelled an hour later after the entire middle school, classroom by classroom, filed silently into the auditorium. Some parents had already arrived, my dad among them, although I did not know that until he walked across the stage decorated with pumpkins and warty gourds and hanging goblins and such. Gigantic fruit bats. Wicked, wild-haired, long-fingernailed witches with pointed hats straight out of *The Wizard of Oz*. Nests of black rubber spiders and snakes that writhed under the slow current of an eight-volt battery that Mr. Hulgrottom had rigged up like always—every October. At least since I'd been a student at Kirtland. And which also rotated the moveable white-boned cardboard knee and elbow joints of those oversized grinning human skeletons that hung from the rafters. Under other circumstances, it might have looked pretty neat, not that I'd made plans to attend the Halloween dance, because I hadn't. I'd thought about it, how maybe "The Monster Mash" would be blaring over those huge stereo speakers, but that's as far as that thought went.

My dad was dressed in one of his tailored suits, and when he stopped stage center he seemed for a few interminable seconds to be searching for me. He introduced himself at the stand-up microphone by name only. "I'm Mr. Angel," he said, and I slunk immediately down in my seat, as low as I could go without falling off and onto the floor. I stayed like that while he led us in prayers of hope and renewal, as if he were a man of the cloth, a priest or a minister or a rabbi or a trained chaplain, and not merely some spur-of-the-moment stand-in, some religious fraud. I wondered if he ever secretly prayed for guidance, and I figured probably not. Probably he never did, and so on this day I did not trust the messenger.

Why they called on him to address us remains a mystery to me, except that he was known and respected by just about everybody in the community—the adults anyway. Mom said once as a kind of joke that if he were to run for public office, he just might win. From mortician to mayor. There'd be no stopping his ascent.

Just joking, but in truth, Mom said, he *was* a good and decent man in spite of his reserve with his own family. Fine, but I posited nonetheless that he certainly was not a sainted man with any burning message, and less and less so it seemed as the seasons drifted by. I mean, he never consulted my mom about anything, and hardly a single gentle word escaped his lips anymore. So I was glad he stuck to his familiar memorized scriptures, stayed relatively brief, nodded and smiled a dutiful I-wish-all-good-things-ahead-for-us smile before taking a couple backward steps to where, without hesitation, he sat down on one of the two straw bales. I could smell them, even from twenty rows back, and I wished then that I could simply sleepwalk right out of there and wake up outside on a different day in the middle of some enormous empty field.

A few teachers followed him to the stage, talking calmly, reassuringly through a smattering of auditorium sniffles. But not Mrs. Whitman. I could tell as soon as she clasped her trembling hands up under her chin in a painful act of contrition that she'd arrived on stage still in utter shock and disbelief. Her voice quavered the loneliest falsetto I'd ever heard—I'd estimate a full few seconds' worth—before she was able to form and then say an actual word, and then a whole sentence. "Oh, honest to goodness.

How?" she wanted to know. "And why? And sweet God our merciful savior this-cannot-be, not here," and when she broke down in uncontrollable sobs, a bunch of the girls did too, tears suddenly flowing from their eyes. I breathed in a few deep gutfuls of air, my throat contracting, and I swallowed hard, attempting to regain *my* composure. My dad, in his practiced way, in the grab bag of what my mom used to call his countless solemnities, stood and cupped Mrs. Whitman's elbow, placed his other hand on her back, and escorted her away, out of sight and eventually out of earshot.

In the end it felt not like a healing assembly, but a whole lot more like a funeral. After the vice-principal cut the school day short and canceled the annual Halloween dance, I sneaked immediately outside through the side exit door without even stopping at my locker to get my jacket and my math homework. I'd already resolved not to drive home with my dad in the Rambler, or to even see him for awhile, and face what nobody else had to face, or even suspect of him—his private eruptions of anger which sometimes, especially lately, even bordered on rage.

I wanted to walk by myself, and so I circled wide beyond the cordoned-off crime scene, trying to visualize how Derald, presumably by himself, had managed to hoist that porcupine up there to stiffen and hang all night in the dark. And tied off the rope, and then, first thing this morning all that weight and speed and velocity descending on unsuspecting Dr. Laday. Who, in white shirt and tie but without his suit jacket, and with a single inadvertent tug, had set all those unstoppable gravitational forces in motion: flesh and quills and teeth and skull and bulbous blue-black swollen tongue. Like a guillotine, though I hoped what had happened was only the crazy physics of a teenage prank gone bad, and not an attempted decapitation.

Just yesterday on the school bus Derald had said to me, "Ah hell," as though it might be time to put some of what he called those enema-bag laws of physics we'd learned to the test. Of course that's only one interpretation, my logical and factual after-the-fact brain working in overdrive to make some coherent sense of it all: the sheriff, the handcuffs, Derald's scared face alight in the fall sun before being driven away like some psychotic adolescent criminal.

It's possible he might merely have meant, as he'd said again to me just one week earlier, that by all rights he ought to have been passed along last year instead of being held back a second time. "A double whammy," as he put it. "Like I'm some stupid-ass inbred," he said, while tapping his loose boot sole on the floor. "Some second-class hopeful dopeful with limited space in the brain-pan." He said of all the degrading things he couldn't get out of in this life—and there'd been plenty—staying back again was far and away the worst, the most hurtful, the most humiliating. "Who do they think they're dealing with here? Somebody's punching dummy?" He said, "You shave, you shouldn't be *in* the eighth grade, no matter for what. Bastards," he called them. "Chicken-fart gas-bag phonies. Every stinking time they open their gobs, and that's the God's honest truth, pure and simple."

But he'd made no direct payback threats that I could recall. Mentioned no names, no enemy number one or two or three. No secret year-in-the-making hit list he'd completed and secretly filed away. Not that day, not ever since I'd known him. From time to time he'd use cuss words like "asswipe" or "suckwad" or "buttlicker," but always in the general scheme of things, like nothing personal, it was just the way of the world. And even though he boasted once that maybe he'd flush an M-80 or two down one of the boys' toilets, I knew he never would. He merely wanted to show them to me—half a dozen three-inch silver depth charges that he claimed would rupture the plumbing, and maybe even shut down the entire educational operation, "'cause where would anybody pinch a loaf—inside the desks or the wastebaskets?" Not likely. And may God strike him dead, he said, if he didn't damn well mean what he said. Derald was angry is all, and who wouldn't be spouting off, venting a little steam under similar circumstances?

If I were called to testify at a trial, I'd swear to that under oath. I'd say some kids I naturally warmed to and others I didn't, and that Derald Pozar, for all his slip-ups, still fit that better profile.

Which was true, and I didn't care if other smarter, popular, sometimes vicious do-gooder hoity-toity types—those spoiled, arro-
gant eye-rollers—*did* see fit to call him a weirdo, a freako, real
demeaning behind-his-back stuff like that. In my book he was
anything but, and I wouldn't have minded one bit if he'd put the
knuckles to Kenny Lamont or Cody McIntire. On their best day
they were still jerks and always would be. Always antagonizing
and wisecracking and unlike Derald they sure didn't have perfect
attendance. I'd mention that fact too. Not that whatever *I* said
would have any bearing on the outcome, bad or good, but at least
I'd have the satisfaction of befriending the underdog, the perpetual loner who, for days on end, wouldn't hear a single affirming,
kind thing said to or about him.

That day, same as always, Derald just seemed sad and kind of
tired and resigned on the back seat of the bus, and when I cleared
my throat to speak, he pointed at me and shook his head no.
"This ain't where you come in, Angel. I like you fine, but I don't
need no bright-boy tutor so don't go offering me that no more,
all right? Just don't. This ain't your fight. This really ain't your
problem."

He didn't test well, in or out of class. Not even on true or false
or multiple guess. Which maybe made sense to his teachers and
counselors, but not to me, given how he knew the names of all the
NASCAR drivers, their current rank in the standings, what kind
of cars they drove, how many horses and cubic inches thundered
under the hoods. Pole positions in what races, their individual
sponsors, who had the fastest pit crews, everything you could
imagine to ask. Who crashed on what lap at Daytona or Talladega
or Dover Downs, and who and in what year, dating back to before
he was even born, won the Busch Series or the Winston Cup.
The exact number of collective fatalities at a given raceway, and
why that might be, and the age and gender of every child in the
respective mourning families who'd been left behind.

Plus he'd all but memorized every single episode of *The Hardy
Boys*. If he had a knack for that—for retaining the minutest details
of description and dialogue and plot—then why hadn't they
encouraged him to join the theater class? Wasn't the positive, as

we'd been taught, always worth highlighting? If so, why was everyone chomping at the bit to put Derald down? Things didn't add up as far as I was concerned, and I couldn't help but wonder if the problem was entirely his. Whether it was or not, it shouldn't have been summed up—not ever, not by anyone—in such calculatedly hurtful terms as "cretin" or "moron" or "mush for brains." Knuckle noggin. Zombie. Simpleton. Retread. Super doofus. Ignoramus. Mental midget. Flunky and clueless and dipstick and dimwit and dummy D. How could it be fair, I wanted to know, to marshal such a long and hateful vocabulary against Derald Pozar, or against anyone for that matter.

"I'm just hangin' till I turn sixteen," he'd said, popping a yellow gumball into his mouth. "Then I'm long gone. Good as already signed off 'cause this Timbuktu of a town's a million frigging miles from anywhere I mean to be. Stay here it'll smother your nuts sure as methane's made from the steam of cow shit. Right there's your x equals y, and the sum fuck of the parts. That's them complete and paid for, and they sure don't smell like roses from where I'm sitting. Besides, who gives a rat's fanny about isosceles triangles, or about objects staying at rest anyway? Or people when you come right down to it. Or anything else."

———

"Not me," my dad says. "Not one iota. Comes a time to lower the boom, juvenile or not, and you can quote me on that. Cold-blooded is cold-blooded and goddangit these . . . these what? Works in progress? Bunk to that . . . he'll serve with his track record for trouble this time . . . up the river and good riddance. Judge throws the book at him right now we'll all be better off. The town, everyone. Petty hooligan crimes are one thing, but this? No sir . . . I for one am darn sick and tired of the wrist-slaps and the wishy-washy lip-service tongue-lashings doled out to criminals these days. Why is it nobody wants to do the decent dirty work anymore? It's a cinch you mollycoddle these younger dangerous types, it'll come back to haunt you, sure as we're sitting here. A decent man's in critical condition, a young decent family man, and I say let the punishment fit the crime for a change. Call it what it is. Attempted murder.

"Twenty to life," he says, "and incarcerate him in Jackson. And then—if Dr. Laday does die—let that Pozar kid stay there until he decomposes."

This was the most he'd had to say on any subject in months, so my mom and I were staying quiet.

Then, fork in hand, tines high and speared right through a sliced dill pickle, he offers up a farewell salute, a permanent wish-you-weren't-here to Derald Pozar, and to the spreading pathological perverseness, as he says, alive in this beastly, evil-minded, falling-from-the-sky, quill-infested world.

I can't tell for sure if my mom's listening. She's been a long time giving up, but she has, I think, finally done just that. Mostly she seems far away now, her eyes opaque and not even blinking, and fixed on nothing that I can see as my dad continues to talk us down with his fusillade of what I think are overly harsh, short-sighted indictments.

My mom has appeared for dinner wearing one of her many silk headscarfs, fastened with a tiara, like she intends to trick-or-treat as a genie or sultan or as Pope Joan or somebody straight out of *The King and I*. All I know for certain is that the red cut-glass stone pin on her forehead looks like a hematoma.

Her skin is white, her bathrobe pink, and you'd think at first glance that maybe she's just come from the shower. It's the chemo that's done this, and she generally has no appetite for food or for conversations of any kind. Certainly not this contentious, single-minded harangue initiated by my dad. A slugfest, really, with him hurling all the punches. Her arguing exists only in the past, in absentia, back before the cancer and the new-market wonder drugs that help stave off her depressions before they ever start. I guess that's good, but in most ways they've made her a different person—quiet, inert, reluctant to stand her ground anymore on any front. By suppertime she barely exists.

She's not afraid, I don't think. She's not a cringer or crier, not even when my dad announces in his patriotic, grandiloquent exuberance that President Richard Milhous Nixon is a lock for a second term and this time by a landslide. In her crazy right mind my mom would never have remained silent for this, and it makes me sad that she won't cast a vote in this election to cancel his out. My dad seems to contradict everything I've been feeling lately, about him and me and the world at large, and about the war that's dragged on and on. About what it means to be mirthful and dreaming good dreams for a change. What it means heading into the holidays as an openly loving family.

I look over at him and he looks like somebody he's not in that black sweater vest and orange tie—bright shiny orange, more like an overripe tangerine. Leprechaun green for St. Patrick's Day, ultra-orange for Halloween. A man of the town with a public nod and smile and proper attire for every season. All things to all people, but a distant figure, more respected than loved. He's got no close friends that I've ever met, no one he ever mentions by name, and this is not, as anyone can clearly see, a bustling metropolis. Twelve thousand tops. Nobody ever calls socially or stops by on a whim, and there's nobody he goes out with for a beer, or to bowl, or to take in a matinee or an area high school football game. No saved seat for him at any of the various tables during chess or bingo or poker nights at the VFW or Lion's Club or at the armory with the WWII tank out front.

My mom doesn't push her plate away. She simply folds her hands on the table edge, and sometimes she smiles over at me, but never even glances at my dad when he gets like this, fiery-eyed and edgy and, like now, so verbally antagonistic.

He's overworked, way overextended—I understand this. That he's been doing all the grocery shopping and cooking—tonight Jimmy Dean sausage biscuits, three and a half minutes from freezer to microwave to our empty dinner plates. Last night he served Chicken-in-a-Bag Delux, the night before that, instant Chinese, minus the rice and soy sauce and fortune cookies. Booth food, he calls it, straight from the Peking Palace, although it's been several months since we've eaten out anywhere, and even longer since I've heard steaks sizzling under the broiler. Not since my mom began her second round of chemo, following those post-surgery radiation treatments. My dad marks the appointment times in red pen on the Angel & Sons calendar, and he always helps her get dressed and drives her to the hospital and back. He waits right there with her, no matter how long it takes. Some nights, to relieve her fever, he'll sit bedside and patiently fan her face. Other times he'll soothe her split lips or cold sores with ice chips, or sponge-bathe and towel-dry her entire body. Twice already he's had to lance her engorged bed blisters, and then treat them with cotton balls and hydrocortisone. He's also the one who changes her bedding daily, and if she can't get her mouth to the vomit pan he'll clean that up too, and light a fragrant candle, and start the soiled laundry going right away.

He attends her without clumsiness or hesitation. I know. He always leaves the bedroom door ajar, and although I don't mean to, I can't help but look. Sometimes I'll hear him crying when I get home from school. Sobbing even, like he's forever and ever worshipped the very ground on which she walks. But other times I'll find him like this, angry and agitated as all get-out. There's simply no predicting his wild mood swings anymore, or if he'll find some permanent middle ground to occupy.

The way he's explained it, there's precious little the doctors can do for my mom anymore. Everything humanly possible has been tried, every new medical option explored. She's in the hands of good people, the best around, he assures me. But he's also confided—"You need to know, Arch," he said, "so you can prepare your emotions like a grown-up"—that her time is limited. Terminal's terminal. Weeks possibly, months at most, and he's referred a number of times to her dying, in advance of that end, as a blessing. It's like he's wishing her life away for her, as if he's already administered last rites. He always concludes these conversations by saying, "May God rest her soul."

He's mentioned hospice. He's mentioned that she's already stage four, the final. The cancer has metastasized again—it's much more aggressive now that it has entered her brain—and he says that remission is a hopelessly irresponsible word for me to use anymore. It's miracle-wishing at this point, he says, and, for the betterment of all concerned, he advises that we cease to speak aloud in such nebulous dreamy terms, and that we grab the bull by the horns instead . . . yes? And face up to the inevitable. He says, "Have you felt her hands and feet, Arch? Have you in just the past few days? If so, you know how cold they are, don't you? And what that means?"

He does not call these medical updates. He calls them communiqués. I don't want them to be true, and so I tend even now to believe her instead when she claims the poems are helping as always, and she's started quoting Emily Dickinson all over the place. Loves her. Refers to her as that kind and compassionate spirit nurse. Her bright and guiding light. Needs her nearby now more than ever, she says: "The props assist the house."

But there's been no scaffolding erected here, no new renovations of any kind, inside or outside, to make her stay on earth more enduring. There are, however, more pills than ever lined up above the bromides and aspirin bottles and peroxide and sore-throat sprays, and she uses a three-pronged lightweight aluminum walker now to get from bedroom to bath, bath to kitchen and back. Dad has to carry her up and down the stairs, which sometimes starts him coughing so hard he can hardly stop. These constitute the major changes in the household. This is pretty much what she's come home to, her skin so thin now it's almost see-through, like the fine disappearing smoke of a candle. She can't weigh eighty-five pounds, this woman who, and not so long ago, as she'll still maintain from time to time, "supped with dignitaries and kings." In recurring dreams, she says, though it's more a deep drowse than a real sleep she enters, be it day or night or any dying time in between.

"How in God's name did those quills puncture all that way to the liver and pancreas?" my dad says. "I ask you, what are the odds of someone suffering such a fate?" No one answers and he shakes his head. "A damn porcupine falling out of the sky. What a mess."

The same could be said, but isn't, for the husband and wife downstairs in the mortuary, victims of a head-on collision. The Smiths: married forty-two years and just out alone for a leisurely evening, peak-color scenic autumn drive. A Mercury Sable and a Mayflower moving van. Never knew what hit them. Four kids.

Eleven grandkids, nine of them boys, all towheads. A sheltie who also did not survive impact. Looked like somebody'd taken after both man and beast with the claw-end of a hammer. Faces shredded. That's all my dad has said about them so far, and I have no idea who's at fault for their being here, mangled and laid out side by side on the stainless steel tables. Because duty calls, my dad's been working overtime, and he's got to rush off again. Due to the unscheduled school visit he's running way behind. It seems, he tells us, that *every* hour lately is the appointed hour, and he shifts position, wipes his mouth, balls up his paper napkin with both hands, and asks: "Did you hear? Jackie Robinson died. You still got his rookie card, Arch, you hang onto it, you hear me? Don't go trading it away now. Should be worth a few bucks down the road. First Negro in the majors and a great, great ballplayer. A real credit to the game. You should have seen him run the bases. It's a crying shame," he says, but he doesn't sound all that broken up. He never does when people pass away. He says, "How about those A's though? How's that for closing out a World Series?"

He doesn't wait for an answer. He pushes back his chair, massages his forehead with both hands, and leaves me alone with my mom and the leftovers and the dirty dishes. As soon as he's gone she says weakly, "Could you get me a glass of water, sweetheart? Please?"

"Sure," I say, and, as I wait at the sink while the tap flow gets good and cold, I'm positive I'm going to choke up and cry. I can already feel the hot salt welling on the bottoms of my eyes. I'm not even sure what for other than everything this day has both become and failed to become. If I had a costume to go house to house for the night it would *not* be my old cowboy outfit that's stored away in the attic—chaps and vest and six-guns from when I was ten—but rather an elaborate arrow-stuck St. Sebastian. There's a gold-framed painting of him in the basement of Sacred Heart, the massive red flood of the blood-wounds pooling at his feet. There's the strangest unformed look on his face, like he's confused about how to feel: mad or sorry or forgiving or scared. Maybe all these emotions circling in at once as he just stands there, waiting for the archers—who are not visibly in the painting—to draw back a second time, and release. Funny, that's Dr. Laday's first name—Sebastian—and all these gory overlapping images of saints and terminal sickness and death sentences at dinner collide as I stand at the sink, the water overflowing the glass.

"Here," I say, pouring some out, and before I even place it on the table the doorbell rings. Which it never has before on Halloween, not a single solitary time that I can recall. We don't even stock any candy or candy apples or popcorn balls to hand out, although my dad, as always, has carved a couple of large pumpkins with his scalpel, the round incision of the crania so fine I can't even see the lines until I pull up on the stems. No seeds or slimy fibrous gunk, the insides scooped out cleaner than clean, and my only job—my only part in any of this—is to light the candles each night. Family events have long ago become a thing of the past. Father-son events too. No more trips to the cabin with my mom so sick. And I can't remember the last time my dad asked if I wanted to help with pumpkin carving. Or even accompany him to the farmers' market to pick out the pumpkins. They're smiling their toothy companion-glow smiles on the porch stairs, like two bemused sentries.

"Trick-or-treaters," I say to my mom. "They'll most likely go away if we don't answer."

She nods, takes a slow, tremor-lipped sip, but when the doorbell rings a second time, and then a third, she points to the pocket-size Gospel of John, the new International Version, copies of which my dad has fanned out on the table like playing cards. They've been there since early morning, a subtle blend of heavenly blue and earthy brown, and on the back cover: "Light Has Come into the World." Gifts for the soon-to-be mourners, courtesy of Angel & Sons. Not for sale or resale, but rather for distribution to the masses, this miniature, on-the-spot, mass-produced pamphlet offered here, free to help with the redemption of wandering souls.

I can't remember ever answering the front door before for anything, but whoever is there has abandoned the buzzer and is now rapping frantically on the smoky glass oval. Nobody's laid out tonight in the viewing parlors, but the lingering, densely layered smell of flowers has flooded even the hallway stairs. It's sub-dermal, as my mom once said. It's alive and silently breathing behind the fading wallpaper, under the mortuary's thick cosmetic skin.

"I'm coming," I say to myself. "I'm coming already," and when I unlock and open the front door, there's a man standing on the stoop. He's short and completely bald and whiskery and kind of pinch-mouthed. Weather-beaten, real wiry, and he's not holding open a paper sack. In fact, he's already shoved both hands into his pants pockets, and he's taken an abrupt step backwards, as if surprised that somebody's all of a sudden standing here in front of him.

He's got eyes all over his shirt, blue and green like on a peacock's tail, but I don't think that's what he's supposed to be. I think it's just the way he's dressed—though why would anyone choose to put on anything so strange and wrinkled, what has to be a bargain-bin purchase, probably worn and washed and hand-wrung a thousand times and left on a line overnight to dry. The chinos too, everything hanging limp and tired on his body.

I mean, he's not wearing a beak or feathers or a plume on his crown, and no coat, so maybe he's stopped because his truck's broken down. I can see it under the streetlight, a smaller truck converted into a larger one, the visibly tilted plywood sides of the bed rising quite a ways above the cab. I can't quite read the crooked bold lettering, but I can make out that someone's watching us from the passenger's side.

"You . . . you're Archie Angel?" he says, his chin jutting out, like he's daring me to either confirm or deny the obvious. Like somehow he's implicating me in something bad.

I swallow and nod and stay right where I am, my hand ready to slam the door shut on this nut if that's what he turns out to be. How does he know my name anyway? It's not all adding up, which naturally makes me kind of nervous and pretty anxious to leave.

"I'm Clive Pozar," he says. "Derald's dad. That's his mom. That's Eileen." He turns and points at the truck. "We just come from the jail and the hospital both, and I'm on my way in a minute here to pick up an old water heater." He says it hoarsely, and so matter-of-factly that it makes such an arcane sequence of nightly rounds sound almost plausible, almost routine.

"Here?" I say, as if maybe my dad's wheeled a dead water heater curbside on a hand dolly, along with the trash for tomorrow morning's pick-up.

"No," he says. "Over on Wheeler. Across town." He pauses, and then he says, "This where they bring in the dead? Through here?"

"Around back," I say, and he single nods his raised head, and he says back to me, his skinny chest swelling, "Tell me it's something dumb Derald did on a dare. Some airhead prank maybe, but not malicious. A harebrained stunt intended not to hurt nobody is all I can hope for at this point. That's why we come. For the truth of it, if you can find right to do that by us. If you know. Can you do that, Archie? For Eileen and me? Can you help us believe in our hearts that we're not all wrong about our son? He ain't perfect, we won't argue that. He ain't one of the gifteds, but he mentioned you. At first I thought he meant an actual angel. You know . . . some *guardian* angel or something he said he sometimes talked to on the school bus, like he'd flipped his lid or maybe started messin' around in the drugs and heard voices. Had to be, but the whole time it's you, the Angel he's talkin' about. A friend, he said."

He averts his eyes as a car passes, and framed by the doorjamb he suddenly seems even shorter, stunted, as if this mourner's entrance has been constructed for the sole purpose of determining human proportion. I'm wearing my slippers, and when I step down onto the porch I'm still taller than Mr. Pozar. If Derald were standing with us he'd dwarf his dad, a sort of physical flip-flop of father and son. It's not at all like that in our household, where things appear, at least outwardly, to be much more normal, even with the cancer having already half devoured my mom's insides.

"Look," he says, pulling out a snapshot from a crinkled plastic slot in his wallet. "Here, you hold it," and he reaches for and hoists one of the jack-o'-lanterns shoulder high so that the coppery candle glow casts its light across the glossy emulsion. The edges are all crooked, scalloped-like, as if the standard print size has been modified with a pair of fingernail scissors.

The woman is pretty and young-looking, redheaded like Derald, but in the candle flicker they appear—all three of them—to drift in and out of focus, their smiles kind of eerie, almost like sneers. In the picture Mr. Pozar's got a glinting gold tooth, which I hadn't noticed until now.

"That's Eileen," he says. "And that's Derald at six or seven. Yep, that's him all right," he says, "when I could still carry him fireman style. Heft him right up there. Now he could carry me like that no trouble. That's my boy," and he looks slowly left and right as if he's not quite sure in what direction he'd have to point to indicate the whereabouts of the county jail. "But what's he likely to amount to now?" Mr. Pozar says. "What's even half possible with folks 'round here always so quick to condemn, but not all that quick to forgive those that never did quite fit in? We tend to keep to ourselves best we can—the Pozars do—but I been to them PTA meetings. I talked with the brain trust there enough times to know that Derald ain't nobody's favorite, and I don't guess he's gonna be. That much . . . it's a foregone conclusion. For sure it is now. They figure he's short on tools. Up here," he says, and taps his forehead.

"I don't think he meant to hurt anyone," I say. "He's not a bully or anything. He doesn't give Indian rope burns or make any of the smaller kids strip after school. And he doesn't back-talk to the teachers. Sometimes he'll show me pressure points and that kind of hurts when he presses down, and once demonstrating the Heimlich maneuver he kind of bruised my ribs, but other than that . . ."

Mr. Pozar shifts and steadies the pumpkin on his shoulder, so it appears like he's got two heads, mismatched Siamese, but both of them shiny. It's turned a lot colder, and there's heat vapor rising from the pumpkin's cut-away eyes and mouth and wide triangular nose. At first I think Mr. Pozar's started to shiver in that short-sleeved shirt, but I can see now that he's started to cry.

"We're grabbing at straws," he says. "Me and Eileen . . . we don't know anymore. What to do or think with that bail set so high. He's fifteen and this . . . it's such a terrible thing what's happened. That poor Principal Laday and his family. We feel just awful. All day Eileen she just prayed and prayed for them. Won't stop. Ever since we first heard. Got all prettied up in a nice dress and prayed the rosary over and over again. That's what she's doing now, asking help from the Lord. But those charges . . . they sound all wrong. Sure, Derald's always been a pistol of a kid, and he's seen a good bit of trouble for his age, but this . . . these charges," he says again. "They sound . . ." but he doesn't finish. He licks his lips and shifts the pumpkin to his other shoulder.

"Maybe Dr. Laday will be okay," I say. "Maybe he'll get better. My dad says only time will tell for sure."

"Well nobody's telling us," he says. "Nobody. We ask but the only one says much of anything's the sheriff, and all he says is: 'My advice to you? Get yourselves a darn good attorney, Clive.'"

Mr. Pozar sniffles, and then he quick wipes his nose with the back of his free hand. "I don't know what to do no more," he says again. "Rescue that water heater and refurbish it if I can. If not, salvage what parts I can and see what I get out of it? A few bucks American? Done. But I don't guess you go out and hire Mr. Perry Mason on that amount. Do you?"

The way he's got the pumpkin steadied with both hands now I'm almost certain he's going to turn and heave it down onto the lawn, or maybe carry it to the street and bust it into pieces against the curbstone. I wish he would, and then leave, or at least just put it back down. It's hard to look at him like this—the pumpkin aglow and steaming and all those different-colored blue and green shirt eyes without emotion or eyebrows staring right out at me.

I feel disoriented, dizzy, and even more so as the hallway light flashes on and off, on and off every couple seconds like a migraine, like someone's tap-tapping the back of my skull with a reflex mallet.

"Here," I say, and inadvertently hand Mr. Pozar the Gospel of John instead of his wallet snapshot. The pamphlet falls naturally open to those middle pages where the two staples puncture its spine. The print is tiny and he leans nearly forehead to forehead with the pumpkin, the text held so close I don't know how he can possibly read from it. But he does, and without glasses. He says, *We know he is our son, and we know he was born blind. But how he can see now, or who opened his eyes, we don't know. Ask him. He is of age; he will speak for himself.*

Mr. Pozar doesn't stumble over a single word. He reads it beautifully. He says, "Thank you." He says, motioning toward the porch light, "Someone's calling."

"My mom," I say. "She's sick and can't use the stairs anymore. It hurts her throat when she tries to call or even talk loud. The special lozenges—they don't really work that great either. Not anymore."

He stoops and looks past me up the polished hallway stairs, but they're too steep to see to the landing.

"Better go," he says, and carefully lowers the pumpkin to the porch. But before he reaches for the snapshot and makes his way back to his truck and his waiting wife Eileen, he looks directly at me and me at him. We hold each other's gaze in a way I'm not used to, not with anyone except occasionally a frightened, half-starved stray cat I wish would let me help. Then he nods and walks to his truck, and I wait until he drives all the way to the end of the block, and brakes, and turns left out of sight, before I go back inside.

I'm grateful that my mom does not ask me any questions, other than if everything is all right.

Fine, I tell her. Nobody's soaped the windows or toilet-papered the porch. That's all I say before turning away to fill the sink with steamy water and suds. I can feel my mom watching me as I wash and rinse and stack. The intercom is right next to me on the wall, and if I were to open the circuit I'm sure I'd hear my dad whistling down there, as if to entertain himself, or maybe to entertain the abruptly departed Mr. and Mrs. Smith.

Up here I'm trying to unscramble in my head how anyone comes to calculate anything correctly, anything that matters enough to permanently alter a person. Why Derald did what he did. Or why the weight of my mom's weariness tonight seems both equal and unequal to the sum of its parts. She can barely move or even speak after that one brief trip to the head of the stairs to rescue me. I know that Mr. Hulgrottom did not cause any of this, and I've come to think that the world is much more hit-and-miss, much more unpredictable than he wants and even expects us to believe in the controlled surroundings of science class. Maybe I'll say that on the test next week, and write "Derald Pozar" where *my* name's supposed to go. I always get 100 percent on my quizzes and tests, and if he wants to fail me for making an ethical point, for speaking out like my mom always did before her illness, then let him.

My mom does not lift her hands as I wipe the kitchen table clean, and I'm careful not to bump them. If I do they'll bruise. I get close but go real slow around the bony white-knuckled fingers and thumbs, folded the way they are, loosely, as if the effort to squeeze any harder would zap every ounce of her remaining strength.

"Can I get you anything?" I ask, but my dad on the intercom interrupts whatever it is she's about to say. When I answer it he says, back in his better mood, "Name and rank?"

He'll never come right out and apologize like I wish he would. He'll never take anything he says back, never admit for once that he'd been wrong. Not directly he won't. Instead he'll clown around with these kinds of senseless questions, which for sure is a whole lot better than him staying mad and fuming and lording his haughty fathership over me, but in another way it just complicates everything. Too much guesswork, too much uncertainty with him feeling the need to sound the all clear all the time. It's like we're under siege. Up down, up down—it makes me afraid to laugh or relax or joke around or say what I think, and it makes my mom go stiff in the shoulder blades. It's no good for anyone.

I push the talk button and say, "It's me. It's Archie." I don't really know my rank. *Kid*, I guess, but that seems a dumb thing to announce to your own dad who shouldn't have to be reminded—not tonight, not ever—of such an obvious fact. So I don't respond, and his attempt to fill the all too credible silence with his Jim Nabors impersonation is a flop.

My mom does not smile, and I don't either, though the goofy nasal-whining voice of Gomer Pyle reverberates on up for awhile, just one more distraction to conclude the night. "Over and out," my dad says, this time in his own personal and jocular dialect.

At first I don't quite hear my mom, but when I sit down next to her she says, "It's on the tip of my tongue."

I figure she means a line from a poem. Her memory's not what it was even two or three weeks ago, and she's even missed on my name a couple of times.

"It'll come," I say, "and if not that's fine. That's okay. Everybody forgets stuff."

But she doesn't let it go. I can see her groping around in her mind, and now she's started muttering in whispers about how that never should have happened, and where was her God, where, when an infant so desperately needed help. Needed more than a mother's love.

"To Dr. Laday?" I say. "Happened to *him*, you mean? He's the principal now, not Mrs. Motif anymore. She left last year, remember? After that operation for varicose veins. And Derald—he's fifteen, Mom. He's almost a legal adult. That's one of the big concerns. All the trouble he's been in over the years. You heard what Dad said."

"Your sister," she says. "Criseide."

"I wouldn't mind one," I say, but I'm not telling her anything she hasn't already heard. I've complained plenty, from the time I was little, about being an only child, a criticism that's always caused my mom to close her eyes and get all wrought up and turn abruptly away from me. Something she'd never do otherwise, not for any other reason. Not unless you count her running away to Wisconsin like she did for all that time.

That was the stretch where I'd make up names of imaginary siblings, and silently mouth the different syllables, a trick I taught myself to help me fall asleep. Baby sisters and brothers. I'd try to add at least one new name to the list every night, but Criseide—I've sure never heard that one before. It's got to be literary.

"That'd be good," I say. "I like it a lot."

"You'll watch her then while I take a quick nap?" she asks. "You won't take your eyes off her? You won't go outside?"

"I promise," I say, and it's weird, but I imagine clearly a little girl named Criseide who looks like me—blue eyes, dark wavy hair—sitting right here opposite me at this very table, playing house, playing the good mother by creating a happy make-believe family environment.

"It's exhausting . . . this business of being awake. But you wake me right up anyway if she starts to cry," my mom says, and I steady her as she rises from her chair.

"I will," I say, and I guide her into the bedroom, her head hanging like a mother whose burden's so deep and private and real that I sense there *is* another presence alive here. That same identical ghostly something I felt during my mom's extended absence. And why, whenever I mentioned it back then, did my dad get so angry? "What basis in fact?" he'd say. "Tell me, Arch," but of course I had none, and in that way he'd put a quick end to the conversation.

I'm the one who set the thermostat at seventy, and I can hear the forced hot air swirling through the ventilation ducts, so I know it's more than warm enough in here. Still, I feel a sudden chill as I lift the tiara from my mom's head, the gray thin staticky wisps of hair standing straight up, her scalp pearly in the moonlight's film.

"Criseide," she whispers again, but this time she's holding onto my wrists with more strength than I've seen from her in months, pleading with her eyes in a way she never does anymore. "You watch her," she says again. "You always have: always, always, always. Remember, she lives inside you, Archie," she says, like she's attempting to cast a spell, or to reveal to me some final unkeepable blood secret that I've never coveted, and that I don't much want to hear now either. But it's only when I repeat that strange name back to her that she releases her grip and willingly reclines—with my help—slowly into the pillow, her face suddenly unfamiliar, exposed like it is in the half shadows, her eyes still open.

I cover her first with the sheet, and then the light cotton blanket. She can't take any more weight than that. The night-light's on as always, and I sit with her for a few minutes while my dad's voice rises again, crackling some new quips from downstairs, a deliberate and confusing up-tumble of words.

It's like I occupy some distorted middle distance between their voices, between these parents who almost never speak to each other anymore, and me this go-between who's here only to interpret their separate and desperate needs, and without ever making either of them the object of my pity. But sometimes, like now, I have to sit down on the floor in the deepest corner of the pantry and put my head in my hands, fingers spread wide apart, and squeeze as hard as I can. It doesn't hurt. And in this way every single human sound in the world becomes the sound of my own breathing. Mother, father, missing sister, imaginary kid brothers with common names like Joey and Pete and George and Henry. The Angels, though I'm not sure what to believe or disbelieve or imagine about anyone anymore. I'm only thirteen. I still drink Welch's grape juice at dinner. There's most likely still a half ring of it staining my upper lip right now.

Just a costumeless kid with sweet-tasting purple lips, all alone and safely hidden, at least for a little while, in the pantry of a haunted house on Halloween.

THIRTEEN

Rodney & Rhea

All the way to the Pig and back the hearse virtually purred, but the engine refuses to turn over another time this morning, the battery worn down by my insistence that it'll start, trust me, I know this vehicle. It's never yet let me down.

Rodney's sitting next to me, shelling peanuts and tossing the shells past my face into the driveway. So far he hasn't made a peep. Rhea's next to him, riding shotgun and exuding truly abusive vibes, and Copperfield's perched like a sea lion on the windshield, purring and staring in at me. His paws are crossed and he punctuates the interior human tension every couple seconds with a slow-motion blink. We've locked eyes for the moment—he and I—as if to silently co-calculate the large degree of my fuckdom.

"Hey, listen to me," I say. "I mean, we don't *have* to drive two hours to catch the Arnold-line ferryboat to transport us on turbulent seas all the way to Mackinac Island, do we? If it's breezy here, this early, imagine what it's going to be like out on Lake Michigan. We shove off on a west blow we'll be into five-, six-footers easy. They'll be coming right down the chute through the Straits. And maybe, like you say, you're *not* prone—either one of you—to motion sickness, but take it from me you will be, standing rail-side next to a couple hundred seasick weekend voyagers. Everybody soaked and miserable and packed in like sardines. And

158

for what? So we can then pay through the nose to be taken by horse and buggy on a tour around an island with a boring fort and a fudge and smoothie monopoly? Or stop in at the Chamber of Commerce where they hire college kids full-time for two solid months for the sole purpose of shoveling road apples from the blacktop? And where the Grand Hotel—the one famous land-mark—charges the rank-and-file—namely us—simply to step on-grounds to snap a vacation souvenir snapshot for posterity's sake?"

Which is simply another nearsighted regurgitation of my forceful failed droning-on argument of last night, when I was soundly voted down two to one. All style and no content, they said. And it was not, by the way, as it isn't in the immediate early-morning present, a good-natured ganging up. They've made up their minds. They—the two of them, team girlfriend-and-son—want to go. Case closed.

They've awakened without complaint well before first light. Not a single yawny whine between them when the alarm clock rang. They've each passed on the sausage and scrambled eggs and blueberry pie à la mode (Archie's famous Bigfoot breakfast) in favor of a slice of cantaloupe, and a glass of high-fiber something or other Rodney brought with him from his *primary* home. While I washed and dried and put away the dishes they packed a few essentials—granola bars and bottled springwater—for their much anticipated day-long excursion. And now, after last night's triumphant "Yessss," this sudden and serious chink in the plans.

"That's great," Rhea says. "Eloquent. But just what alternative non-event do you have in mind, other than sitting out here and studying for another hour or two that gooey silver slug's trail on the windshield? But you are right about making the best of a bad situation. Because that's what this is—bad—and we'd better figure something out."

It's true we haven't formulated a two-thirds-majority plan B, and given the anti-Archie alliance that's already been formed between Rodney and Rhea, none of my optional local casting about has the slightest chance to fly. They made perfectly clear after the long drive back last night from the Pig that they don't want to fish or float—any and all manner of river recreation is out—it's a no-go, a bust. Rhea says, "Thanks a lot, Archie, for putting such a positive spin on a Mackinac Island trip, where I for one have never been. Sorry I ever even mentioned it." Followed by Rodney's insistence that "Mom said she would have had a fantastic time on the island if we'd gone without you. Just me and her instead. I can't remember it, I was too little."

I flinch inwardly, remembering the few choice words Z saved—until we stepped safely back onto the mainland—to make clear to me how I'd single-handedly annihilated that weekend getaway.

"Only kidding," I finally say to Rhea and Rodney. "Only kidding." I wasn't, of course, though I might just as well have suggested that we trail back inside and snuggle up—a happy fun-loving threesome—on the kitchen floor, and read aloud very long sections from Sir Francis Bacon.

"Okay, three's a crowd on a motorcycle," I say, "so here's the deal. I'll shoot down to Buck's—he's open twenty-four hours—and see if he can give us a tow. Maybe it's something simple. A bad battery or gummed-up carburetor. A loose wire. That shouldn't take long. While I'm gone you two can confer on what you want to do. Whatever you decide. Anything's fine. I'm totally flexible."

"Why don't we just call him?" Rodney says. "That'd be a lot faster."

"Because that's where the phone *is*," I say. "That's where I call you from. I don't have a phone here, you know that."

"But I do," he says. "A cellular. In my backpack. Mom says I can't be up here anymore without one. She says in case of emergencies on either end. Guess she's right again."

"Right as right gets right," Rhea says, as if it's worth repeating that one word as often as humanly possible in a single short declarative sentence. Like it's suddenly the most irresistible and longest pronounceable pure monosyllable in the language. To identify it is to identify its opposite, and the odds of me being right keep worsening by the minute.

"You really oughta get one, Dad," Rodney says. "You could

call me from anywhere. Right from on the river. Nobody'd be the wiser. Unless you told me I could I wouldn't give your number out. I promise. Not even to Mom. If only I had it you'd know every time it rang that it was me. You wouldn't even need caller ID. I hate that we get to talk only at appointed times."

I nod. "I'll think about it," I say. "I will, I promise," and I shake my head no when he offers me a peanut.

There's still no timeline for how long Rhea intends to stick around. She's clearly less than fully committed, but mostly she seems content here. We've browsed a few antique malls, walked the dunes, cooled off in different stretches of river. I enjoy her company a lot, although a hairsbreadth less so at this moment.

Which, I suppose, is just another way to say that I did not send her packing the instant she suggested a laptop—so many RAMS and megahertz and gigabytes—and a direct-market fly-fishing Web site. Sound-bites, river graphics, the creation of files, chat rooms to chit-chat about the big one that got away. She hasn't brought up that or any other business stratagems in front of Rodney, who likes and knows all that computer stuff cold. He's hooked on genealogics, and claims that maybe he and I are descended from the very same angels who comforted Christ and assisted him in warding off the devil's temptations. He's read and researched it all on-line, where he's learned that sometimes only women can see angels. He made me a bookmark for my birthday this year with a quote from St. Augustine: *Every visible thing in this world is put in the charge of an angel.* "You in charge of me," he said, "and me in charge of you." It's far and away the best birthday present I've ever received, from him or from anyone. I keep it bedside for safekeeping, and I fully intend to give it back to him some future day as a gift so he can pass it along in the opposite direction, to his firstborn. And so on like that in the ageless, slow-growing litany of Angel fathers and sons.

Copperfield yawns, then turns away as Rhea and Rodney continue their personal and structural makeover expansionist plans for another few minutes before, and by unpopular demand, I bring it to a halt.

I'm not discounting what they say. I'm simply not ready or

willing to check out Radio Shack at the Cherryland Mall in Traverse City, where the cellular-phone kiosk barkers peddle their wares. "You speak, it dials." Already the cancerous growth rate of durable goods and the need for service space have induced the town fathers to engage in serious chatter about a bypass, one of the truly ugly words in the quickly deteriorating language of northern landscapes. Every time I'm forced to drive in there my heart beats like a tom-tom at the first Taco Bell I pass. But Rhea and Rodney could care less; they've moved on to bigger, more pressing transportation matters: like how about a practical hatchback? Maybe a reliable, late-model Toyota or Honda so I can still haul my river gear without having to break down the rods?

"A Jeep Cherokee like the one we used to have—you liked it," Rodney says. "Mom would've sold it cheap if you'd ever wanted to get rid of the hearse. That's what she said. It's too late now, it's gone already. She said you really blew that."

Even Copperfield gets back into the act, shifting position and stretching as if for the sole purpose of elevating and aiming his puckered pink manx anus into proper thermometer position directly in front of my face. I love him dearly—I do—but I hate his cynical flair for drama at exactly the wrong moment. I mean, Rhea's the veterinary technician here, not me. In fact, she started just yesterday at the new animal clinic—All God's Creatures Large and Small—out on U.S. 31, which is why she didn't make the trip with me to the Pig. Probably a good thing after the Omar fiasco, though Rhea says she'd welcome the opportunity to formally meet Z. Names, handshakes. Thinks now that they'd get along.

Women in arms, as Rhea says, and she's taken an instant liking to Dr. Susan, whom she assists, the two animal lovers inducing labor on some guy's prized miniature potbellied Vietnamese sow yesterday after-hours. "North or South?" I asked, but she didn't even smile, and said only that the pig's name was Josephine and that her owner—the breeder—was a dead ringer for George Stephanopoulos, except for the blondish hair swept back and the onyx stud in his left nostril. Of course that might just be a disguise, but regardless, he really was quite handsome in a schnauzer sort of way, and did I happen to know how tall George stands in actual life? "Short," I said. "He's very short," and Rhea said back, "Maybe it *was* him then—five-foot-five at best. But why would he be up here in the northern boonies under an alias? Vincent Van-wormer, if you can imagine that—and half bonkers with worry over a pregnant and apparently quite happy but overdue potbellied pig. Pretty improbable, isn't it? A brush with political greatness so far from the nation's capital?"

"Extremely," I said, while revealing nothing about how, in a clearer than clear and recent dream, I guided the Dalai Lama (not in waders but in rope sandals and simple white raiments) on all three major area rivers—Platte, Betsie, and Boardman—at the same time. One was all and all one and the waters flowed not around but through us, fish and mayflies and a muskrat with silky green cress flowing out both sides of its mouth. Before I could even explain certain basic fly-casting techniques, the Dalai Lama splashed right by me, and without pause and without a rod or a net, stopped exactly at mid-river. Far from being spooked, the trout swam in amassing silver schools, surrounding and fanning him with their tails. The Dalai Lama, whose anti-predatory riverness made me feel as holy as I've ever felt there or anywhere. What one might call essence or being, I suppose, and without the predictable tinge of falsehood or embarrassment I usually feel using—or hearing used—such pompously inflated words. So who's to say who's here among us or not? Who's been here and gone? Who it is we've recognized or missed or simply imagined?

I do like how Rodney and Rhea have hit it off—bosom buddies already—even if I am suddenly the odd man out. They refer to themselves as R&R.

"Okay," I say, "all right," and Rodney crawls over the seat into the back, and before he can even hand me the cell phone Rhea says, "This isn't a setup, is it? You didn't pull a spark-plug wire or something like that, did you?"

"What?" I say.

"Sabotage. I'd just like your assurance that this all happened on its own. You know, of natural mechanical causes. Because to me it seems awfully convenient."

She's helped herself to one of my T-shirts, and to a pair of Z's old shorts, an old Angel–St. James mix and match. And squeezed Z's goose-feather pillow between her thighs last night, and had a terrific sound sleep. She's well rested, and Rodney too, and he's all serious-faced and nodding in emphatic corroboration behind me that he wouldn't mind me answering that simple question either.

"So that's the consensus? I dreamed this up? You really believe I'd do that?"

"Mom's car always starts," Rodney says. "Every morning."

"Of course it does, it's a brand-spanking-new BMW," I say, "the Mother Superior of automobiles, for crying out loud. So let's everyone just cool their jets a minute, okay? Just lighten up. Granted, Mackinac Island's not my first choice—that's no big secret. But a vote's a vote and I lost, and I accepted that, so get off my case. Just zip it with this I-nixed-the-trip-on-purpose. That's the most ludicrous thing I've ever heard. I mean, you two are serious, aren't you?"

"I am," Rhea says. "You make it hard not to be. Sorry, but I'm not buying it until I hear the mechanic's verdict."

"Uh-huh. For sure," Rodney says. "Yup. She's right. Here," he says. "Here's the phone, Dad."

Next thing I know they're both out in the driveway, backing slowly away from each other and flinging a Frisbee back and forth across the hood. It's approximately six forty-five A.M., the sky still pink, and Copperfield's fully concentrated, even feverish in his leaping attempts to bat the Frisbee down like some flat, white, round plastic pigeon. Let a warm-blooded bird with feathers and a heartbeat fly by and he'll curl up in the sun and grab instead some much-unneeded shut-eye. I attribute the broken necks of the two chickadees to Rhea's having washed the riverside windows, two Windex-inflicted deaths, which constitutes double the Copperfield carnage since the very first time I fed him.

Rodney's not half bad with his throws, but Rhea's the pro. An ambidextrous female Oddjob who might, just to re-clarify the tenuous lay of the land, decapitate the wood sculpture of Icarus in waders that I bought from Its. I don't doubt she can do it, at sixty-plus feet, with a simple elbow bend and a quick flick of her wrist.

It's a dance she does—a graceful series of pivots and pirouettes and near splits. Catches it between her legs, behind her back, one-fingered above her head like someone balancing a spinning dinner plate on a dowel. It's an impressive coordination display, but nothing compared to the way she takes off running like a long-jumper after Rodney sails the Frisbee as high and far as he can downwind. It appears to rise and fall and rise slow motion again in the air current. Even Copperfield stands on the hearse roof for a better look. I lean forward, the ringing cell phone pressed to my ear.

Buck answers at the instant Rhea goes airborne at the river's edge, her long legs still pumping hard until, impossibly angled upward behind her arched spine, she snares the Frisbee between ankles and ass and still manages to transfer it to her hand before an almost splashless entry. It's amazing how limber, how kid-bendable someone in her thirties can be. Rodney's cheering like this is some brand-new Olympic event. He's jumping up and down, wind-milling his arms, and I say, "Yeah, it's me, Archie. Right, it's a long story," and before I hang up Buck assures me that I am indeed up Shit Creek, but that he does, in fact, have a paddle. A loaner if I don't mind the miles and the faded white door stars, the sometimes temperamental windshield wipers, and, of course, no top, but no rain's in the immediate forecast either, and who needs all those whistles and bells anyhow? He's talking about his late-fifties-vintage military-issue Willys. Buck's a homegrown wrench extraordinaire, but maybe not, as he some-times claims to be after bouts of heavy sudsing, a retired and highly decorated Navy Seal. Whatever his background, actual or invented, Rodney likes him. Likes, among other things, the way Buck always snaps a match into flame with his thumbnail when-ever he lights a cigar.

Still, it surprises me that Rodney opts to ride into town with us in the wrecker, abandoning Rhea to defend the home front on her own. She hasn't lifted the wet T-shirt away from her body, and her black hair's slicked back, and she looks all of about seventeen just standing there barefoot in the early river-reflected sunlight. The Frisbee's still in her hand, and the wings of half a dozen monarchs keep opening and closing on the heads of the wildflowers. Nobody's mentioned anything about squeezing Rhea in, and it's not until we hit the Deadstream Road and hang a right that Buck announces, "Priority parcel. When, my friend, did those goods arrive? No wonder I ain't seen hide nor hair of you lately. Send her my way all wet like that and *I'd* be hard-pressed to leave my chambers long-term too."

"I've been in," I say.

"Oh? Then clear up for me why I got half a dozen messages waiting for you and not all of them what I'd call entirely friendly. Hell, you're gassed up and out the yard like a horny roadrunner, and now I know why. You'll be lucky they don't lock your cradle-robbing ass up, and toss the goddamn key."

Rodney laughs and looks up at me like he always does whenever Buck spins into one of his I-gotcha-now riffs, regardless of the subject. Everything from rice-burners (Japanese compacts), to the price of solar panels, to Monica Lewinski's lips and withers and how she's under *his* desk he sure the fuck ain't picking up to take any incoming red-alert phone calls. So let's just put the uncivilized world on hold for one additional minute. Hummer's better than a stress test any day, he says, and he's curious to know where this country's sense of humor's gone to these last few years anyhow. The most powerful man in the world on trial for what? A chubby intern tooting his piccolo? A-B-C-D-E-F-Geeee-fucking whiz let's lighten up already. It's way too early in this beautiful new century for so much envy and partisan political revenge. What's in dispute here is a simple health issue, you ask me. It ain't like he got caught cross-dressing or screwing a starfish in the Lincoln Bedroom for Christ's sake.

Rodney's been reminded and re-reminded that Buck is Buck, and yes, he certainly does swear to beat the band during his crass and fruit-loopy monologues. "I sure wish he wouldn't in front of you," I tell Rodney. But keep in mind he's kid-deprived and doesn't mean any harm. It's just his way. He opens his mouth he maxes out whether or not anyone can make heads or tails of any of it after awhile. What you see, et cetera, et cetera, and "The less Z hears about all this the better for everyone," I always remind

Rodney. "Because spilling the beans sure won't help our lot in life, will it?" His comeback is always the same: "Rule one," he says. "Works both ways."

"So what's the holdup? What's the U.S. government postmark say there, Archie?"

He means where's Rhea from, and after an evasive couple of hems and haws, Rodney intercedes to identify her first of all by name. "Rhea," he says. "She's sometimes from the Pig downstate, but now she fixes them. She did yesterday already. The mom. Eleven healthy tiny pink babies, which is a real lot for a minia-ture. Usually they'll have like . . . oh, only five or six. The dad, he's a grand champ."

Apparently this makes perfect sense to Buck who nods, shifts into third, and checks all three mirrors to make sure the hearse is still riding backwards behind us, the yellow and red emergency lights coptering across its tilted roof and hood. He engages and disengages and double-clutches and power-shifts like we're in a wrecker race.

We're driving away from the sun, and Buck keeps lifting and moving a toothpick from one side of his mouth to the other with the tip of his tongue, flipping it forward now and then like a snake. It's hard to pinpoint his exact age, somewhere between thirty-seven and sixty, the age discrepancy a function of his per-petually youthful smiling eyes. Deep brown and deeply set. But young Buck or older Buck, he's always stout and beer-bellied, forearms muscle-corded from a lifelong love affair with engine blocks. He's missing most of his ring finger on his left hand—two knuckles worth—and from the neck up he looks not unlike Moe from the Three Stooges. Same goofy bowl-floppy black haircut. Same frenetic impulse to correct the asocial behavior of fools.

He owns, along with his father, the combination mini-mart, gas station, body-repair and bait shop, plus the bare-bones four-unit motel where my clients generally stay cut-rate if they want to rough it up here in the tundra. A multitask operation, as Buck says, the likes of which, in some alternative upscale venue, would have made him a king. The locals refer to it without irony as Buck's Empire. He's been married three times, each a study in contrasts, but always a whole raft more contrast than study. I'm not exactly sure what he means by that and I've never asked. Nor, as far as I know, have I ever run into Buck-X-One, as he calls her, or Buck-X-Two, or Buck-X-Three, like their getting away had something to do with them busting off, and Buck then going to an even stronger leader and tippet.

His line-item domestic paraphrase goes something like this: three brides, no kids, no pets, negative population growth. He nonetheless describes himself as a self-endowed optimist, and sometimes right out of the blue he'll say, as he does now, "Outstanding."

"What is?" Rodney says. "What's outstanding?" and Buck says back, "That right there," and he points across his body toward the open window where Rhea has just this instant pulled up alongside. We're doing maybe fifty-five, and for a few seconds I'm convinced she's going to reach over and high-five Buck and then disappear for good. Maybe first to Mackinac Island, and from there to parts unknown. She reaches instead and lifts her face shield and shouts over the deep mellow roar of the Harley's pipes, "I'm going to get a newspaper . . . so we can check out what's playing at the movies. Maybe there's a concert over at the arts camp, or at the casino. I think I heard there is. Lyle Lovett or someone."

When I flash her a thumbs-up she flips me the bird, cranks on the throttle and cuts so sharply in front of us I'm sure she's going to clip the front bumper wench and then crash and burn. She doesn't, but it's close as she straightens the bike, and leans forward over the handlebars, and by the time we round the next bend she's already out of sight.

"Howdy-howdy," Buck says. "Life is short my name's not important I swear I ain't one of them dainties I'm a man among men and therefore come writhe with me my lovely Aphrodite live free and be brave I promise what's mine is yours lock stock and barrel and hey-oh-hey-dee-hey-hey-hey."

"Yeah, wishful thinking," I say. "Try again."

"Sure," Buck says back, and without missing a beat: "I'll take one hot meal to go and you keep the jar of wieners and oh you sweet daughter of the pleasure gods I swear. Yeehaah," he says, "fire in the hole," and he lolls his tongue, toothpick-tipped, and then starts barking his way down the Deadstream, jowls shaking like a bulldog's.

"She's my dad's girlfriend," Rodney says. "She's in her thirties and she's real nice."

Buck pauses in his farcical wrecker-guy-in-heat act, his face dead serious when he looks down at Rodney, and says, "Woof." He says, "Woof" again, and Rodney laughs and just like that they're barking back and forth at each other, louder and louder, each of them busting a gut, and they've got me laughing pretty good too. "Woof, woof," and then together they turn on me and we're all suddenly woofing it up in chaotic canine uproar, Rhea already halfway to Honor. Halfway, and no doubt still plenty pissed at what's transpired, and so easily outrunning the hounds.

"A raison d'être?" I say. "Do you know what it means? And when did you start talking French anyway?"

"Omar. He speaks . . . maybe five different languages. Major ones. He taught me a bunch of phrases. It means . . . hmmm . . . sort of like don't make up reasons for things?"

Major languages? I think. As opposed to what, Yanomamul or pig Latin? But I don't say that. I say, "Why, was somebody lying?"

"No."

"Then what's the deal? Why'd it even come up in the first place?"

"It just did, that's why. Stuff comes up at dinner all the time, not that he's there every night but when he is, like for a special occasion."

"Oh?"

"Yeah, for my birthday was one. He's really smart about sports and classical music and food and about all these different places 'cause he's been everywhere all over the world that I've never heard of. Not even in school when we spin the globe. Bucharest, that's one."

169

"Romania," I say.

"Maybe. I guess. Anyway, he knows like a kazillion jokes. Mom says he makes the meals more . . . I think she said, fun and—oh yeah—multicultural. No, cross-cultural. One of those, I can't remember. More civilized. Omar, he's a food and wine connoisseur."

"A gourmand?" I say. "Like me."

"No, not like you. When *he* cooks it's like always the best by far. He makes flaming desserts and the fire it's really, really blue. Just like at his restaurant. It's neat. He pours it right over the ice cream and it turns all to caramel."

"Sounds good," I say, though I've always been a lousy liar, and Rodney just turns away, his eyes following the flight of the dozen or so buffleheads heading for Little Platte Lake. "Okay, so give me a hypothetical then so I'll know how you use the phrase. A made-up example," I say.

Rodney's turned cautious—we're perilously close to violating rule one—but after a few seconds he says, turning to look at me, "I don't know. Maybe like why we're not on our way to Mackinac Island isn't really the real reason. The raison d'etre."

"And what's the real reason? I mean, hey, if the hearse doesn't start it doesn't start, *capiche*? I told you straight-out it had nothing to do with me. Don't kid yourself, cars do break down. Not all the time of course, but when it happens people don't start in accusing other people of sabotage like you guys did. Talk about a crummy deal. We always see one or two cars abandoned on the side of the highway, don't we? Every trip up and back. That's why they're called breakdown lanes. That's what they're there for."

"Mom says . . ."

"Never mind Mom. She's not part of this discussion. She's completely beside the point . . . it's *our* conversation. I want to hear what you think."

We've already topped off the gas tank—the gauge doesn't work—and we're on our slow bumpy way back to the cabin, the long knobless stick shift vibrating in my hand as I grind the gears trying to find fourth. There's no rear seat, no radio or air conditioning or cruise control, no cigarette lighter, no airbags or empty casket space behind us, and certainly, with the wind whipping around, no hothouse smells. It's bare bones—just a chassis, a roll bar, and four balanced wheels that so far keep turning over.

"I think the hearse . . . maybe it got heatstroke."

"You mean overheated?"

"No. More like it's old and shouldn't be on the road for how you use it to come and get me at the Pig from so far away. I liked riding in the wrecker, that was fun. But I hate getting stuck like happened this morning when we had plans, and now everyone's disappointed. Me and Rhea anyway."

"And I'm not?"

"Yeah, you are, but only 'cause we're upset, and not because we didn't get to go. You didn't want to and it's too late now, and Rhea's on call tomorrow. All day. And that's the real reason today's all ruined. You, you're the raison d'etre and not the hearse, but maybe now you'll get rid of it. And I don't care anymore that Grandpa left it to you in his will. It isn't something you can save forever and give to me. Even if you could, I don't want it."

"It was never meant to be that," I say. "It ran great and that's all I ever asked. Besides, it never had any trade-in value anyway. None. I checked around. Nobody wanted it, not then, and for sure not now. Seemed nonsensical to just give it away and spend a lot of money on something new and expensive. It served our needs, didn't it?"

"Well it doesn't now, and Rhea . . . she likes you a lot, I can tell, but I bet not so much after today. You better think of something good, and not like a sundae or lunch at Money's. And I don't want to go to the trestle, not today, okay? Or any garage sales. They're always just junky and I think kind of creepy too. And like Mom says, sad."

He's right, or Z's right—no honored guests sipping champagne at those events. Just an open invitation to every small-hope passerby who imagines one great find there among the discarded princess phones and roller-skate keys and twined-up stacks of old *Life* magazines. Cigar boxes lined with empty thread spools and mismatched buttons. A mountain-gorilla mask, the plastic as shiny black and slippery as a fish scale. A dying, underinflated set of water wings.

"Can't you think of something fun we've never done before? Please?" Rodney says. "Please, can you? Can you, Dad?"

———

Because the sun is the wind's source, hot air ballooning, if one is not attempting to circle the globe, is done primarily in the mornings and evenings. Still, thrown off course by the stiff Lake Michigan breeze, we lost the chase crew early on and ended our ride by bounce-landing along that stretch of nude beach at Otter Creek, the topless sun-junkies—those few who were left—screaming as they fled their blankets. But then, more curious than frightened, they drifted partway back. And when Camille, our lost pilot, sounded her ardent call for sisterly assistance, those semi-naked beach nymphs, without shyness or hesitation, took hold of the four tether lines and dug their heels in deep against the wind's persistent tugs. Arms and thighs and flat stomachs in serious strain—and all I could think at that precarious juncture was bless their merciful hearts and hard-rounded early-twenty-something-ish look-alike behinds.

I had two frames left on the roll of thirty-six, and although I toyed inwardly with throwing caution to the wind for art's sake, I didn't in the end even remove the lens cap from the Pentax, not with the theme of the day being personal recovery. Still, it was definitely a significant image. A once-in-a-lifetime, and who back in the heyday of the Fox Den would believe such a thing without indisputable visual glossy evidence? No matter, I wasn't ready to risk deep-sixing a voyage that had all but redeemed me. A drift in which we rose, weightless in our fiery propane ascendance, to over two thousand feet, where we viewed, off one side, the Wisconsin shoreline, off another the UP, Michigan's Upper Peninsula, almost a hundred miles away. A commanding view wherever we looked.

"We should have brought a camcorder," Rhea said, draping her arm around my neck, and leaning in to kiss me. Rodney kept looking up at us and smiling like I was Orville Wright, and Rhea Amelia Earhart minus the scarf. The orchards were red with apples à la Pissarro, and I thought if we listened intently enough we might hear one fall to the ground. It was that quiet up there, almost hollow, the balloon's shadow darkening the farmhouses and the barns and the silos as we passed over. Cows, cornfields and cribs and dense perennial gardens, occluded irrigation ponds I could obliterate merely by holding out my fist. The empty floating rowboat made me think of sunfish.

I liked the feeling of Rhea's weight against me. I liked how she drew my hand to her lips and kissed my knuckles. And most of all how our feet on wicker floated above this quilted patchwork landscape, and even without a bottle of Good Harbor chardonnay and a few glasses to toast our success I felt pretty buzzed. Airy even in my groin when I thought of the basket as a boat and how half-smashed clients of mine in their clumsiness did occasionally tumble overboard.

Camille of the bountiful flowing chestnut hair had never, in seventeen years of ballooning, suffered a single casualty. "Knock on wicker," I said, but better yet she uncorked a vial of holy water (from where she didn't say) and asked us each, for ritual's sake, to sprinkle a few drops.

Indeed we had drifted a bit off course, Camille said, but being in no immediate danger of blowing away for good, she relaxed and pointed out the Chain of Lakes and Lake Mitchell, Cadillac and Higgins, the two Manitou Islands. Plus Fox and Beaver Islands, the Old Mission Peninsula, the Sleeping Bear Dunes. All this spectacular geological splendor in less than two hours, and already we were back safe and sound on good old terra firma.

Rodney was first to climb out of the basket, and Rhea followed, while Captain Camille turned off the burners, and the multicolored ripstop nylon envelope slowly collapsed. I marveled at the pliable muscular young backs almost parallel to the sand. Of all the breasts I'd ever witnessed live, none had ever stared so dramatically skyward. I nearly applauded and, if I'd had a stash with me, I would have seriously considered torching off a string or two of ladyfingers on their behalf. Camille at ground zero had given me a boutonniere of poppies, and I suppose I could have plucked and thrown the red petals into the wind as a showy offering. Instead I thanked each of the tether holders with a nod, brief enough to appear appropriately thankful and discreet, and just long enough to commit the moment to everlasting memory.

The chasers, who'd stayed in constant radio contact, finally arrived, one of them driving the Willys right down onto the beach. She stopped and got out and handed me back the ignition key. I'd met her earlier while negotiating the barter: a hot air balloon ride for a future evening of terrestrial fishing (fire ants or katydids or foam wing hoppers) with Camille and her partner Julia Marie Bouvier. "No relation to Jacqueline," she said without any prompting.

She asked if I was interested in selling the Willys, and it pained me to respond in the negative. How could it not, with her militarily adorned in camouflage bush shorts and matching T-shirt, tight-fitting and tucked in and, even with the sun's fire paling to salmon pink on the western rim, a pair of those silver one-way mirror shades, and a camouflage flap-hat? To further authenticate the rough-and-tumble drill-sergeant look, silver dog tags. A female Desert Fox, and if she'd ordered me to fall in I believe I would have, a battalion of one. I couldn't help but imagine a machine gun mounted to the roll bar and Julia Marie Bouvier patrolling, on her off-hours and on highest alert, for any sign of a naval invasion of Michigan's Third Coast, the longest of our nation's three.

Julia did finally take off her shades and I swear her eyes were the color of Fresca. Lovely dilating feline eyes. I was already worried for the fish, but grateful that Julia, in front of Rhea and Rodney, crooned loud and clear that a future day with me and Camille on the river was exactly what their analyst had prescribed.

The day being what it had become, I did not admonish Rhea and Rodney to "Hey, listen up. Listen to Julia Bouvier, whose shrink's personal marching orders are to get on the river and cast all those petty worries aside."

No, I did not crow or cavil or engage in any river sermon on the beach. Instead I put the Willys in four-wheel and headed across the dry white sand and away from the lake, Rodney beside me and Rhea on her knees between us in the back. For maybe three or four consecutive minutes nobody said a thing, as if the image of where we'd just been continued to hover overhead. I did not look up quite that high, but rather into the rearview mirror where, and not altogether to my surprise, all eyes were focused: mine and Rodney's and Rhea's locked on each other. We were moving slowly in second gear, the wind barely lifting our hair. Without anybody saying so it was clear that all three of us separately and together were happy just to be. Out of love we'd become. Together the day. All of it very. Every arrangement thereof.

FOURTEEN

When Everything That Ticked—Has Stopped

Although I've carefully sculpted my cheeks and chin with my dad's steaming Gillette Foamy, I'm not intending to shave for real. I'm practicing for when that time arrives, but at this moment I still feel a whole lot more like a kid than a grown-up.

I wish I'd locked the door, or that my dad had at least knocked so I could have quick rinsed and towel-dried my face instead of standing here all lathered up like this, the bladeless double-edged razor squeezed in my raised hand. It's mid-November, a cold, snow-spitting late Sunday afternoon, and I haven't yet even physically matured to the peach fuzz stage.

"You need to use the bathroom?" I say, and he nods, and I step aside as he slowly opens the mirrored medicine cabinet and takes out one of my mom's pill containers from the upper shelf, lines up the white arrows and clicks the top open and checks the number of capsules, half green, half black. I can see only three in his open palm. Then he puts the medication back.

I've already fake shaved from my ears to midway down my jaw line, and I feel pretty conspicuous standing around in nothing but my jockey shorts, and sporting a gleaming white Fu Manchu. I figure there are probably hundreds of ways to look ridiculous in front of your dad, and that this takes a back seat to none of them. The odd thing is that he doesn't even comment or throw me a single sidelong glance. He simply says, "I need to talk to you, Arch. So finish up and get dressed and meet me downstairs."

"Where downstairs?" I ask, and he says back, "All the way down. I'll be waiting for you. Five minutes."

I'd been down there only the one time, three years ago, and once was plenty. "How come not in the living room?" I say. "Or in the kitchen. That'd save a lot of time and trouble, wouldn't it?"

"You let me be the judge of that," he says, and he turns on both the hot and cold water taps and hands me a face cloth from the rack. "Five minutes," he says again, and backs out into the hallway, eyes suddenly narrowed and his index finger pointing at me like "not another word."

As far as I know the mortuary is empty, as it has been all month. My dad even quipped that maybe he should hang a vacancy sign out front. He said that's the problem with the dead—no referrals. But he made clear in his tone that it wasn't a ha-ha sort of whimsy, which served only to heighten the tension we'd both been feeling all week, my mom slipping in and then out of day-long comas.

And there's sure nothing funny about how he's taken to wearing a medical frock around the house. If he means to impersonate a doctor, he's sadly mistaken. His demeanor is entirely wrong, his face all puffy from lack of sleep. He does check on my mom a lot, which I like. At half-hour intervals lately, but in between times he'll pace and pace the upstairs rooms, from one to another, and sometimes stop at the kitchen window to stare outside at the headstones below. He hasn't added any more lately, but some evenings at dinner he'll circle certain order numbers in his headstone catalogues, and mark certain pages with paper clips, but never when my mom is present, or even awake. She's not in traction, of course, but there's been a double hand stirrup contraption installed above her bed in case she needs to pull herself up. Which she can't anymore.

"Five minutes," I whisper, and even though I don't slam the bathroom door, the metal slide engages the lock pretty loud when

I turn it hard, and I hope my dad's heard it too. I hope he's gotten *my* message.

With careful downward strokes, I finish shaving, and dry my face, and hand-pat not one drop of his Old Spice onto my skin. I wet and comb my hair back off my forehead, and stare close-up at my reflection, the hot-water steam clouding the mirror. People sometimes remark how much I resemble my dad, and I figure even more so when, in the privacy of my bedroom, I open my closet door and take out and dress to a T in my latest Robert Hall pallbearer suit, the only suit I own. Just another impostor, I think, another stand-in, as I straighten and snug up my half-Windsor, the knot my dad prefers and taught me to tie. Polished shoes, cufflinks—all standard issue on burial days at Angel & Sons. It's clear my mom's impending death coincides in some direct way with whatever it is he intends to say down there in his chambers. And I want him to know at the first sight of me that I'm both ready and not ready to discuss the inevitable, as a kid *and* as an adult, and that most likely I'll hold this about-to-be conversation against him forever.

I pause at the doorway to my mom's room at the head of the stairs. *Going down*, I think, but there's no elevator here, and she's breathing so lightly under the sheet that I believe she might rise with each slow descending step I take. Three steep flights—the multiple round trips of which my dad makes daily, given how his business has thrived over the years. Downright spooky, he said just yesterday, the way nobody has passed on. Not a single drop-off or alert-call all week long. Like the entire town's on hold, waiting, as we've been, he said, for God to reclaim my mom before allowing life's normal dying cycle to continue on.

I've imagined two fold-up chairs pulled close and facing each other, and my dad already seated, his fingers loosely interlaced between his knees. But he's not sitting when I enter. He's standing beside an open casket—a hand-tinted color photo portrait of my mom propped against the satin pillow. She's younger and more beautiful than I ever imagined her, hair thick and wavy and glamorous in a way I've never seen it fixed before. For a few interminable seconds I can't avert my eyes. She's smiling, and so is my dad, first at her and then back at me. His face, I notice now under the harsh glare of the fluorescent lights, is bristled gray.

An inlaid trellis of roses, a profusion of white climbers, surrounds the casket. "Ivory," my dad says, "and mother of pearl," and he brushes with his fingertips the fine plaited vines and the leaves and the full-bellied blossoms, as if, over a lifetime, he has secretly handcrafted it himself, the knotless mahogany turned dark as a night absent of fire. No moon or stars or northern lights. Only those garlanded, incandescent flowers exploding upward in bunches through the imaginary ash.

"You like it?" he asks.

"Like you've got it now, you mean—with only the picture? I guess so," I say, my on-the-spot compromise response a hedge against whatever other plan he might have in mind. It's way too late to ask but maybe a memorial-type wake after the cremation would be okay with her. Lid open and my mom looking normal and kind of lost-in-thought. A poem or two laid out next to the portrait for the mourners to read, though I can't imagine there will be more than a few. My dad and me and my aunt Esther maybe, if she can even be located anymore. Omaha. That's the last anybody's heard, and that was over a year ago. There have been small wakes in the past. "That's death for you," I've heard my dad say. "Seems wasted, but sometimes you just can't predict a turnout."

Why he checks his watch I'm not sure. Time already for my mom's medicine? Or is he simply marking this moment eternal when he says, "Arch . . . listen to me," but I don't. I shake my head no because it's undeniably clear as he picks up the portrait that it's to show me what my mom will look like again in the cold hard flesh. "Like herself," he says. "Before the onset of that horrible disease."

I'm not sure which one he means, the cancer or the depression. Or both. Doesn't matter, because "You can't. It's not fair," I say. "It's not at all what she wants."

"Oh? What makes you such an expert, Arch? You're reading her thoughts now, are you, is that it? Or maybe she consulted you about the service arrangements."

"Yes," I lie. "She did, a bunch of times."

"And said what exactly?"

"Something about clothing and corruption and being cremated and not being stared at by people who never cared about her. People she didn't even know. Total strangers. She said you'd betray her just like you're going to. Aren't you?"

He glances at the coffin and then back at me. "Madness makes its own claims, Arch. Defective claims, and it's our job to root out what's right and what's wrong. So much of what she's said . . . it's simply beyond our powers of comprehension. You know that. Nonsense and double-talk, all that indecipherable gibberish that goes back years and years before you were ever born. Trust me—whenever you make important personal decisions like this one you've got to take a person's condition into account. You've got to interpret for them sometimes and come up with a more intact version of who they are and were and what it is they really want."

"Did you when you first got married? Did you even back then? Did you ever?"

Now he's staring right at me, not stymied-like exactly, but confounded just the same, as if he doesn't have a ready answer, and instead places the portrait carefully back into the casket and closes the lid, those roses bunched even thicker on top, and tinted blue. We're standing maybe three feet apart is all, so when he steps closer my entire body tenses. He's back to the pointing, this time thudding his stiff right index finger against my chest, right above my silver tie clasp. Not hard, but more like for emphasis.

"Nobody's perfect," he says, "and it's fairly certain few of us are destined for sainthood. And I'm not one of them—I can't right every wrong—but I did do my best. Overall I did, but the big mistake I made . . . do you want to hear this, Arch? Is this the time? Do you? Because here's what I did: I loved your mom for her weaknesses, not for her strengths, and that's the wrong way to be let in. The wrong and very worst way, and made even worse over a lifetime. She was married once before me—briefly—before we ever met. I suppose she told you that too?"

I don't know why, or why I'm suddenly shaking so badly inside, but I lie again, or half lie or whatever it is when the mind's recall is so distant that every might-have-been-said word lingers right there at the far edge of consciousness. "Yes, she told me that," I say, this strange metal taste forming at the back of my mouth. "She told me everything," and I believe in my sudden light-headedness that I'm going to hyperventilate, and then panic and bolt back up those stairs, two or three at a time into my mom's bedroom, and lock that door, and protect her from him forever.

"High school sweethearts," he says. "Usually ends there. Didn't though—they stayed together right through college. But you're privy to all this? And how her first husband ended up here, in my care?" He steps away and motions with both arms extended as if in our peripheral vision lurk the dark hidden secrets of every nonliving person ever to have entered this room.

"Maybe," I say. "I don't remember for sure. She said I had a sister named Criseide."

"Who died in infancy?"

I nod and my dad says, "And her father before her—in Korea. You've heard of that, the war that followed the Good War? Drafted right out of college and shipped home dead six weeks later, just days before that conflict officially ended. Never even knew your mom was pregnant. The last letter she sent him arrived back stateside two weeks after he did. Unopened. You want his name?"

At first I think he means to keep, to make mine, but no, it's only for the record, and any time I want him to stop with the details, the irrefutable facts, as he says, just say so. Say, "Enough," and we'll quick close this tell-all conversation down. We'll bury it for good—all those ghosts who until this moment had so obediently held their tongues. But as always, whatever my mom has confided in me needs to be re-clarified, amended in the way great sadness remembered clearly over time is always the truer version, the deeper flowing river.

But no way am I on his side, and before this wintry fall afternoon turns into evening I could be his mortal enemy, his opposite, his son by birth only, a blood-kin traitor at thirteen. "Where's he buried?" I ask. "And Criseide . . . her too."

"Together," he says. "Side by side in St. Jerome's. Lot number

1473. Two small footstone markers that I picked out and paid for. There's a place reserved for your mom there, but that's not where she'll be interred. The three of us, *this* family, and Grandma and Grandpa Angel of course—we've got our own plot to tend a little higher up on another hill."

"Criseide's real. Everything Mom said is real, isn't it?"

"Real and not real, Arch. How can I make you understand this? The child lived barely two weeks. That's all. Infant fatalities . . . they're not uncommon.

"Your room—that became the nursery—filigree and frills on the crib and stuffed with Raggedy Anns and animals galore and for months afterward your mom hallucinated that baby into being there. She was impervious to the sleeping pills. I'd find her sitting in the rocker in the dead of night, humming sometimes and other times whimpering and hugging herself. Those deaths coming within seven months of each other—husband and baby daughter—she just never recovered. Was never quite all there again. And let me tell you—in those days she did not suffer in silence. Started blaming me for just about everything. Young marrieds but you'd sure never have known it. She said once that I was as unsurprising as I was unexpected. That hurt, Arch. A lot. That I never forgot. A convenience—that'd be me all right, your dad. Convenience and security—that's what she needed at the time and it's what I gave her and it turned out to be the biggest design flaw of all."

He pauses, and I notice for the first time a prism hanging above the embalming table, refracting its shiny chrome light like a mobile for all God's deceased children, young and old alike.

"I've never had trouble making ends meet, Arch. I pride myself on being a good provider. Always have, but every time I bought her a pick-me-up gift—didn't matter what it was, a new dress or a bracelet—she said I made her feel like a charity case. Couldn't even get her to go out to dinner at the Holiday Inn. Last time we did she got up right in mid-meal and without even putting on her coat she walked outside. It was raining cats and dogs and she just stood in that parking lot, sobbing and refusing to get into the car. Next thing I knew she'd taken a job at a dry cleaners of all places, then at a bakery, the bookstore next. All minimum wage. Not even twenty-four years old and war-widowed and remarried. But not out of love, and certainly not out of any interest in what I did. Deep grief and rescue—it's a dangerous mix. I was thirty and settled and already thinking about a family and . . . well, I thought we had plenty of time."

"For Mom to get better, you mean? For her to recover from all that terrible stuff?"

"Which she did," he says, "reading all the time, getting lost in those books of hers. Taking notes, signing up for graduate classes. Heck, I needed a dictionary just to keep up with what she was saying. Words and theories I'd never heard of and even after I did they didn't make any sense. Not really."

He shrugs through a brief sideways shift and sniffle and says, "Then she'd get worse and better and then she'd tumble all over again. There were days I thought sure she'd drowned in the bathtub. She'd be leaning back and staring—who knows for how long—straight at the ceiling, the water ice-cold and up over her lips and her lips already blue. Not a drop of water displaced, like she was deadweight. No movement at all. I'd reach in and pull the plug chain and help her out and she'd start shivering and . . . it was something. Downright frightening. But did I love her? You bet I did, and more than she ever loved me. And things were good after we had you. Nine pounds eight ounces. Twenty-three inches long. Delivered healthy and strong and right on time—the easiest, sweetest baby anybody could imagine. Your mom took to motherhood like it was the cure of all cures. Giddy, downright slaphappy in love with life most days. She'd bathe you in the kitchen sink and you'd kick and splash and smile wide as a Cheshire cat. I half believed back then that nothing would ever forsake her again." He shrugs and laughs a crooked pinched-face nervous laugh and kind of wrings his hands and says, "Sometimes I wish we'd had a dozen kids."

Enough to gather together and confer, I think, and then take a family vote and let that stand as the correct and decent and least offensive funeral plan. "*Did* love," he said about my mom. If I were in charge that's how I'd word the obituary: "Millicent

Angel—survived by her only son Archie who loves her. And by her longtime husband Rod who only *did*, but spared no expense at the end manipulating his remorse into something more akin to pity, and possibly even revenge." The obituaries—the only section of the newspaper he claimed ever to trust. Dead was dead, the most convincing and irrefutable fact in the universe.

"You'll thank me," he says. "You'll see," and he quick nods, as if this confused and wacky anti-burial decree I'm wedded to has finally confronted a reasonable level of doubt. With a little basic deductive reasoning, how could it not, my dad wants to know, but I remain mute. I've got questions of my own that I want answered, but for sure not by him, and maybe not by any mortal person. My mom once said it's the archangel Michael who eventually comes for us all. If so, whose truth-version might *he* listen to and is it really so crazy to believe he'll claim us with song? I hope it's in the voice of a woman—the all but disappeared voice of my mom. My dad's rasp has gotten worse and worse over time. There's almost no music left in him at all.

"I want to be cremated too," I blurt out, "and when I get married it won't be to someone who changes everything around to suit their wishes."

"When you get, Arch? When you get? Like in get lucky or saved or disappointed or—that's right—get married? Let me tell you, it cuts both ways—all those gets and don'ts that collect and evolve to make up a person's life. Well, here's another one," he says with an edge, "but first I want you to tell me if you get what I've been saying so far."

"That you're doing this for yourself, and not to honor Mom." And when he says, "I'm doing it for all of us," I think, liar, liar, liar. And all I can hear as my dad unleashes his barrage of cold background warning shouts is "Get back here, you get back here, Arch." But I'm already in full flight up the windowless triple-decker stairway where all around me the darkness suddenly converges as my dad switches off the lights. I slow down but I don't stop until I reach the top, each wild heartbeat a reminder, as my mom could surely have testified, that nobody walks into or away from this life entirely shameless, entirely sane and justified.

"Who's the selfish one now?" my dad shouts. "Who, Arch? Who?" the words echoing up behind me in a kind of deep gulping sound, like somebody terribly alone and lost, and real, real close to crying.

Even after almost an hour I'm still attempting to regain my bearings. My dad's in the kitchen, fixing sweet diced pickle and ham sandwiches, and succotash from a can. He doesn't post the dinner menu, but his routine of late has been to prepare the same meal on consecutive nights. Less to think about, I guess. Either that or a case of selective amnesia. He's come into my mom's bedroom only once, not to take her pulse or administer medication or console anyone, but to quietly lecture me on how lack of compassion insures that a person will misjudge everything, and that I need to consider both sides, my position *and* his. Before he left, and without raising his voice, he said, "Figure that much out, Arch, and you and me, we're back in business. All squared away like old times. Father and son."

The last thing my mom had to eat was a spoonful of Neapolitan ice cream. That was early this morning, and she's been asleep ever since. I've got her Emily Dickinson out, the fattest volume, but I don't understand a lot of it, and "death" and "despair" and "pain"—they don't sound to me like poetic words, like words I should read aloud to her, and they're everywhere, on nearly every page. I considered editing them out but the poems seemed even stranger that way, crude and incomplete and without a whole lot of conviction. If all else fails maybe I'll just start in and see what happens, but for the time being I've decided to whisper whatever uplifting thoughts pop into my mind. Not like Spiro Agnew resigning or anything, but more like how the usual stays that way, which maybe isn't all that newsworthy, but if she could've seen the noonday clouds pass overhead this morning she'd sure know it was late fall again. "November," I say. "Your favorite season."

I'm sitting bedside, snow ticking the window. When I reach over and tilt the amber lamp glow sideways, those heavy flakes have patterned a perfect clockface on the glass. "It's almost six thirty," I say, and it's already dark out and there's a double-feature Audrey Hepburn on TV tonight should she wake and want to watch it. Just the two of us if my dad's not hogging the set again and still computing with compass and tiny T-square yet another funeral home ad mock-up for next year's yellow pages: "Second Generation Family-Owned and Operated. 24-Hour On Call Personal Service. Veterans Discount and Pre-Planning for that future time when each of us settles back for good." He hasn't run them by me, but he hasn't exactly hidden them from plain view either.

I wonder if my mom might hear me better if I were to lift her fingertips to my lips. The doctor assured my dad that she's not in any pain, and most likely has no idea where she is anymore. A part of me takes it a step further, thinking maybe she's not even inside her own body, at least not all the time. Leaves for awhile for a long walk or a train ride to somewhere far off and comes back is my theory, but that kind of groundless kid speculation is off-limits when talking to my dad. He's got all the bases covered, he says. No brain, no headache. Meaning the burden is his, not mine. I don't tell him that for weeks now my head has been pounding something terrible, like the pulse of a mallet, and that a lot of it's because of him. If I did he'd say what he always does: "This world will survive us all, and we'll be asleep a long, long time. So let's accentuate the positive while we can. Even if your mother doesn't respond she knows we're here. She knows we're close by—I'm certain of it—and in the final analysis that's how each us will be spared. By having somebody we love nearby."

There might be something to that, given how when I close and then reopen my eyes, my mom's are open too. They're so incredibly clear in the brilliant blur of the lamplight, as if cut out of that photo portrait. Maybe my dad could fix what's left of her hair, and dress her, and even if she could manage only a few tiny bites, invite her to sit with us at the table. He calls only me: "Dinner, Arch."

He's in the living room where he's turned the TV on loud enough for us to hear something about a cease-fire somewhere in the world. Egypt and Israel, I think. A good war, I wonder, or a bad one? What's obvious is that my mom's mind is quiet, empty of politics, and even emptier of the world's humongous chaos and clutter and, as she used to say, cruelty. I can tell all that simply by the way she holds my gaze, and by how her chest rises and falls at not even a third the normal rate, as mine does. Because she's been away all day we've got some catching up to do, and I say, "Just nod if you can hear me." She does, so infinitesimally I believe at first that it's only the breeze of the bedroom door opened wider, and my dad standing there. The stare I give him silences whatever he's intended to say. He nods and backs slowly away into the bluish silhouette of himself, where two TV trays are stationed side by side. He turns and sits behind the one minus the glass of milk. I wonder if my mom can see him, all alone out there, lifting his sandwich with both hands. Someday soon, as he's so often pointed out, decades will have vanished, and I'm positive I'll still remember my parents like this, always growing more and more distant in the separate rooms of their silence.

"Archie . . ." my mom whispers, and a whole lifetime passes between those two syllables. It's the first fully formed word to escape her lips in days, and it's strange, but I see it somersaulting toward me. I'm five again, that sudden tumbling motion reversing itself, and we're outside in the backyard. Just the two of us, the leaves floating down in dense vibrant colors onto the lawn no matter which way we lean or sway. What's that word she used? Ochre? Mauve? Whatever, she's about to begin raking. I've got a rake too, a miniature red one, and a Radio Flyer wagon I've been pulling, and a scarf the wind keeps lifting across my face. There's a cardinal at the birdbath, which my mom has not ten minutes ago rinsed out and filled fresh with the hose. Her beret is the exact same red as that bird's brightest wing feathers.

We've already been to the farmers' market. And that sound a little bit ago? Just the car's trunk slamming shut. I helped carry the pumpkins and gourds to the back porch, and I'll bet she's kissed me a hundred times already, which compared to some days isn't even all that many. It's crystal clear to me, even at this age, that that's how you make another person love you. I wonder why my dad doesn't do it more often, to me *and* to my mom.

She calls the yard raking a roundup. I like it best when the piles fatten and get high enough for us to fall backwards, arms outstretched under the flat early-afternoon light, and how our bodies go limp inside those deep leafy indentations. My mom can't stop watching me, nor me her, but of course we can't linger because it's no longer 1965. It's 1973 and back here in her bedroom the odd angle of her knees under the sheet is enough to make me almost weep that past away. Call it up and let it go, and, as my dad always says about imminent death, try and make the best of an unhappy ending.

Her eyes have already glazed over again and all I can think is that a son or daughter should have to live much longer than this to outlive their mom. What I mean is that there's got to be a puzzle on the kitchen table we've yet to complete. Remember? And the chances are still good—aren't they—that the next piece I lift will fit into the continuous blue pattern of the sky? Or is it another fragment of ocean, as my mom thinks it is, guiding my hand just left of the lighthouse? The puzzle-box picture is tilted up because this one's really hard, my mom says, so difficult in fact that when we finally finish we're going to get it framed behind glass for my bedroom wall. It's still hanging there, a puzzle I could take apart and scramble and reassemble now in all of about fifteen minutes. I could do it blindfolded. The way I've so often done it in dreams.

"Mom?" I say, but she does not look away from my dad whose face is momentarily haloed by the TV light—I hear some man say "moons" and "rings" and "Saturn." And leaning forward from the couch my dad quick signals me in. He gives me that emphatic hey, don't-miss-this look, as if some physicist has just calculated a math equation complex enough to unlock another unknowable secret about the universe. Evidence to the contrary is that I don't care, which is why I shake my head no. I'm going to sit tight and listen instead to the slow orbit of my mom's slow breathing. If I could I'd subtract days from my life and give them to her. Not more sick days—happy, healthy ones so she could get out of bed, and dress herself, and walk without any pain to the stove to brew a cup of tea. A ritual she always performed on cold, late-fall days like this one.

My dad hasn't said yet whether or not I have to go to school again tomorrow. Last Friday in biology class Mr. Hurley gathered us all around the lab table and demonstrated the proper technique for dissecting a frog. He identified by name all those tiny internal organs, which he carefully lifted out with silver tweezers and held up to the light. By the end of the hour his fingernails were stained black. Formaldehyde, he said, and smiled and made clear come Monday morning we would work quietly and alone on our own amphibian dissections, observing closely and taking careful notes and making what he termed astute and salient observations. He passed out sheets of ditto paper with smeared numbered purple lines—twenty of them—and a line on top for our names, and he eyeballed each and every one of us as he sometimes does through those thick rimless lenses he wears. He said that he was little amused by the nicknaming of the frogs and he pointed at the lifeless layers of them floating in that murky see-through plastic bucket on the floor. "Take your pick," he said, while making clear they were all the same, prune-skinned and chemically pickled and all identically dead. "So get over the squeamishness, girls," he said to all of us. "Because I expect you to get right in there and poke around and help medical science discover how we can someday—each and every last one of us— grow old and smart and beautiful. This," he said, "believe it or not, might be that initial step."

I'm not that vocal in the class—not unless called on—and here at home it's hard to tell from one minute to the next if I'm even on speaking terms with my dad. He's talked *at* me but I haven't responded, which I've learned is sometimes both the first and last line of defense in a family like ours. Look how my mom's been reduced to living inside a single word: "Archie," and that word spoken just once all day, as if repeating it or any other would be way too much for anyone to bear.

My dad has pretty much worn my name out already, and now he's resorted to hand gestures, cupping the colored TV light as he calls and calls me out to him—three, four, five times in a row. It's not that my mom is holding me back. She's deep asleep again, floating off somewhere on her own. It's more that my dad has changed the station to some cheap game show where the audience is clapping so loudly that the applause has already lifted him from the couch. He's up, he's got that answer too, and the next and the next. He's on a roll and he wants me out there, witness to how he'd fare if he were only one of the chosen. Just your average Midwestern funeral-director contestant with a son and a wife, and a chance at last—one chance, that's all he asks, for half an hour—to be recognized as somebody smart and wise and worth our undivided attention.

"And your point?" my dad said, but I didn't have one I could put into words. Just this ever-expanding aversion to what he'd done over the years to my mom, and vice versa, and what he intended to do now that she was back from the hospital, pronounced dead on arrival—9:07 A.M. Millicent Burns Angel. And already she'd been delivered downstairs.

He hadn't bothered to pick me up from school, or to be waiting for me in the driveway with the news when I stepped off the bus. He wasn't even upstairs, and all I saw when I entered my mom's bedroom was the empty bed already stripped bare to the mattress, and the thermostat set back at sixty-five. No note on the kitchen table, the breakfast dishes still in the sink.

For over an hour I couldn't think straight or catch my breath, and when he still hadn't appeared by dusk I pressed the intercom button. "Dad," I said, "are you down there?" He didn't answer. "Where's Mom?" I said. "Where is she?" and with those questions my legs wobbled so badly I had to sit down on the floor, and that's when I heard him staggering up the stairway, so slow and heavy-footed that for a split second I imagined him carrying a coffin on his back. Hunchbacked, he slowly walked up close to me as if, after all this time, he was visibly crippled by grief. From the inside out, I thought, in a way I'd never seen him before. All silent and swollen-faced like he'd been stung by a swarm of bees, though of course it was way too cold for them to sting or even fly this late in the year.

My teeth almost chattered I was trying so hard not to cry. I hoped he'd say something, but he didn't. He just hovered and stared until his eyes turned even redder, and that's when he turned and left to go lie down on the couch. I got up then and steadied myself. And next thing I knew I'd unfolded the extra blanket at the foot of my bed, and when I made my way back into the living room to cover him I could tell he'd already fallen asleep. You'd think he might at least have taken off his shoes, or that unasked maybe I would have for him, as I used to some evenings for my mom if she was too fatigued. She said whenever I did she knew she'd dream about dancing barefoot across long white beaches in Spain and Portugal, where she hadn't yet visited, but where the purple fires of the sky showered down all around her like nightfall itself. No, never like rain, she said, but that's what I heard hardening into sleet and plinking on the roof. My dad's breathing was pained and audible, and the wind had picked up, and standing in this semidarkness, every separate overlapping sound coalesced into the sound of slow, slow seconds passing.

My dad was on his back, the luminescent green dial of his wristwatch like a single lidless eye ticking just inches above the worn-out carpet. "A time to let go," he'd say. "To sail on. A time for your mother to come closer to God."

Although exhausted by all the secret vows I'd made and broken and remade over the past few months, I nonetheless promised myself this: If my dad forced me to attend the wake, I'd refuse to kneel and look into that casket. And I wouldn't utter a single word to him or to anyone else. Were the preparations, as he always called them, already complete? And I wondered, did she exit this world smiling as I'd seen her smile so briefly just last night when I leaned down and kissed her? Or is the final expression always one of fear? Something every mortician learns early on to manipulate with needle and thread and lip glue? Had he finally cried himself out down there? And even if he didn't mean to, look how he left the lamp on in her bedroom, the only light burning in the house.

Nobody escorts the sleepwalker, not if you're an only child in a large house where your dad's exhaustion over time has silenced even those dream moans you know him by most nights when you wake. But you're not awake now. You're floating bodiless down the dark hallways, following those invisible arrows that lead you without a single misstep around every sharp-edged corner, down every steep staircase, sometimes even into the tiled vestibules and closets and out onto the porches flooded with moonlight impossible to see by. If you ever even imagined this route you'd taken blind so many times you'd be startled, perhaps even terrified. And if someone were there—your mom, let's say—who understood exactly what to do, she'd lead you back through the catacombs to your bed without a faltering word of caution or panic. And tuck you in, and leave immediately, leaving you alone to listen to every lost and lonely inconsolable heartbeat the sleepwalker shares with nobody but himself.

The sleepwalker might—though only in theory, because there is not one nearby—climb the water tower that looms above the town with its name and white numbers. Population unknown, which bears remembering, given how those enormous numerals tend to glisten, like the afterglow of glaciers you've seen in *National Geographic*, how they ignite the predawn fields and meadows below with silver. The danger, of course, is that the sleepwalker will, in sudden full consciousness, discover himself in the very place he's successfully avoided his entire waking life. On the icy bridge railing on the edge of yet another interminable winter, or at the mouth of that dry well's deafening echo shouting back *his* name and not that of the odd little kid who disappeared one night almost a decade ago on Christmas Eve.

And alone down here in the viewing parlor I do snap awake, my knees pressed deep into the kneeler pad, hands folded, not around a rosary, but around a matchbook. So it's probably me who lit these four white votive candles. A fresh sulfur smell hangs in the air, stronger than the scent of warm wax or flowers, the flames still coalescing into perfect liquid spires. My school clothes, I remember, when I went to bed, were discarded in a heap on the floor. But I'm fully dressed again, and my mom is too, in a new blue dress with a flat bridal-white collar. Her hair's not thick but thicker, and instead of a rosary she's holding a book with a ribbon bookmark sticking out. *The Collected Emily Dickinson.* I almost reach in and open it to that page. "Go Not Too Near a House of Rose" is one she'd memorized and said aloud each April like a rite of spring. Maybe it's that one my dad has chosen.

There's a wedding ring back on her finger, and even though I know *she* did not slip it back on at the very end, I'm glad my dad has taken this liberty. Not that the end justifies the means, as he's sometimes prone to lecture, but because maybe he did all along really think of himself as married.

In the same way that I've always thought of myself as a son, even while my mom raged long-distance over the phone for years to me about the accelerating fall of man. And refused steadfastly to come home to us from Wisconsin, though in her absence it was clear we would never entirely be ourselves again.

I did not sleepwalk until the very night she left, and back then I understood exactly nothing about the complex diffusions of blood, how in theory the arteries suddenly crisscross in ways so confusing that the heart literally aches. I read all this a few years later in a book about sudden loss and trauma that I checked out of the public library, and showed it to my dad who said any writer who thought like that should have his head examined. I bet my mom would have understood. I bet she wouldn't have called the guy a quack, and might even have asked if anyone was still awake and listening to the heart's unstoppable sadness pounding away.

"Only me," I whisper. "Only me," and the admission that I'm here is enough to start those candle flames wavering. It's enough to make even me believe that the weight of my dad's passion must have *always* been real and lasting, and this—at least in his mind— is his final act of intimacy. How could it be otherwise? My mom—she looks so peaceful for once, so perfectly content. That blue dress and my dad's fingers smoothing it out, adjusting the collar in the hours before I got home and eventually fell into dreamless sleep, and later sleepwalked down here to be alone with her. Before the scheduled wake and burial. And for sure before I could ever have imagined what he could possibly give to her in her dying. Nothing she said she wanted. Nothing, I believe now, but exactly this.

FIFTEEN

The Northern Lights

"The prognosis? Well," Buck said, "given that it's both good and not so fucking good, let me break it down for you." Which he then did, explaining that "What we got here's a 210,000-mile death-delivery vehicle in dire need of a new timing belt, new brake shoes, a valve job, and this radiator dissolving to rust has all but swallowed the cyanide capsule."

When I asked if he could nonetheless salvage the hearse he said, "Was Warren G. Harding president of these United States? Do fish piss in the river? Damn straight I can fix it." But it would hurt a whole lot less if repairs were made for the county fair's Demo Derby 2000, what he referred to as a very American institution. "It'll get bashed to shit," he said. "Side to side and nose to bunghole but a second life's a second life, and with a frame like a tank you don't play tap and touch out there. You smash-ass for broke and my best estimate says *you* get behind that wheel we don't survive the first frigging heat." But chain the motor down and weld the driver's-side door shut and strap old Buckmaster Andretti into the cockpit and all who enter this kingdom of mud and rubber and sheared axles—"All ye half-baked screwed-blue sandbagging yahoo retreads and buddy bangers and hide-and-seekers—be-fucking-ware."

The winner's purse is a sweet three grand and a fifty-fifty split, as Buck made clear for my benefit and mine alone. "Ain't banker's wages but it ain't bad business neither." Not with the Kalkaska and Manton derbies just a zip code away, and a full week to make alterations for that inaugural competition in Traverse City. He said take it national, there's literally thousands of derbies, and "What we got here's a rig with balls bigger than a '67 Chrysler Imperial," which he admits is hung like a goddamn galloping bull elephant. "Short of that," he said and winked, "we'll be trophy-fucking the winner's circle like a couple of destruction whores banging our way straight to the Midwest Invitational." He means a high-stakes eight-state roundup held once a year for top-ten local fair finishers. Somewhere in Badger land, he says, in Kenosha or Ladysmith—he can't recall exactly, but that's our intended destination, so what say we get this show off the hard-top and onto the crash track.

We even batted around half a dozen or so names—Big Road and Bouncer and Boot Hill and Kiss This—but settled finally on Gravedigger. Buck's got in mind to weld a white cross on the roof, and, in accordance with our bury-the-competition theme, doctor the rear door with a stenciled skull and cross bones superimposed on a mausoleum. "Bad taste?" he said. "What the goddamn hell's that got to do with anything?"

As to the combat alterations: Bias plies and idle ups and flip the manifolds and run the exhaust straight through the hood and maybe weld the spider gears to insure tire traction even after blowouts. Radius the wheel wells and cut off and sharpen the bumper ends and *Mad Max* whatever falls within the rules because as the flier makes clear, "We wrote the book, we know all the tricks, and, in over 25 years, have seen some real cuties. And we will catch you and shut you down. So play the game the right way and you will have no trouble. You don't and you *will* be disqualified."

I mostly listened and nodded until it came time to shake hands and then I said to Buck, "You sponsor me, I drive, win or lose, the hearse is yours free and clear and already battle tested. That's the package."

At first he said nothing. Just stood there expanding his barrel-stave chest as if to huff and puff and blow me right past the gas pumps and clear out of the station.

"What'll it be?" I asked, which prompted an approximate thirty-second first-round rough-draft version of the Muhammad Ali shuffle, his black hightops kicking up thick ground clouds of dust. Then clench-fisted he ducked and juked left and back again, all the while throwing a series of rapid short-arm jabs, followed by a series of right crosses, intentional low blows, a violent non-stop arsenal of anger-management shadow punches before finally punching himself out.

"You done?" I said, once the dust settled. Sucking for air he shook his head no, he damn well wasn't. But he did give it up, as he said after another couple of catch-his-breath minutes—and as if through the fairground's loudspeaker—for "Archie, the hard-bargain-driving hard-on derringer-dick Angel running out of Honor where—apparent even among fishermen and thieves—there is none anymore, not a piss pot's worth of honor left in our enlarged third-string testicle of a township or in any other god-forsaken hellhole on this degenerate planet as far as I can tell."

"Yes or no?" I said, and standing there behind the station where he'd been busting loose truck tires from their rims, he handed me one of the two Swisher Sweets he slid from his shirt pocket. "Got a light?" he said, and I torched both cigar tips with my Zippo while Buck just smirked and nodded and sucked on the unclipped cigar end as if attempting to extract all the tobacco and chew it up and spit the juicy black gob at my boot toes. "Yeah, deal," he said. "And a goddamn exceptional one at that," and he grabbed his sledgehammer—his tool of choice—and with a series of compact uppercut swings sent all four chrome door handles flying skyward. Followed by the Caddy's hood ornament, and the wheel covers and on and on like that.

I did not shudder with a nostalgic last-second change of heart as I figured I might. Instead I pulled a quick 180 and stepped a few yards away and dialed up Rodney on my new cell phone. It wasn't quite dinnertime, and he said he was stir-crazy bored and

just kind of sitting idly on the backside of the garage roof, hoping
I'd call. Wishing and wishing it. He said that's how come he got
it on the very first ring.

I remembered how the two of us used to sit up there together.
Not a tree fort, though we surely would have built one if not for
the neighborhood ordinance strictly enforced against them. So a
ladder it was, and a secret spot was a secret spot, and side by side
we'd lock our heels in the heavy wooden rain gutter, and lie back,
and talk, sometimes well past dusk, watching for the moon and
that first faint glitter of stars. The top I thought I could make spin
sideways on the steep slant of the green asphalt shingles remains
mysteriously lost in the downspout, regardless of the number of
times we snaked the garden hose down and opened the spigot
full-bore. Rodney claims he continues to check after every heavy
rain, but so far nothing but dead leaves and the cat's-eye marbles
he sometimes sends rattling through.

"Now you be careful," I said. "I'm not crazy about you being
up there alone."

"Dad, you don't have to shout, you know. I can hear you good
as if you were right here next to me. Just talk regular." After an
audible pause he said in his sometimes supervisory tone, "Jimmy
McFarland—remember he used to live down the street? Now
he's from San Diego by the ocean and he's got tonsillitis and can't
hardly even say anything above a whisper. Doesn't matter though,
we call each other just the same. Listen," he said, and his every
steady inhale and exhale sounded like the slow, close-up lapping
of waves. I said nothing until he asked, "What's all that noise?"
and I explained to him my newfound passion for hearse wrecking.
And how Buck in less than four or five frenzied minutes had dis-
mantled all of its luxury trim and glitter, and totaled its street and
cemetery life forever and ever amen.

"So like you're taking it for a final spin you mean?" and I
thought, yeah, more or less I guess I am. And once he caught on
to what I was telling him he said, "Wow, Dad," and then he got
the giggles so bad I worried he *would* roll off the roof and onto the
lawn.

"But keep it under your hat," I reminded him, "because what

your mom doesn't know goes a long way toward keeping the peace." And then all serious-like Rodney said no, he *didn't* think my brain was back in the box, a Z phrase for habitual low-minded adult folly. Maybe and maybe not, though Rodney's reverse appeal suddenly made the derby seem like an even better idea, a sly and brilliant brainstorm in the extreme that just might fly. First a hot air balloon ride, he said, and now this, and he's thinking he should just stay up north more because ever since Rhea arrived and fun stuff gets planned he's counting the days again. Me too, I told him, every single solitary minute of.

Rhea tends some days to speak in code. "Gas and Delius," for example. Out of context it sounds refined enough, though at least a touch malodorous. Or even worse, homicidal. But not all that incongruous or menacing when she explained how, at the clinic this morning, they calmed the eye-injured Persian llama with megadoses of classical music before administering anesthesia. "Pre-slumbered her with symphonic song," Rhea said. Which is why she borrowed the CD overnight, and took out my Nancy Griffith and played "Upon the Cuckoo's Arrival in Spring" instead.

I poured us each a glass of Bonterra, a Mendocino County chardonnay for which I'd splurged, along with some fancy water crackers and lox and half a pound of Gorgonzola. Foie gras. Whitefish pâté. About a buck-fifty for each pedigree combination sip and bite—give or take. Plus I'd sliced up a fresh garden watermelon into lightly salted star shapes, which I chilled just short of freezing. A major Deadstream feast celebration for Rhea who's been working ten-hour shifts all week, but who got off far less on the fancy hors d'oeuvres and uptown vino blanco than on making the rim of her long-stemmed wine glass hum with circular ear-piercing monotony.

Her discontent had nothing whatsoever to do with me driving in the derby. She's fine with that, minimal alarm as she put it, even though over dinner she read aloud from the setup tips and checklist and concluded that there could indeed occur great bodily harm. Quote: "Mount bars, chains or wire where windshield used to be. Our preference? Wire. Run about 4 braided strands through and then twist it nice and tight. Why? If hood comes loose, it won't fly in and cut off your head. Decapitations are not flukes."

I listened closely, making every effort to blot out that headless-driver image, but I could not help but picture my torso strapped in behind the steering wheel and the hearse still in reverse motion, still maneuvering to make another fatal hit. I quick corked what little was left in the bottle, and Rhea, in need of an after-dinner power nap, finally switched the CD player off repeat and crashed on the couch. Without pause I turned down the volume and picked up reading exactly where she'd left off.

Quote: "Remove sun visors. Why? Just another thing that may come loose and poke out your eye." Showstoppers, as my dad used to say about other things, and as Buck concurred just yesterday after cutting a round twenty-four-inch hole in the hood. "Why? Easier to put out the fire." And if the gas tank happens to rupture and gas splashes on the driver . . . well, the volunteer fire posse can be slow reacting and *no* diehard survivalist no matter how adept at outwitting disaster is invincible to chemical flame, now is he? Or then again, as Buck offered one final time as a final bail option, we could simply shitcan the entire enterprise. Just string the hearse with flower wreaths and loose hanging ropes of laurel and slow-tow it in among his growing fleet of field junkers while I stand off in the weeds playing taps on his kazoo. Right you are, he said, just one more metal hutch for the wild bunnies and the mice to nest up in and fuck.

"Sure took you long enough to get one," Z said just the day before yesterday, welcoming me into the modern world. Then she thanked me, though only in what I'd call minor thirds, when she explained how hectic the summer had been. And how Omar had seen the Seurat exhibit both in Chicago and in Paris, but had never seen the Upper Peninsula, the Lake Superior coastline, had never tasted its deep-water coastal breezes. Tasted? I thought. *Tasted* its coastal breezes? And then I thought, Jesus, wasn't it sufficient for me to hear Omar's name mentioned without some verbal demonstration of how inspired love changes even the goddamn English language?

But I did not sound the charge. I stayed poised and cordial, my vital signs steady enough, and I even swallowed hard and recommended as a peace offering that they visit Picture Rock on the way up to Copper Country. Seurat it's not, I said, but the glyphs in the rock formations are well worth the viewing and no need for a museum card. Just enough natural daylight and some leisure time.

I'd already embarked on a quiet mission to take up less than my fair share of all Archie and Z conversations, present and future. To listen rather than speak—wired or wireless or face-to-face. Still, when she described their upcoming trip as a driving weekend I couldn't help but recall *our* car time together, which always waylays me first with jealousy and then head-on with loneliness and remorse. She's made clear that her affection for Omar is not pretend, and that I shouldn't pretend that either. She didn't say love but she did say serious, and I stopped just short of hanging up the phone and taking a long solitary walk through the dunes.

The visual images I dredge up after speaking with Z are the most hurtful. Sometimes, if I shut my eyes, she'll be there driving and I'll key immediately on how physical she appears just *sitting* in a car, fully clothed and staring straight ahead and maybe cruising to nowhere more exciting than Walgreens or the Citgo.

Rhea claims that if I can't forgive and let go of the past, if I can't get over it, she's out of here, and yes she'll close the door behind her. "Sort it out," she says. "Get clear of it. But don't do it for me, Archie. Do it for yourself."

What can I say? That cellular-call number one or two to Z, or her return calls to me, weren't overly painful conversations? That the words scraping right tight to the hardpan had neither immediate nor residual effect? Well, they did. But did not—and this must count for something—provoke a single verbal outburst. Not even with her insistent use of the plural pronoun, though clearly it did not and probably never will again include me.

And now the reconfigured "we" of Z and Omar. And no, the Cherry Hut did not sound like a place where they might like to dine, but as it was the "good-eats" destination of my choosing, they'd be happy to drop Rodney there on their way through late Friday afternoon. Just stretch their legs and be on their way.

"Sounds like a plan," I said, and it does save me the long round-trip to the Pig in the Willys. And I figure just relaxing around the cabin might help ease the pre-collision jitters. Rhea's amended version? The pre-Z jitters, because "That's what you mean, don't you?" She quietly points out my reaction's always that same unhealthy muddle of emotions, and I don't blame her for being doubtful.

Just this week she offered to pay rent and split the cost of food and utilities, or just pack up and leave, if that's where this has all been leading anyway.

It's late and she's sound asleep, curled up in the bed with Copperfield. All the music is off and Rodney arrives tomorrow. Not fifteen minutes ago I was half-seriously contemplating whether or not to try and pop all of Omar's knuckles the first time I'm forced to shake his hand. Right, the pleasure's all mine. But that thought passed as the crickets turned silent in the sudden and brilliant shower of silver light. Northern lights, the summer's first, and it's those shotgun shells filled with my dad's ashes that have also filled my mind. I'm sitting alone again out on the porch. The footpath to the Platte appears calcified, bone white, and the river adrift in a kind of late-summer snowlight, the temperature dropping lower than it's been since early May.

I'm reminded that maybe this is the night. I've cleaned out the hearse of course, so the shotgun is in the closet now, inside that same garment bag that still protects my dad's funeral garb from moths. In the past tense: his cabin, his gun, his hearse and his suit, his shoes, his son and grandson. His bedroom, which in due course became mine, and mine Rodney's, and how short-lived all of it, my dad said more and more often toward the end, as if prepping me to endorse that same fatalistic death anthem.

His wheelchair, his troubled deep silences, his surrender to the oxygen and the nitroglycerin pills and finally, and perhaps even with unspoken gratitude, the nursing home. His funeral, though it's my call on exactly what night to wade out and press the wooden gun stock to my cheek and aim for highest range and scatter what remains of him heavenward. No slow quiet boat ride up into Loon Lake or downriver into Lake Michigan, routes I'd much prefer to take into the afterworld. But for him no slow and cautious overturning of the urn.

Rhea claims it's possible to astral project right from wrong. Fine, but how about past from present? That's what I've been wondering, and if it's really true that the very first time my dad held my hand he also held my son's. I have not yet asked Rodney if he wants to wade out into the river with me at midnight while I sight up the twin barrels and blast, and blast away. The truth is I'm not at all positive that I can pull the trigger. His request, but my neck craned back. My solemn promise to him in his slow dying, and my constant worry that such a loud and violent send-off will remind me of the crazy ways we acquiesce and, in so doing, separate ourselves further and further from love.

"New memory implants." That's the phrase Rhea uses, and whenever she French kisses me to drive home that concept of pleasure and good fortune in the present moment she's pretty convincing. Maybe I should wake her so she can witness how the light whirls and spins and gathers itself into trillions and trillions of incandescent silver threads, the purest pure glittering particles of liquid silk spooling and spooling up and down from every-where out of the darkness, like angel hair. This is just the start. In a month they'll be even brighter, more densely evanescent, although there's something magic and more astonishing about the season's first display, something unforgettable, an almost holy illumination.

Or maybe I should get out my dad's Bible—there's sure light enough to read by tonight—and find an appropriate passage or two for his eulogy. Maybe one that Rodney could memorize and deliver during that pause between each ejected shell and that next explosion of muzzle-fire.

These come immediately to mind: "The last shall be first." "In the end is my beginning." Or vice versa, as my dad was wont to challenge. Either way, it all goes, doesn't it? His circulation, his hospital morphine, his cc's, his partial left lung, his voice, his heart, his wife years before him, *his* dad who picked me up before I was named and spoke it and, although I barely remember him, that's who I was from that moment on, Archibald Angel. I am their flesh and blood, the embodiment of our enormous differences and our love, as well as our inability to admit it, and therefore our inevitable separation.

Now the tops of the trees are covered with starlight. The garden glows. My tomatoes, Rodney's pumpkins, my scarecrow canted forward and still wearing my dad's faded flannel shirt, the sleeves rolled back on those outstretched wooden arms. There are other shirts of his folded in a wire basket in my closet. And sweaters too, and a red and black fleece-lined woolen vest I used to put on and trudge to the outhouse in all winter before the bathroom plumbing was installed.

My shovel, my boots, my tracks in the snow, and my dog Buster whose humped grave is also, on this night, shrouded silver, almost platinum glazed. Rodney has never stayed awake late enough to see such cosmic display. He wants to, he says, now that he's older, but I haven't yet mentioned the northern lights to him in a funeral context, and it's possible that I won't. After all, my dad never mentioned anything about Rodney being present. And I sure haven't run any of this by Z or Rhea.

Maybe I will, but for now I think I'll just stare out into the vaporous godlight, the way I did that very first time my dad gently awakened me and ushered me onto the porch, his hand firm and fatherly on my shoulder.

We stopped and stood silent, and the only word he uttered was "Mercy," and when I looked up into his face I could see he was holding back tears, his cheeks already shiny with the effort. That's when I took his hand. I don't remember who squeezed first—him, I think—*his* squeeze, although it wasn't until I squeezed back that he said, "This . . . only this." He said it haltingly as if to be sure there was nothing else—just the two of us, me and him—covered in light as thin and perfect as heavenly mist.

SIXTEEN

Demolition Derby

This is not entirely a dream, but rather an actual childhood occurrence. An Angel family outing that got dreamed later, and then recurred often, and after thirty-six or thirty-seven years they've merged—dream and memory, memory and dream—switchbacks that render their separateness indistinguishable. Like light from the honey, let's say. Like the onlooker from the view, the shooting from the star. The lesson learned and forgotten and, in both deep and restless slumber, learned all over again.

It's my mom who's sitting next to me. The attendant, his wallet chained to his belt loops, hasn't yet engaged the power switch lever so the bumper cars are still parked all helter-skelter. From far above they might resemble boats at their moorings, but they are not boats, no matter what corridor of recollection or sleep I walk down. A multicar accident—it could be that—or a bottleneck of tanks or even an open-topped cage of giant crustaceans or immobilized land tortoises. Grand pianos perhaps. And for sure I wouldn't rule out the possibility that they exist, and always have, as scattered immovable hunks of some charred, deep-space asteroid. But most of the time they are what they are—bumper cars—and standing in the ticket line everyone always appears sane and patient and just respectful enough to go pretty much unnoticed.

My mom's the only adult out here, the only female, woman or

girl. She's wearing high heels and a re-hemmed below-the-knee-length dress the color and sheen of ripe red garden peppers and lipstick to match because, as my dad has said to me in private, she is not lately in full command of her senses. They come and go and *her* understanding is that we were headed not to Riverside Amusement Park but rather to the planetarium in East Lansing. "But didn't you say a little bit ago . . . ?" and my dad firing back at her "What? What didn't I say a little bit ago or whenever I didn't say it?" and my mom then turning around to me in the back seat of the Rambler, and gone instantly was every trace of happiness from her face. We'd hardly gotten going and already the day was all messed up, already on a collision course with tension so sharp and silent I can still feel it spreading across the inside of my forehead.

We're surrounded, trapped in the middle of the pack, and she's not even gripping the steering wheel. She's staring up instead in a planetary manner, into the illusion of some greater space of rising constellations, but all other eyes—all of them—are suddenly dark and bead-hard and trained entirely on us. It's blood they see. It's weakness they're after and the fifty million light years—the distance in time and space to the farthest and oldest stars—means nothing to them. It's Saturday afternoon and they are on their own and the object of this particular amusement ride is vehemence and fury.

My dad's decided to sit this one out, even though he's the one who led us here and it's going to be our very first ride of the day. He's leaning on the railing, his forearms crossed, his eyelids sweaty. The half-smoked cigarette smoldering between his fingers is almost upright, his other hand clinched loosely into a fist. He's wearing a fedora, neatly creased and tipped back on his forehead, and a tie but no coat. It's early summer and warm and so his white shirt is short-sleeved, the collar starched stiff, and he's nodding as I glance back, the floor gritty and dark as graphite. Like always he *meant* to bring his camera. "My mistake," he said. "My oversight. Next time for sure. Scout's honor."

The whole place is kind of dank and sour-smelling like pee and nobody's smiling so this might not make for the greatest picture anyway. But I bet the carousel would. I can hear the distant music from over there, which is where I'd much rather be, the kids all younger, quieter—more my age and size. Everybody going up and down in slow motion, the chrome poles shiny as mirrors and the ponies tame and ornately painted with bright enamel colors, their tails plumed and their muzzles bridled silver and gold, their manes wavy and thick and beautiful. I like how they all follow in the same circle, in their same calm, unhurried direction. No mad clatter of hooves—just the calliope and the ponies floating as if through a peaceful dream. My mom said to me when we first passed them that it's not easy to imagine them indifferent to love.

Unlike these bumper cars, which are flat solid colors, black and gray and red, and heavy like ancient hurled boulders. It's only because I'm accompanied by my mom—because I'm in her care—that the attendant has allowed me to ride on them. I'm not sure why she's agreed, except that maybe she doesn't quite grasp the concept yet. Maybe she thinks they're miniature airships and this attendant will somehow release the ballast and we'll rise and float through a make-believe three-dimensional galaxy into another universe. I know my mom's got some folded star charts in her handbag because I watched her put them there before we ever left the house.

Then again maybe she just feels duped and wants some immediate distance from my dad who's complained all week: "What in this world, pray tell, is she even thinking or talking about? How does anybody get so discombobulated, so completely turned around? It's absurd," he says, and whenever I ask, "What is?" he gets all over the way she exists in her head. "All that thinking alone doesn't constitute a living life," he says. "It's all make-believe." He says he wants her to be more practical-minded and show some interest in what he deems to be your normal, basic everyday fun things. But she doesn't grapple well with ordinary confusions, with surprises and circumstances like this. At such moments there's one and always only one version of the world—my dad's, and whatever else anyone, especially my mom, might think hardly counts. One truth. "One way," as he says, "tested and proven right over time." Whenever he gets like that my mom's unresisting, helpless.

Those older, bigger kids who deferred so we could go first have not broken in slow quiet tempo behind us out onto the floor. They've gotten a running start, their sneakers pealing a stampeding frequency so high it's impossible to dispel, in either the actual moment or the recurring dream, so I don't even bother to cover my ears anymore. It's clear, at least in backward-running time, that someone seeing you so easily seized by such a mild frenzy of noise will demean you in a forum such as this. They will not fan out. They will close quickly and confront you with their ugliness and sudden invasive bold fury, lisping "fairy" or "queerbait" or "you're dead." Fortified in numbers they will always press that advantage. They will single you out the instant the electrified blue sparks ignite and crack across the dark iron grid of the ceiling. I know— once again every heavy-nosed bumper car but ours has turned suddenly hyperkinetic, and there's that thick hovering magnetic stink I hate. It's so pungent it burns my nostrils and throat.

"Mom," I say, but her shoulders stay drooped, her hands folded tightly in her lap, and she doesn't even brace herself against the initial impact, which whiplashes us and knocks her glasses crooked on her nose. She doesn't even bother to straighten them, and the next time we're rear-ended they fly forward right off her face. Maybe she's playing possum, but when they refuse to leave us alone I shout, "Stop it. All of you, stop it, stop it, stop it," but they won't, not then or now or most likely not ever. My weak terror-pleas exist solely for the amusement of their growing up. They are in charge and the world for them exists without alternate focus, without beginning or end. It exists only at this moment and only for them.

I don't understand why my mom doesn't rise from her seat and warn them away with that stare she sometimes uses at home to silence my dad. Or why she doesn't at least press down on the pedal so we can make our way safely back to him. There's already a bruise forming on my left wrist and another on my bare knee and my mom appears pale and weak and aging in speeded-up time. Because I can't slow it down, and because I have no idea how to disentangle us from this relentless assault, I'm awfully close to tears.

It's no laughing matter but that's what they're doing, laughing and whooping and ramming us full-force from all sides, like we've been mistakenly confused with people these kids hate, or their parents hate and have forever, and the mere sight of us has sent their sons into fits of rage. They're screaming like spider monkeys and glaring with such unprovoked contempt that I guess my mom has no recourse but to close her eyes. Below us her shattered lenses reflect back like bits of starlight from the grimy black floor, the frames mangled.

The jolt of every vocal insult—words and grunts and whistles—directed at us from everywhere at once makes me dizzy. I'm shaking my mom's arm. "Wake up," I say, because this is all a dream—it's just a bad dream but the attendant's voice over the intercom keeps instructing her to press down on the pedal, ma'am, and turn the wheel. These are simple commands and this—clear to me now in memory but not then--is why my dad has sent my mom and me out here in the first place, alone. This is a test. He is the competent parent. He is the one who is coming toward us, one arm raised, his brow furrowed as he keeps shouting above the din, "Do *not* get out, do not leave the car. Stay right where you are." He and he alone is positioned to be the victor, he—my dad.

But by the time he gets to us the madness has abated, those boys already on their feet, already on the lookout for whoever might tell them to put out those smokes, though banded together they are carefree and cocky now and punching each other's biceps. They are twelve, maybe thirteen, and as wiry and sinewy as whippets. The attendant keeps chortling and shaking his head. We're the misfits here, the outsiders. Even the English sparrows are undaunted. The electrical current is off again and so they're flying down from the trusses and through the squares of iron grid and out under the overhang into the bright light of the midway. I can hear the baby birds chirp-chirping right above me in their nests.

My mom sits stock-still. In the aftermath of what has just happened, in this world absent of poets, she is equal parts fear and humiliation and quiet rage. I can feel it all, and unlike me she does not take my dad's hand when he offers it. There are white frills on the collar of her red dress, and a gathered front, impairments of both reason and suitable public attire, as my dad says about almost everything she wears anymore. That sweater with the grinning monkey on the front, and the black and white accordion fanned open, shoulder to shoulder across the back? Where does she shop? Where does she find these grandmotherly castoffs? He asks me these questions, he says, so as not to shirk the duty of his fatherhood. He's a man of principle and decorum and sometimes her moonstruck version of the world needs tempering, needs proportion. If he is footsore from standing all day above the deceased, then my mom is the absence of gravity. If he is time-release—steady and consistent and solid over the long haul—then she is the frivolous moment stolen and lost. I don't yet understand all this, which he insists is precisely the point, but I keep missing it, every, every time, no matter the number of harsh lessons.

It could be that he waited until she dressed this morning and only then decided where we'd end up. A plan betokening—as he'd argue for years to come—an act of love. Love? Like in a kind of double helix or a trick of mirrors? Or is it always, as it seemed so clearly back then, an act of sabotage and cruelty? Does *he* even know? Might he ever? Look at his shoes—resoled and spit-shined. New laces. He picks his feet up when he walks. He picks me up. And it's only when he turns to leave without my mom that she climbs down unassisted from the car—that same unfocused stare on her face—and follows us.

"Brainy," that's another unfortunate and careless dad label used to describe my mom. "Dilettante," and later on, before scavenging through the final sad rubble of their lives both together and apart: "demented," "crazy," "out of reach" and "out of touch." Better that, I figure, better to exist in another dimension than to obsess—as he did leading up to the very end—on one's own forlorn, self-regarding disappointments. Which, no doubt, I've been in danger of doing, too. So I'll take crazy anytime. I'll take loony and out of touch and, whenever possible, fun-loving. Not that my mom was *that*—not very often she wasn't—but why not add it to the mix? And if death doesn't love us for it then screw him too. Time-wise we're not in bad shape. Rhea doubts seriously that hope springs eternal, but she's in anyway, and Rodney's pumped, as he says, and since Z's cruising the UP with Omar, it's almost the wrecking hour down here.

Rhea and Rodney are sitting in the front row. No printed programs to roll up and shout encouragement through, but they've got my strongest pair of Bushnell binoculars, and I'm facing the grandstand, which is packed, and Buck's back in the pit area with his wrecker and welder and tools and emergency replacement parts. I'm buckled in and staring out the windowless windshield, reviewing—as best I can remember them—his final instructions for a final time. My palms and fingers are already white with rosin, and underneath my loose-fitting navy blue one-piece mechanics jumpsuit, my skin's all pins and needles. No STP or Quaker State or Fuji film patches. Just my name, Gravedigger, embroidered in bright yellow cursive above the pocket.

As Buck's made clear, you don't brake through a glass wall, do you? No, you hit it full speed ahead and in that way avoid the other hundred or so bad-choice variables that get you mud-stuck or fender-locked or trunk-humped right out of the competition. The meek may for all he knows inherit the earth, but this ain't the Good Book so don't go New Testament on him. Covet and lust and plunder-fuck for those are the commandments in this the hearse that Buck rebuilt.

It's everything he said it would be, and more, and when I first laid eyes on it I fell silent and almost called a halt to the whole shebang right then and there, the ludicrous enterprise of it all. But on closer examination—after eyeballing the competition and hoisting myself through the driver's-side window—I felt remarkably less squeamish and unjustly self-chastened. And ridiculous with a capital *R* turned immediately lowercase. In fact, I'm ready, the deep derangement of it all seeming oddly poetic, almost tranquil in that calm pre-twister kind of way. I don't know, blame it on the battle-design modifications of the demo cars and their names and the comic confusion of both theme and tone, the decidedly Keystone chaos of what's about to transpire. There's a grunge band going to play right here in the engorged mud pit following the derby. They call themselves Monophyle and the Amoebolites. Neither Rhea nor Rodney has ever heard of them, and neither have I.

The car to my immediate right is dubbed the Palomino, a well-ridden Buick Electra with a white hood and trunk, honey-colored fenders and a leather pommel fastened on top, a giant stirrup painted on both front doors. I'm still waiting for Rex Allen there to tighten a ten-gallon Stetson over the bald Teflon skull of his helmet and then grab for the reins.

There's Assassin II and Fireball and a Dodge Dart called Pisces, which can't have a whole lot of fight left in him. Just a half-decayed old moldy Joe of a milted-out salmon, flat black and fungal, the current of years having already peeled away its silver scales, the chromium incandescent glitter of its skin. Bean Blue OBI looks battle-tested and bruised and plenty durable, apparently no stranger to such events. I have no clue about the make, model or message, although when he first fired up it sounded like a detonation. The county fair queen and her entire court pressed their palms to their ears in sweet and cowering pageantry. They're wearing bright tight strapless gowns as shiny green and fluid as radiator coolant. Extending from the queen's right shoulder to her opposite hip is a wide white ribbon, the whole package accentuated by a crown of cherries.

I'm second from the end, and to the left of me in this line of eight demomobiles is the only woman entered in the derby. Even under the headgear she's a dead ringer for Mary Lou Retton. She's beaming that trademark ear-to-ear. At least until she glances over at me, the eternal footman with a smile of my own and a four-finger salute from which she turns immediately away. She's driving a '66 Imperial, what Buck referred to earlier as a highly evolved and cool-running organism.

I said, "Mary Lou Retton. America's favorite gymnast," and Buck said back, "No shit?" and when I said, "None," he said, "Perfect. First backflip she attempts you stick it to her full nuts and tenderloin. It's us. We're it. So haul your starstruck ass out there and get mean and pulverize whatever gets in your way. You are the Gravedigger and, lest we forget, your mission is to search and destroy, to eradicate all visible signs of any other automotive life. Now get out there and bruise and contuse and seize the goddamn day."

It's sunny, broken clouds scattered against the bright robin's-egg sky and, at least so far, no sign of the Blue Angels in tight fly-over formation. Not a drop of rain in the near forecast, but the bare ground is anything but dry. It has been hosed to limit both traction and speed and to keep the dust to a minimum and the spectacle something less than death-defying. Still, there's an ambulance and a fire truck parked side by side just beyond the demolition field. Which, by the way, is entirely earth-bermed, as if ready to be bulldozed forward for mass entombment immediately following the as-advertised pandemonium and carnage.

There's no hovering Goodyear blimp, no worldwide satellite TV coverage. But high up in the broadcast booth Irish Danny O'Shea, DJ for the golden oldies radio station out of T.C. commands us in deep baritone through the dual loudspeakers to "Start your engines, gentlemen," as if this were the Detroit Grand Prix.

Right before turning the key I pantomime a quick champagne toast to Rhea and Rodney who rise clapping with the rest of the crowd, the collective straight-pipe engine roar as deafening as the throat of a tuba. For a second I'm not even certain where I am anymore or who this flag-bearer squalling through the dirt and mud from behind us even is. He's wearing a Day-Glo orange vest and wielding with both hands a long baton above his head. He seems, until the instant he stops on top of the low scarp and turns back toward us, to be in full retreat with his white flag of surrender. But when he whips the baton tip down to the ground the cars are off like Pavlov's hounds chasing after the last known warm-blooded hare on the planet.

They're scattering every which way, forward and back, left and right. Everybody but me, that is, because my tires keep spinning in place. If the hearse were still speedometer-wired the needle would be buried. It's the double-dose rush of inexperience and adrenaline and general sensory overload that's anchored me right here under the great crusting shower of my own cascading dirt spumes. It's pouring down and I don't know if it's blind luck or what, but the instant I ease off the accelerator I'm ass-ended and launched clear of the deep double ruts and within seconds I'm banking like a bat out of hell around the harder-packed rim of the battlefield proper. My dad should see me now, assailed not by hothouse odors and the lingering deaths of some four thousand days during which *he* slow-chauffeured this hearse, but by a cadaverous fish, an astrological horse, an OBI, a second-generation assassin, a fireball, a pawnbroker, a Cyclops and a Wheaties-box gymnast. And his one and only grandson's cheering me on from the far field of the bleachers.

I've often hit twenty-five or thirty miles per hour down the better two-tracks to the rivers, and I'm goosing the hearse to at least that and no doubt doubled if impact is head-on with anyone closing fast from the opposite direction. Nobody is, so I've sighted in on Fireball who's backing out of the tidal mud, pearly gray-blue smoke already drifting up from under its hood. My reflex is to honk but of course there's no horn anymore, and that's hardly the point. No brakes either, and when I blindside him the car collapses like a ruptured water bag. It literally sags, settles, its wheels buckled inward.

Though I feel not unlike a crash dummy I'm not hurt and already I'm in reverse, the hearse in a slight serpentine swing that crushes Pawnbroker's left front fender. That same side tire's blown too and I pull forward and then I back up and slam him again and then again, and Mary Lou of the cute tumbling Olympic gold fanny scores a perfect ten with a full-powered rear-end maneuver that's just about separated pawn from its broker. We've got him sandwiched and before Mary Lou and I can gain tactical separation and squeeze him again he reaches out and breaks off his orange "I surrender" dowel. Each of us has one—required issue—and it dawns on me in the midst of this mayhem how my mom on those bumper cars had had at her disposal no such clear and easy way to announce her defeat. If it hadn't been for the ride-time expiring and my dad to the rescue I'm convinced she would have silently endured the untempered repetition of those cruel blow-by-blows all day and all night long.

It could be these are those identical kids grown paunchy and middle-aged, and if so this one's for you, Mom, and I brace myself as I sight in on Cyclops who's fishtailing right into my path. The traction's decent at this even-keeled speed and I can almost feel my dad in the stands. Not sitting with Rodney and Rhea, but off by himself, shaking his head in disbelief.

Nevertheless, the hit is perfect, the filed edge of the hearse's raised front bumper penetrating deep into that single painted blue eye, the radiator exploding in steam so thick and hot that I'm momentarily blinded. And then blindsided by OBI, and by what physics his battery finds its Diehard way onto the top of my hood is far beyond my comprehension. The battery is upside down, the acid seeping out.

I try reverse and forward and reverse again, back and forth like that, but nothing doing. I rock a little is all and then bog right down, tires spinning and spitting. I'm locked up somewhere, and I can't pull loose or move either of these two derby stiffs another inch. They're hanging on like death, and when I close my eyes and breathe in deeply and think, okay, what's next? what's the deal here? my dad's back behind the wheel. No big surprise. I figured at some point he would be. That's the way with the past—which it never quite is with its inevitable resurrecting.

I blink my eyes open and he's gone, *this* day alive with its din and mud and motorized madness. I shut them and it's quiet, the hearse freshly waxed and shiny black, and the engine's idle is so low again I can barely even hear it, a whisper is all, a slow and distant breathing. No cheering from anywhere anymore, no noise or motion, not even a breeze. We're parked on the road's edge, just the two of us on another of our drives, but I can't remember exactly where to this time. Somewhere out in the country. I know this because there's a mortar and fieldstone structure he keeps pointing to. It's mostly underground, the dandelions and weed shoots growing right out of the humped roof. A single door but no windows, like structures I've seen in the cemeteries, but my dad says no, it's a potato cellar. It's dark and cool inside. Dirt floor. It keeps the harvest from the sunlight and the rain, from rotting in the open expanse of those fields.

On these drives, on every last one of them, there's always something like this to anchor and help while away the evenings, to help bring another day without my mom to a close. He doesn't say that, of course. He points instead to the farmhouse already collapsed. The double chimneys are still standing, but I doubt for too much longer given the way they're tipped toward one another. It might be fun to traipse over there and investigate, but he'd sooner forfeit these father-son outings than assist in something as unforeseen as that. He enjoys the solemn, stationary comfort of the air-conditioned hearse, so we're always sitting at a distance from whatever is being acknowledged or observed. As I did thirty years later, the engine idling for maybe half an hour before I finally got out and walked alone up the long driveway to the crematorium and back. A different hearse and my dad in the passenger seat this time, already reduced to bone ash in a silver urn.

But there he is again in the stands, the incised lines of his forehead seeming to deepen, his dismayed eyes staring so close-up into mine that I can almost see the pupils dilate and expand. It's as if he's been shocked into silence, shunted and ridiculed, and laden with disappointment so final that all he can do now is shake his head. And who could blame him when, at day's end, we've ended up here like this.

Go ahead, I think, but he nods instead. Nods a few times, but it's not until he smiles at me that my chest begins to rise and fall— I can feel it—in perfect sync with his. "It's all right," he whispers. "It's all good," his gaze still fixed on me as I switch off the ignition, and break off the surrender stick.

I only hope that Rodney's not too disappointed. I've got no ship-to-shore to call him, but when I lean right and look over in that direction there he is. He's got the binoculars to his eyes and with his free hand he's waving to me because even in the anticlimax of the derby crashing on without me, this is a win-win and no way imaginable could I ever be better recompensed. His eyes on me at nine-power. In full magnification at fifty yards max I'm right there, close enough to kiss him, this kid I love so much that my every facial smile muscle has already begun to tighten and ache. So much so that I start laughing like a madman delirious amidst this landscape of smoking metal and seized engines and ruptured radiators and twisted frames and sheared-off valve stems, cracked and bleeding crankcases, all of it just spectacular enough for a story. I know I'll tell it, though probably without mention of my dad. But for sure this part about how an early middle-aged man trapped in a stripped-down, smashed-to-shit hearse could not stop from laughing and flashing a victory sign to his kid. And this from a serious potential front-runner eliminated halfway through the very first heat. I take off the splatter goggles Rhea borrowed for me from the clinic so I can wipe away the tears, as deliciously warm and heavy as wax. And only then do I pay attention to how the demolition plays out without me.

Like I really care that we're down to the last two crippled but willing survivors: Mary Lou versus the fish? My belly hurts but I can't stop the howls of laughter from bursting up from my diaphragm now that I've gotten started all over again. And why would I want to stop? It's been a long go since that feeling's come on so strong and I fully intend to abide its welcome for as long as I possibly can. And maybe walk the midway after awhile. Whatever Rodney and Rhea decide—it's entirely their call. Throw darts at oblong balloons, softballs at pyramided milk bottles made of cement. Ride on the Ferris wheel, I hope, at least once before we exit the fairgrounds. The three of us squeezed in together— Rodney in the middle with some cotton candy—and who knows what we'll be thinking or saying or even secretly praying for up there above the town? Or who, at that slow, forward musical descent, might point down at Buck's wrecker towing an embattled hearse out of the fairgrounds? "Where? No, I don't. Point again." And right then the white cross catching just enough of the dying light for each of us to see it.

SEVENTEEN

The River

We did not rise before dawn and hit the ground running, although I am currently the proud owner of a vintage International Scout. Forest green. A one-owner with every service and repair receipt bound in a folder, plus a warranty twelve years expired. Like adoption papers, Buck said, the kind of scrupulous documentation that testifies to its seventy-two thousand babied miles, to its being barely even broken in. Without a moment's inclination to mull or dicker I paid the full asking price, cash on the barrelhead. And why wouldn't I? No noticeable rust. Never plowed. Garaged every winter, the engine steam-cleaned once a year and, on all subzero nights, plugged into a heater coil. Front bumper wench, roof rack. Other than the absence of airbags, there's no downside that I can detect, and the transaction as far as a cry gets from breaking the bank.

Rhea and I rose well after the first choruses of bird songs and the multiple refills of strong black coffee out on the porch. After the thin plumes of mist had already evaporated from the river's surface. The Scout's parked just up from the river mouth, and we have maybe three or four more float miles before we get there and load the drift boat onto the trailer and drive home in time for a late dinner.

The pungent wild summer honeysuckle has turned odorless

and disappeared into the damp layers of sediment, of fetid sea-sonal musk, a kind of reverse blooming fragrance that I happen to like. But every smell and image lost to the grandeur of Rhea who, after breaking off in the tag alder branches on her backcast for the third time, jumps from the boat in her flip-flops and shorts. And this maneuver after not having dipped a toe or a hand all morning and well into the afternoon.

She's wending out waist-deep to where she finally stops mid-river on the packed bottom-sand. And shouts back that she likes how the grains tickle her ankles each time she takes a step. Another couple and she'll be over the shelf and over her head. Her ribbed-sweater bottom and elbows are soaked, the water temperature a good ten degrees below what it was only two weeks ago, and the river traditionally at this time of year not fishing terribly well. I wish I'd thought to stuff a towel and a change of clothes in a rucksack, although her sudden H$_2$O immersion wasn't part of anybody's plan, and I've never once in almost twenty years of river guiding capsized while on the Platte.

"That tea-colored water, that coppery line—see it? Right there's where it gets really deep," I say. "So be careful. Don't get any closer than what you already are."

She doesn't answer or acknowledge in any way, awaits no further instruction pointers or professional on-site evaluation. And I think, indeed: once the fishing rod is mistaken for the sword there is every reason to sheath it. Meaning the guide should never show up his client, and should never insist beyond the client's angling capabilities or willingness to listen and respond—that rule-of-thumb doctrine quadrupled for lovers and wives. So I anchor the boat right up against the bank and offer no additional tips, and let her re-rig on her own, tippet to leader, and the terrestrial of her choosing tied on with a surgeon's knot, and snipped. A Chernobyl ant pattern, although I'd earlier suggested a cricket, explained why that particular hunch, and demonstrated correct presentation, the mend, and the soft V wake of the drift. "Like this. See? And again like this with a nice light easy rhythm," a couple of false casts followed by the loop turned over just short of the opposite bank, and this time I can tell her fly has drifted right into the undercut. She's already blown a few tries on rising rainbows, but suddenly the hookup's clean, the line tight and straight to the trout's upper lip. It's nothing lake-run but when it boils I can see from its shoulders that it's real decent size, particularly for mid-day, head-thrashing and then powering out in a ten- or twelve-foot rip toward the logjam.

A pure method's practitioner she'll never be, so chalk it up to will and instinct that she's exerting exactly the right amount of torque, the rod tip held high and firm, wrist locked straight to elbow. No panic whatsoever, not even when the fish double-cart-wheels away and turns wide and moves slowly back upriver behind her in a way a fish this hot and this size rarely will. As soon as he figures what's what and lowers his nose into the downward current he'll be punching out on a novice like Rhea, good instincts or not.

Instead he moves into the holding water where he's hers if she doesn't press, if she simply takes her time and holds that tension. She does, and after another five minutes I offer to hop in too and stalk a quiet half circle behind the fish and net him for her but she's already backing up to the boat, into the shallows and still in complete control. There's a hemostat hanging from her lanyard, and kneeling she reels in and brings the fish to hand and extracts the barbless hook, a single quick twist and tug. Then she's cup-ping that played-out rainbow's white belly in both hands, her fingers splayed, rod handle tucked into the crook of her arm. It's in the instant that she rises and pivots slowly around that I'm wit-ness to the resplendent roseate gill plates and the full-length body stripe held toward me, and that's when I snap the picture.

"It's a keeper," I say, meaning the snapshot. But also the fish if she wants to, my feeling being that if it's not a catch-and-release stretch then the guide—this guide anyway—will from time to time gut and clean and cook up a trout right on the riverbank. Exactly, as fresh as fresh will ever get. Salt and lemon pepper. Wild chives. Some olive oil, a dapple of pickled ginger, all staples currently on board in the Coleman cooler. Plus a bottle of Good Harbor chardonnay we picked up on a leisurely drive up the peninsula last weekend. The grill is stored under my seat, but Rhea says no, she's landed her very first fish on a fly rod and wants only to let it go.

She's not squeamish, doesn't wince or hesitate to ask, "How's the best way to do this?"

"Hold and face him upriver," I say. "Firm but not so tight that he can't swim away on his own. Let go too soon and he's apt to go belly-up and not recover. That's what's key—*his* desire to go and only when he's good and ready. Only then can you be sure he won't drown, and who knows, maybe you'll get a crack at him another time. They do get smarter and more cautious, though, with every passing summer, a whole lot harder to fool. But that's when it gets really fun. That's when the IQ part of it comes into play." I tap my temple for emphasis and Rhea says, "Of course. An annual meeting of the minds."

"All I'm saying is that trophy fishing is more than a matter of luck. And that you've done great. You were fun to watch. You've got a real knack for this."

The water distorts the shape of her thighs, which are thin and pale and wavering slightly, and between them the pink gills of that rainbow open and close, and the tail-fan motion is already steadier, stronger. But still it takes another few minutes, and I can tell from the audible way Rhea's breathing that she's cold. In the day's sequence of stills, snapped or not, I know I'll remember her like this, down on both knees and working patiently to resuscitate a deep-girth Platte River trout, the waterline up to her breasts. It's clear to me already that this moment stands to survive as one of those pure indelible moments we only rarely own unaltered by either desire or time.

A gorgeous backyard rainbow, eighteen inches maybe, a farewell catch as it turns out, although I don't know this yet. After all, we're still linked, wet or dry, warm or cold, to everything the river gods have bestowed on us, and I've done my part by guiding us here.

"Some sight, isn't it?" I say. "All this? I could float it forever and never get bored. String out all the floats I've made on this river and I bet I've been halfway around the world without ever leaving home. Sounds nuts, I know, but get an eyeful in any direction and why go anywhere else?"

Upriver, the Angel trestle where we didn't stop earlier, but stared up as we passed silently beneath, emerging from its hard, sharp-edged dark abutment shadow and back into the sunlight, the river film tinted silver. And where I haven't come to sit and drink alone at night since Rhea arrived over two months ago. Around the next bend that clump of swamp oaks, the giant root mass grown out from the bank like a beaver lodge. Just last year I counted a group of fifteen deer feeding there on acorns in a sudden heavy snow. Perched above them on the twisted limbs at least twice that many crows, a flock as still and shiny black as obsidian, and their eyes in that low pre-winter light aglow with the color of pale amethyst. I drifted by not twenty-five yards away without a single bird or beast up and taking flight. All reasons, I suppose, to uncork this chilled bottle of local wine and pour to half-full these two long-stemmed glasses I had the forethought to pack.

"To you," I say. "To a great day," and we clink glasses, and with my free hand I take the rod and store it out of the way. Then I help her back into the boat, and as soon as I begin to disrobe she says, "Don't. Don't, Archie." She says, "Because even if you do I won't wear it."

"Why not? Come on, don't be ridiculous—it's no big deal. I'll be fine. Just slip off your sweater and put on my shirt until you warm up. Then we'll get hauling straight away and get you back to the Scout and test out what that old heater's got to say."

She sips from her glass and shakes her head no. She says, "Let's not argue this," and when she sits down and hunches forward I can see cleavage and breastbone until she pinches closed the open neckline with her free hand. The flotation vest won't help a whole lot but I offer it anyway, without success.

"Then let me at least light the Hibachi. It'll take ten, fifteen minutes at most but we get a load of coals glowing good and put it right here on the floor between us . . ."

"No," she says. "No, no, no. It's not even about that really—about getting warm. Car heaters and portable river fires and wearing or not wearing your shirt or life vest. Archie, can't you see that this is all about you and me? About us? More me it's pretty clear, although I didn't think that for quite awhile, but I think so now. I know so."

The outline of her lips in this slight head-tilt of a pose makes me want to lean forward and kiss her, but as soon as I do her whole face pinches up.

"You okay?" I ask, and when she shakes her head no, I say, "Hang on, we're out of here," and I put down my wineglass and pull anchor and push off and really lean into the oars.

The breeze is hardly arctic but we have been on the river since early morning, almost eight hours, and now Rhea's wet all the way to her chest, arms included, and even if she won't admit to being cold she's already started to shiver. Which is why I reverse the boat so that drifting backwards what's left of the late-day sun throws just enough heat in her direction to hopefully cut the chill. It's not a dangerous maneuver at all on a river absent of whitewater and steep-walled gorges, of rapids and rips. The Platte meanders—pools and riffles and extended slicks—and I can easily improvise the remainder of the trip this way. I could do it on a cloud-covered, moon-barren night or I could do it blindfolded. Another thirty minutes at most and we're there, home free. That's what I tell her, half an hour, and she nods and with the wet backs of her wrists she wipes her eyes.

Rodney starts school in less than a week and the public schools are already in session. I haven't yet put on the storm door, but the nights have turned cool enough to zip in our coat liners to walk the dunes or the lakeshore at dusk. Plus I saw an ad just yesterday in the *Northern Express* for snow plowing and roof shoveling, and for seasoned cordwood. I haven't mentioned it to Rhea, but there's no missing how the days have grown shorter, and the pay-raise incentive to keep her at the animal clinic has not, I gather, deterred her ensuing leave of absence. It's obviously not an official request, and who but a tenured college professor leaves a job only to come back anyway? Who does that, disappears for months and then comes back? I doubt she's whispered word one about it at work. But to me she just has, about a two-minutes-ago heads-up, and I can't stop staring at her, backlit against the sun's low western angle. The sky behind her is streaked salmon and dark blue, and her eyes are as silver liquid as poured mercury. She's wearing a black beret and red lipstick, and for a second I imagine exchanging these oars for a palette and brush, and painting her exactly like this: an on-the-river portrait to hang on the living room wall after she's gone.

Just last week I'd interpreted Rhea's conditions for staying to mean an extra bureau drawer and some closet-cleaning, a quick trip or two to Goodwill. But that's not what she meant at all, and when I attempt some eye-to-eye she momentarily looks away, every wincing body-gesture in clear response to the sunlight having suddenly gone so cold. Even I, bone-dry, can feel it descending now.

She's finished her wine and she's doubled up hugging herself, palms to elbows, forearms on her thighs, and I think, So this is how it ends. This is how I lose her. Not to boredom or bad love or idle plans, but to the tundra itself, those anticipated ice fields and frozen lakes, the unabated winds and the snow on top of snow on top of snow. For whatever I've missed it's clear to me now that the months of intense deep-freeze to come are already depressing her, though the ululating gurgle of the black feeder stream we're passing sounds precisely like the season it still is—early fall. The leaves have already begun turning along the banks, russets and yellows and multiple mutations of reds, and against this display the green spires of the cedars are tinged bronze. There's still plenty of time, plus the inevitability of Indian summer, a season unto itself. So why now? But it's not the weather that's on Rhea's mind.

"Sometimes I get completely lost in the logic," Rhea says. "Like there are only two settings in my brain and they're both the same. Confusion and more confusion and I can't think sensibly anymore. I can't sort out the positives from the negatives and whenever that happens I just want out. It's what I do, remember? It's what I've always done. I told you that—commit to nothing other than me. One life—that's enough responsibility. Pound rescues or strays—you'd think I could handle that at least, a dog or a cat. And of course I want to adopt every single one but I start thinking that way and I get the shivers, like now, but bone-deep. Next thing I know I'm stealing away. Here and gone. It's not a willed thing, Archie, do you understand that? It's most likely a survival instinct. Like you always bolting to the river."

She forces a lopsided smile. She says, "This," and motions with her arms to both sides of the river, her palms turned up inside the sleeves, and only her fingertips showing, and in this light they appear to be on fire. "It's idyllic, beautiful and quiet and mostly I believe I could stay. And you, Archie, and Rodney—he's a fantastic kid, smart and nice and vulnerable just like you. Believe me, it's not a tough sell. You happened along just at the right time and I wanted this to be easy but what's ever easy anyway?"

"Island rum and a hand-rolled cigar?"

"It's no joke," she says. "I've got things to sort out and so do you. Some time apart might not be such a bad thing." She pauses, sniffles, clears her throat. Neither of us looks away. "Well?" she says.

I don't respond, afraid I might reveal to her how, on way too many late-winter nights, I'd storm out of the cabin and get into the hearse, the windows and windshield frozen, and squeeze the steering wheel until my knuckles turned bloodless. I wouldn't even start the engine. I'd just sit and sit for as long as it took to determine that there was nowhere else on earth to go, not from this far north, the snow coming down hard and fast and the roads unplowed. Nowhere to go but back inside to stoke the wood-stove, and open a book, or take out a sketch pad and design a new dry fly or two for the season ahead. No TV back then, although I wished I owned one with a movie channel that ran old black and white films nonstop all night long. Anything to stop me from musing about the past. Shack-wacky, as the locals describe it.

"Has anything happened for you here?" I say. "Anything you might come back for?"

"Don't ever doubt that. Ever."

"A time frame?" I ask.

"Thanksgiving maybe, but don't pin me down, Archie," she

says. "Please don't," and she reaches and picks up the Pentax from the floor. There's only one frame left on this roll of thirty-six. Together we've already arrested the best moments in a continuous series of stills. Double prints on these, no doubt, a Kodachrome set for each of us to line up in sequence and watch like a silent filmstrip. I can only guess what the face framed in this final shot will mean after enough time passes and reshapes the memory of this brilliant late-September day.

She focuses for at least another full minute in which nobody speaks. Then she says, stammering a little, "Ready?" and I let go of the oars, which drag in their locks, the float boat following the current down through the tailout into the heaviness of the slower holding water. We're not stationary, but almost, and behind Rhea three hooded mergansers I hadn't seen tucked into the reeds wing-beat the water in hasty retreat. She doesn't turn around, and the sudden faint reverse chop on the surface means that the waves on the Big Lake are hammering down, although we're not quite close enough to hear them, nor the howl of the wind funneled up the gut as if in mourning. None of it's audible yet, and won't be for another two or three bends.

What we both hear instead is the sound of the shutter as it clicks open and shuts. She's shaking pretty badly now. She's cold and crying harder and not until I reach out and snap the lens cap back on does she lower the camera. Then she closes both eyes, the anti-pigment of the lids so white they appear almost blue, almost translucent. Red lipstick, black beret, blue fluttering eyelids.

Fact: A man on the river will believe what he wants, and what I want is this woman named Rhea and this day back, and then back again, and again, over and over so that nothing about them, together or alone, is ever forgotten or lost.

EIGHTEEN

The Garden

Rodney's in the garden harvesting pumpkins—the mid-spring planting's final bounty, and it's a good one. I've already lopped them from the vines, about twenty, all real decent-size. Two-handers, and the biggest of them big enough to cut open and reach elbow-deep inside and scrape the innards clean with a trowel. Rodney will no doubt have to wheel those few out in the wagon. But right now he's hefting and carrying what he can, one by one, and lining them up—best side facing us—so Z and I can make our picks first before he chooses for himself and for Timmy Reminschider and for Timmy's younger sister Ruth Anne. We'll carve a few here, as we always do, and wash and lightly salt and cook up the seeds on cookie sheets. The remaining pumpkins we'll donate tomorrow to the church youth group in town. From this vantage point the thickly curved and twisting fibrous dry stems appear to be mottled blue.

It's late October. Rhea's been gone a month, and Z has driven up from New Buffalo, driven back down the Deadstream after how many years? And then down the two-track driveway, and parked, and although Rodney bounded right in calling, "Dad, we're here," Z knocked and waited at the front door until I appeared and offered cautious, nervous welcome and invited her inside. Although I said, "No need," she stepped out of her shoes and placed them carefully beside mine on the mat. I did not in preparation for her visit make an extra dump run, but I have vacuumed and swept and made the beds, palm-smoothed the creases from the bedspreads. Went semi-wild with Windex and lemon-scented Pledge, and laid out bathroom towels fresh from the dryer, and stocked the refrigerator with Deja Blue and vanilla yogurt, and a half dozen strawberry Danishes that look pretty irresistible under Cling Wrap on the counter just in case anybody's snacking today. Took a damp cloth to the baseboards. An entire morning's worth of housecleaning. I stopped short of replacing the stand-up framed color snapshots of fish with pictures of Z. Even worse, of me and Z together, younger versions thereof, our arms draped around each other like sticky jungle vines. Had we stayed as mirthfully married as those stored-away snapshots illusioned, we would have celebrated our tenth wedding anniversary early last month.

She and Rodney arrived maybe half an hour ago, but Z and I have yet to confront the not-so-mysterious nature of her visit. She's not wearing a ring of any kind, band or diamond, and unless they're out in the car, no bridal magazines for her to flip through while we chat our way to the more serious matter at hand. So it could be that I've intuited all wrong, but it's unlikely that she's driven four hours to the outskirts of nowhere to talk to me offhandedly about the South of France or Mary Queen of Scots. Not likely at all, and we'll get down to it before long, whatever it is, but for now we're sitting quietly out on the porch, the evening seeming to warm up as it closes in around us.

That's the forecast: a promise of slightly rising temperatures throughout the evening hours. Sweatshirt weather and Z's wearing one that says UNCONSCIOUS DRIVER. It's true, she makes every right move on the roads but rarely remembers a single detail's worth of where she's been outside the city limits. I wonder if any of it's familiar, this jaunt through miles and miles of no-man's-land only to end up back here right in the heart of the matter. In Plato's cave as Z once called it—the books and the darkness and not a whole lot else in those early pre-skylight days, the stars and the moon and the noctilucent clouds drifting by unseen.

A decade ago when she first stepped foot inside the cabin she was all floating eye, silently appraising the possibility of this and that and sizing it up in a matter of minutes as a handyman's special. Or maybe not so much a place in decline as a novelty, a quirky, fun destination where one morning we'd wake and break camp and that would be the end of it—as impermanent as cinders scattered in a campfire. I burned oil lanterns back then and I remember asking her one night, the two of us drinking shots of Jägermeister, where she'd rather be during a power outage, here or on the third floor of some Ramada. All she said was, "Why? Is there one close by?"

So I did not anticipate nor did I hear a single note of nostalgic ache in her voice this time around. Compliments on the multiple renovations, the comfortable, lived-in quality of the cabin. Not the Pierce-Arrow of homes, but in its own slow and careful makeover some awfully nice touches and an enthusiastic "Yes, absolutely" to my mention of the sauna I'm considering yet this fall, right out there by the wood sculpture. But still, not a single exultant ache for the sake of "what was," what identified us for awhile.

"Gadzooks," Z says, and I shore up her undulant praise by saying down to Rodney, "Looking good there. Looking mighty darn respectable."

His nose is scrinkled up and he grunts lowering another pumpkin onto the ground. Then he takes a deep breath and waves and smiles up at us, his parents sitting together without argument and clasping mugs of mulled cider and intermittently inhaling its soothing cinnamon vapor and slowly breathing it out. It's got what Rodney calls a strong zingy taste.

"He's what happened here," Z says. "For that I can love it too. Not like he does or you do, Archie, but this feels good for a change, doesn't it to you?"

"Yes," I say—quick to agree but meaning it more in the context of a dream I might wake from happy enough to weep. A hurtful happiness and it takes all my willpower not to reach up and stroke her hair with the backs of my fingers.

In all my rehearsing of what I might do or say or attempt to atone for I hadn't anticipated Z moving the white wicker table and repositioning the porch chairs so we'd be sitting quite this close together, side by side, our shoulders almost touching. It's such an odd and proximate dislocation, this space between us so fragile and thin that if we simultaneously relaxed and exhaled, we'd be leaning against each other again.

I point at Copperfield, at Mr. Wondercat, who has just moments ago left my lap to go sprawl outside in the sharp shadowy squares of the late-day sunshine widening below the badminton net. He's licking the pads of both front paws and rubbing them across his ears and face, his eyes shut.

Last night's heavy frost has weakened the leaf stems and the slightest breeze sends them cascading down. Rodney pauses on his way back to the garden and stares up into this slow-falling shower of gold, into its whispered rustle so melancholy it makes my eardrums hum, the sound itself a kind of distant hush. "Imagine, all those leaves and no two the same," I say, extolling little more than a cliché, but that's enough for Z to reach over anyway and take my hand.

Neither of us takes our eyes off Rodney, as if doing so would be to lose hold of every small blessing the past has bestowed. I squeeze and Z squeezes back, and Rodney says, "Dad, look," and he points high up into those already bare and sparser branches where the remains of a kite billow and slowly settle back. A kite I designed and built to resemble a flying fish and argued could most definitely *not* be launched in such confinement, not with its nose-heavy design and against the natural down draft the clearing creates. A kite that I first field-tested alone from the top of the dunes, and for over an hour hand-fed all three hundred yards of twine into the featureless sky. So tiny swimming up there I could barely even see it, the silver fins aflutter, and the tug heavier by far than any water fish I'd ever felt. It took twice as long to land as it did to watch it rise and drift and dip only to thrust even higher up. Rhea thinks I should patent and market them and really rake in the bucks, but as I said to her, "It's just for fun." So a one-of-a-kind it was, and the truth is she and Rodney came within a few feet of proving me wrong. He wants to help design and build the next one. He's got some wicked neat ideas, he says, and no scales this time—he wants it stripy and bright and square, a box kite or biplane construction, and as I always remind him, "Pal, you just say the word."

For the past week Canada geese have been migrating south, enormous barking Vs of them, the single shadow of each flock gliding across the ground like a giant black arrowhead. But today only the sporadic, ritual shedding of the hardwoods, a kind of shh-shh, which syncopates in perfect harmony with what Z is saying as she presses her index finger to my lips. "Shh, no, please, Archie, let me finish."

I nod, and because she's turned her chair and is staring right at me, she nods too. And Rodney takes off his vest and drapes it over one arm of the scarecrow whose faded and tattered wardrobe was upgraded by Rhea just a few days before she left, not to frighten anything away but rather to dignify. A bright yellow turtleneck and thin, shiny charcoal tie. She was dressed up too, a white blouse and a long flower-print skirt that covered her feet so that when she turned away she didn't look real, like she was floating down the footpath toward the river. She sat on the dock for a long time alone, knees to her chin, and Copperfield curled and purring beside her as she sipped the hot, steamy tea I'd brought down to her.

I'm not sure how the conversation has come around to this but Z says, "He misses Rhea. It's clear he likes her a lot, but he's so guarded about what he says. He'll get started and go silent in mid-sentence as if he's betraying you. It's not healthy, you know."

"Did you tell him that?"

"I said she sounded nice, which she does, and that he shouldn't feel like he can't mention her around me. You have a different take on this, I know, but really, how long is it going to continue? After all, somewhere, somehow we blinked and it got to be the year 2000, Archie. All those zeroes lining up. And these secret separate lives—it messes everything up, and it does nothing but complicate what's already complicated enough. Don't misunderstand. I'm not suggesting we drag out all the old skeletons, but maybe it *is* time we closed the book on all that rule-one stuff.

More and more it just confuses him, and you know what? It confuses me too."

Behind Z there's a near pileup of pumpkin and kid. Rodney's attempting to keep pace with the weight his stooped-over body is chasing out of the garden. He doesn't quite make it, but even arm-weary he refuses to relent, lowering the pumpkin to the ground with a dense thud and then, in squat position, rolling it the rest of the way. The line of pumpkins already spans the entire length of the porch.

"Wagon time," I say, and Z turns back around and Rodney says, "Just three more . . . then you can pick. They're monsters, Dad. They're like the biggest ones ever. What'd you call 'em, the Percherons? That's what they are all right. Yup, the Percherons." He's breathing hard, and between breaths he says, "Do you . . . think we could maybe weigh them . . . later? On the bathroom scale, that'd work. Just to see?"

"Sure. Of course we can," I say, "nothing to it," and Z says, "Tell your dad how much *you* weighed yesterday morning. First time ever."

"One hundred pounds," he says, and sounding just like me, "on the button."

"Okay then, off with the shoes and shirt and the cargo shorts and then we'll see about triple figures. You don't look all that massive and chiseled to me."

He grins and juts up his chin and turning sideways he impersonates my "this-way-to-the-beach" muscleman pose, and the way he breaks up laughing makes me go suddenly weak all over. I wonder if Z can feel it in my fingers, in the thumb that brushes across her knuckles.

"Soon as I come in," he says. "You'll see," and he places one foot flat in the center of the wagon and with the other he pushes off as if on a raised red skateboard, and steers with the metal handle, the hard rubber wheels sinking just a fraction into the earth. Z shouts out after him, "If they're too heavy you ask your father for help," and Rodney flashes her a thumbs-up with his free hand.

"Clearly this is true," I say, and Z says, "Context?" and I say back, "You know, what you said a couple minutes ago about what's off-limits—conversation-wise. That's fine. Really, we can dispense with all that."

"Can or should?"

"Either way," I say. "However you want to word it, but that's not really why you're here, I don't believe. We probably could've capped that one on the phone. I guess what I'm saying is that we don't need to put off whatever you've come to tell me. It'd be easier all around if you just said it. I mean, as long as you've driven all the way up here it probably merits a mention."

She lets go of my hand and tucks the folds of her skirt between her thighs. Interlocks both hands, as if a moment of prayer is needed before lowering the boom, her face downturned. I imagine her mind both avoiding and slowly forming the words, or word, a name, and even with my blood surging through the semilunar chambers of my heart I say it for her, and as gently as I can: "Omar."

Her right ankle rests on her left knee, and if I break down it'll be due to nothing beyond that beautiful sad contour of her instep. Or the shiny gray streaks in her hair. Or the rattle of the wagon echoing toward us, the warp-speed at which Rodney is growing, and the greater portion of this day already gone, the light just beginning to wane.

"Wow," Z says.

"When?" I ask. "How soon?"

"We haven't set a date. But in any case not right away," she says. "It's not even a formal engagement yet," and when she looks back up at me and wets her lips I lean forward and kiss her, and whatever Rodney's about to say to us is left unsaid. He's standing and cupping both hands like a visor on his forehead. It's as if Z can feel his eyes on us and she slides her cheek against mine and whispers in my ear. "No," she says, "he doesn't know. Not yet," and we both rise from our chairs and, standing above him, we lean our foreheads against the screen, and Z says, "That one," because the afternoon is already getting on. As much as she'd like to stay for dinner—shish kebabs on the grill—she doesn't want to drive home in the dark. The pumpkin she's pointing at is the last one in the garden.

"It's the biggest one," Rodney says. "I think Dad should help me."

"Let's all three of us do it," I say, and as soon as Z leaves to go get her shoes, Rodney lowers his head. Then he lifts it, up and down in five- or six-second intervals, as if calculating the approximate collective weight of the pumpkins he and I planted from seed almost half a year ago. Which in and of itself is worth our full attention, though I doubt that's what's going through his mind at the moment.

I open the screen door and step outside, and when Z walks into view from the other side of the cabin I say, "Hey."

"Hey," she says, and now Rodney's looking from me to his mom, back and forth. I'm already down the three stairs to the ground, and for however confused Rodney momentarily seems, there's no mistaking this convergence of his parents coming toward him under this even heavier swirl of yellow leaves cascading down around us.

"Omar can lift it out," Z says, and when Rodney stops dead in his tracks and stares wide-eyed at me, I ask, "Well, is that true? Can he?" and Rodney nods. "All right then," I say, "let's get it up and out of here."

"Don't look at *me*," Z says. "Help your dad so he doesn't go straining his back again."

"On three," I say, and we lift and load it together and I steady its awkward oblong weight from behind as Rodney pulls the wagon, the miniature wheel ruts deepening just a hair more. "To the right," I tell him. "Go that way around the cabin to the car. It'll be easier."

Z takes the other, the longer but faster route, and she has already popped the trunk by the time we get there. She's bent over, clearing a few things out of the way. Her skirt clings to her hips and the breeze blows those few loose strands of hair across her mouth when she turns back around. She kisses Rodney on the top of his head. And then she hugs me. It's brief and alarmingly uncomplicated and Rodney and I stand watching until she turns right out of the driveway. Although we can't see the car, we can hear the distant blurred whine of the tires on the pavement as she gains speed. Maybe twenty seconds worth, and then there's only silence.

"Dad, you want to pick yours now?" Rodney says.

"I sure do," I say.

"You didn't want Mom's, I hope. Did you?"

"I want Mom to have Mom's," I say.

"Promise?"

"Scout's honor."

"Because they're really ours, yours and mine, you know."

"All of ours," I say, "and Rhea's too if she were here."

"I wish," Rodney says. "I wish I knew when she's coming back."

She's been sending us postcards, one per week. Rodney's been making a collection of them, and summoning the forces some nights by lining them all up on the kitchen table. Chiseled, sad and beautiful faces mostly: Chief Joseph, Georgia O'Keefe, Virginia Woolf, and most recently Leonard Nimoy musing, no doubt, about the great human folly of desire and imperfection.

"Do you love her?"

"Yes," I say. "I do. Much more than I knew."

"Me too."

"I know and so does Rhea and she's pretty darn partial to you when it comes right down to it."

"To you too, and that's the truth. She said so lots of times. She said you're real good at pool but not all that great at foosball and that next time maybe I can play too when you go to the Fox Den. In the back room."

I shrug and smile and flick out a feathery left jab and cover up because it *is* the truth. All of it, all that he's just said. And what I think now is that my dad was right about how easy it is to always be so hard on ourselves—to wear a bull's-eye over our hearts. Rodney pulls down my guard and that's right where he pats me. It's something he used to do when he was a little kid, from the time he was maybe three years old. Softly pat my heart with his palm, saying, "It's okay." And I'd do it back, sometimes very late at night when he was asleep, after I'd arrived back home from the cabin after too many days away. Before the separation, before the divorce, before I strayed so far afield I wondered if I'd ever get back to him safely. Before everything that perished and didn't. Before everything that led to us standing here, Z no more than a mile down the Deadstream, and Rhea's whereabouts unknown for now. And Rodney already slide-stepping toward and pointing at his impressive line of pumpkins, the more immediate father-and-son business at hand.

NINETEEN

The Light

The radio's playing and Chuck Berry keeps inquiring: "Maybelline, why can't you be true?" Rodney's the one who selected the station. And the predominant oldies mood for the night? Exactly—another and then another miserable pining wretch's pathetic sad wail as he falls head over heels yet again for that next wrong woman to love. Rodney's unfamiliar with the lyrics but he's in and out of the beat, kind of dancing on his knees between punctures and deep, clean incisions. I've sharpened my Swiss Army Knife on the whetstone, and Rodney's being deliberate and careful and wearing gloves. With real proficiency he's drawn and scored and then carved a pumpkin first for himself—five-point-star eyes and a wide, single-tooth smile—and he's just now finishing up one for Rhea, its face a sad polar opposite. We've got newspapers spread out on the porch floor, and some wooden spoons and two deep seed bowls and on the glass-topped wicker table the twelve cartridge loops of my hunting vest are filled with shotgun shells. Outside the evening keeps darkening ahead of the moon, and I think, Pumpkins and early-sixties rock 'n' roll tunes that my dad scorned with a vengeance, and the notion of liberating him tonight by dispatching his ashes heavenward feels dubious at best and possibly even downright loony.

But as my dad so often pointed out, life's mission is pretty darn elemental: from ashes to ashes and dust to dust. Life, he maintained, is life until it isn't. "Just like for those ducks," he said, and he pointed at a pair of mallards, hell-bent in flight away from the two of us who might have stepped riverward for no other reason than to kill and consume. For what it's worth I can't remember the last time I purchased a waterfowl or small-game license, or even thought about doing so. And for sure Rodney has never shown any interest in that. It seems odd that my dad never mentioned where he got the shotgun, or why, and that I never asked. He never once loaded and fired it himself, at least not that I'm aware of, and up north here is where he would have done it and certainly nowhere else.

Wing-shoot my dad never did, though occasionally he'd break open the double barrels from the breechblock just to hear the intricate click of the action. "That's real craftsmanship," he'd say. "That's surgical precision," which he also referred to as love. "You care this way about things, this deeply, Arch, they'll stand the test of time all right." He'd say, "Come over here and feel this," and he'd take my hand in his and feather my fingertips slowly back and forth across the fancy blue-black engraving. He'd say, "Shut your eyes," and as soon as I did I could almost feel that startled pheasant rising from right under the tiny pulse of my touch. "Understand?" my dad would say and I'd whisper, "Yes," and that's as close as we'd come for years to engaging in what I'd call any intimate conversations.

But in the natural world he was entirely out of his element, a man without a single imaginable course of action. Had I asked him to I doubt he could even have identified that frenetic, unmistakable drumming of grouse, although come fall we'd hear them every morning on the far side of the river. Over there was all primeval forest to him, dark and forbidden—Sasquatch country, as he called it. Whenever I'd ask him to explore it with me— maybe just to jump across a few feeder creeks—he'd say, "And where would that get anybody but lost or hurt, and I sure don't want to be on the wrong end of that. Right here's good. Right here's plenty far enough." Then he'd nod as if his denials were reassurances, and I'd nod back like I understood, but of course I didn't. He had it covered, he'd say, meaning from right there on the porch where, pale-skinned and slump-shouldered, he smoked and nodded off in the shade of the overhang, and sometimes drank but never into intoxication. I'd read years later how, in advanced age, everybody retained *some* youthful trait. Some single accented physical detail eternal: an eye twinkle or smile or maybe, momentarily muted in a particular slant of evening light, a whole entire face preserved in that instant before it turned away from the window as if to forestall the passing of yet another day. But my dad did not look young ever. Not that I recall. Instead I remember how he made just sitting there getting older and older his primary hobby, his final, unabated passion.

If he included woodcock or quail or canvasback in a sentence, he was merely echoing names he'd heard me say as I identified them by either sight or sound. His use of them existed only in the vaguest of contexts, and in that way hunting became nothing more than the new wild next-thing intention that just never got any father-son traction. Right: a collector's-grade shotgun that in his hands posed no threat to any living warm-blooded thing. And now, half a lifetime later, it comes down to this, to the use for which the shotgun must always have been intended, and in this way maybe the ceremony is not entirely contradictory to who he was. Within limits, that is.

Rodney's decided he does want to wade out mid-river with me. And then push upstream and onto the sandbar where the footing is solid, and where the water is no higher than his waist. We've had no practice service and I've made clear that funeral-wise it does seem like a strange sort of occasion, doesn't it? No formal dressing up. No missal or rosary, and not even any newly memorized Bible passages to help get him into heaven. I suggested a few "Our Fathers" in tandem might be the way to go: *thy kingdom come, thy will be done.* Or better yet maybe we could alternate verses—him, me, him, me—and pause just long enough between each verse to blast away. Nothing to it: spoken prayer lines balanced by the point-blank shotgun's roar. Given our limited options it sounded like valid thinking, and Rodney, without batting an eyelash, said fine but that sometimes prayers made him think of everything other than God and was that okay because he did love his grandpa and didn't want to louse up the ceremony. I told him that's what God is, everything, the world without end, and that whatever came into somebody's mind was perfectly all right as long as they were good thoughts. It's what his grandpa would want.

"Will his ashes fall on us?" he asked, and I said, "No, I don't think so, not if there's no breeze and I shoot upriver in an arch. Maybe they'll drift down and then drift by us and by the cabin and I'm sure he'd like that. Don't you think?"

He didn't answer. Instead he asked, "There aren't, you know, all that many ways to be buried, are there? Like only a few, but Grandpa he wanted us to do this 'cause it's different or something? Is that what you mean?"

"I don't know for sure. He didn't say."

"But why do you think?"

"Well, I remember he said one time right before we drove away from the cabin that there'd come a day he'd never come back up here, and that that day—it'd be a real sad one. And he sounded sad when he said it, like he'd already started to miss this place."

"Did you ever think *not* to shoot him up into the sky like he asked?"

"For sure, lots of times," I said, but that it was his grandpa's deathbed wish and that didn't leave an only son a whole lot of room or time to bargain or resist, no matter how illogical or crazy-seeming the request. Plus a promise was a promise and however we chose to go into the afterlife probably ought to be on our own terms, though I admitted that I sure wouldn't have thought of such a sendoff myself, for him or for me or for anybody.

What I had considered a thousand times at least was that quiet traditional cemetery burial my dad enacted against my mom's wishes, and I wondered if that alone was sufficient to act against his. My out if I ever needed it, I thought, but I said nothing about that to Rodney, nor about how the dead in my dad's book were always worthy of forgiveness. No—not so, I think now. Redemption, possibly, as I've come to believe, but never forgiveness, and I'm not sure who in the end would even want that granted without just cause.

And I still have ashes enough in the urn to inter next to my mom—a kind of silent counter-barrage to the uproar service of what in short order will come echoing off the river. Part of him here and part there, which, in the name of uncertainty, seems, not cowardly, but only fair.

So we've come to this, or I have anyway, and when I say, "Hey, d'you still want to go?" Rodney shakes off the question by furrowing his brow, an ageless, kid-quizzical scold for his old man's tentative ruminations.

"You?" he says, and I say, "I guess," and I point outside at the blurred shapes of the ghost-faced bats zigzagging like shadows through the perimeter haze of the yard light. My cue to slowly rise and walk over and switch it off. And once I do, there's the moon, still two days shy of full, but the revised weather report is for clouds and drizzle after midnight, and then the cold front dropping down from Canada and the possibility by first light of everything being shrouded in the season's original snow.

"Better go for it then," I say. "Looks like our only opening," and in the few minutes it takes us to get into our waders and step outside, the sky is entirely star-strewn, the lightspill spreading like trillions of bits of silver across the landscape. On the line the clothespins gleam white. The few that Rodney clipped together earlier in the day resemble hanging wooden crosses, and below them, Copperfield's unblinking agate eyes appear clear as liquid, the tree trunks whitewashed along the swamp edge. The night is as suddenly bright as if illuminated by flares, so I don't even bother to light the Coleman lantern. I leave it right where it is on the bottom stair, an almost century-old heirloom of a shotgun already broken open across my left forearm.

Rodney's face is upturned—befuddled and awestruck both—but I refuse to debate yet again whether or not to just call the whole thing off, and this time for good. Just give it up. Laugh it off and swagger back inside and get those pumpkin seeds salted and buttered and onto the cookie sheet and into the oven. Instead

I say, "All set?" and he says back, "Okay, uh-huh, I guess. What was that?"

He means the sudden flat muscular thwap of the beaver's tail right out front of the cabin. "It's just that same beaver," I say, but it's as if I've just named a constellation, and stargazing again Rodney says, "Yeah. And there's Orion. There's Pegasus too, and Cassiopeia, and that green star, that real bright one over there kind of moving around, that's Venus, right?"

We're walking down the path, me breaking trail through puddles of particle light and Rodney bringing up the rear. I say, "It sure is, and there's the Southern Fish and the Sculptor," but it's the upside-down sightless face of the moon mirrored in the river that stops us in our tracks. I've never thought of the moon before as blind or bloated or openly weeping but I do now as Rodney shields his eyes and says, "It looks so sad up close like this. How come?"

We're standing side by side on the riverbank, and I say, "Well, your grandma—she always said we should never have landed a man up there. That that's when the moon first lost heart. She said ever since the dawn of time the moon had always been a muse. You know, like an inspiration for poets?"

He stares up at me as if no, he doesn't get what that means, not entirely, but nonetheless when I squat he hugs me around the neck from behind, his left cheek pressing against my right ear. I don't hoist and cinch him up with my arms as I usually do for a piggyback. "So just hang on," I say, and I straighten and step down and slosh knee-deep before maneuvering diagonally out into the trough, the shotgun held high. Even on my tiptoes with Rodney in tow, I take in a little water, and Rodney says, "Whoa, Dad," because he's been told one wrong step and we could both be under.

"We're fine," I say, "just hold tight," and he says back, "A hundred pounds. I bet you believe me now."

"That I do," I say, "and then some." And by comparison I calculate the total deadweight of my dad in ounces, and how in a few brief minutes he'll be scrawled visibly loud and clear, and suspended there for how long I don't know before his slow ashy decent from the heavens. In all manner of vanishing, eventually we do go, and if my dad taught me anything he taught me that.

We turn straight upriver into the current, into the chrome-like glint of this night, and already my thighs tremble and ache, and Rodney's breathing in half grunts from the effort of hanging on. The rubber bottoms of his waders are buoyant and their double rudder-like toe drag makes him even heavier. There's still a good twenty-five yards to go. Which in my mind has doubled at least, and I say, "How we doing?"

Without missing a beat Rodney says, "Dad, look behind us," and when I stop and turn, the left eye of the moon has opened in the shimmering V wake that widens and ripples behind us. Then the other eye opens too, the whole face re-forming in a muted, burnished glow that seems to rise and waver just inches below the surface, the water itself like a clear liquid veil.

I've brought a couple of candles to light—they're zip-locked in plastic bags inside my wader pouch—plus some stick matches and a striker. Intermittent scrims of mist keep floating by, and this feels entirely dreamlike now, the moon afloat no matter which way I step. But stationary too so that whenever I turn or glance back it's right there behind us, a pale flesh-colored meniscus, the fat cheeks lilting back and forth like weightlessness itself.

But mostly I'm bent forward, sucking wind and focused on what's directly ahead, my legs as heavy as waterlogged tree stumps. But in my exhaustion I'm not entirely certain where we are until my knee comes down hard, as if in emphatic genuflection, on the sandbar's rim. Followed by the other knee, and it's not until Rodney dismounts and is standing in front of me and helping me with my balance that I'm able to stand up too. I'm sweat-soaked and panting hard and Rodney says, "I guess we're here," and I nod, thinking, Oh, Jesus, yes, and how I never slogged my way so determinedly upriver like this toward a rising brown or rainbow. Though I certainly have, after slow and careful approach, fished from my knees, ad-libbing a silent "take it, take it" prayer for what miracle rise might be that close at hand.

Rodney opens both of his hands, palms up, and then he closes his fingers around the candle I've just offered him, which he then holds out to me to light. In the soft glow he looks like an altar boy, the wax already starting to pool under the spitting blue flame of the wick.

I touch the match head to the water—not even a hiss—and then I put it back in my pouch and slide the first two shells into the double chambers, and click the barrels closed.

"Our Father," Rodney says, and I step forward, legs spread wide, and wedge each boot sole back and forth until they sink and grab in the hard-packed sand. "Who art in heaven," and I raise stock to shoulder and level the shotgun, lifting it slowly until the tiny sight bead is visible against all that heavenly light showering down. Only then do I slide the safety off, and I think, Say it, and Rodney does: ". . . on earth as it is," and aiming into that vast, sweeping silver grommet of stars, I fire.

Maybe it's the light loads—there's almost no recoil. And the double blast, the repetitive blam-blam, is more concussive than loud, like the slow rumbling echo of distant thunder, and it seems not so much the powder charge as it does this brilliant night that carries his remains skyward.

I'd expected something—I don't know—charred and clotted, a couple of dull, scudding barrel-spumes of smoke that disappeared without us hardly even noticing. But this—it's more like a light show, and after I reload and appeal to God that we be given this day, I touch off another couple rounds. Followed by two more and two more again and then, without prayer pause, the rapid-fire grand finale.

For a few long seconds my dad seems to hover above us like a cloud of powdered silk, these final and highest-trajectory explosions of ash spreading out in waves tipped with phosphor. The glow they give off shimmers like a halo before it slowly dissolves. And before it does entirely I remember how, whenever my dad sat on the cabin porch, his trouser cuffs would ride up beyond his ankles and socks, the flesh there so white I imagined it in miles or even in years. It saddened me like nothing else ever did, as if the narrow span of his entire life could be measured by that single inch of exposed and shiny skin.

Now the ejected spent shells are bunched in my pouch, all twelve of them, which is why I'm holding a lighted candle too.

Rodney and I are facing each other, our heads bowed, and I know a footfall on the water is a lot to claim. But I swear somebody has tiptoed by, touching a son and a father, or a father and a son who stand together alone in a river at midnight in late October. And where, between them, candle vapors rise like incense into the predicted chill of the early-morning air.

"Dad?" Rodney whispers, and it's as if, opening my eyes upon him for the very first time, I find again and again in that single, mortal, forever looked-for sound, the thing I am among all things infinite, and all things blessed.